BERNARD CORNWELL

Heretic

D0029070

HARPER

NEW YORK · LONDON · TORONTO · SYDNEY

Heretic is for
Dorothy Carroll,
who knows why

HARPER

First published in Great Britain in 2003 by HarperCollins Publishers.

A hardcover edition of this book was published in 2003 by HarperCollins Publishers.

HarperCollins books may be purchased for educational, business, or sales promotional use. For information, please e-mail the Special Markets Department at SPsales@harpercollins.com.

FIRST HARPER PAPERBACK PUBLISHED 2007.

The Library of Congress has catalogued the hardcover edition as follows:
Cornwell, Bernard.
    Heretic / Bernard Cornwell.—1st ed.
            355 p. ; 24 cm.
        ISBN-13: 978-0-06-053049-5
        ISBN-10: 0-06-053049-9
        1. Hundred Years' War, 1339–1453—Fiction. 2. Heretics, Christian—Fiction. 3. British—France—Fiction. 4. Revenge—Fiction. 5. Archers—Fiction. 6. Grail—Fiction. 7. Gascony (France)—Fiction. I. Title.
PR6053.O75 H47 2003
823/.914 22   2004270344
ISBN: 978-0-06-074828-9 (pbk.)
ISBN-10: 0-06-074828-1 (pbk.)

    17 18 19 20   ID/RRD   20 19 18 17 16

Contents

CALAIS, 1347

THE ROAD CAME from the southern hills and crossed the marshes by the sea. It was a bad road. A summer's persistent rain had left it a strip of glutinous mud that baked hard when the sun came out, but it was the only road that led from the heights of Sangatte to the harbors of Calais and Gravelines. At Nieulay, a hamlet of no distinction whatever, it crossed the River Ham on a stone bridge. The Ham was scarcely worth the title of river. It was a slow stream that oozed through fever-ridden marshlands until it vanished among the coastal mudflats. It was so short that a man could wade from its source to the sea in little more than an hour, and it was so shallow that a man could cross it at low tide without getting his waist wet. It drained the swamps where reeds grew thick and herons hunted frogs among the marsh grass, and it was fed by a maze of smaller streams where the villagers from Nieulay and Hammes and Guîmes set their wicker eel traps.

Nieulay and its stone bridge might have expected to slumber through history, except that the town of Calais lay just two miles to the north and, in the summer of 1347, an army of thirty thousand Englishmen was laying siege to the port and their encampment lay thick between the town's formidable walls and the marshes. The road which came from the heights and crossed the Ham at Nieulay was the only route a French relief force might use, and in the height of the summer, when the inhabitants of Calais were close to starvation, Philip of Valois, King of France, brought his army to Sangatte.

Twenty thousand Frenchmen lined the heights, their banners thick in the wind blowing from the sea. The oriflamme was there, the sacred war pennant of France. It was a long flag with three pointed tails, a blood-red ripple of precious silk, and if the flag looked bright that was because it was new. The old oriflamme was in England, a trophy taken on the wide green hill between Wadicourt and Crécy the previous summer. But the new flag was as sacred as the old, and about it flew the standards of France's great lords: the banners of Bourbon, of Montmorency and of the Count of Armagnac. Lesser flags were visible among the noble standards, but all proclaimed that the greatest warriors of Philip's kingdom were come to give battle to the English. Yet between them and the enemy were the River Ham and the bridge at Nieulay that was defended by a stone tower around which the English had dug trenches. These they had filled with archers and men-at-arms. Beyond that force was the river, then the marshes, and on the higher ground close to Calais's high wall and its double moat was a makeshift town of houses and tents where the English army lived. And such an army as had never been seen in France. The besiegers' encampment was bigger than Calais itself. As far as the eye could see were streets lined with canvas, with timber houses, with paddocks for horses, and between them were men-at-arms and archers. The oriflamme might as well have stayed unfurled.

"We can take the tower, sire." Sir Geoffrey de Charny, as hard a soldier as any in Philip's army, gestured down the hill to where the English garrison of Nieulay was isolated on the French side of the river.

"To what end?" Philip asked. He was a weak man, hesitant in battle, but his question was pertinent. If the tower did fall and the bridge of Nieulay was thus delivered into his hands, what would it serve? The bridge merely led to an even greater English army, which was already arraying itself on the firm ground at the edge of its encampment.

The citizens of Calais, starved and despairing, had seen the French banners on the southern crest and they had responded by hanging their own flags from their ramparts. They displayed images of the Virgin, pictures of St. Denis of France and, high on the citadel, the blue and yellow royal standard to tell Philip that his subjects still lived, still fought. Yet the brave display could not hide that they had been besieged for eleven months. They needed help.

"Take the tower, sire," Sir Geoffrey urged, "and then attack across the bridge! Good Christ, if the Goddamns see us win one victory they might lose heart!" A growl of agreement came from the assembled lords.

The King was less optimistic. It was true that Calais's garrison still held out, and that the English had hardly damaged its walls, let alone found a way to cross the twin moats, but nor had the French been able to carry any supplies to the beleaguered town. The people there did not need encouragement, they needed food. A puff of smoke showed beyond the encampment and a few heartbeats later the sound of a cannon rolled across the marshes. The missile must have struck the wall, but Philip was too far away to see its effect.

"A victory here will encourage the garrison," the Lord of Montmorency urged, "and put despair in the English hearts."

But why should the English lose heart if the tower of Nieulay fell? Philip thought it would merely fill them with a resolve to defend the road on the far side of the bridge, but he also understood that he could not keep his rough hounds leashed when a hated enemy was in sight and so he gave his permission. "Take the tower," he instructed, "and God give you victory."

The King stayed where he was as the lords gathered men and armed themselves. The wind from the sea brought the smell of salt, but also a scent of decay which probably came from rotting weed on the long tidal flats. It made Philip melancholy. His new astrologer had refused to attend the King for weeks, pleading that he had a fever, but Philip had learned that the man was in fine health, which meant that he must have seen some great disaster in the stars and simply feared to tell the King. Gulls cried beneath the clouds. Far out to sea a grubby sail bellied towards England, while another ship was anchoring off the English-held beaches and ferrying men ashore in small boats to swell the enemy ranks. Philip looked back to the road and saw a group of around forty or fifty English knights riding towards the bridge. He made the sign of the cross, praying that the knights would be trapped by his attack. He hated the English. Hated them.

The Duke of Bourbon had delegated the organization of the assault to Sir Geoffrey de Charny and Edouard de Beaujeu, and that was good. The King trusted both men to be sensible. He did not doubt they could carry the tower, though he still did not know what good it would do; but he supposed it was better than letting his wilder noblemen carry their lances in a wild charge across the bridge to utter defeat in the marshlands. He knew they would love nothing better than to make such an attack. They thought war was a game and every defeat only made them more eager to play. Fools, he thought, and he made the sign of the cross again, wondering what dire prophecy the astrologer was hiding from him. What we need, he thought, is a miracle. Some great sign from God. Then he twitched in alarm because a nakerer had just beaten his great kettledrum. A trumpet sounded.

The music did not presage the advance. Rather the musicians were warming their instruments, ready for the attack. Edouard de Beaujeu was on the right where he had assembled over a thousand cross-bowmen and as many men-at-arms, and he plainly intended to assault the English from one flank while Sir Geoffrey de Charny and at least five hundred men-at-arms charged straight down the hill at the English entrenchments. Sir Geoffrey was striding along the line shouting at the knights and men-at-arms to dismount. They did so reluctantly. They believed that the essence of war was the cavalry charge, but Sir Geoffrey knew that horses were no use against a stone tower protected by entrenchments and so he was insisting they fight on foot. "Shields and swords," he told them, "no lances! On foot! On foot!" Sir Geoffrey had learned the hard way that horses were pitiably vulnerable to English arrows, while men on foot could advance at the crouch behind stout shields. Some of the higher-born men were refusing to dismount, but he ignored them. Even more French men-at-arms were hurrying to join the charge.

The small band of English knights had crossed the bridge now and looked as if they intended to ride straight up the road to challenge the whole French battle line, but instead they checked their horses and gazed up at the horde on the ridge. The King, watching them, saw that they were led by a great lord. He could tell that by the size of the man's banner, while at least a dozen of the other knights carried the square flags of bannerets on their lances. A rich group, he thought, worth a small fortune in ransoms. He hoped they would ride to the tower and so trap themselves.

The Duke of Bourbon trotted his horse back to Philip. The Duke was in plate armor that had been scoured with sand, vinegar and wire until it shone white. His helmet, still hanging from his saddle's pommel, was crested with feathers dyed blue. He had refused to dismount from his destrier, which had a steel chanfron to protect its face and a trapper of gleaming mail to shield its body from the English archers who were no doubt stringing their bows in the entrenchments. "The oriflamme, sire," the Duke said. It was supposed to be a request, but somehow sounded like an order.

"The oriflamme?" The King pretended not to understand.

"May I have the honor, sire, of carrying it to battle?"

The King sighed. "You outnumber the enemy ten to one," he said, "you hardly need the oriflamme. Let it stay here. The enemy will have seen it." And the enemy would know what the unfurled ori-flamme meant. It instructed the French to take no prisoners, to kill everyone, though doubtless any wealthy English knight would still be captured rather than killed, for a corpse yielded no ransom. Still, the unfurled triple-tongued flag should put terror into English hearts. "It will remain here," the King insisted.

The Duke began to protest, but just then a trumpet sounded and the crossbowmen started down the hill. They were in green and red tunics with the grail badge of Genoa on their left arms, and each was accompanied by a foot soldier holding a pavise, a huge shield that would protect the crossbowman while he reloaded his clumsy weapon. A half-mile away, beside the river, Englishmen were running from the tower to the earth entrenchments that had been dug so many months before that they were now thickly covered with grass and weeds. "You will miss your battle," the King said to the Duke who, forgetting the scarlet banner, wheeled his great armored warhorse towards Sir Geof-frey's men.

"*Montjoie St. Denis!*" The Duke shouted France's war cry and the nakerers thumped their big drums and a dozen trumpeters blared their challenge at the sky. There were clicks as helmet visors were lowered. The crossbowmen were already at the foot of the slope, spreading right to envelop the English flank. Then the first arrows flew: English arrows, white-feathered, fluttering across the green land, and the King, leaning forward in his saddle, saw that there were too few archers on the enemy side. Usually, whenever the damned English gave battle, their archers outnumbered their knights and men-at-arms by at least three to one, but the outpost of Nieulay seemed mostly to be gar-risoned by men-at-arms. "God speed you!" the King called to his sol-diers. He was suddenly enthused because he could scent victory.

The trumpets sounded again and now the grey metallic tide of men-at-arms swept down the slope. They roared their war cry and the sound was rivaled by the drummers who were hammering their taut goatskins and the trumpeters who were playing as if they could defeat the English with sound alone. "God and St. Denis!" the King shouted.

The crossbow quarrels were flying now. Each short iron bolt was fitted with leather vanes and they made a hiss as they streaked towards the earthworks. Hundreds of bolts flew, then the Genoese stepped behind the huge shields to work the ratchets that bent back their steel-reinforced bows. Some English arrows thumped into the pavises, but then the archers turned towards Sir Geoffrey's attack. They put bodkin-headed arrows on their strings, arrows that were tipped with three or four inches of narrow-shafted steel that could pierce mail as if it were linen. They drew and shot, drew and shot, and the arrows thumped into shields and the French closed ranks. One man was pierced in the thigh and stumbled and the men-at-arms flowed around him and closed up again. An English archer, standing to loose his bow, was hit in the shoulder by a crossbow bolt and his arrow flew crazily into the air.

"Montjoie St. Denis!" The men-at-arms bellowed their challenge as the charge reached the flat ground at the foot of the slope. The arrows hammered into shields with sickening force, but the French held their tight formation, shield overlapping shield, and the cross-bowmen edged closer to aim at the English archers who were forced to stand high in their trenches to loose their weapons. A bolt went clean through an iron sallet to pierce an English skull. The man toppled sideways, blood spilling down his face. A volley of arrows whipped from the tower's top and the answering crossbow bolts rattled on the stones as the English men-at-arms, seeing that their arrows had not checked the enemy, stood with unsheathed swords to meet the charge.

"St. George!" they shouted, then the French attackers were at the first entrenchment and stabbing down at the English beneath them. Some Frenchmen found narrow causeways piercing the trench and they streamed through to attack the defenders from the rear. Archers in the two rearmost trenches had easy targets, but so did the Genoese crossbowmen who stepped from behind their pavises to rain iron on the enemy. Some of the English, sensing the slaughter to come, were leaving their entrenchments to run towards the Ham. Edward de Beaujeu, leading the crossbowmen, saw the fugitives and shouted at the Genoese to drop their crossbows and join the attack. They drew swords or axes and swarmed at the enemy. "Kill!" Edward de Beaujeu shouted. He was mounted on a destrier and, his sword drawn, he spurred the big stallion forward. "Kill!"

The Englishmen in the forward trench were doomed. They struggled to protect themselves from the mass of French men-at-arms, but the swords, axes and spears slashed down. Some men tried to yield, but the oriflamme was flying and that meant no prisoners, so the French swamped the slick mud at the trench's bottom with English blood. The defenders from the rearward trenches were all running now, but the handful of French horsemen, those too proud to fight on foot, spurred across the narrow causeways, shoved through their own men-at-arms and screamed the war cry as they drove their big horses into the fugitives beside the river. Stallions wheeled as swords chopped. An archer lost his head beside the river that turned sudden red. A man-at-arms screamed as he was trampled by a destrier, then stabbed with a lance. An English knight held his hands in the air, offering a gauntlet as a token of surrender, and he was ridden down from behind, his spine pierced with a sword, then another horseman cut an axe into his face. "Kill them!" the Duke of Bourbon shouted, his sword wet, "Kill them all!" He saw a group of archers escaping towards the bridge and shouted at his followers, "With me! With me! *Montjoie St. Denis!*"

The archers, nearly thirty of them, had fled towards the bridge, but when they reached the straggle of reed-thatched houses beside the river they heard the hoofbeats and turned in alarm. For a heartbeat it seemed they would panic again, but one man checked them. "Shoot the horses, boys," he said, and the bowmen hauled on their cords, loosed, and the white-fledged arrows slammed into the destriers. The Duke of Bourbon's stallion staggered sideways as two arrows drove through its mail and leather armor, then it fell as another two horses went down, hooves flailing. The other riders instinctively turned away, looking for easier pickings. The Duke's squire yielded his own horse to his master, then died as a second English volley hissed from the village. The Duke, rather than waste time trying to mount his squire's horse, lumbered away in his precious plate armor, which had protected him from the arrows. Ahead of him, around the base of Nieulay's tower, the survivors from the English trenches had formed a shield wall that was now surrounded by vengeful Frenchmen. "No prisoners!" a French knight shouted, "No prisoners!" The Duke called for his men to help him into the saddle.

Two of the Duke's men-at-arms dismounted to help their master onto the new horse, and just then they heard the thunder of hooves. They turned to see a group of English knights charging from the village. "Sweet Jesus!" The Duke was half in, half out of the saddle, his sword scabbarded, and he began to fall backwards as the men helping him drew their own swords. Where the hell had these English come from? Then his other men-at-arms, desperate to protect their lord, slammed down their visors and turned to meet the challenge. The Duke, sprawling on the turf, heard the clash of armored horsemen.

The English were the group of men the French King had seen. They had paused in the village to watch the slaughter in the entrenchments and had been about to ride back across the bridge when the Duke of Bourbon's men had come close. Too close: a challenge that could not be ignored. So the English lord led his household knights in a charge that tore into the Duke of Bourbon's men. The Frenchmen had not been ready for the attack, and the English came in proper array, knee to knee, and the long ash lances, carried upright as they charged, suddenly dropped to the killing position and tore through mail and leather. The English leader was wearing a blue surcoat slashed with a diagonal white band on which three red stars were blazoned. Yellow lions occupied the blue field that turned suddenly black with enemy blood as he rammed his sword up into the unprotected armpit of a French man-at-arms. The man shook with pain, tried to backswing his sword, but then another Englishman hammered a mace into his visor that crumpled under the blow and sprang blood from a dozen rents. A hamstrung horse screamed and toppled. "Stay close!" the Englishman in the gaudy surcoat was shouting at his men. "Stay close!" His horse reared up and flailed its hooves at an unhorsed Frenchman. That man went down, helmet and skull crushed by a horseshoe, and then the rider saw the Duke standing helpless beside a horse; he recognized the value of the man's shining plate armor and so spurred at him. The Duke fended the sword blow with his shield, swung his own blade that jarred on the enemy's leg armor and suddenly the horseman was gone.

Another Englishman had pulled his leader's horse away. A mass of French horsemen was coming down the hill. The King had sent them in hope of capturing the English lord and his men, and still more Frenchmen, unable to join the attack on the tower because too many of their fellows were assembling to help kill the garrison's remnant, were now charging the bridge. "Back!" the English leader called, but the village street and the narrow bridge were blocked by fugitives and threatened by Frenchmen. He could cut his way through, but that would mean killing his own archers and losing some of his knights in the chaotic panic, so instead he looked across the road and saw a path running beside the river. It might lead to the beach, he thought, and there, perhaps, he could turn and ride east to rejoin the English lines.

The English knights slashed their spurs back. The path was narrow, only two horsemen could ride abreast; on one side was the River Ham and on the other a stretch of boggy swamp, but the path itself was firm and the English rode it until they reached a stretch of higher ground where they could assemble. But they could not escape. The small piece of higher ground was almost an island, reachable only by the path and surrounded by a morass of reeds and mud. They were trapped.

A hundred French horsemen were ready to follow along the path, but the English had dismounted and made a shield wall, and the thought of hacking their way through that steel barrier persuaded the French to turn back to the tower where the enemy was more vulnerable. Archers were still shooting from its ramparts, but the Genoese crossbowmen were replying, and now the French slammed into the English men-at-arms drawn up at the tower's foot.

The French attacked on foot. The ground was slippery because of the summer's rain and the mailed feet churned it to mud as the leading men-at-arms bellowed their war cry and threw themselves onto the outnumbered English. Those English had locked their shields and they thrust them forward to meet the charge. There was a clash of steel on wood, a scream as a blade slid under a shield's edge and found flesh. The men in the second English rank, the rear rank, flailed with maces and swords over their comrades" heads. "St. George!" a shout went up, "St. George!" and the men-at-arms heaved forward to throw the dead and dying off their shields. "Kill the bastards!"

"Kill them!" Sir Geoffrey de Charny yelled in return and the French came back, stumbling in their mail and plate across the wounded and dead, and this time the English shields were not touching rim to rim and the French found gaps. Swords crashed onto plate armor, thrust through mail, beat in helmets. A few last defenders were trying to escape across the river, but the Genoese crossbowmen pursued them and it was a simple matter to hold an armored man down in the water until he drowned, then pillage his body. A few English fugitives stumbled away on the farther bank, going to where an English battle line of archers and men-at-arms was forming to repel any attack across the Ham.

Back at the tower a Frenchman with a battle-axe swung repeatedly at an Englishman, cracking open the espalier that protected his right shoulder, slashing through the mail beneath, beating the man down to a crouch, and still the blows came until the axe had laid open the enemy's chest and there was a splay of white ribs among the mangled flesh and torn armor. Blood and mud made a paste underfoot. For every Englishman there were three enemies, and the tower door had been left unlocked to give the men outside a place where they could retreat, but instead it was the French who forced their way inside. The last defenders outside the tower were cut down and killed, while inside the attackers began fighting up the stairs.

The steps turned to the right as they climbed. That meant the defenders could use their right arms without much encumbrance while the attackers were forever balked by the big central pillar of the stairs, but a French knight with a short spear made the first rush and he disemboweled an Englishman with the blade before another defender killed him with a sword thrust over the dying man's head. Visors were up here, for it was dark in the tower, and a man could not see with his eyes half covered with steel. And so the English stabbed at French eyes. Men-at-arms pulled the dead off the steps, leaving a trail of guts behind, and then two more men charged up, slipping on offal. They parried English blows, thrust their swords up into groins, and still more Frenchmen pushed into the tower. A terrible scream filled the stairwell, then another bloodied body was hauled down and out of the way: another three steps were clear and the French shoved on up again. *"Montjoie St. Denis!"*

An Englishman with a blacksmith's hammer came down the steps and he beat at French helmets, killing one man by crushing his skull and driving the others back until a knight had the wit to seize a crossbow and sidle up the stairs until he had a clear view. The bolt went through the Englishman's mouth to lift off the back of his skull and the French rushed again, screaming hate and victory, trampling the dying man under their gore-spattered feet and carrying their swords up to the very top of the tower. There a dozen men tried to shove them back down the steps, but still more French were thrusting upwards. They forced the leading attackers onto the swords of the defenders and the next men clambered over the dying and the dead to rout the last of the garrison. All the men were hacked down. One archer lived long enough to have his fingers chopped off, then his eyes prized out, and he was still screaming as he was thrown off the tower onto the waiting swords below.

The French cheered. The tower was a charnel house, but the banner of France would fly from its ramparts. The entrenchments had become graves for the English. Victorious men began to strip the clothes from the dead to search for coins, when a trumpet called.

There were still some Englishmen on the French side of the river. There were horsemen trapped on a patch of firmer ground.

So the killing was not done.

THE *ST. JAMES* ANCHORED off the beach south of Calais and ferried its passengers ashore in rowboats. Three of the passengers, all in mail, had so much baggage that they paid two of the *St. James*'s crew to carry it into the streets of the English encampment where they sought the Earl of Northampton. Some of the houses had two stories, and cobblers, armorers, smiths, fruiterers, bakers and butchers had all hung signs from their upper floors. There were whorehouses and churches, fortune-tellers' booths and taverns built between the tents and houses. Children played in the streets. Some had small bows and shot blunt arrows at irritated dogs. The nobles' quarters had their banners displayed outside and mail-clad guards standing at their doors. A cemetery spread into the marshes, its damp graves filled with men, women and children who had succumbed to the fever that haunted the Calais swamps.

The three men found the Earl's quarters, which was a large wooden dwelling close to the pavilion that flew the royal flag, and there two of them, the youngest and the oldest, stayed with the baggage while the third man, the tallest, walked towards Nieulay. He had been told that the Earl had led some horsemen on a foray towards the French army. "Thousands of the bastards," the Earl's steward had reported, "picking their noses up on the ridge, so his lordship wants to challenge some of them. Getting bored, he is." He looked at the big wooden chest that the two men were guarding. "So what's in that?"

"Nose pickings," the tall man had said, then he shouldered a long black bowstave, picked up an arrow bag and left.

His name was Thomas. Sometimes Thomas of Hookton. Other times he was Thomas the Bastard and, if he wanted to be very formal, he could call himself Thomas Vexille, though he rarely did. The Vexilles were a noble Gascon family and Thomas of Hookton was an illegitimate son of a fugitive Vexille, which had left him neither noble nor Vexille. And certainly not Gascon. He was an English archer.

Thomas attracted glances as he walked through the camp. He was tall. Black hair showed beneath the edge of his iron helmet. He was young, but his face had been hardened by war. He had hollow cheeks, dark watchful eyes and a long nose that had been broken in a fight and set crooked. His mail was dulled by travel and beneath it he wore a leather jerkin, black breeches and long black riding boots without spurs. A sword scabbarded in black leather hung at his left side, a haversack at his back and a white arrow bag at his right hip. He limped very slightly, suggesting he must have been wounded in battle, though in truth the injury had been done by a churchman in the name of God. The scars of that torture were hidden now, except for the damage to his hands, which had been left crooked and lumpy, but he could still draw a bow. He was twenty-three years old and a killer.

He passed the archers' camps. Most were hung with trophies. He saw a French breastplate of solid steel that had been pierced by an arrow hung high to boast what archers did to knights. Another group of tents had a score of horsetails hanging from a pole. A rusty, torn coat of mail had been stuffed with straw, hung from a sapling and pierced by arrows. Beyond the tents was marshland that stank of sewage. Thomas walked on, watching the French array on the southern heights. There were enough of them, he thought, far more than had turned up to be slaughtered between Wadicourt and Crécy. Kill one Frenchman, he thought, and two more appear. He could see the bridge ahead of him now and the small hamlet beyond, and behind him men were coming from the encampment to make a battle line to defend the bridge because the French were attacking the small English outpost on the farther bank. He could see them flooding down the slope, and he could also see a small group of horsemen who he assumed were the Earl and his men. Bchind him, its sound dulled by distance, an English cannon launched a stone missile at Calais's battered walls. The noise rumbled over the marshes and faded, to be replaced by the clash of weapons from the English entrenchments.

Thomas did not hurry. It was not his fight. He did, however, take the bow from his back and string it, and he noted how easy that had become. The bow was old; it was getting tired. The black yew stave, which had once been straight, was now slightly curved. It had followed the string, as archers said, and he knew it was time to make a new weapon. Yet he reckoned the old bow, which he had colored black and onto which he had fixed a silver plate showing a strange beast holding a cup, still had a few Frenchmen's souls in it.

He did not see the English horsemen charge the flank of the French attack because the hovels of Nieulay hid the brief fight. He did see the bridge fill with fugitives who got in each other's way in their haste to escape the French fury, and above their heads he saw the horsemen ride towards the sea on the river's far bank. He followed them on the English side of the river, leaving the embanked road to jump from tussock to tussock, sometimes splashing through puddles or wading through mud that tried to steal his boots. Then he was by the river and he saw the mud-colored tide swirling its way inland as the sea rose. The wind smelt of salt and dccay.

He saw the Earl then. The Earl of Northampton was Thomas's lord, the man he served, though the Earl's rein was loose and his pursc generous. The Earl was watching the victorious French, knowing that they would come to attack him, and one of his men-at-arms had dismounted and was trying to find a path firm enough for the armored horses to reach the river. A dozen more of his men-at-arms wcre kneeling or standing across the French approach path, ready to meet a charge with shield and sword. And back at the hamlet, wherc the slaughter of the English garrison was finished, the French were turning wolfishly towards the trapped men.

Thomas waded into the river. He held his bow high, for a wet string would not draw, and he waded through the tide's tug. The water came to his waist, then he was pushing out onto the muddy bank and he ran to where the men-at-arms waited to receive the first French attackers. Thomas knelt just beside them, out in the marsh; he splayed his arrows on the mud, then plucked one.

A score of Frenchmen were coming. A dozen were mounted and those horsemen kept to the path, but on their flanks dismounted men-at-arms splashed through the swamps and Thomas forgot them, they would take time to reach the firm ground, so instead he began shooting at the mounted knights.

He shot without thinking. Without aiming. This was his life, his skill and his pride. Take one bow, taller than a man, made from yew, and use it to send arrows of ash, tipped with goose feathers and armed with a bodkin point. Because the great bow was drawn to the ear it was no use trying to aim with the eye. It was years of practice that let a man know where his arrows would go and Thomas was shooting them at a frantic pace, one arrow every three or four heartbeats, and the white feathers slashed across the marsh and the long steel tips drove through mail and leather into French bellies, chests and thighs. They struck with the sound of a meat-axe falling on flesh and they stopped the horsemen dead. The leading two were dying, a third had an arrow in his upper thigh, and the men behind could not pass the wounded men in front because the path was too narrow and so Thomas began shooting at the dismounted men-at-arms. The force of an arrow's strike was enough to throw a man backwards. If a Frenchman lifted a shield to protect his upper body Thomas put an arrow into his legs, and if his bow was old, then it was still vicious. He had been at sea for more than a week and he could feel the ache in his back muscles as he hauled the string back. Even pulling the weakened bow was the equivalent of lifting a grown man bodily, and all that muscle was poured into the arrow. A horseman tried to splash through the mud but his heavy destrier floundered in the soggy ground; Thomas selected a flesh arrow, one with a broad, tanged head that would rip through a horse's guts and blood vessels and he loosed it low, saw the horse shudder, picked a bodkin from the ground and let it fly at a man-at-arms who had his visor up. Thomas did not look to see if any of the arrows were on target, he shot and picked another missile, then shot again, and the bowstring whipped along the horn bracer that he wore on his left wrist. He had never bothered to pro-tect his wrist before, reveling in the burn left by the string, but the Dominican had tortured his left forearm and left it ridged with scar so now the horn sheath guarded the flesh.

The Dominican was dead.

Six arrows left. The French were retreating, but they were not beaten. They were shouting for crossbowmen and for more men-at-arms and Thomas, responding, put his two string fingers in his mouth and let loose a piercing whistle. Two notes, high and low, repeated three times, then a pause and he blew the double notes again and he saw archers running towards the river. Some were the men who had retreated from Nieulay and others came from the battle line because they recognized the signal that a fellow archer needed help.

Thomas picked up his six arrows and turned to see that the first of the Earl's horsemen had found a passage to the river and were lead-ing their heavily armored horses across the swirling tide. It would be minutes before they were all across, but archers were splashing towards the farther bank now and those closest to Nieulay were already shooting at a group of crossbowmen being hurried towards the unfinished fight. More horsemen were coming down from the heights of Sangatte, enraged that the trapped English knights were escaping. Two galloped into the marsh where their horses began to panic in the treacherous ground. Thomas laid one of his last arrows on the string, then decided the marsh was defeating the two men and an arrow would be superfluous.

A voice came from just behind him. "Thomas, isn't it?"

"Sire." Thomas snatched off his helmet and turned, still on his knees.

"You're good with that bow, aren't you?" The Earl spoke ironically.

"Practice, sire."

"A nasty mind helps," the Earl said, motioning Thomas to stand. The Earl was a short man, barrel-chested, with a weatherbeaten face that his archers liked to say looked like the backside of a bull, but they also reckoned he was a fighter, a good man and as hard as any of his men. He was a friend of the King's, but also a friend of any who wore his badge. He was not a man to send others into battle unless he led them, and he had dismounted and removed his helmet so that his rearguard would recognize him and know that he shared their danger. "I thought you were in England," he said to Thomas.

"I was," Thomas said, speaking now in French for he knew the Earl was more comfortable in that language, "then I was in Brittany."

"Now you're rescuing me." The Earl grinned, revealing the gaps where he had lost his teeth. "I suppose you'll want a pot of ale for this?"

"As much as that, my lord?"

The Earl laughed. "We rather made fools of ourselves, didn't we?" He was watching the French who, now that a hundred or more English archers lined the riverbank, were thinking twice before launching another attack. "We thought we might tempt forty of their men to a battle of honor by the village, then half their bloody army comes down the hill. Do you bring me news of Will Skeat?"

"Dead, my lord. Died in the fight at La Roche-Derrien."

The Earl flinched, then made the sign of the cross. "Poor Will. God knows I loved him. No better soldier ever breathed." He looked at Thomas. "And the other thing. Do you bring me that?"

He meant the Grail. "I bring you gold, my lord," Thomas said, "but not that."

The Earl patted Thomas's arm. "We shall talk, but not here." He looked at his men and raised his voice. "Back now! Back!"

His dismounted rear guard, their horses already led to safety through the rising tide, now hurried to the river and crossed. Thomas followed and the Earl, his sword drawn, was the last man to wade the deepening water. The French, denied their valuable quarry, jeered at his retreat.

And that day's fighting was done.

THE FRENCH ARMY did not stay. They had killed the Nieulay garrison, but even the most hot-blooded among them knew they could do no more. The English were too many. Thousands of archers were just praying for the French to cross the river and offer battle, so instead Philip's men marched away, leaving the trenches of Nieulay filled with the dead and the windswept ridge of Sangatte empty, and next day the town of Calais surrendered. King Edward's first instinct was to slaughter every inhabitant, to line them beside the moat and cut the heads from their emaciated bodies, but his great lords protested that the French would then do the same to any English-held town they captured in Gascony or Flanders and so the King reluctantly reduced his demand to just six lives.

Six men, hollow-cheeked and dressed in the robes of penitents, with hanging nooses draped about their necks, were brought from the town. They were all leading citizens, merchants or knights, men of wealth and standing, the kind of men who had defied Edward of England for eleven months. They carried the keys of the town's gates on cushions that they laid before the King, then prostrated themselves in front of the wooden platform where the King and Queen of England and the great magnates of their realm were seated. The six men pleaded for their lives, but Edward was angry. They had defied him, and so the executioner was summoned, but again his great lords argued that he invited reprisals, and the Queen herself knelt to her husband and begged that the six men be spared. Edward growled, paused while the six lay motionless beneath the dais, then let them live.

Food was taken to the starving citizens, but no other mercy was shown. They were evicted, allowed to take nothing except the clothes they wore and even those were searched to ensure that no coins or jewels were being smuggled past the English lines. An empty town, with houses for eight thousand people, with warehouses and shops and taverns and docks and a citadel and moats, belonged to England. "A doorway into France," the Earl of Northampton enthused. He had taken a house that had belonged to one of the six, a man who now wandered Picardy like a beggar with his family. It was a lavish stone house beneath the citadel with a view of the town quay that was now crowded with English ships. "We'll fill the town with good English folk," the Earl said. "You want to live here, Thomas?"

"No, sire," Thomas said.

"Nor me," the Earl admitted. "A pig sty in a swamp, that's what it is. Still, it's ours. So what do you want, young Thomas?"

It was morning, three days after the town's surrender, and already the confiscated wealth of Calais was being distributed to the victors. The Earl had found himself even richer than he expected, for the great chest Thomas had brought from Brittany was filled with gold and silver coins captured in Charles of Blois's camp after the battle outside La Roche-Derrien. One-third of that belonged to Thomas's lord and the Earl's men had counted the coins, setting aside a third of the Earl's share for the King.

Thomas had told his story. How, on the Earl's instructions, he had gone to England to search his dead father's past for a clue to the Grail. He had found nothing except a book in which his father, a priest, had written about the Grail, but Father Ralph had wits that wandered and dreams that seemed real and Thomas had learned nothing from the writings, which had been taken from him by the Dominican who had tortured him. But the book had been copied before the Dominican took it and now, in the Earl's new sunlit chamber above the quay, a young English priest tried to make sense of the copy.

"What I want," Thomas told the Earl, "is to lead archers."

"God knows if there'll be anywhere to lead them," the Earl responded gloomily. "Edward talks of attacking Paris, but it won't happen. There's going to be a truce, Thomas. We'll plead eternal friendship, then go home and sharpen our swords." There was the crackle of parchment as the priest took up a new page. Father Ralph had written in Latin, Greek, Hebrew and French, and evidently the priest understood them all. He made an occasional note on a scrap of parchment as he read. Barrels of beer were being unloaded on the quay, the rumble of the great tuns sounding like thunder. The flag of England's King, leopards and fleur de lys, flew from the captured citadel above the French standard, which was hung upside down as a mark of derision. Two men, Thomas's companions, stood at the edge of the room, waiting for the Earl to include them. "God knows what employment there'll be for archers," the Earl went on, "unless it's guarding fortress walls. Is that what you want?"

"It's all I'm good for, my lord. Shooting a bow." Thomas spoke in Norman French, the language of England's aristocracy and the language his father had taught him. "And I have money, my lord." He meant that he could now recruit archers, equip them with horses and take them on the Earl's service, which would cost the Earl nothing, but the Earl could then take one-third of everything they plundered.

That was how Will Skeat, common-born, had made his name. The Earl liked such men, profited from them, and he nodded approvingly. "But lead them where?" he asked. "I hate truces."

The young priest intervened from his table by the window. "The King would prefer it if the Grail were found."

"His name's John Buckingham," the Earl said of the priest, "and he's Chamberlain of the Receipt of the Exchequer, which may not sound much to you, young Thomas, but it means he serves the King and he'll probably be Archbishop of Canterbury before he's thirty."

"Hardly, my lord," the priest said.

"And of course the King wants the Grail found," the Earl said, "we all want that. I want to see the damn thing in Westminster Abbey! I want the King of damned France crawling on his bloody knees to say prayers to it. I want pilgrims from all Christendom bringing us their gold. For God's sake, Thomas, does the bloody thing exist? Did your father have it?"

"I don't know, my lord," Thomas said.

"Much bloody use you are," the Earl grumbled.

John Buckingham looked at his notes. "You have a cousin, Guy Vexille?"

"Yes," Thomas said.

"And he seeks the Grail?"

"By seeking me," Thomas said. "And I don't know where it is."

"But he was searching for the Grail before he knew you existed," the young priest pointed out, "which suggests to me that he possesses some knowledge denied to us. I would advise, my Lord, that we seek this Guy Vexille."

"We'd be two dogs chasing each other's tails," Thomas put in sourly.

The Earl waved Thomas to silence. The priest looked back at his notes. "And, opaque though these writings are," he said disapprovingly, "there is one thread of light. They seem to confirm that the Grail was at Astarac. That it was hidden there."

"And taken away again!" Thomas protested.

"If you lose something valuable," Buckingham said patiently, "where do you begin your search? At the place where it was last seen. Where is Astarac?"

"Gascony," Thomas said, "in the fief of Berat."

"Ah!" the Earl said, but then was silent.

"And have you been to Astarac?" Buckingham asked. He might have been young, but he had an authority that came from more than his job with the King's Exchequer.

"No."

"Then I suggest you go," the priest said, "and see what you can learn. And if you make enough noise in your searching then your cousin may well come looking for you, and you can find him and discover what he knows." He smiled, as if to suggest that he had solved the problem.

There was silence except that one of the Earl's hunting dogs scratched itself in a corner of the room and on the quays a sailor let loose a stream of profanities that might have brought a blush to the devil's face. "I can't capture Guy by myself," Thomas protested, "and Berat offers no allegiance to our King."

"Officially," Buckingham said, "Berat offers allegiance to the Count of Toulouse, which today means the King of France. The Count of Berat is definitely an enemy."

"No truce is signed yet," the Earl offered hesitantly.

"And won't be for days, I suspect," Buckingham agreed.

The Earl looked at Thomas. "And you want archers?"

"I'd like Will Skeat's men, sire."

"And no doubt they'd serve you," the Earl said, "but you can't lead men-at-arms, Thomas." He meant that Thomas, not nobly born and still young, might have the authority to command archers, but men-at-arms, who considered themselves of higher rank, would resent his leadership. Will Skeat, worse born than Thomas, had managed it, but Will had been much older and far more experienced.

"I can lead men-at-arms," one of the two men by the wall announced.

Thomas introduced the two. The one who had spoken was an older man, scarred, one eye missing, hard as mail. His name was Sir Guillaume d'Evecque, Lord of Evecque, and he had once held a fief in Normandy until his own King turned against him and now he was a landless warrior and Thomas's friend. The other, younger man was also a friend. He was a Scot, Robbie Douglas, taken prisoner at Durham the year before. "Christ's bones," the Earl said when he knew

Robbie's circumstances, "but you must have raised your ransom by now?"

"I raised it, my lord," Robbie admitted, "and lost it."

"Lost it!"

Robbie stared at the floor, so Thomas explained in one curt word. "Dice."

The Earl looked disgusted, then turned again to Sir Guillaume. "I have heard of you," he said, and it was a compliment, "and know you can lead men-at-arms, but whom do you serve?"

"No man, my lord."

"Then you cannot lead my men-at-arms," the Earl said pointedly, and waited.

Sir Guillaume hesitated. He was a proud man, thirty-five years old, experienced in war, with a reputation that had first been made by fighting against the English. But now he possessed no land, no master, and as such he was little more than a vagabond and so, after a pause, he walked to the Earl and knelt before him and held up his hands as though in prayer. The Earl put his own hands round Sir Guillaume's. "You promise to do me service," he asked, "to be my liege man, to serve no other?"

"I do so promise," Sir Guillaume said earnestly and the Earl raised him and the two men kissed on the lips.

"I'm honored," the Earl said, thumping Sir Guillaume's shoulder, then turned to Thomas again. "So you can raise a decent force. You'll need, what? Fifty men? Half archers."

"Fifty men in a distant fief?" Thomas said. "They won't last a month, my lord."

"But they will," the Earl said, and explained his previous, surprised reaction to the news that Astarac lay in the county of Berat. "Years ago, young Thomas, before you were off your mother's tit, we owned property in Gascony. We lost it, but we never formally surrendered it, so there are three or four strongholds in Berat over which I have a legitimate claim." John Buckingham, reading Father Ralph's notes again, raised an eyebrow to suggest that the claim was tenuous at best, but he said nothing. "Go and take one of those castles," the Earl said, "make raids, make money, and men will join you."

"And men will come against us," Thomas observed quietly.

"And Guy Vexille will be one," the Earl said, "so that's your opportunity. Take it, Thomas, and get out of here before the truce is made."

Thomas hesitated for a heartbeat or two. What the Earl suggested sounded close to insanity. He was to take a force into the deep south of French territory, capture a fortress, defend it, hope to capture his cousin, find Astarac, explore it, follow the Grail. Only a fool would accept such a charge, but the alternative was to rot away with every other unemployed archer. "I shall do it, my lord," he said.

"Good. Be off with you, all of you!" The Earl led Thomas to the door, but once Robbie and Sir Guillaume were on the stairs, he pulled Thomas back for a private word. "Don't take the Scotsman with you," the Earl said.

"No, my lord? He's a friend."

"He's a damned Scot and I don't trust them. They're all god-damned thieves and liars. Worse than the bloody French. Who holds him prisoner?"

"Lord Outhwaite."

"And Outhwaite let him travel with you? I'm surprised. Never mind, send your Scottish friend back to Outhwaite and let him molder away until his family raises the ransom. But I don't want a bloody Scotsman taking the Grail away from England. You under-stand?"

"Yes, my lord."

"Good man," the Earl said and clapped Thomas's back. "Now go and prosper."

Go and die, more like. Go on a fool's errand, for Thomas did not believe the Grail existed. He wanted it to exist, he wanted to believe his father's words, but his father had been mad at times and mischievous at others, and Thomas had his own ambition, to be a leader as good as Will Skeat. To be an archer. Yet the fool's errand gave him a chance to raise men, lead them and follow his dream. So he would pursue the Grail and see what came.

He went to the English encampment and beat a drum. Peace was coming, but Thomas of Hookton was raising men and going to war.

Part One

THE DEVIL'S PLAYTHING

T HE COUNT OF BERAT was old, pious and learned. He had lived sixty-five years and liked to boast that he had not left his fiefdom for the last forty of them. His stronghold was the great castle of Berat. It stood on a limestone hill above the town of Berat, which was almost surrounded by the River Berat that made the county of Berat so fertile. There were olives, grapes, pears, plums, barley and women. The Count liked them all. He had married five times, each new wife younger than the last, but none had provided him with a child. He had not even spawned a bastard on a milkmaid though, God knew, it was not for lack of trying.

That absence of children had persuaded the Count that God had cursed him and so in his old age he had surrounded himself with priests. The town had a cathedral and eighteen churches, with a bishop, canons and priests to fill them, and there was a house of Dominican friars by the east gate. The Count blessed the town with two new churches and built a convent high on the western hill across the river and beyond the vineyards. He employed a chaplain and, at great expense, he purchased a handful of the straw that had lined the manger in which the baby Jesus had been laid at his birth. The Count encased the straw in crystal, gold and gems, and placed the reliquary on the altar of the castle's chapel and prayed to it each day, but even that sacred talisman did not help. His fifth wife was seventeen and plump and healthy and, like the others, barren.

At first the Count suspected that he had been cheated in his purchase of the holy straw, but his chaplain assured him that the relic had come from the papal palace at Avignon and produced a letter signed by the Holy Father himself guaranteeing that the straw was indeed the Christ-child's bedding. Then the Count had his new wife examined by four eminent doctors and those worthies decreed that her urine was clear, her parts whole and her appetites healthy, and so the Count employed his own learning in search of an heir. Hippocrates had written of the effect of pictures on conception and so the Count ordered a painter to decorate the walls of his wife's bedchamber with pictures of the Virgin and child; he ate red beans and kept his rooms warm. Nothing worked. It was not the Count's fault, he knew that. He had planted barley seeds in two pots and watered one with his new wife's urine and one with his own, and both pots had sprouted seedlings and that, the doctors said, proved that both the Count and Countess were fertile.

Which meant, the Count had decided, that he was cursed. So he turned more avidly to religion because he knew he did not have much time left. Aristotle had written that the age of seventy was the limit of a man's ability, and so the Count had just five years to work his miracle. Then, one autumn morning, though he did not realize it at the time, his prayers were answered.

Churchmen came from Paris. Three priests and a monk arrived at Berat and they brought a letter from Louis Bessières, Cardinal and Archbishop of Livorno, Papal Legate to the Court of France, and the letter was humble, respectful and threatening. It requested that Brother Jerome, a young monk of formidable learning, be allowed to examine the records of Berat. "It is well known to us," the Cardinal Archbishop had written in elegant Latin, "that you possess a great love of all manuscripts, both pagan and Christian, and so entreat you, for the love of Christ and for the furtherance of His kingdom, to allow our Brother Jerome to examine your muniments." Which was fine, so far as it went, for the Count of Berat did indeed possess a library and a manuscript collection that was probably the most extensive in all Gascony, if not in all southern Christendom, but what the letter did not make clear was why the Cardinal Archbishop was so interested in the castle's muniments. As for the reference to pagan works, that was a threat. Refuse this request, the Cardinal Archbishop was saying, and I shall set the holy dogs of the Dominicans and the Inquisitors onto your county and they will find that the pagan works encourage heresy. Then the trials and the burnings would begin, neither of which would affect the Count directly, but there would be indulgences to buy if his soul was not to be damned. The Church had a glutton's appetite for money and everyone knew the Count of Berat was rich. So the Count did not want to offend the Cardinal Archbishop, but he did want to know why His Eminence had suddenly become interested in Berat.

Which was why the Count had summoned Father Roubert, the chief Dominican in the town of Berat, to the great hall of the castle, which had long ceased to be a place of feasting, but instead was lined with shelves on which old documents moldered and precious handwritten books were wrapped in oiled leather.

Father Roubert was just thirty-two years old. He was the son of a tanner in the town and had risen in the Church thanks to the Count's patronage. He was very tall, very stern, with black hair cut so short that it reminded the Count of the stiff-bristled brushes the armorers used to burnish the coats of mail. Father Roubert was also, this fine morning, angry. "I have business in Castillon d'Arbizon tomorrow," he said, "and will need to leave within the hour if I am to reach the town in daylight."

The Count ignored the rudeness in Father Roubert's tone. The Dominican liked to treat the Count as an equal, an impudence the Count tolerated because it amused him. "You have business in Castillon d'Arbizon?" he asked, then remembered. "Of course you do. You are burning the beghard, are you not?"

"Tomorrow morning."

"She will burn with or without you, father," the Count said, "and the devil will take her soul whether you are there to rejoice or not." He peered at the friar. "Or is it that you like to watch women burn?"

"It is my duty," Father Roubert said stiffly.

"Ah yes, your duty. Of course. Your duty." The Count frowned at a chessboard on the table, trying to work out whether he should advance a pawn or retract a bishop. He was a short, plump man with a round face and a clipped beard. He habitually wore a woolen cap over his bald head and, even in summer, was rarely without a fur-lined gown. His fingers were perpetually ink-stained so that he looked more like a fussy clerk than the ruler of a great domain. "But you have a duty to me, Roubert," he chided the Dominican, "and this is it." He gave the Cardinal Archbishop's letter to the Dominican and watched as the friar read the long document. "He writes a fine Latin, does he not?" the Count said.

"He employs a secretary who is properly educated," Father Roubert said curtly, then he examined the great red seal to make certain the document was genuine. "They say," the friar sounded respectful now, "that Cardinal Bessières is regarded as a possible successor to the Holy Father."

"So not a man to offend?"

"No churchman should ever be offended," Father Roubert answered stiffly.

"And certainly not one who might become Pope," the Count concluded. "But what is it he wants?"

Father Roubert went to a window screened with a lead lattice supporting scraped horn panes that let a diffuse light into the room, but kept out rain, birds and some of winter's cold winds. He lifted the lattice from its frame and breathed the air which, this high up in the castle's keep, was wonderfully free of the latrine stink in the lower town. It was autumn and there was the faint smell of pressed grapes in the air. Roubert liked that smell. He turned back to the Count. "Is the monk here?"

"In a guest room," the Count said. "He's resting. He's young, very nervous. He bowed to me very properly, but refused to say what the Cardinal wants."

A great clash in the yard below prompted Father Roubert to peer through the window again. He had to lean far forward for even here, forty feet up the keep, the walls were nearly five feet thick. A horseman in full plate armor had just charged the quintain in the yard and his lance had struck the wooden shield so hard that the whole contraption had collapsed. "Your nephew plays," he said as he straightened from the window.

"My nephew and his friends practice," the Count corrected the friar.

"He would do better to look to his soul," Father Roubert said sourly.

"He has no soul, he's a soldier."

"A tournament soldier," the friar said scornfully.

The Count shrugged. "It is not enough to be wealthy, father. A man must also be strong and Joscelyn is my strong arm." The Count said it forcibly, though in truth he was not sure that his nephew was the best heir for Berat, but if the Count had no son then the fief must pass to one of his nephews and Joscelyn was probably the best of a bad brood. Which made it all the more important to have an heir. "I asked you here," he said, choosing to use the word "asked" rather than "ordered," "because you might have some insight into His Eminence's interest."

The friar looked at the Cardinal's letter again. "Muniments," he said.

"I noticed that word too," the Count said. He moved away from the open window. "You're causing a draught, father."

Father Roubert reluctantly replaced the horn screen. The Count, he knew, had deduced from his books that for a man to be fertile he must be warm and the friar wondered how folk in cold northern countries ever managed to breed. "So the Cardinal isn't interested in your books," the Dominican said, "but only in the county's records?"

"So it would seem. Two hundred years of tax rolls?" The Count chuckled. "Brother Jerome will enjoy deciphering those."

The friar said nothing for a while. The sound of clashing swords echoed from the castle's curtain wall as the Count's nephew and his cronies practiced their weapons in the yard. Let Lord Joscelyn inherit here, the friar thought, and these books and parchments would all be put to the flames. He moved closer to the hearth in which, though it was not cold outside, a great fire burned and he thought of the girl who must be burned to death next morning in Castillon d'Arbizon. She was a heretic, a foul creature, the devil's plaything, and he remembered her agony as he had tortured the confession from her. He wanted to see her burn and hear the screams that would announce her arrival at the gates of hell, and so the sooner he answered the Count the sooner he could leave.

"You're hiding something, Roubert," the Count prompted him before the friar could speak.

The friar hated being called by his simple Christian name, a reminder that the Count had known him as a child and had paid for his elevation. "I hide nothing," he protested.

"So tell me why a Cardinal Archbishop would send a monk to Berat?"

The friar turned from the fire. "Do I need to remind you," he said, "that the county of Astarac is now a part of your domain?"

The Count stared at Father Roubert, then realized what the friar was saying. "Oh, dear God, no," the Count said. He made the sign of the cross and returned to his chair. He peered at the chessboard, scratched an itch beneath his woolen cap and turned back to the Dominican. "Not that old story?"

"There have been rumors," Father Roubert said loftily. "There was a member of our order, a fine man, Bernard de Taillebourg, who died this year in Brittany. He was pursuing something, we were never told what, but the rumors say that he made common cause with a member of the Vexille family."

"Good Christ Almighty," the Count said. "Why didn't you tell me this before?"

"You wish me to bother you with every vaporous story that gets told in the taverns?" Father Roubert retorted.

The Count did not answer. Instead he was thinking of the Vexilles. The old Counts of Astarac. They had been powerful once, great lords of wide lands, but the family had become entangled with the Cathar heresy and when the Church burned that plague from the land the Vexille family had fled to its last stronghold, the castle of Astarac, and there they had been defeated. Most had been killed, but some had succeeded in running away, even, the Count knew, as far as England, while ruined Astarac, home to ravens and foxes, had been swallowed into the fiefdom of Berat and with the ruined castle had come a persistent story that the defeated Vexilles had once held the fabled treasures of the Cathars in their keeping, and that one of those treasures was the Holy Grail itself. And the reason, of course, that Father Roubert had made no mention of the new stories was because he wanted to find the Grail before anyone else discovered it. Well, the Count would forgive him that. He looked across the wide room. "So the Cardinal Archbishop believes the Grail will be found among those things?" He gestured at his books and papers.

"Louis Bessières," the friar said, "is a greedy man, a violent man and an ambitious man. He will turn the earth upside down to find the Grail."

The Count understood then. Understood the pattern of his life. "There was a story, wasn't there," he mused aloud, "that the keeper of the Grail would be cursed until he gave the cup back to God?"

"Stories," Father Roubert sneered.

"And if the Grail is here, father, even if it is hidden, then I am its keeper."

"If," the Dominican sneered again.

"And so God cursed me," the Count said in wonderment, "because all unknowingly I hold his treasure and have not valued it." He shook his head. "He has withheld a son from me because I have withheld his son's cup from him." He shot a surprizingly harsh look at the young friar. "Does it exist, father?"

Father Roubert hesitated, then gave a reluctant nod. "It is possible."

"Then we had best give the monk permission to search," the Count said, "but we must also make sure that we find what he is looking for before he does. You will go through the muniments, Father Roubert, and only pass on to Brother Jerome those records that do not mention treasures or relics or grails. You understand?"

"I will seek the permission of my regent to perform that duty," Father Roubert responded stiffly.

"You will seek nothing but the Grail!" The Count slapped the arm of his chair. "You will start now, Roubert, and you will not stop till you have read every parchment on those shelves. Or would you rather I evicted your mother, your brothers and sisters from their houses?"

Father Roubert was a proud man and he bridled, but he was not a foolish man and so, after a pause, he bowed. "I will search the documents, my lord," he said humbly.

"Starting now," the Count insisted.

"Indeed, my lord," Father Roubert said, and sighed because he would not see the girl burn.

"And I will help you," the Count said enthusiastically. Because no Cardinal Archbishop would take from Berat the holiest treasure on earth or in heaven. The Count would find it first.

THE DOMINICAN FRIAR ARRIVED at Castillon d'Arbizon in the autumn dusk, just as the watchman was shutting the western gate. A fire had been kindled in a big brazier that stood inside the gate's arch to warm the town's watchmen on what promised to be the first chill night of the waning year. Bats were flickering above the town's half-repaired walls and about the tower of the high castle which crowned Castillon d'Arbizon's steep hill.

"God be with you, father," one of the watchmen said as he paused to let the tall friar through the gate, but the watchman spoke in Occitan, his native tongue, and the friar did not speak that language and so he just smiled vaguely and sketched a sign of the cross before he hitched up his black skirts and toiled up the town's main street towards the castle. Girls, their day's work finished, were strolling the lanes and some of them giggled, for the friar was a fine-looking man despite a very slight limp. He had ragged black hair, a strong face and dark eyes. A whore called to him from a tavern doorway and prompted a cackle of laughter from men drinking at a table set in the street. A butcher sluiced his shopfront with a wooden pail of water so that dilute blood swilled down the gutter past the friar while above him, from a top-floor window where she was drying her washing on a long pole, a woman screamed insults at a neighbor. The western gate crashed shut at the foot of the street and the locking bar dropped into place with a thud.

The friar ignored it all. He just climbed to where the church of St. Sardos crouched beneath the pale bastion of the castle and, once inside the church, he knelt at the altar steps, made the sign of the cross and then prostrated himself. A black-dressed woman praying at the side altar of St. Agnes, disturbed by the friar's baleful presence, made the sign of the cross too and hurried from the church. The friar, lying flat on the top step, just waited.

A town sergeant, dressed in Castillon d'Arbizon's livery of gray and red, had watched the friar climb the hill. He had noticed that the Dominican's robe was old and patched and that the friar himself was young and strong, and so the sergeant went to find one of the town's consuls and that official, cramming his fur-trimmed hat onto his gray hair, ordered the sergeant to bring two more armed men while he fetched Father Medous and one of the priest's two books. The group assembled outside the church and the consul ordered the curious folk who had gathered to watch the excitement to stand back. "There is nothing to see," he said officiously.

But there was. A stranger had come to Castillon d'Arbizon and all strangers were cause for suspicion, and so the crowd stayed and watched as the consul pulled on his official robe of gray and red cloth trimmed with hare fur, then ordered the three sergeants to open the church door.

What did the people expect? A devil to erupt from St. Sardos's? Did they think to see a great charred beast with crackling black wings and a trail of smoke behind his forked tail? Instead the priest and the consul and two of the sergeants went inside, while the third sergeant, his stave of office showing the badge of Castillon d'Arbizon, which was a hawk carrying a sheaf of rye, guarded the door. The crowd waited. The woman who had fled the church said that the friar was praying. "But he looks evil," she added, "he looks like the devil," and she hurriedly made the sign of the cross once more.

When the priest, the consul and the two guards went into the church the friar was still lying flat before the altar with his arms spread wide so that his body made the shape of the cross. He must have heard the nailed boots on the nave's uneven flagstones, but he did not move, nor did he speak.

"*Paire!*" Castillon d'Arbizon's priest asked nervously. He spoke in Occitan and the friar did not respond. "Father?" The priest tried French.

"You are a Dominican?" The consul was too impatient to wait for any response to Father Medous's tentative approach. "Answer me!" He also spoke in French, and sternly too, as befitted Castillon d'Arbizon's leading citizen. "Are you a Dominican?"

The friar prayed a moment longer, brought his hands together above his head, paused for a heartbeat, then stood and faced the four men.

"I have come a long way," he said imperiously, "and need a bed, food and wine."

The consul repeated his question. "You are a Dominican?"

"I follow the blessed St. Dominic's way," the friar confirmed. "The wine need not be good, the food merely what your poorest folk eat, and the bed can be of straw."

The consul hesitated, for the friar was tall, evidently strong and just a bit frightening, but then the consul, who was a wealthy man and properly respected in Castillon d'Arbizon, drew himself up to his full height. "You are young," he said accusingly, "to be a friar."

"It is to the glory of God," the Dominican said dismissively, "that young men follow the cross instead of the sword. I can sleep in a stable."

"Your name?" the consul demanded.

"Thomas."

"An English name!" There was alarm in the consul's voice and the two sergeants responded by hefting their long staves.

"*Tomas*, if you prefer," the friar said, seemingly unconcerned as the two sergeants took a menacing pace towards him. "It is my baptismal name," he explained, "and the name of that poor disciple who doubted Our Lord's divinity. If you have no such doubts then I envy you and I pray to God that he grants me such certainty."

"You are French?" the consul asked.

"I am a Norman," the friar said, then nodded. "Yes, I am French." He looked at the priest. "Do you speak French?"

"I do." The priest sounded nervous. "Some. A little."

"Then may I eat in your house tonight, father?"

The consul would not let Father Medous answer, but instead instructed the priest to give the friar the book. It was a very old book with worm-eaten pages and a black leather cover that the friar unwrapped.

"What do you want of me?" the friar demanded.

"Read from the book." The consul had noticed that the friar's hands were scarred and the fingers slightly twisted. Damage, he thought, more fitting for a soldier than a priest. "Read to me!" the consul insisted.

"You cannot read for yourself?" the friar asked derisively.

"Whether I read or not," the consul said, "is not your business. But whether you can read, young man, is our business, for if you are not a priest then you will not be able to read. So read to me."

The friar shrugged, opened a page at random and paused. The consul's suspicions were roused by the pause and he raised a hand to beckon the sergeants forward, but then the Dominican suddenly read aloud. He had a good voice, confident and strong, and the Latin words sounded like a melody as they echoed from the church's painted walls. After a moment the consul held up a hand to silence the friar and looked quizzically at Father Medous. "Well?"

"He reads well," Father Medous said weakly. The priest's own Latin was not good and he did not like to admit that he had not entirely understood the echoing words, though he was quite sure that the Dominican could read.

"You know what the book is?" the consul demanded.

"I assume," the friar said, "that it is the life of St. Gregory. The passage, as you doubtless recognized," there was sarcasm in his voice, "describes the pestilence that will afflict those who disobey the Lord their God." He wrapped the limp black cover about the book and held it out to the priest. "You probably know the book as the *Flores Sanctorum*?"

"Indeed." The priest took the book and nodded at the consul.

That official was still not entirely reassured. "Your hands," he said, "how were they injured? And your nose? It was broken?"

"As a child," the friar said, holding out his hands, "I slept with the cattle. I was trampled by an ox. And my nose was broken when my mother struck me with a skillet."

The consul understood those everyday childhood accidents and visibly relaxed. "You will understand, father," he said to the friar, "that we must be cautious of visitors."

"Cautious of God's priests?" the Dominican asked caustically.

"We had to be sure," the consul explained. "A message came from Auch which said the English are riding, but no one knows where."

"There is a truce," the friar pointed out.

"When did the English ever keep a truce?" the consul retorted.

"If they are indeed English," the Dominican said scornfully. "Any troop of bandits is called the English these days. You have men," he gestured at the sergeants who did not understand a word of the French conversation, "and you have churches and priests, so why should you fear bandits?"

"The bandits are English," the consul insisted. "They carried war bows."

"Which does not alter the fact that I have come a long way, and that I am hungry, thirsty and tired."

"Father Medous will look after you," the consul said. He gestured at the sergeants and led them back down the nave and out into the small square. "There is nothing to worry about!" the consul announced to the crowd. "Our visitor is a friar. He is a man of God."

The small crowd dispersed. Twilight wreathed the church tower and closed about the castle's battlements. A man of God had come to Castillon d'Arbizon and the small town was at peace.

THE MAN OF GOD ate a dish of cabbage, beans and salt bacon. He explained to Father Medous that he had made a pilgrimage to Santiago de Compostela in Spain to pray at the tomb of St. James and now he was walking to Avignon to fetch new orders from his superiors. He had seen no raiders, English or otherwise.

"We have seen no English in many years," Father Medous replied, making a hasty sign of the cross to avert the evil he had just mentioned, "but not so long ago they ruled here." The friar, eating his meal, appeared not to be interested. "We paid taxes to them," Father Medous went on, "but then they went and now we belong to the Count of Berat."

"I trust he is a godly man?" Friar Thomas asked.

"Very pious," Father Medous confirmed. "He keeps some straw from the manger at Bethlehem in his church. I would like to see that."

"His men garrison the castle?" the friar demanded, ignoring the more interesting topic of the baby Jesus' bedding.

"Indeed," Father Medous confirmed.

"Does the garrison hear Mass?"

Father Medous paused, obviously tempted to tell a lie, then settled for a half-truth. "Some do."

The friar put down his wooden spoon and stared sternly at the uncomfortable priest. "How many are they? And how many of them hear Mass?"

Father Medous was nervous. All priests were nervous when Dominicans appeared, for the friars were God's ruthless warriors in the fight against heresy and if this tall young man reported that the folk of Castillon d'Arbizon were less than pious then he could bring the Inquisition and its instruments of torture to the town. "There are ten of them in the garrison," Father Medous said, "and they are all good Christians. As are all my people."

Friar Thomas looked skeptical. "All of them?"

"They do their best," Father Medous said loyally, "but . . ." He paused again, evidently regretting that he had been about to add a qualification and, to cover his hesitation, he went to the small fire and added a log. The wind fretted at the chimney and sent a back-draught of smoke whirling about the small room. "A north wind," Father Medous said, "and it brings the first cold night of the autumn. Winter is not far off, eh?"

"But?" The friar had noted the hesitation.

Father Medous sighed as he took his seat. "There is a girl. A heretic. She was not from Castillon d'Arbizon, God be thanked, but she stayed here when her father died. She is a beghard."

"I did not think the beghards were this far south," the friar said. Beghards were beggars, but not just any importunate folk. Instead they were heretics who denied the Church and denied the need to work and claimed all things came from God and therefore that all things should be free to all men and women. The Church, to protect itself against such horrors, burned the beghards wherever they were found.

"They wander the roads," Father Medous pointed out, "and she came here, but we sent her to the bishop's court and she was found guilty. Now she is back here."

"Back here?" The friar sounded shocked.

"To be burned," Father Medous explained hurriedly. "She was sent back to be burned by the civil authorities. The bishop wants the people to see her death so they know the evil is gone from among them."

Friar Thomas frowned. "You say this beghard has been found guilty of heresy, that she had been sent here to die, yet she is still alive. Why?"

"She is to be burned tomorrow," the priest said, still hastily. "I had expected Father Roubert to be here. He is a Dominican like yourself and it was he who discovered the girl's heresy. Perhaps he is ill? He did send me a letter explaining how the fire was to be made."

Friar Thomas looked scornful. "All that's needed," he said dismissively, "is a heap of wood, a stake, some kindling and a heretic. What more can you want?"

"Father Roubert insisted that we use small faggots and that they stand upright." The priest illustrated this requirement by bunching his fingers like sticks of asparagus. "Bundles of sticks, he wrote to me, and all pointing to heaven. They must not lay flat. He was emphatic about that."

Friar Thomas smiled as he understood. "So the fire will burn bright, but not fierce, eh? She will die slowly."

"It is God's will," Father Medous said.

"Slowly and in great agony," the friar said, relishing the words, "that is indeed God's will for heretics."

"And I have made the fire as he instructed," Father Medous added weakly.

"Good. The girl deserves nothing better." The friar mopped his dish with a piece of dark bread. "I shall watch her death with joy and then walk on." He made the sign of the cross. "I thank you for this food."

Father Medous gestured at his hearth where he had piled some blankets. "You are welcome to sleep here."

"I shall, father," the friar said, "but first I shall pray to St. Sardos. I have not heard of him, though. Can you tell me who he is?"

"A goatherd," Father Medous said. He was not entirely sure that Sardos had ever existed, but the local people insisted he had and had always venerated him. "He saw the lamb of God on the hill where the town now stands. It was being threatened by a wolf and he rescued it and God rewarded him with a shower of gold."

"As is right and proper," the friar said, then stood. "You will come and pray to the blessed Sardos with me?"

Father Medous stifled a yawn. "I would like to," he said without any enthusiasm.

"I shall not insist," the friar said generously. "Will you leave your door unbarred?"

"My door is always open," the priest said, and felt a pang of relief as his uncomfortable guest stooped under the door's lintel and went into the night.

Father Medous's housekeeper smiled from the kitchen door. "He's a good-looking one for a friar. Is he staying tonight?"

"He is, yes."

"Then I'd better sleep in the kitchen," the housekeeper said, "because you wouldn't want a Dominican to find you between my legs at midnight. He'll put us both on the fire with the beghard." She laughed and came to clear the table.

The friar did not go to the church, but instead went the few paces down the hill to the nearest tavern and pushed open the door. The noise inside slowly subsided as the crowded room stared back at the friar's unsmiling face. When there was silence the friar shuddered as though he was horrified at the revelry, then he stepped back into the street and closed the door. There was a heartbeat of silence inside the tavern, then men laughed. Some reckoned the young priest had been looking for a whore, others merely supposed he had opened the wrong door, but in a moment or two they all forgot about him.

The friar limped back up the hill to St. Sardos's church where, instead of going into the goatherd's sanctuary, he stopped in the black shadows of a buttress. He waited there, invisible and silent, noting the few sounds of Castillon d'Arbizon's night. Singing and laughter came from the tavern, but he was more interested in the footsteps of the watchman pacing the town wall that joined the castle's stronger rampart just behind the church. Those steps came towards him, stopped a few paces down the wall and then retreated. The friar counted to a thousand and still the watchman did not return and so the friar counted to a thousand again, this time in Latin, and when there was still nothing but silence above him he moved to the wooden steps that gave access to the wall. The steps creaked under his weight, but no one called out. Once on the wall he crouched beside the high castle tower, his black robe invisible in the shadow cast by the waning moon. He watched down the wall's length where it followed the hill's contour until it turned the corner to the western gate where a dim red glow showed that the brazier was burning strongly. No watchmen were in sight. The friar reckoned the men must be warming themselves at the gate. He looked up, but saw no one at the castle's rampart, nor any movement in the two half-lit arrow slits that glowed from lanterns inside the tall tower. He had seen three liveried men inside the crowded tavern and there might have been others that he had not seen, and he reckoned the garrison was either drinking or asleep and so he lifted his black skirts and unwound a cord that had been wrapped about his waist. The cord was made of hemp stiffened with glue, the same kind of cord that powered the dreaded English war bows, and it was long enough so that he was able to loop it about one of the wall's crenellations and then let it drop to the steep ground beneath. He stayed a moment, staring down. The town and castle were built on a steep crag around which a river looped and he could hear the water hissing over a weir. He could just see a gleam of reflected moonlight glancing from a pool, but nothing else. The wind tugged at him, chilled him, and he retreated to the mooncast shadow and pulled his hood over his face.

The watchman reappeared, but only strolled halfway up the wall where he paused, leaned on the parapet for a time, then wandered back towards the gate. A moment later there was a soft whistle, jagged and tuneless like the song of a bird, and the friar went back to the cord and hauled it up. Knotted to it now was a rope, which he tied around the crencllation. "It's safe," he called softly in English, and then flinched at the sound of a man's boots scuffing on the wall as he climbed the rope.

There was a grunt as the man hauled himself up the rampart and a loud crash as his scabbard thumped on the stone, but then the man was over and crouching beside the friar. "Here." He gave the friar an English war bow and a bag of arrows. Another man was climbing now. He had a war bow slung on his back and a bag of arrows at his waist. He was more nimble than the first man and made no noise as he crossed the battlement, and then a third man appeared and crouched with the other two.

"How was it?" the first man asked the friar.

"Frightening."

"They didn't suspect you?"

"Made me read some Latin to prove I was a priest."

"Bloody fools, eh?" the man said. He had a Scottish accent. "So what now?"

"The castle."

"Christ help us."

"He has so far. How are you, Sam?"

"Thirsty," one of the other men answered.

"Hold these for me," Thomas said, giving Sam his bow and arrow bag, and then, satisfied that the watchman was out of sight, he led his three companions down the wooden steps to the alley which led beside the church to the small square in front of the castle's gate. The wooden faggots piled ready for the heretic's death were black in the moonlight. A stake with a chain to hold the beghard's waist jutted up from the waiting timber.

The castle's tall gates were wide enough to let a farm cart enter the courtyard, but set into one leaf was a small wicket gate and the friar stepped ahead of his companions and thumped the small door hard. There was a pause, then a shuffle of feet sounded and a man asked a question from the gate's far side. Thomas did not answer, but just knocked again, and the guard, who was expecting his companions to come back from the tavern, suspected nothing and pulled back the two bolts to open the door. Thomas stepped into the flamelight of two high torches burning in the inner archway and in their flickering glow he saw the guard's look of astonishment that a priest had come to Castillon d'Arbizon's castle in the darkness, and the man still looked astonished as the friar hit him hard, straight in the face, and then again in the belly. The guard fell back against the wall and the friar clamped a hand across the man's mouth. Sam and the other two came through the gate, which they locked behind them. The guard was struggling and Thomas brought up a knee which made the man give a muffled squeal. "Look in the guardroom," Thomas ordered his companions.

Sam, with an arrow on his bow's string, pushed open the door which led from the castle's entrance. A single guard was there, standing by a table on which was a skin of wine, two dice and a scatter of coins. The guard stared at Sam's round, cheerful face and he was still gazing open-mouthed when the arrow took him in the chest and threw him back against the wall. Sam followed, drawing a knife, and blood slashed up the stones as he cut the man's gullet.

"Did he have to die?" Thomas asked, bringing the first guard into the room.

"He was looking at me funny," Sam said, "like he'd seen a ghost." He scooped up the cash on the table and dropped it into his arrow bag.

"Shall I kill him too?" he asked, nodding at the first guard.

"No," Thomas said. "Robbie? Tie him up."

"What if he makes a noise?" Robbie, the Scotsman, asked.

"Then let Sam kill him."

The third of Thomas's men came into the guardroom. He was called Jake and he was a skinny man with crossed eyes. He grinned at the sight of the fresh blood on the wall. Like Sam he carried a bow and an arrow bag, and had a sword at his waist. He picked up the wine skin.

"Not now, Jake," Thomas said and the lanky man, who looked older and far more cruel than the younger Thomas, meekly obeyed. Thomas went to the guardroom door. He knew the garrison numbered ten men, he also knew that one was dead, one was a prisoner and at least three were still in the tavern. So five men could be left. He peered into the courtyard, but it was empty except for a farm wagon heaped with bales and barrels, and so he crossed to the weapon rack on the guardroom wall and selected a short sword. He tested the edge and found it sharp enough. "Do you speak French?" he asked the captive guard.

The man shook his head, too terrified to speak.

Thomas left Sam to guard the prisoner. "If anyone knocks on the castle gate," he said, "ignore it. If he makes a noise," he jerked his head towards the prisoner, "kill him. Don't drink the wine. Stay awake." He slung his bow on his shoulder, pushed two arrows into the rope belting his friar's robe, then beckoned to Jake and Robbie. The Scotsman, dressed in a short mail hauberk, had his sword drawn. "Keep it silent," Thomas said to them, and the three slipped into the courtyard.

Castillon d'Arbizon had been at peace for too long. The garrison was small and careless, its duties little more than to levy tariffs on goods coming to the town and dispatching the taxes to Berat where their lord lived. The men had become lazy, but Thomas of Hookton, who had pretended to be a friar, had been fighting for months and his instincts were those of a man who knew that death could be waiting at every corner. Robbie, though he was three years younger than Thomas, was almost as experienced in war as his friend, while cross-eyed Jake had been a killer all his life.

They began with the castle's undercroft where six dungeons lay in fetid darkness, but a flickering rushlight showed in the jailer's room where they found a monstrously fat man and his equally corpulent wife. Both were sleeping. Thomas pricked the man's neck with the sword's point to let him smell blood, then marched the couple to a dungeon where they were locked away. A girl called from another of the cells, but Thomas hissed at her to be quiet. She cursed him in return, then went silent.

One down, four to go.

They climbed back to the courtyard. Three servants, two of them boys, were sleeping in the stables and Robbie and Jake took them down to the cells, then rejoined Thomas to climb the dozen broad steps to the keep's door, then up the tower's winding stair. The servants, Thomas guessed, would not be numbered among the garrison, and there would doubtless be other servants, cooks and grooms and clerks, but for now he worried only about the soldiers. He found two of them fast asleep in the barracks room, both with women under their blankets, and Thomas woke them by tossing in a torch he took from a becket on the stairway. The four sat up, startled, to see a friar with an arrow nocked on his drawn bow. One woman took breath to scream, but the bow twitched and the arrow was pointing straight at her right eye and she had the sense to stifle her alarm.

"Tie them up," Thomas said.

"Quicker to slit their gizzards," Jake suggested.

"Tie them up," Thomas said again, "and stuff their mouths."

It did not take long. Robbie ripped a blanket into strips with his sword and Jake trussed the four. One of the women was naked and Jake grinned as he tied her wrists and then hoisted her up to a hook on the wall so that her arms were stretched. "Nice," he said.

"Later," Thomas said. He was at the door, listening. There could be two more soldiers in the castle, but he heard nothing. The four prisoners were all being half suspended from the big metal hooks that normally held swords and mail shirts and, when the four were silenced and immobilized, Thomas went up the next winding stair to where a great door blocked his path. Jake and Robbie followed him, their boots making a slight noise on the worn stone steps. Thomas motioned them to silence, then pushed on the door. For a moment he thought it must be locked, but he pushed again, harder, and the door jerked open with a terrible shriek of rusted metal hinges. The sound was fit to wake the dead and Thomas, appalled, found himself staring into a great high room hung with tapestries. The squeal of the hinges died away, leaving silence. The remnants of a fire burned in a big hearth and gave enough light to show that the hall was empty. At its far end was a dais where the Count of Berat, the Lord of Castillon d'Arbizon, would sit when he visited the town and where his table would be placed for any feasts. The dais was empty now, except that at its rear, hidden by a tapestry, there was an arched space where another flicker of light showed through the moth-eaten weave.

Robbie slipped past Thomas and crept up the side of the hall beneath the slit windows, which let in slanting bars of silvered moonlight. Thomas put an arrow on the black bow, then drew the cord and felt the immense power of the yew stave as he took the string back to his right ear. Robbie glanced at him, saw he was ready, and reached out with his sword to pull back the threadbare tapestry.

But before the blade even touched the tapestry it was swept aside as a big man charged Robbie. He came roaring and sudden, astonishing the Scot who tried to bring his sword back to meet the attack, but Robbie was too slow and the big man leaped on him, fists flailing. Just then the big black bow sang. The arrow, which could strike down an armored knight at two hundred paces, slid through the man's rib cage and spun him around so that he flailed bloodily across the floor. Robbie was still half under him, his fallen sword clattering on the thick wooden floorboards. A woman was screaming. Thomas guessed the wounded man was the castellan, the garrison's commander, and he wondered if the man would live long enough to answer some questions, but Robbie had drawn his dagger and, not knowing that his assailant was already pierced by an arrow, was flailing the short blade at the man's fat neck so that a sheet of blood spilled dark and shining across the boards and even after the man had died Robbie still gouged at him. The woman screamed on. "Stop her noise," Thomas said to Jake and went to pull the heavy corpse off the Scot. The man's long white nightshirt was red now. Jake slapped the woman and then, blessedly, there was silence.

There were no more soldiers in the castle. A dozen servants were sleeping in the kitchens and storerooms, but they made no trouble. The men were all taken down to the dungeons, then Thomas climbed to the keep's topmost rampart from where he could look down on the unsuspecting roofs of Castillon d'Arbizon, and there he waved a flaming torch. He waved it back and forth three times, threw it far down into the bushes at the foot of the steep slope on which the castle and town were built, then went to the western side of the rampart where he laid a dozen arrows on the parapet. Jake joined him there. "Sam's with Sir Robbie at the gate," Jake said. Robbie Douglas had never been knighted, but he was well born and a man-at-arms, and Thomas's men had given him the rank. They liked the Scotsman, just as Thomas did, which was why Thomas had disobeyed his lord and let Robbie come with him. Jake laid more arrows on the parapet. "That were easy."

"They weren't expecting trouble," Thomas said. That was not entirely true. The town had been aware of English raiders, Thomas's raiders, but had somehow convinced themselves that they would not come to Castillon d'Arbizon. The town had been at peace for so long that the townsfolk were persuaded the quiet times would go on. The walls and the watchmen were not there to guard against the English, but against the big companies of bandits that infested the countryside. A dozy watchman and a high wall might deter those bandits, but it had failed against real soldiers. "How did you cross the river?" he asked Jake.

"At the weir," Jake said. They had scouted the town in the dusk and Thomas had seen the mill weir as the easiest place to cross the deep and fast-flowing river.

"The miller?"

"Scared," Jake said, "and quiet."

Thomas heard the crackling of breaking twigs, the scrape of feet and a thump as a ladder was placed against the angle between the castle and the town wall. He leaned over the inner parapet. "You can open the gate, Robbie," he called down. He put an arrow on his string and stared down the long length of moonlit wall.

Beneath him men were climbing the ladder, hoisting weapons and bags that they tossed over the parapet and then followed after. A wash of flamelight glowed from the open wicket gate where Robbie and Sam stood guard, and after a moment a file of men, their mail clinking in the night, went from the wall's steps to the castle gate. Castillon d'Arbizon's new garrison was arriving.

A watchman appeared at the wall's far end. He strolled towards the castle, then suddenly became aware of the sound of swords, bows and baggage thumping on stone as men clambered over the wall. He hesitated, torn between a desire to get closer and see what was really happening and a wish to find reinforcements, and while he hesitated both Thomas and Jake loosed their arrows.

The watchman wore a padded leather jerkin, protection enough against a drunkard's stave, but the arrows slashed through the leather, the padding and his chest until the two points protruded from his back. He was hurled back, his staff fell with a clatter, and then he jerked in the moonlight, gasped a few times and was still.

"What do we do now?" Jake asked.

"Collect the taxes," Thomas said, "and make a nuisance of ourselves."

"Until what?"

"Until someone comes to kill us," Thomas said, thinking of his cousin.

"And we kill him?" Jake might be cross-eyed, but he held a very straightforward view of life.

"With God's good help," Thomas said and made the sign of the cross on his friar's robe.

The last of Thomas's men climbed the wall and dragged the ladder up behind them. There were still half a dozen men a mile away, across the river and hidden in the forest where they were guarding the horses, but the bulk of Thomas's force was now inside the castle and its gate was again locked. The dead watchman lay on the wall with two goose-feathered shafts sticking from his chest. No one else had detected the invaders. Castillon d'Arbizon either slept or drank.

And then the screams began.

I T HAD NOT OCCURRED to Thomas that the beghard girl who was to die in the morning would be imprisoned in the castle. He had thought the town would have its own jail, but she had evidently been given into the garrison's keeping and now she was screaming insults at the newly imprisoned men in the other cells and her noise was unsettling the archers and men-at-arms who had climbed Castillon d'Arbizon's wall and taken the castle. The jailer's plump wife, who spoke a little French, had shouted for the English to kill the girl. "She's a beghard," the woman claimed, "in league with the devil!"

Sir Guillaume d'Evecque had agreed with the woman. "Bring her up to the courtyard," he told Thomas, "and I'll hack off her damn head."

"She must burn," Thomas said. "That's what the Church has decreed."

"So who burns her?"

Thomas shrugged. "The town sergeants? Maybe us, I don't know."

"Then if you won't let me kill her now," Sir Guillaume said, "at least shut her goddamned mouth." He drew his knife and offered it to Thomas. "Cut her tongue out."

Thomas ignored the blade. He had still not found time to change out of his friar's robe, so he lifted its skirts and went down to the dungeons where the girl was shouting in French to tell the captives in the other cells that they would all die and that the devil would dance on their bones to a tune played by demons. Thomas lit a rush lantern from the flickering remnants of a torch, then went to the beghard's cell and pulled back the two bolts.

She quietened at the sound of the bolts and then, as he pushed the heavy door open, she scuffled back to the cell's far wall. Jake had followed Thomas down the steps and, seeing the girl in the lantern's dim light, he sniggered. "I can keep her quiet for you," he offered.

"Go and get some sleep, Jake," Thomas said.

"No, I don't mind," Jake persisted.

"Sleep!" Thomas snapped, suddenly angry because the girl looked so vulnerable.

She was vulnerable because she was naked. Naked as a new-laid egg, arrow-thin, deathly pale, flea-bitten, greasy-haired, wide-eyed and feral. She sat in the filthy straw, her arms wrapped about her drawn-up knees to hide her nakedness, then took a deep breath is if summoning her last dregs of courage. "You're English," she said in French. Her voice was hoarse from her screaming.

"I'm English," Thomas agreed.

"But an English priest is as bad as any other," she accused him.

"Probably," Thomas agreed. He put the lantern on the floor and sat beside the open door because the stench in the cell was so overwhelming. "I want you to stop your screaming," he went on, "because it upsets people."

She rolled her eyes at those words. "Tomorrow they are going to burn me," she said, "so you think I care if fools are upset tonight?"

"You should care for your soul," Thomas said, but his fervent words brought no response from the beghard. The rush wick burned badly and its horn shade turned the dim light a leprous, flickering yellow. "Why did they leave you naked?" he asked.

"Because I tore a strip from my dress and tried to strangle the jailer." She said it calmly, but with a defiant look as though daring Thomas to disapprove.

Thomas almost smiled at the thought of so slight a girl attacking the stout jailer, but he resisted his amusement. "What's your name?" he asked instead.

She was still defiant. "I have no name," she said. "They made me a heretic and took my name away. I'm cast out of Christendom. I'm already halfway to the next world." She looked away from him with an expression of indignation and Thomas saw that Robbie Douglas was standing in the half-open door. The Scot was gazing at the beghard with a look of wonderment, even awe, and Thomas looked at the girl again and saw that under the scraps of straw and embedded filth she was beautiful. Her hair was like pale gold, her skin was unscarred from pox and her face was strong. She had a high forehead, a full mouth and sunken cheeks. A striking face, and the Scotsman just stared at her and the girl, embarrassed by his frank gaze, hugged her knees closer to her breasts.

"Go," Thomas told Robbie. The young Scotsman fell in love, it seemed to Thomas, like other men became hungry, and it was plain from Robbie's face that he had been struck by the girl's looks with the force of a lance hammering into a shield.

Robbie frowned as though he did not quite understand Thomas's instruction. "I meant to ask you," he said, then paused.

"Ask me what?"

"Back in Calais," Robbie said, "did the Earl tell you to leave me behind?"

It seemed an odd question in the circumstances, but Thomas decided it deserved a response. "How do you know?"

"That priest told me. Buckingham."

Thomas wondered why Robbie had even talked to the priest, then realized that his friend was simply making conversation so he could stay near to the latest girl he had fallen so hopelessly in love with. "Robbie," he said, "she's going to burn in the morning."

Robbie shifted uneasily. "She doesn't have to."

"For God's sake," Thomas protested, "the Church has condemned her!"

"Then why are you here?" Robbie asked.

"Because I command here. Because someone has to keep her quiet."

"I can do that," Robbie said with a smile, and when Thomas did not respond the smile turned into a scowl. "So why did you let me come to Gascony?"

"Because you're a friend."

"Buckingham said I'd steal the Grail," Robbie said. "He said I'd take it to Scotland."

"We have to find it first," Thomas said, but Robbie was not listening. He was just looking hungrily at the girl who huddled in the corner. "Robbie," Thomas said firmly, "she's going to burn."

"Then it doesn't matter what happens to her tonight," the Scotsman said defiantly.

Thomas fought to suppress his anger. "Just leave us alone, Robbie," he said.

"Is it her soul you're after?" Robbie asked. "Or her flesh?"

"Just go!" Thomas snarled with more force than he meant and Robbie looked startled, even belligerent, but then he blinked a couple of times and walked away.

The girl had not understood the English conversation, but she had recognized the lust on Robbie's face and now turned it on Thomas. "You want me for yourself, priest?" she asked in French.

Thomas ignored the sneering question. "Where are you from?"

She paused, as if deciding whether or not to answer, then shrugged. "From Picardy," she said.

"A long way north," Thomas said. "How does a girl from Picardy come to Gascony?"

She hesitated again. She was, Thomas thought, perhaps fifteen or sixteen years old, which made her overripe for marriage. Her eyes, he noticed, had a curious piercing quality, which gave him the uncomfortable sensation that she could see right through to the dark root of his soul. "My father," she said. "He was a juggler and flame-eater."

"I've seen such men," Thomas said.

"We went wherever we wished," she said, "and made money at fairs. My father made folk laugh and I collected the coins."

"Your mother?"

"Dead." She said it carelessly as if to suggest she could not even remember her mother. "Then my father died here. Six months ago. So I stayed."

"Why did you stay?"

She gave him a sneering look as if to suggest the answer to his question was so obvious that it did not need stating, but then, presuming him to be a priest who did not understood how real people lived, she gave him the answer. "Do you know how dangerous the roads are?" she asked. "There are *coredors*."

"*Coredors?*"

"Bandits," she explained. "The local people call them *coredors*. Then there are the routiers who are just as bad." Routiers were companies of disbanded soldiers who wandered the highways in search of a lord to employ them and when they were hungry, which was most of the time, they took what they wanted by force. Some even captured towns and held them for ransom. But, like the *coredors*, they would regard a girl traveling alone as a gift sent by the devil for their enjoyment. "How long do you think I would have lasted?" she asked.

"You could have traveled in company?" Thomas suggested.

"We always did, my father and I, but he was there to protect me. But on my own?" She shrugged. "So I stayed. I worked in a kitchen."

"And cooked up heresy?"

"You priests do so love heresy," she said bitterly. "It gives you something to burn."

"Before you were condemned," Thomas said, "what was your name?"

"Genevieve."

"You were named for the saint?"

"I suppose so," she said.

"And whenever Genevieve prayed," Thomas said, "the devil blew out her candles."

"You priests are full of stories," Genevieve mocked. "Do you believe that? You believe the devil came into the church and blew out her candles?"

"Probably."

"Why didn't he just kill her if he's the devil? What a pathetic trick, just to blow out candles! He can't be much of a devil if that's all he does."

Thomas ignored her scorn. "They tell me you are a beghard."

"I've met beghards," she said, "and I liked them."

"They are the devil's spawn," Thomas said.

"You've met one?" she asked. Thomas had not. He had only heard of them and the girl sensed his discomfort. "If to believe that God gave all to everyone and wants everyone to share in everything, then I am as bad as a beghard," she admitted, "but I never joined them."

"You must have done something to deserve the flames."

She stared at him. Perhaps it was something in his tone that made her trust him, but the defiance seemed to drain out of her. She closed her eyes and leaned her head against the wall and Thomas suspected she wanted to cry. Watching her delicate face, he wondered why he had not seen her beauty instantly as Robbie had done. Then she opened her eyes and gazed at him. "What happened here tonight?" she asked, ignoring his accusation.

"We captured the castle," Thomas said.

"We?"

"The English."

She looked at him, trying to read his face. "So now the English are the civil power?"

He supposed she had learned the phrase at her trial. The Church did not burn heretics, they merely condemned them, and then the sinners were handed to the civil power for their deaths. That way the Church kept clean hands, God was assured that his Church was undefiled and the devil gained a soul. "We are the civil power now," Thomas agreed.

"So the English will burn me instead of the Gascons?"

"Someone must burn you," Thomas said, "if you are a heretic."

"If?" Genevieve asked, but when Thomas did not answer she closed her eyes and rested her head on the damp stones again. "They said I insulted God." She spoke tiredly. "That I claimed the priests of God's Church were corrupt, that I danced naked beneath the lightning, that I used the devil's power to discover water, that I used magic to cure people's ills, that I prophesied the future and that I put a curse on Galat Lorret's wife and on his cattle."

Thomas frowned. "They did not convict you of being a beghard?" he asked.

"That too," she added drily.

He was silent for a few heartbeats. Water dripped somewhere in the dark beyond the door and the rushlight flickered, almost died and then recovered. "Whose wife did you curse?" Thomas asked.

"Galat Lorret's wife. He's a cloth merchant here and very rich. He's the chief consul and a man who would like younger flesh than his wife."

"And did you curse her?"

"Not just her," Genevieve said fervently, "but him too. Have you never cursed anyone?"

"You prophesied the future?" Thomas asked.

"I said they would all die, and that is an evident truth."

"Not if Christ comes back to earth, as he promised," Thomas said.

She gave him a long, considering look and a small smile half showed on her face before she shrugged. "So I was wrong," she said sarcastically.

"And the devil showed you how to discover water?"

"Even you can do that," she said. "Take a forked twig and walk slowly across a field and when it twitches, dig."

"And magical cures?"

"Old remedies," she said tiredly. "The things we learn from aunts and grandmothers and old ladies. Take iron from a room where a woman is giving birth. Everyone does it. Even you, priest, touch wood to avert evil. Is that piece of magic sufficient to send you to the fire?"

Again Thomas ignored her answer. "You insulted God?" he asked her.

"God loves me, and I do not insult those who love me. But I did say his priests were corrupt, which you are, and so they charged me with insulting God. Are you corrupt, priest?"

"And you danced naked under the lightning," Thomas concluded the indictment.

"To that," she said, "I plead guilty."

"Why did you dance?"

"Because my father always said that God would give us guidance if we did that."

"God would do that?" Thomas asked, surprised.

"So we believed. We were wrong. God told me to stay in Castillon d'Arbizon and it only led to torture and tomorrow's fire."

"Torture?" Thomas asked.

Something in his voice, a horror, made her look at him, and then she slowly stretched out her left leg so that he could see her inner thigh and the raw, red, twisted mark that disfigured the white skin. "They burned me," she said, "again and again. That was why I confessed to being what I was not, a beghard, because they burned me." She was crying suddenly, remembering the pain. "They used red-hot metal," she said, "and when I screamed they said it was the devil trying to leave my soul." She drew up her leg and showed him her right arm, which had the same scars. "But they left these," she said angrily, suddenly revealing her small breasts, "because Father Roubert said the devil would want to suck them and the pain of his jaws would be worse than anything the Church could inflict." She drew her knees up again and was silent for a while as the tears ran down her face. "The Church likes to hurt people," she continued after a while. "You should know that."

"I do," Thomas said, and he very nearly lifted the skirts of his Dominican's robe to show her the same scars on his body, the scars

of the hot iron that had been pressed on his legs to make him reveal
the secrets of the Grail. It was a torture that drew no blood for the
Church was forbidden to draw blood, but a skilled man could make
a soul scream in torment without ever breaking the skin. "I do,"
Thomas said again.

"Then damn you," Genevieve said, recovering her defiance,
"damn you and damn all the damned priests."

Thomas stood and lifted the lantern. "I shall fetch you something
to wear."

"Frightened of me, priest?" she mocked.

"Frightened?" Thomas was puzzled.

"By this, priest!" she said and showed him her nakedness and
Thomas turned away and closed the door on her laughter. Then, when
the bolts were shot, he leaned on the wall and stared at nothing. He
was remembering Genevieve's eyes, so full of fire and mystery. She
was dirty, naked, unkempt, pale, half starved and a heretic and he had
found her beautiful, but he had a duty in the morning and he had not
expected it. A God-given duty.

He climbed back to the yard to find everything quiet. Castillon
d'Arbizon slept.

And Thomas, bastard son of a priest, prayed.

THE TOWER STOOD in woodland a day's ride east of Paris, on a low
ridge not far from Soissons. It was a lonely place. The tower had once
been home to a lord whose serfs farmed the valleys on either flank
of the ridge, but the lord had died without children and his distant rel-
atives had squabbled over ownership which meant the lawyers had
become rich and the tower had decayed and the fields had been over-
grown by hazel, and then by oak, and owls had nested in the high
stone chambers where the winds blew and the seasons passed. Even
the lawyers who had argued over the tower were now dead and the
small castle was the property of a Duke who had never seen it and
would never dream of living there, and the serfs, those that remained,

worked fields closer to the village of Melun where the Duke's tenant had a farm.

The tower, the villagers said, was haunted. White spirits wreathed it on winter nights. Strange beasts were said to prowl the trees. Children were told to stay away, though inevitably the braver ones went to the woods and some even climbed the tower to find it empty.

But then the strangers came.

They came with the faraway Duke's permission. They were tenants, but they did not come to farm or to thin the ridge of its valuable timber. They were soldiers. Fifteen hard men, scarred from the wars against England, with mail coats and crossbows and swords. They brought their women who made trouble in the village and no one dared to complain because the women were as hard as the soldiers, but not as hard as the man who led them. He was tall, thin, ugly, scarred and vengeful. His name was Charles and he had not been a soldier and he never wore mail, but no one liked to ask him what he was or what he had been for his very glance was terrifying.

Stonemasons came from Soissons. The owls were ejected and the tower repaired. A new yard was made at the tower's foot, a yard with a high wall and a brick furnace, and soon after that work was finished a wagon, its contents hidden by a linen canopy, arrived at the tower and the new gate in the yard's wall slammed shut behind it. Some of the braver children, curious about the strange happenings at the tower, sneaked into the woods, but they were seen by one of the guards and they fled, terrified, as he pursued them, shouting, and his crossbow bolt narrowly missed a boy. No child went back. No one went there. The soldiers bought food and wine in the market, but even when they drank in Melun's tavern they did not say what happened at the tower. "You must ask Monsieur Charles," they said, meaning the ugly, scarred man, and no one in the village would dare approach Monsieur Charles.

Smoke sometimes rose from the yard. It could be seen from the village, and it was the priest who deduced that the tower was now the home of an alchemist. Strange supplies were taken up the ridge and one day a wagon loaded with a barrel of sulphur and ingots of lead paused in the village while the carter drank wine. The priest smelt the sulphur. "They are making gold," he told his housekeeper, knowing she would tell the rest of the village.

"Gold?" she asked.

"It is what the alchemists do." The priest was a learned man who might have risen high in the Church except that he had a taste for wine and was always drunk by the time the angelus bell sounded, but he remembered his student days in Paris and how he had once thought that he might join the search for the philosopher's stone, that elusive substance which would meld with any metal to make it gold. "Noah possessed it," he said.

"Possessed what?"

"The philosopher's stone, but he lost it."

"Because he was drunk and naked?" the housekeeper asked. She had a dim memory of the story of Noah. "Like you?"

The priest lay on his bed, half drunk and fully naked, and he remembered the smoky workrooms of Paris where silver and mercury, lead and sulphur, bronze and iron were melted and twisted and melted again. "Calcination," he recited, "and dissolution, and separation, and conjunction, and putrefaction, and congelation, and cibation, and sublimation, and fermentation, and exaltation, and multiplication, and projection."

The housekeeper had no idea what he was talking about. "Marie Condrot lost her child today," she told him. "Born the size of a kitten, it was. All bloody and dead. It had hair though. Red hair. She wants you to christen it."

"Cupellation," he said, ignoring her news, "and cementation, and reverberation, and distillation. Always distillation. *Per ascendum* is the preferred method." He hiccuped. "Jesus," he sighed, then thought again. "Phlogiston. If we could just find phlogiston we could all make gold."

"And how would we make gold?"

"I just told you." He turned on the bed and stared at her breasts that were white and heavy in the moonlight. "You have to be very clever," he said, reaching for her, "and you discover phlogiston which is a substance that burns hotter than hell's fires, and with it you make the philosopher's stone that Noah lost and you place it in the furnace with any metal and after three days and three nights you will have gold. Didn't Corday say they built a furnace up there?"

"He said they made the tower into a prison," she said.

"A furnace," he insisted, "to find the philosopher's stone."

The priest's guess was closer than he knew, and soon the whole neighborhood was convinced that a great philosopher was locked in the tower where he struggled to make gold. If he was successful, men said, then no one would need to work again for all would be rich. Peasants would eat from gold plate and ride horses caparisoned in silver, but some people noted that it was a strange kind of alchemy for two of the soldiers came to the village one morning and took away three old ox-horns and a pail of cow dung. "We're bound to be rich now," the housekeeper said sarcastically, "rich in shit," but the priest was snoring.

Then, in the autumn which followed the fall of Calais, the Cardinal arrived from Paris. He lodged in Soissons, at the Abbey of St-Jean-de-Vignes which, though wealthier than most monastic houses, could still not cope with all the Cardinal's entourage and so a dozen of his men took rooms in a tavern where they airily commanded the landlord to send the bill to Paris. "The Cardinal will pay," they promised, and then they laughed for they knew that Louis Bessières, Cardinal Archbishop of Livorno and Papal Legate to the Court of France, would ignore any trivial demands for money.

Though of late His Eminence had been spending it lavishly. It had been the Cardinal who restored the tower, built the new wall and hired the guards, and on the morning after he arrived at Soissons he rode to the tower with an escort of sixty armed men and fourteen priests. Halfway to the tower they were met by Monsieur Charles who was dressed all in black and had a long, narrow-bladed knife at his side. He did not greet the Cardinal respectfully as other men would, but nodded a curt acknowledgement and then turned his horse to ride beside the prelate. The priests and men-at-arms, at a signal from the Cardinal, kept their distance so they could not overhear the conversation.

"You look well, Charles," the Cardinal said in a mocking voice.

"I'm bored." The ugly Charles had a voice like iron dragging through gravel.

"God's service can be hard," the Cardinal said.

Charles ignored the sarcasm. The scar went from his lip to his cheekbone, his eyes were pouchy, his nose broken. His black clothes hung from him like a scarecrow's rags and his gaze constantly flicked from side to side of the road as though he feared an ambush. Any travelers, meeting the procession, had they dared raise their eyes to see the Cardinal and his ragged companion, would have taken Charles to be a soldier, for the scar and the sword suggested he had served in the wars, but Charles Bessières had never followed a war banner. He had cut throats and purses instead, he had robbed and murdered, and he had been spared the gallows because he was the Cardinal's eldest brother.

Charles and Louis Bessières had been born in the Limousin, the eldest sons of a tallow merchant who had given the younger son an education while the elder ran wild. Louis had risen in the church as Charles had roamed dark alleys, but different though they were, there was a trust between them. A secret was safe between the tallow merchant's only surviving sons and that was why the priests and the men-at-arms had been ordered to keep their distance.

"How is our prisoner?" the Cardinal asked.

"He grumbles. Whines like a woman."

"But he works?"

"Oh, he works," Charles said grimly. "Too scared to be idle."

"He eats? He is in good health?"

"He eats, he sleeps and he nails his woman," Charles said.

"He has a woman?" The Cardinal sounded shocked.

"He wanted one. Said he couldn't work properly without one so I fetched him one."

"What kind?"

"One from the stews of Paris."

"An old companion of yours, perhaps?" the Cardinal asked, amused. "But not one, I trust, of whom you are too fond?"

"When it's all done," Charles said, "she'll have her throat cut just like him. Simply tell me when."

"When he has worked his miracle, of course," the Cardinal said.

They followed a narrow track up the ridge and, once at the tower, the priests and the armed men stayed in the yard while the brothers dismounted and went down a brief winding stair that led to a heavy door barred with three thick bolts. The Cardinal watched his brother draw the bolts back. "The guards do not come down here?" he asked.

"Only the two who bring food and take away the buckets," Charles said, "the rest know they'll get their throats cut if they poke their noses where they're not wanted."

"Do they believe that?"

Charles Bessières looked sourly at his brother. "Wouldn't you?" he asked, then drew his knife before he shot the last bolt. He stepped back as he opened the door, evidently wary in case someone beyond the door attacked him, but the man inside showed no hostility, instead he looked pathetically pleased to see the Cardinal and dropped to his knees in reverence.

The tower's cellar was large, its ceiling supported by great brick arches from which a score of lanterns hung. Their smoky light was augmented by daylight that came through three high, small, thickly barred windows. The prisoner who lived in the cellar was a young man with long fair hair, a quick face and clever eyes. His cheeks and high forehead were smeared with dirt, which also marked his long, agile fingers. He stayed on his knees as the Cardinal approached.

"Young Gaspard," the Cardinal said genially and held out his hand so the prisoner could kiss the heavy ring that contained a thorn from Christ's crown of death. "I trust you are well, young Gaspard? You eat heartily, do you? Sleep like a babe? Work like a good Christian? Rut like a hog?" The Cardinal glanced at the girl as he said the last words, then he took his hand away from Gaspard and walked further into the room towards three tables, on which were barrels of clay, blocks of beeswax, piles of ingots, and arrays of chisels, files, augers and hammers.

The girl, sullen, red-haired and dressed in a dirty shift that hung loose from one shoulder, sat on a low trestle bed in a corner of the cellar. "I don't like it here," she complained to the Cardinal.

The Cardinal stared at her in silence for a good long time, then he turned to his brother, "If she speaks to me again, Charles, without my permission," he said, "whip her."

"She means no harm, your eminence," Gaspard said, still on his knees.

"But I do," the Cardinal said, then smiled at the prisoner. "Get up, dear boy, get up."

"I need Yvette," Gaspard said, "she helps me."

"I'm sure she does," the Cardinal said, then stooped to a clay bowl in which a brownish paste had been mixed. He recoiled from its stench, then turned as Gaspard came to him, dropped to his knees again, and held up a gift.

"For you, your eminence," Gaspard said eagerly, "I made it for you."

The Cardinal took the gift. It was crucifix of gold, not a hand's breadth high, yet every detail of the suffering Christ was delicately modeled. There were strands of hair showing beneath the crown of thorns, the thorns themselves could prick, the rent in his side was jagged edged and the spill of golden blood ran past his loincloth to his long thigh. The nail heads stood proud and the Cardinal counted them. Four. He had seen three true nails in his life. "It's beautiful, Gaspard," the Cardinal said.

"I would work better," Gaspard said, "if there was more light."

"We would all work better if there were more light," the Cardinal said, "the light of truth, the light of God, the light of the Holy Spirit." He walked beside the tables, touching the tools of Gaspard's trade. "Yet the devil sends darkness to befuddle us and we must do our best to endure it."

"Upstairs?" Gaspard said. "There must be rooms with more light upstairs?"

"There are," the Cardinal said, "there are, but how do I know you will not escape, Gaspard? You are an ingenious man. Give you a large window and I might give you the world. No, dear boy, if you can produce work like this"—he held up the crucifix—"then you need no more light." He smiled. "You are so very clever."

Gaspard was indeed clever. He had been a goldsmith's apprentice in one of the small shops on the Quai des Orfèvres on the Île de la Cité in Paris where the Cardinal had his mansion. The Cardinal had always appreciated the goldsmiths: he haunted their shops, patronized them and purchased their best pieces, and many of those pieces had been made by this thin, nervous apprentice who had then knifed a fellow apprentice to death in a sordid tavern brawl and been condemned to the gallows. The Cardinal had rescued him, brought him to the tower and promised him life.

But first Gaspard must work the miracle. Only then could he be released. That was the promise, though the Cardinal was quite sure that Gaspard would never leave this cellar unless it was to use the big furnace in the yard. Gaspard, though he did not know it, was already at the gates of hell. The Cardinal made the sign of the cross, then put the crucifix on a table. "So show me," he ordered Gaspard.

Gaspard went to his big work table where an object was shrouded in a cloth of bleached linen. "It is only wax now, your eminence," he explained, lifting the linen away, "and I don't know if it's even possible to turn it into gold."

"It can be touched?" the Cardinal asked.

"Carefully," Gaspard warned. "It's purified beeswax and quite delicate."

The Cardinal lifted the gray-white wax, which felt oily to his touch, and he carried it to one of the three small windows that let in the shadowed daylight and there he stood in awe.

Gaspard had made a cup of wax. It had taken him weeks of work. The cup itself was just big enough to hold an apple, while the stem was only six inches long. That stem was modeled as the trunk of a tree and the cup's foot was made from the tree's three roots that spread from the bole. The tree's branches divided into filigree work that formed the lacy bowl of the cup, and the filigree was astonishingly detailed with tiny leaves and small apples and, at the rim, three delicate nails. "It is beautiful," the Cardinal said.

"The three roots, your eminence, are the Trinity," Gaspard explained.

"I had surmised as much."

"And the tree is the tree of life."

"Which is why it has apples," the Cardinal said.

"And the nails reveal that it will be the tree from which our Lord's cross was made," Gaspard finished his explanation.

"That had not escaped me," the Cardinal observed. He carried the beautiful wax cup back to the table and set it down carefully. "Where is the glass?"

"Here, your Eminence." Gaspard opened a box and took out a cup that he offered to the Cardinal. The cup was made of thick, greenish glass that looked very ancient, for in parts the cup was smoky and elsewhere there were tiny bubbles trapped in the pale translucent material. The Cardinal suspected it was Roman. He was not sure of that, but it looked very old and just a little crude, and that was surely right. The cup from which Christ had drunk his last wine would probably be more fit for a peasant's table than for a noble's feast. The Cardinal had discovered the cup in a Paris shop and had purchased it for a few copper coins and he had instructed Gaspard to take off the ill-shapen foot of the glass which the prisoner had done so skillfully that the Cardinal could not even see that there had once been a stem. Now, very gingerly, he put the glass cup into the filigree wax bowl. Gaspard held his breath, fearing that the Cardinal would break one of the delicate leaves, but the cup settled gently and fitted perfectly.

The Grail. The Cardinal gazed at the glass cup, imagining it cradled in a delicate lacework of fine gold and standing on an altar lit by tall white candles. There would be a choir of boys singing and scented incense burning. There would be kings and emperors, princes and dukes, earls and knights kneeling to it.

Louis Bessières, Cardinal Archbishop of Livorno, wanted the Grail and, some months before, he had heard a rumor from southern France, from the land of burned heretics, that the Grail existed. Two sons of the Vexille family, one a Frenchman and the other an English archer, sought that Grail as the Cardinal did, but no one, the Cardinal thought, wanted the Grail as much as he did. Or deserved it as he did. If he found the relic then he would command such awesome power that kings and pope would come to him for blessing and when Clement, the present Pope, died, then Louis Bessières would take his throne and keys—if only he possessed the Grail. Louis Bessières wanted the Grail, but one day, staring unseeing at the stained glass in his private chapel, he had experienced a revelation. The Grail itself was not necessary. Perhaps it existed, probably it did not, but all that mattered was that Christendom believed that it existed. They wanted a Grail. Any Grail, so long as they were convinced it was the true and holy, one and only Grail, and that was why Gaspard was in this cellar, and why Gaspard would die, for no one but the Cardinal and his brother must ever know what was being made in the lonely tower among the windswept trees above Melun. "And now," the Cardinal said, carefully lifting the green glass from its wax bed, "you must make the common wax into heavenly gold."

"It will be hard, your eminence."

"Of course it will be hard," the Cardinal said, "but I shall pray for you. And your freedom depends on your success." The Cardinal saw the doubt on Gaspard's face. "You made the crucifix," he said, picking up the beautiful gold object, "so why can you not make the cup?"

"It is so delicate," Gaspard said, "and if I pour the gold and it does not melt the wax then all the work will be wasted."

"Then you will start again," the Cardinal said, "and by experience and with the help of God you will discover the way of truth."

"It has never been done," Gaspard said, "not with anything so delicate."

"Show me how," the Cardinal ordered and Gaspard explained how he would paint the wax cup with the noxious brown paste that had repelled the Cardinal. That paste was made from water, burned ox-horn that had been pounded to powder and cow dung, and the dried layers of the paste would encase the wax and the whole would then be entombed in soft clay, which had to be gently pressed into place to cradle the wax, but not distort it. Narrow tunnels would run through the clay from the outside to the entombed wax, and then Gaspard would take the shapeless clay lump to the furnace in the yard where he would bake the clay and the beeswax inside would melt and run out through the tunnels and, if he did it well, he would be left with a hard clay mass within which was concealed a delicate cavity in the shape of the tree of life.

"And the cow dung?" the Cardinal asked. He was genuinely fascinated. All beautiful things intrigued him, perhaps because in his youth he had been denied them.

"The dung bakes hard," Gaspard said. "It makes a hard shell around the cavity." He smiled at the sullen girl. "Yvette mixes it for me," he explained. "The layer closest to the wax is very fine, the outer layers are coarser."

"So the dung mixture forms the hard surface of the mold?" the Cardinal asked.

"Exactly." Gaspard was pleased that his patron and savior understood.

Then, when the clay was cold, Gaspard would pour molten gold into the cavity and he must hope that the liquid fire would fill every last cranny, every tiny leaf and apple and nail, and every delicately modeled ridge of bark. And when the gold had cooled and become firm the clay would be broken away to reveal either a grail-holder that would dazzle Christendom or else a mess of misshapen gold squiggles. "It will probably have to be done in separate pieces," Gaspard said nervously.

"You will try with this one," the Cardinal ordered, draping the linen cloth back over the wax cup, "and if it fails you will make another and try again, and then again, and when it works, Gaspard, I shall release you to the fields and to the sky. You and your little friend." He smiled vaguely at the woman, made the sign of a blessing over Gaspard's head, then walked from the cellar. He waited as his brother bolted the door. "Don't be unkind to him, Charles."

"Unkind? I'm his jailer, not his nurse."

"And he is a genius. He thinks he is making me a Mass cup, so he has no idea how important his work is. He fears nothing, except you. So keep him happy."

Charles moved away from the door. "Suppose they find the real Grail?"

"Who will find it?" the Cardinal asked. "The English archer has vanished and that fool of a monk won't find it in Berat. He'll just stir up the dust."

"So why send him?"

"Because our Grail must have a past. Brother Jerome will discover some stories of the Grail in Gascony and that will be our proof, and once he has announced that the records of the Grail exist then we shall take the cup to Berat and announce its discovery."

Charles was still thinking of the real Grail. "I thought the Englishman's father left a book?"

"He did, but we can make nothing of it. They are the scribblings of a madman."

"So find the archer and burn the truth from him," Charles said.

"He will be found," the Cardinal promised grimly, "and next time I'll loose you on him, Charles. He'll talk then. But in the meantime we must go on looking, but above all we must go on making. So keep Gaspard safe."

"Safe now," Charles said, "and dead later." Because Gaspard would provide the means for the brothers to go to Avignon's papal palace and the Cardinal, climbing to the yard, could taste the power already. He would be Pope.

AT DAWN THAT DAY, far to the south of the lonely tower near Soissons, the shadow of Castillon d'Arbizon's castle had fallen across the heap of timbers ready for the heretic's burning. The firewood had been well constructed, according to Brother Roubert's careful instructions, so that above the kindling and around the thick stake to which a chain had been stapled there were four layers of upright faggots that would burn bright, but not too hot and without too much smoke, so that the watching townsfolk would see Genevieve writhe within the bright flame and know that the heretic was going to Satan's dominion.

The castle's shadow reached down the main street almost to the west gate where the town sergeants, already bemused by the discovery of the dead watchman on the walls, stared up at the bulk of the castle's keep outlined by the rising sun. A new flag flew there. Instead of showing the orange leopard on the white field of Berat it flaunted a blue field, slashed with a diagonal white band that was dotted with three white stars. Three yellow lions inhabited the blue field and those fierce beasts appeared and disappeared as the big flag lifted to an indifferent wind. Then there was something new to gape at, for as the town's four consuls hurried to join the sergeants, men appeared at the top of one of the bastions that protected the castle gate and they dropped a pair of heavy objects from the rampart. The two things dropped, then jerked to a stop at the end of ropes. At first the watching men thought that the garrison was airing its bedding, then they saw that the lumps were the corpses of two men. They were the castellan and the guard, and they hung by the gate to reinforce the message of the Earl of Northampton's banner. Castillon d'Arbizon was under new ownership.

Galat Lorret, the oldest and richest of the consuls, the same man who had questioned the friar in the church the previous night, was the first to gather his wits. "A message must go to Berat," he ordered, and he instructed the town's clerk to write to Castillon d'Arbizon's proper lord. "Tell the Count that English troops are flying the banner of the Earl of Northampton."

"You recognize it?" another consul asked.

"It flew here long enough," Lorret responded bitterly. Castillon d'Arbizon had once belonged to the English and had paid its taxes to distant Bordeaux, but the English tide had receded and Lorret had never thought to see the Earl's banner again. He ordered the four remaining men of the garrison, who had been drunk in the tavern and thus escaped the English, to be ready to carry the clerk's message to distant Berat and he gave them a pair of gold coins to hasten their ride. Then, grim-faced, he marched up the street with his three fellow consuls. Father Medous and the priest from St. Callic's church joined them and the townsfolk, anxious and scared, fell in behind.

Lorret pounded on the castle gate. He would, he decided, face the impudent invaders down. He would scare them. He would demand that they leave Castillon d'Arbizon now. He would threaten them with siege and starvation, and just as he was summoning his indignant words the two leaves of the great gate were hauled back on screeching hinges and facing him were a dozen English archers in steel caps and mail hauberks, and the sight of the big bows and their long arrows made Lorret take an involuntary step back.

Then the young friar stepped forward, only he was no longer a friar, but a tall soldier in a mail haubergeon. He was bare-headed and his short black hair looked as if it had been cut with a knife. He wore black breeches, long black boots and had a black leather sword belt from which hung a short knife and a long plain sword. He had a silver chain about his neck, a sign that he held authority. He looked along the line of sergeants and consuls, then nodded to Lorret. "We were not properly introduced last night," he said, "but doubtless you remember my name. Now it is your turn to tell me yours."

"You have no business here!" Lorret blustered.

Thomas looked up at the sky, which was pale, almost washed out, suggesting that more unseasonably cold weather might be coming. "Father," he spoke to Medous now, "you will have the goodness to translate my words so everyone can know what is going on." He looked back to Lorret. "If you will not talk sense then I shall order my men to kill you and then I shall talk to your companions. What is your name?"

"You're the friar," Lorret said accusingly.

"No," Thomas said, "but you thought I was because I can read. I am the son of a priest and he taught me letters. Now, what is your name?"

"I am Galat Lorret," Lorret said.

"And from your robes," Thomas gestured at Lorret's fur-trimmed gown, "I assume you have some authority here?"

"We are the consuls," Lorret said with what dignity he could muster. The other three consuls, all younger than Lorret, tried to look unworried, but it was difficult when a row of arrow heads glittered beneath the arch.

"Thank you," Thomas said courteously, "and now you must tell your people that they have the good fortune to be back under the Earl of Northampton's rule and it is his lordship's wish that his people do not stand about the street when there is work to be done." He nodded at Father Medous who offered a stammering translation to the crowd. There were some protests, mainly because the shrewder folk in the square understood that a change of lordship would inevitably mean more taxes.

"The work this morning," Lorret said, "is burning a heretic."

"That is work?"

"God's work," Lorret insisted. He raised his voice and spoke in the local language. "The people were promised time from their labor to watch the evil burned from the town."

Father Medous translated the words for Thomas. "It is the custom," the priest added, "and the bishop insists that the people see the girl burn."

"The custom?" Thomas asked. "You burn girls often enough to have a custom about it?"

Father Medous shook his head in confusion. "Father Roubert told us we must let the people see."

Thomas frowned. "Father Roubert," he said, "that's the man who told you to burn the girl slowly? To stand the faggots upright?"

"He is a Dominican," Father Medous said, "a real one. It was he who discovered the girl's heresy. He should be here." The priest looked about him as if expecting to see the missing friar.

"He'll doubtless be sorry to miss the amusement," Thomas said, then he gestured to his row of archers who moved aside so that Sir Guillaume, armored in mail and with a great war sword in his hand, could bring Genevieve out of the castle. The crowd hissed and jeered at the sight of her, but their anger went silent when the archers closed up behind the girl and hefted their tall bows. Robbie Douglas, in a mail haubergeon and with a sword at his side, pushed through the archers and stared at Genevieve who now stood beside Thomas. "This is the girl?" Thomas asked.

"She is the heretic, yes," Lorret said.

Genevieve was staring at Thomas with some disbelief. The last time she had seen him he had been wearing a friar's robes, yet now he was palpably not a priest. His mail haubergeon, a short coat that came to his thighs, was of good quality and he had polished it during the night, which he had spent guarding the cells so that no one would abuse the prisoners.

Genevieve was no longer ragged. Thomas had sent two of the castle's kitchen maids to her cell with water, cloths and a bone comb so she could clean herself, and he had provided her with a white gown that had belonged to the castellan's wife. It was a dress of expensively bleached linen, embroidered at its neck, sleeves and hem with golden thread, and Genevieve looked as though she had been born to wear such finery. Her long fair hair was combed back to a plait secured with a yellow ribbon. She stood beside him, surprizingly tall, with her hands tied before her as she stared defiantly at the townsfolk. Father Medous timidly gestured towards the waiting timbers as if to suggest that there was no time to waste.

Thomas looked again at Genevieve. She was dressed as a bride, a bride come to her death, and Thomas was astonished at her beauty. Was that what had offended the townsfolk? Thomas's father has always declared that beauty provoked hate as much as love, for beauty was unnatural, an offense against the mud and scars and blood of common life, and Genevieve, so tall and slender and pale and ethereal, was uncommonly lovely. Robbie must have been thinking the same for he was staring at her with an expression of pure awe.

Galat Lorret pointed at the waiting pyre. "If you want folk to work," he said, "then get the burning done."

"I've never burned a woman," Thomas said. "You must give me time to decide how best to do it."

"The chain goes round her waist," Galat Lorret explained, "and the blacksmith fastens it." He beckoned to the town's smith who was waiting with a staple and hammer. "The fire will come from any hearth."

"In England," Thomas said, "it is not unknown for the executioner to strangle the victim under the cover of smoke. It is an act of mercy and done with a bowstring." He took just such a string from a pouch at his belt. "Is that the custom here?"

"Not with heretics," Galat Lorret said harshly.

Thomas nodded, put the bowstring back in the pouch, then took Genevieve's arm to walk her to the stake. Robbie started forward, as if to intervene, but Sir Guillaume checked him. Then Thomas hesitated. "There must be a document," he said to Lorret, "a warrant. Something which authorizes the civil power to carry out the Church's condemnation."

"It was sent to the castellan," Lorret said.

"To him?" Thomas looked up at the fat corpse. "He failed to give it to me and I cannot burn the girl without such a warrant." He looked worried, then turned to Robbie. "Would you look for it? I saw a chest of parchments in the hall. Perhaps it's there? Search for a document with a heavy seal."

Robbie, unable to take his eyes from Genevieve's face, looked as if he intended to argue, then he abruptly nodded and went into the castle. Thomas stepped back, taking Genevieve with him. "While we wait," he told Father Medous, "perhaps you will remind your townsfolk why she is to burn?"

The priest seemed flummoxed by the courteous invitation, but gathered his wits. "Cattle died," he said, "and she cursed a man's wife."

Thomas looked mildly surprised. "Cattle die in England," he said, "and I have cursed a man's wife. Does that make me a heretic?"

"She can tell the future!" Medous protested. "She danced naked under the lightning and used magic to discover water."

"Ah." Thomas looked concerned. "Water?"

"With a stick!" Galat Lorret interjected. "It is the devil's magic."

Thomas looked thoughtful. He glanced at Genevieve who was trembling slightly, then he looked back to Father Medous. "Tell me, father," he said, "am I not right in thinking that Moses struck a rock with his brother's staff and brought water from the stone?"

It had been a long time since Father Medous had studied the scriptures, but the story seemed familiar. "I remember something like it," he admitted.

"Father!" Galat Lorret said warningly.

"Quiet!" Thomas snarled at the consul. He raised his voice. "'*Cumque elevasset Moses manum,*'" he was quoting from memory, but thought he had the words right, "'*percutiens virga bis silicem egressae sunt aquae largissimae.*'" There were not many advantages to being the bastard son of a priest or to having spent some weeks at Oxford, but he had picked up enough learning to confound most churchmen. "You have not interpreted my words, father," he told the priest, "so tell the crowd how Moses struck the rock and brought forth a gush of water. And then tell me that if it pleases God to find water with a staff, how can it be wrong for this girl to do the same with a twig?"

The crowd did not like it. Some shouted and it was only the sight of two archers appearing on the rampart above the two dangling corpses that quietened them. The priest hurried to translate their protests. "She cursed a woman," he said, "and prophesied the future."

"What future did she see?" Thomas asked.

"Death." It was Lorret who answered. "She said the town would fill with corpses and we would lie in the streets unburied."

Thomas looked impressed. "Did she foretell that the town would return to its proper allegiance? Did she say that the Earl of Northampton would send us here?"

There was a pause and then Medous shook his head. "No," he said.

"Then she does not see the future very clearly," Thomas said, "so the devil cannot have inspired her."

"The bishop's court decided otherwise," Lorret insisted, "and it is not up to you to question the proper authorities."

The sword came from Thomas's scabbard with surprizing speed.

The blade was oiled to keep it from rusting and it gleamed wetly as he prodded the fur-trimmed robe at Galat Lorret's chest. "I am the proper authorities," Thomas said, pushing the consul backwards, "and you had best remember it. And I have never met your bishop, and if he thinks a girl is a heretic because cattle die then he is a fool, and if he condemns her because she does what God commanded Moses to do then he is a blasphemer." He thrust the sword a last time, making Lorret step hurriedly back. "What woman did she curse?"

"My wife," Lorret said indignantly.

"She died?" Thomas asked.

"No," Lorret admitted.

"Then the curse did not work," Thomas said, returning the sword to its scabbard.

"She is a beghard!" Father Medous insisted.

"What is a beghard?" Thomas asked.

"A heretic," Father Medous said rather helplessly.

"You don't know, do you?" Thomas said. "It's just a word for you, and for that one word you would burn her?" He took the knife from his belt, then seemed to remember something. "I assume," he said, turning back to the consul, "that you are sending a message to the Count of Berat?"

Lorret looked startled, then tried to appear ignorant of any such thing.

"Don't take me for a fool," Thomas said. "You are doubtless concocting such a message now. So write to your Count and write to your bishop as well, and tell them that I have captured Castillon d'Arbizon and tell them more . . ." He paused. He had agonized in the night. He had prayed, for he tried hard to be a good Christian, but all his soul, all his instincts, told him the girl should not burn. And then an inner voice had told him he was being seduced by pity and by golden hair and bright eyes, and he had agonized even more, but at the end of his prayers he knew he could not put Genevieve to the fire. So now he cut the length of cord that tied her bonds and, when the crowd protested, he raised his voice. "Tell your bishop that I have freed the heretic." He put the knife back in its sheath and put his right arm around Genevieve's thin shoulders and faced the crowd again. "Tell your bishop that she is under the protection of the Earl of Northampton. And if your bishop wishes to know who has done this thing, then give him the same name that you provide to the Count of Berat. Thomas of Hookton."

"Hookton," Lorret repeated, stumbling over the unfamiliar name.

"Hookton," Thomas corrected him, "and tell him that by the grace of God Thomas of Hookton is ruler of Castillon d'Arbizon."

"You? Ruler here?" Lorret asked indignantly.

"And as you have seen," Thomas said, "I have assumed the powers of life and death. And that, Lorret, includes your life." He turned away and led Genevieve back into the courtyard. The gates banged shut.

And Castillon d'Arbizon, for lack of any other excitement, went back to work.

FOR TWO DAYS Genevieve did not speak or eat. She stayed close to Thomas, watching him, and when he spoke to her she just shook her head. Sometimes she cried silently. She made no noise when she wept, not even a sob, she just looked despairing as the tears ran down her face.

Robbie tried to talk with her, but she shrank from him. Indeed she shuddered if he came too close and Robbie became offended. "A bloody goddamned heretic bitch," he cursed her in his Scottish accent and Genevieve, though she did not speak English, knew what he was saying and she just stared at Thomas with her big eyes.

"She's frightened," Thomas said.

"Of me?" Robbie asked indignantly, and the indignation seemed justified for Robbie Douglas was a frank-faced, snub-nosed young man with a friendly disposition.

"She was tortured," Thomas explained. "Can't you imagine what that does to a person?" He involuntarily looked at the knuckles of his hands, still malformed from the screw-press that had cracked the bones. He had thought once he would never draw a bow again, but Robbie, his friend, had persevered with him. "She'll recover," he added to Robbie.

"I'm just trying to be friendly," Robbie protested. Thomas gazed at his friend and Robbie had the grace to blush. "But the bishop will send another warrant," Robbie went on. Thomas had burned the first, which had been discovered in the castellan's iron-bound chest along with the rest of the castle's papers. Most of those parchments were tax rolls, pay records, lists of stores, lists of men, the small change of everyday life. There had been some coins too, the tax yield, the first plunder of Thomas's command. "What will you do?" Robbie persisted. "When the bishop sends another warrant?"

"What would you like me to do?" Thomas asked.

"You'll have no choice," Robbie said vehemently, "you'll have to burn her. The bishop will demand it."

"Probably," Thomas agreed. "The Church can be very persistent when it comes to burning people."

"So she can't stay here!" Robbie protested.

"I freed her," Thomas said, "so she can do whatever she likes."

"I'll take her back to Pau," Robbie offered. Pau, a long way to the west, was the nearest English garrison. "That way she'll be safe. Give me a week, that's all, and I'll take her away."

"I need you here, Robbie," Thomas said. "We're few and the enemy, when they come, will be many."

"Let me take her back—"

"She stays," Thomas said firmly, "unless she wants to go."

Robbie looked as if he would argue, then abruptly left the room. Sir Guillaume, who had been listening in silence and who had understood most of the English conversation, looked grim. "In a day or two," he said, speaking English so that Genevieve would not understand, "Robbie will want to burn her."

"Burn her?" Thomas said, astonished. "No, not Robbie. He wants to save her."

"He wants her," Sir Guillaume said, "and if he can't have her then he'll decide no one should have her." He shrugged, then changed to French. "If she was ugly," he looked at Genevieve as he asked the question, "would she be alive?"

"If she were ugly," Thomas said, "I doubt she would have been condemned."

Sir Guillaume shrugged. His illegitimate daughter, Eleanor, had been Thomas's woman until she had been killed by Thomas's cousin, Guy Vexille. Now Sir Guillaume looked at Genevieve and recognized that she was a beauty. "You're as bad as the Scotsman," he said.

That night, the second night since they had captured the castle, when the men who had been raiding for food were all safe home and the horses were fed and the gate was locked and the sentries had been set and the supper eaten, and when most of the men were sleeping, Genevieve edged from behind the tapestry where Thomas had given her the castellan's bed and came to the fire where he was sitting read-ing the copy of his father's strange book about the Grail. No one else was in the room. Robbie and Sir Guillaume both slept in the hall, along with Thomas, but Sir Guillaume had charge of the sentries and Robbie was drinking and gambling with the men-at-arms in the chamber below.

Genevieve, dressed in her long white gown, stepped delicately off the dais, came close to his chair and knelt by the fire. She stared into the flames for a while, then looked up at Thomas and he marvelled at the way the flames lit and shadowed her face. Such a simple thing, a face, he thought, yet hers enthralled him.

"If I were ugly," she asked, speaking for the first time since he had released her, "would I be alive?"

"Yes," Thomas said.

"So why did you let me live?" she asked.

Thomas pulled up a sleeve and showed her the scars on his arm. "It was a Dominican who tortured me too," he said.

"Burning?"

"Burning," Thomas said.

She rose from her knees and put her arms about his neck and her head on his shoulder and held him. She said nothing, nor did he, neither did they move. Thomas was remembering the pain, humiliation, terror, and suddenly felt as if he wanted to cry.

And then the hall door squealed open and someone came in. Thomas had his back to the door so could not see who it was, but Genevieve raised her head to look at whoever had interrupted them and there was a moment's silence, then the sound of the door closing and footsteps going back down the stairs. Thomas knew it had been Robbie. He did not even need to ask.

Genevieve put her head back on his shoulder. She said nothing. He could feel her heart beating.

"The nights are the worst," she said.

"I know," Thomas said.

"In daylight," she said, "there are things to look at. But in the dark there are only memories."

"I know."

She pulled her face back, leaving her hands linked behind his neck, and she looked at him with an expression of intense seriousness. "I hate him," she said, and Thomas knew she was talking of her torturer. "He was called Father Roubert," she went on, "and I want to see his soul in hell."

Thomas, who had killed his own torturer, did not know what to say, so retreated into an evasion. "God will look after his soul."

"God seems very far away sometimes," Genevieve said, "especially in the dark."

"You must eat," he said, "and you must sleep."

"I can't sleep," she said.

"Yes," Thomas said, "you can," and he took her hands from his neck and led her back to the dais and behind the tapestry. He stayed there.

And next morning Robbie was not talking to Thomas, but their estrangement was diffused because there was so much work to be done. Food had to be levied from the town and stored in the castle. The blacksmith had to be taught how to make English arrow heads, and poplars and ash were cut to make the shafts. Geese lost their wing feathers to fledge the arrows, and the work kept Thomas's men busy, but they were still sullen. The jubilation that had followed their easy capture of the castle had been replaced by unrest and Thomas, whose first command this was, knew he had reached a crisis.

Sir Guillaume d'Evecque, much older than Thomas, made it explicit. "It's about the girl," he said. "She must die."

They were again in the great hall and Genevieve, sitting by the fire, understood this conversation. Robbie had come with Sir Guillaume, but now, instead of looking at Genevieve with longing, he watched her with hatred.

"Tell me why," Thomas said. He had been rereading the copy of his father's book with its strange hints about the Grail. It had been copied in a hurry and some of the handwriting was barely decipherable, and none of it made much sense, but he believed that if he studied it long enough then some meaning would emerge.

"She's a heretic!" Sir Guillaume said.

"She's a goddamned witch," Robbie put in vehemently. He spoke some French now, enough to understand the conversation, but preferred to make his protest in English.

"She wasn't accused of witchcraft," Thomas said.

"Hell, man! She used magic!"

Thomas put the parchment aside. "I've noticed," he said to Robbie, "that when you are worried you touch wood. Why?"

Robbie stared at him. "We all do!"

"Did a priest ever tell you to do it?"

"We do it! That's all."

"Why?"

Robbie looked angry, but managed to find an answer. "To avert evil. Why else?"

"Yet nowhere in the scriptures," Thomas said, "and nowhere in the Church Fathers' writings will you find such a command. It is not a Christian thing, yet you do it. So must I send you to the bishop to stand trial? Or should I save the bishop's time and just burn you?"

"You're blathering!" Robbie shouted.

Sir Guillaume hushed Robbie. "She is a heretic," the Norman said to Thomas, "and the Church has condemned her and if she stays here she will bring us nothing but ill luck. That's what's worrying the men. Jesus Christ, Thomas, but what good can come from harboring a heretic? The men all know it will bring evil."

Thomas slapped the table, startling Genevieve. "You," he pointed at Sir Guillaume, "burned my village, killed my mother and murdered my father who was a priest, and you tell me of evil?"

Sir Guillaume could not deny the charges any more than he could explain how he had become a friend of the man he had orphaned, but nor would he back down in the face of Thomas's anger. "I know evil," he said, "because I have done evil. But God forgives us."

"God forgives you," Thomas asked, "but not her?"

"The Church has decided otherwise."

"And I decided otherwise," Thomas insisted.

"Sweet Jesus," Sir Guillaume said, "do you think you're the bloody Pope?" He had become fond of English curse words and used them interspersed with his native French.

"She's bewitched you," Robbie growled. Genevieve looked as if she would speak, then turned away. Wind gusted at the window and brought a spatter of rain onto the wide floorboards.

Sir Guillaume looked at the girl, then back to Thomas. "The men won't stand her," he said.

"Because you worry them," Thomas snarled, although he knew

that it was Robbie, not Sir Guillaume, who had caused the unrest. Ever since Thomas had cut Genevieve's bonds he had worried about this, knowing his duty was to burn Genevieve and knowing he could not. His father, mad and angry and brilliant, had once laughed at the Church's idea of heresy. What was heretical one day, Father Ralph had said, was the Church's doctrine the next, and God, he had said, did not need men to burn people: God could do that very well for himself. Thomas had lain awake, agonizing, thinking, and knowing all the while that he wanted Genevieve too badly. It was not theological doubt that had saved her life, but lust, and the sympathy he felt for another soul who had suffered the Church's torture.

Robbie, usually so honest and decent, managed to control his anger. "Thomas," he said quietly, "think why we are here, and consider whether God will give us success if we have a heretic among us."

"I have thought of little else," Thomas said.

"Some of the men are talking of leaving," Sir Guillaume warned him. "Of finding a new commander."

Genevieve spoke for the first time. "I will leave," she said. "I will go back north. I won't be in your way."

"How long do you think you'll live?" Thomas asked her. "If my men don't murder you in the yard then the townsfolk will kill you in the street."

"Then what do I do?" she asked.

"You come with me," Thomas said and he crossed to an alcove beside the door where a crucifix hung. He pulled it from its nail and beckoned to her and to Sir Guillaume and Robbie. "Come," he said.

He led them to the castle yard where most of his men were gathering to discover the result of Sir Guillaume and Robbie's deputation to Thomas. They murmured unhappily when Genevieve appeared and Thomas knew he risked losing their allegiance. He was young, very young to be the leader of so many men, but they had wanted to follow him and the Earl of Northampton had trusted him. This was his first test. He had expected to meet that test in battle, but it had come now and he had to solve it, and so he stood on the top of the steps that overlooked the yard and waited until every man was staring at him. "Sir Guillaume!" Thomas called. "Go to one of the priests in the town and ask for a wafer. One that has already been consecrated. One kept for the last rites."

Sir Guillaume hesitated. "What if they say no?"

"You're a soldier, they're not," Thomas said and some of the men grinned.

Sir Guillaume nodded, glanced warily at Genevieve, then gestured two of his men-at-arms to accompany him. They went unwillingly, not wanting to miss whatever Thomas was about to say, but Sir Guillaume growled at them and they followed him through the gate.

Thomas held the crucifix high. "If this girl is the devil's creature," he said, "then she cannot look at this and she cannot bear its touch. If I hold it in front of her eyes she will go blind! If I touch her skin it will bleed. You know that! Your mothers told you that! Your priests told you that!"

Some of the men nodded and all stared open-mouthed as Thomas held the crucifix in front of Genevieve's open eyes, and then touched it to her forehead. Some men held their breath and most looked puzzled when her eyes remained whole and her clear, pale skin unblemished.

"She has the devil's help," a man growled.

"What kind of a fool are you?" Thomas spat. "You claim she can escape by using the devil's trickery? Then why was she here? Why was she in the cells? Why didn't she unfold great wings and fly away?"

"God prevented it."

"Then God would have made her skin bleed when the crucifix touched her," Thomas said, "wouldn't He? And if she's the devil's creature she'll have cat's feet. You all know that!" Many of the men muttered agreement for it was well known that those whom the devil favored were given cats' paws so they could creep about in the dark to work their evil. "Take your shoes off," Thomas ordered Genevieve, and when her feet were bare he pointed at them. "Some cat, eh? She won't catch many mice with paws like that!"

Two or three other men offered argument, but Thomas put them to scorn, and then Sir Guillaume came back and Father Medous accompanied him with a small silver casket that he kept ready to take the sacraments to a dying person. "It isn't seemly," Father Medous began, but stopped when Thomas glared at him.

"Come here, priest," Thomas said and Father Medous obeyed. Thomas took the silver casket from him. "She has passed one test," he said, "but all of you know, *all* of you, even in Scotland they know this," he paused and pointed at Robbie, "that the devil himself cannot save his creatures from the touch of Christ's body. She will die! She will writhe in agony. Her flesh will fall away and the worms will wriggle where she stood. Her screams will be heard in heaven. You all know that!"

They did know it and they nodded, and they watched as Thomas took a small piece of dry bread from the box and held it towards Genevieve. She hesitated, looking worriedly into Thomas's eyes, but he smiled at her and she obediently opened her mouth and let him put the thick wafer on her tongue.

"Kill her, God!" Father Medous called. "Kill her! Oh Jesus, Jesus, kill her!"

His voice echoed from the castle's yard, then the echo died away as every man in the yard stared at the tall Genevieve as she swallowed.

Thomas let the silence stretch, then he looked pointedly at Genevieve who still lived. "She came here," he told his men in English, "with her father. He was a juggler who collected pennies at fairs and she carried the hat. We've all seen folk like that. Stilt-walkers, fire-eaters, bear-handlers, jugglers. Genevieve collected the coins. But her father died and she was left here, a stranger, among folk who spoke a different language. She was like us! No one liked her because she came from far away. She didn't even speak their language! They hated her because she was different, and so they called her a heretic. And this priest says she's a heretic! But on the night I came here I was in his house and he has a woman who lives in his house and cooks for him and cleans for him, but he only has one bed." That got a laugh as Thomas had known it would. For all he knew Father Medous had a dozen beds, but the priest did not know what was being said. "She is no beghard," Thomas said, "you have just seen that for yourself. She is only a lost soul, like us, and folk took against her because she was not like them. So, if any of you still fear her and still think she will bring us bad luck, kill her now." He stepped back, arms folded, and Genevieve, who had not understood anything he said, looked at him with worry on her face. "Go on," Thomas said to his men. "You have bows, swords, knives. I have nothing. Just kill her! It won't be murder. The Church says she must die, so if you want to do God's work, do it." Robbie took a half-pace forward, then sensed the mood in the yard and stayed still.

Then someone laughed, and suddenly they were all laughing and cheering and Genevieve still looked puzzled, but Thomas was smiling. He quietened them by raising his hands. "She stays," he said, "she lives, and you have work to do. So go and bloody do it."

Robbie spat in disgust as Thomas took Genevieve back to the hall. Thomas hung the crucifix in its niche and closed his eyes. He was praying, thanking God she had passed the test of the wafer. And, better still, that she was staying.

T HOMAS SPENT HIS FIRST fortnight readying for a siege. Castillon d'Arbizon's castle possessed a well, which brought up a discolored and brackish water but meant his men would never die of thirst; the old garrison's storerooms, however, had contained only a few sacks of damp flour, a barrel of sprouting beans, a jar of rancid olive oil and some moldering cheeses. So, day after day, Thomas sent his men to search the town and the nearby villages and now food was piling into the undercroft. Once those sources had been exhausted, he began raiding. This was war as he knew it, the kind of war that had ravaged Brittany from end to end and reached almost to the gates of Paris. Thomas would leave ten men as a castle guard and the rest would follow him on horseback to some village or farm that owed allegiance to the Count of Berat and they would take the livestock, empty the barns and leave the place burning. After two such raids Thomas was met by a delegation from a village who brought money so that his men would spare them from pillage, and next day two more embassies arrived with bags of coin. Men also came offering their services. Routiers heard there was money and plunder to be gained in Castillon d'Arbizon and before he had been in the town ten days Thomas commanded over sixty men. He had two mounted raiding parties leave each day, and almost every day he sold excess plunder in the marketplace. He divided the money into three parts, one for the Earl of Northampton, one for himself which he shared with Sir Guillaume and Robbie, and the third part for the men.

Genevieve rode with him. Thomas had not wanted that. Taking women on raids was a distraction and he forbade any of the other men to bring their women, but Genevieve still feared Robbie and the handful of men who seemed to share his hatred of her, and so she insisted on riding alongside Thomas. She had discovered a small haubergeon in the castle stores and polished it with sand and vinegar until her hands were red and sore and the mail glowed like silver. It hung loose on her thin frame, but she belted it with a strip of yellow cloth and hung another strip of the same color from the crown of her polished helmet, which was a simple iron cap padded with a leather liner. The people of Castillon d'Arbizon, when Genevieve of the silver mail rode into town at the head of a line of mounted men leading packhorses heaped with plunder and driving stolen cattle, called her a *draga*. Everyone knew about *dragas*, they were devil's girls, capricious and deadly, and they dressed in glowing white. Genevieve was the devil's woman, they said, and she brought the Englishmen the devil's own luck. Strangely, that rumor made the majority of Thomas's men proud of her. The archers among them had become accustomed to being called the *hellequin* in Brittany and they were perversely proud of that association with the devil. It made other men fearful, and so Genevieve became their symbol of good luck.

Thomas had a new bow. Most archers, when their old bows wore out, simply purchased a new one from the supplies that were shipped from England, but there were no such supplies in Castillon d'Arbizon and, besides, Thomas knew how to make the weapon and loved doing it. He had found a good yew branch in Galat Lorret's garden and he had sawed and slashed away the bark and outer wood until he had a straight staff that was dark as blood on one half and pale as honey on the other. The dark side was the yew's heartwood that resisted compression, while the golden half was the springy sapwood; when the bow was finished the heartwood would fight against the cord's pull and the sapwood would help snap the bow straight so the arrow would fly like a winged demon.

The new weapon was even bigger than his old bow and sometimes he wondered if he was making it too big, but he persisted, shaping the wood with a knife until it had a thick belly and gently tapering ends. He smoothed, polished and then painted the bow, for the wood's moisture had to be trapped in the timber if the bow was not to break, and then he took the horn nocks from his old bow and put them on the new. He also took the silver plate from the old bow, the piece of Mass cup that bore his father's badge of a yale holding a grail, and he pinned it to the outer belly of the new bow that he had rubbed with beeswax and soot to darken the wood. The first time he strung it, bending the new staff to take the cord, he marvelled at the strength he needed, and the first time he shot it he watched astonished as the arrow soared out from the castle battlements.

He had made a second bow from a smaller bough, this one a child's bow that needed hardly any strength to draw, and he gave it to Genevieve who practiced with blunt arrows and amused the men as she sprayed her missiles wildly about the castle's yard. Yet she persevered, and there came a day when arrow after arrow struck the inner side of the gate.

That same night Thomas sent his old bow to hell. An archer never threw a bow away, not even if it broke on him; instead, in a ceremony that was an excuse for drinking and laughter, the old bow was committed to the flames. It was being sent to hell, the archers said, going ahead to wait for its owner. Thomas watched the yew burn, saw the bow bend for the last time, then snap in a shower of sparks, and he thought of the arrows it had sent. His archers stood respectfully around the great hall's hearth, and behind them the men-at-arms were silent, and only when the bow was a broken strip of ash did Thomas raise his wine. "To hell," he said in the old invocation.

"To hell," the archers agreed and the men-at-arms, privileged to be admitted to this archers' ritual, echoed the words. All but Robbie, who stood apart. He had taken to wearing a silver crucifix about his neck, hanging it above his mail coat to make it obvious that it was there to ward off evil.

"That was a good bow," Thomas said, watching the embers, but the new one was just as good, maybe better, and two days later Thomas carried it when he led his biggest raid yet.

He took all his men except the handful needed to guard the castle. He had been planning this raid for days and he knew it would be a long ride and so he left long before dawn. The sound of the hooves echoed from the house fronts as they clattered down to the western arch where the watchman, now carrying a staff decorated with the Earl of Northampton's badge, hurriedly pulled apart the gates, then the horsemen trotted across the bridge and vanished into the southern trees. The English were riding, no one knew where.

They were riding east, to Astarac. Riding to the place where Thomas's ancestors had lived, to the place where perhaps the Grail had once been hidden. "Is that what you expect to find?" Sir Guillaume asked him. "You think we'll trip over it?"

"I don't know what we'll find," Thomas admitted.

"There's a castle there, yes?"

"There was," Thomas said, "but my father said it had been slighted." A slighted castle was one that had been demolished, and Thomas expected to find nothing but ruins.

"So why go?" Sir Guillaume asked.

"The Grail," Thomas answered curtly. In truth he was going because he was curious, but his men, who did not know what he sought, had detected there was something unusual in this raid. Thomas had merely said they were going to a distant place because they had plundered everything that was close, but the more thoughtful of the men had noticed Thomas's nervousness.

Sir Guillaume knew the significance of Astarac, as did Robbie, who now led the advance guard of six archers and three men-at-arms who rode a quarter-mile ahead to guard against ambush. They were guided by a man from Castillon d'Arbizon who claimed to know the road and who led them up into the hills where the trees were low and scanty and the views unrestricted. Every few minutes Robbie would wave to signify that the way ahead was clear. Sir Guillaume, riding bare-headed, nodded at the distant figure. "So that friendship's over?" he asked.

"I hope not," Thomas said.

"You can hope what you bloody like," Sir Guillaume said, "but she came along." Sir Guillaume's face had been disfigured by Thomas's cousin, leaving the Norman with only his right eye, a scarred left cheek and a streak of white where the sword had cut into his beard. He looked fearsome, and so he was in battle, but he was also a generous man. He looked now at Genevieve who rode her grey mare a few yards to the side of the path. She was in her silver armor, her long legs in pale grey cloth and brown boots. "You should have burned her," he said cheerfully.

"You still think that?" Thomas asked.

"No," Sir Guillaume admitted. "I like her. If Genny's a beghard then let's have more of them. But you know what you should do with Robbie?"

"Fight him?"

"Christ's bones, no!" Sir Guillaume was shocked that Thomas should even suggest such a thing. "Send him home. What's his ransom?"

"Three thousand florins."

"Christ in his bucket, that's cheap enough! You must have that much coin in the chests, so give it to him and send him packing. He can buy his freedom and go and rot in Scotland."

"I like him," Thomas said, and that was true. Robbie was a friend and Thomas hoped that their old closeness could be restored.

"You might like him," Sir Guillaume retorted tartly, "but you don't sleep with him, and when it comes to a choice, Thomas, men always choose the one who warms their bed. It may not give you a longer life, but it will certainly be a happier one." He laughed, then turned to search the lower ground for any enemy. There was none. It appeared that the Count of Berat was ignoring the English garrison that had so suddenly taken a part of his territory, but Sir Guillaume, who was older in war than Thomas, suspected that was only because the Count was marshalling his forces. "He'll attack when he's ready," the Norman said. "And have you noticed that the *coredors* are taking an interest in us?"

"I have," Thomas said. On every raid he had been aware of the ragged bandits watching his men. They did not come close, certainly not within bowshot, but they were there and he expected to see them in these hills very soon.

"Not like bandits to challenge soldiers," Sir Guillaume said.

"They haven't challenged us yet."

"They're not watching us for amusement," Sir Guillaume added dryly.

"I suspect," Thomas replied, "that there's a price on our heads. They want money. And they'll get brave one day. I hope so." He patted the new bow, which was holstered in a long leather tube sewn to his saddle.

By midmorning the raiders were crossing a succession of wide fertile valleys separated by high rocky hills that ran north and south. From the summit of the hills Thomas could see dozens of villages, but once they descended and were among the trees again, he could see none. They saw two castles from the heights, both small, both with flags flying from their towers, but both were too far away to distinguish the badge on the flags, which Thomas assumed would be that of the Count of Berat. The valleys all had rivers running north, but they had no trouble crossing them for the bridges or fords were not guarded. The roads, like the hills and valleys, went north and south and so the lords of these rich lands did not guard against folk traveling east or west. Their castles stood sentinel over the valley entrances where the garrisons could skim taxes from the merchants on the roads.

"Is that Astarac?" Sir Guillaume asked when they crossed yet another ridge. He was staring down at a village with a small castle.

"Astarac's castle is ruined," Genevieve answered. "It's a tower and some walls on a crag, nothing like that."

"You've been there?" Thomas asked.

"My father and I always went for the olive fair."

"Olive fair?"

"On the feast of St. Jude," she said. "Hundreds of folk came. We made good money."

"And they sold olives?"

"Jars and jars of the first pressing," she said, "and in the evening they soaked young pigs with the oil and people tried to catch them. There was bull-fighting and dancing." She laughed at the memory, then spurred on. She rode well, straight-backed and with her heels down, while Thomas, like most of his archers, rode a horse with all the grace of a sack of wheat.

It was just past midday when they rode down into Astarac's valley. The *coredors* had seen them by now and a score of the ragged bandits were dogging their footsteps, but not daring to come close. Thomas ignored them, staring instead at the black outline of the broken castle that stood on its rocky knoll a half-mile south of a small village. Farther north, in the distance, he could see a monastery, probably Cistercian for its church had no tower. He looked back at the castle and knew his family had once held it, that his ancestors had ruled these lands, that his badge had flown from that broken tower, and he thought he ought to feel some strong emotion, but instead there was only a vague disappointment. The land meant nothing to him, and how could something as precious as the Grail belong to that pathetic pile of shattered stone?

Robbie rode back. Genevieve moved aside and he ignored her. "Doesn't look like much," Robbie said, his silver crucifix shining in the autumn sun.

"It doesn't," Thomas agreed.

Robbie twisted in his saddle, making the leather creak. "Let me take a dozen men-at-arms to the monastery," he suggested. "They might have full storerooms."

"Take a half-dozen archers with you as well," Thomas suggested, "and the rest of us will ransack the village."

Robbie nodded, then looked back at the distant *coredors*. "Those bastards won't dare attack."

"I doubt it," Thomas agreed, "but my suspicion is that there's a price on our heads. So keep your men together."

Robbie nodded and, still without even glancing at Genevieve, spurred away. Thomas ordered six of his archers to go with the Scotsman, then he and Sir Guillaume rode down to the village where, as soon as the inhabitants saw the approaching soldiers, a great fire was lit to spew a plume of dirty smoke into the cloudless sky. "A warning," Sir Guillaume said. "That'll happen everywhere we go now."

"A warning?"

"The Count of Berat has woken up," Sir Guillaume said. "Everyone will be ordered to light a beacon when they see us. It warns the other villagers, tells them to hide their livestock and lock away their daughters. And the smoke will be seen in Berat. It tells them where we are."

"We're a long damn way from Berat."

"They won't ride today. They'll never catch us," Sir Guillaume agreed.

The purpose of the visit, so far as Thomas's men was concerned, was to plunder. In the end, they believed, such depredations would bring out the forces of Berat and so they would have a chance to fight a proper battle in which, if God or the devil favored them, they would take some valuable prisoners and so make themselves even richer, but for now they simply stole or destroyed. Robbie rode to the monastery, Sir Guillaume led the other men into the village while Thomas and Genevieve turned south and climbed the rough path to the ruined castle.

It was ours once, Thomas was thinking. It was here that his ancestors had lived, yet still he could feel nothing. He did not think of himself as a Gascon, let alone a Frenchman. He was English, yet still he gazed at the ruined walls and tried to imagine when the castle was whole and his family had been its masters.

He and Genevieve picketed their horses at the broken gate, then stepped over fallen stone into the old courtyard. The curtain wall was almost entirely gone, its stones carried away to make houses or barns. The biggest remnant was the tower keep, but even that was half shattered, its southern side open to the wind. A hearth showed halfway up the northern wall and there were great stones jutting from the inner flank to show where the joists supporting the floors had once been. A broken stair wound up the eastern side, leading to nothing.

Beside the tower, sharing the highest part of the rock crag, were the remnants of a chapel. Its floor was flagstones and on one of them was Thomas's badge. He put his bow down and crouched by the stone, trying to feel some sense of belonging.

"One day," Genevieve was standing on the broken southern wall, staring south down the valley, "you'll tell me why you're here."

"To raid," Thomas said shortly.

She took off her helmet and shook out her hair, which she wore loose, like a young girl. The blonde strands lifted in the wind as she smiled. "Do you take me for a fool, Thomas?"

"No," he said warily.

"You travel a long way," she said, "from England, and you come to a little town called Castillon d'Arbizon, and then you ride here. There were a dozen places we could have raided on the way, but it is here we come. And here there is the same badge as the one you carry on your bow."

"There are many badges," Thomas said, "and they often resemble each other."

She shook her head dismissively. "What is that badge?"

"A yale," he said. A yale was a beast invented by the heralds, all teeth, claws, scales and threat. Thomas's badge, the one pinned to his bow, showed the yale holding a cup, but the yale on the flagstone held nothing in its taloned paw.

Genevieve looked past Thomas to where Sir Guillaume's men were herding livestock into a pen. "We used to hear so many stories," she said, "my father and I, and he liked stories so he tried to remember them, and in the evenings he would tell them to me. Tales of monsters in the hills, of dragons flying across the rooftops, reports of miracles at holy springs, of women giving birth to monsters. A thousand tales. But there was one story we heard again and again whenever we came to these valleys." She paused.

"Go on," Thomas said. The wind gusted, lifting the long fine strands of her hair. She was more than old enough to tie it up, to mark herself as a woman, but she liked it unbound and Thomas thought it made her look still more like a *draga*.

"We heard," Genevieve said, "about the treasures of the Perfect."

The Perfect had been forerunners of the beghards, heretics who had denied the authority of the Church, and their evil had spread through the south until the Church, with the help of the French King, had crushed them. The fires of their deaths had died a hundred years ago, yet still there were echoes of the Cathars, as the Perfect had been called. They had not spread into this part of Gascony, though some churchmen claimed the heresy had infested all Christendom and was still hidden away in its remotest parts. "The treasures of the Perfect," Thomas said tonelessly.

"You come to this little place," Genevieve said, "from far away, yet you carry a badge that comes from these hills. And whenever my father and I came here we heard stories of Astarac. They still tell them here."

"Tell what?"

"How a great lord fled here for refuge and brought the treasures of the Perfect with him. And the treasures, they say, are still here."

Thomas smiled. "They would have dug them up long ago."

"If a thing is hidden well," Genevieve said, "then it is not found easily."

Thomas looked down at the village where bellows and screeches and bleatings came from the pen where the livestock was being slaughtered. The best cuts of bleeding, fresh meat would be tied to the saddles and taken back for salting or smoking, while the villagers could have the horns, offal and hides. "They tell stories everywhere," he said dismissively.

"Of all the treasures," Genevieve said softly, ignoring his disparagement, "there is one that is prized above all the others. But only a Perfect can find it, they say."

"Then God alone can find it," Thomas said.

"Yet that doesn't stop you looking, Thomas, does it?"

"Looking?"

"For the Grail."

The word was said, the ridiculous word, the impossible word, the name of the thing that Thomas feared did not exist, yet which he sought. His father's writings suggested he had possessed the Grail, and Thomas's cousin, Guy Vexille, was certain that Thomas knew where the relic was, and so Vexille would follow Thomas to the ends of the earth. Which was why Thomas was here, in Astarac, to draw his murderous cousin within range of the new bow. He looked up at the tower's ragged top. "Sir Guillaume knows why we are here," he told her, "and Robbie knows. But none of the others do, so don't tell them."

"I won't," she said, "but do you think it exists?"

"No," he said with far more certainty than he felt.

"It does," Genevieve said.

Thomas went to stand beside her and he stared southwards to where a stream twisted soft through meadows and olive groves. He could see men there, a score of them, and he knew they were *coredors*. He would have to do something about them, he thought, if his men were not to be dogged by the ragged bands through the winter. He did not fear them, but he did fear that one of his men would wander off the path and be seized, so it would be better to frighten the bandits off before that happened.

"It does exist," Genevieve insisted.

"You can't know that," Thomas said, still watching the ragged men who watched him.

"The Grail is like God," Genevieve said. "It is everywhere, all around us, obvious, but we refuse to see it. Men think they can only see God when they build a great church and fill it with gold and silver and statues, but all they need do is look. The Grail exists, Thomas, you just need to open your eyes."

Thomas strung his bow, took one old arrow from his bag, then pulled the cord back as far as it would go. He could feel the muscles in his back aching from the unexpected strain of the new bow. He held the arrow low, level with his waist, and cocked his left hand high so that when he released the string the arrow flew into the sky, the white feathers getting smaller and smaller, and then it plummeted to earth, thumping into the stream bank over three hundred yards away. The *coredors* understood the message and backed away.

"Waste of a good arrow," Thomas said. Then he took Genevieve's arm and went to find his men.

ROBBIE MARVELED at the monastery's lands, all tended by white-robed Cistercians who gathered up their skirts and ran when they saw his mailed men ride out from the village. Most of the fields were given over to vines, but there was a pear orchard and an olive grove, a pasture of sheep and a fish pond. It was, he thought, a fat land. For days now he had been hearing how the harvest in southern Gascony had been poor, yet it seemed to him that this was a very heaven compared to the hard, thin lands of his northern home. A bell began to toll its alarm from the monastery.

"They've got to have a treasure house." Jake, one of his archers, spurred alongside Robbie and nodded at the monastery. "And we'll kill *him*," he spoke of a solitary monk who had come from the monastery gatehouse and now walked calmly towards them, "then the rest won't be no trouble."

"You'll kill no one," Robbie snapped. He motioned his men to stop their horses. "And you'll wait here," he told them, then he swung out of his saddle, threw his reins to Jake and walked towards the monk, who was very tall, very thin and very old. He had wispy white hair about his tonsure, and a long, dark face that somehow conveyed wisdom and gentleness. Robbie, striding in his coat of mail with his shield slung on his back and his uncle's long sword at his side, felt clumsy and out of place.

The right sleeve of the monk's white robe was smeared with ink, making Robbie wonder if the man was a scrivener. He had plainly been sent to negotiate with the raiders, perhaps buy them off or try to persuade them to respect God's house, and Robbie thought how he had helped plunder the great priory of the Black Canons at Hexham, just across the English border, and he remembered the friars pleading with the invaders, then threatening God's vengeance, and how the Scots had laughed at them, then stripped Hexham bare. But God had wreaked his vengeance by letting the English army win at Durham, and that memory, the sudden realization that perhaps the desecration of Hexham had led directly to the defeat at Durham, gave Robbie pause so that he stopped, frowned and wondered what exactly he would say to the tall monk, who now smiled at him. "You must be the English raiders?" the monk said in very good English.

Robbie shook his head. "I'm a Scot," he retorted.

"A Scot! A Scot riding with the English! I once spent two years in a Cistercian house in Yorkshire and the brothers never said a good word of the Scots, yet here you are, with the English, and I thought I had witnessed every marvel that this sinful world has to offer." The monk still smiled. "My name is Abbot Planchard and my house is at your mercy. Do what you will, young man, we will not fight you." He stepped to one side of the path and gestured towards the monastery as if inviting Robbie to draw his sword and start the plunder.

Robbie did not move. He was thinking of Hexham. Thinking of a friar dying in the church there, his blood running from beneath his black robe and trickling down a step, and of the drunken Scottish soldiers stepping over the man with their spoils: candlesticks, crosses and embroidered copes.

"Of course," the abbot said, "if you prefer, you can have some wine? It's our own wine and not the best. We drink it too young, but we have some fine goat cheese and Brother Philippe makes the best bread in the valley. We can water your horses, but alas I have little hay."

"No," Robbie said abruptly, then turned and shouted at his men. "Go back to Sir Guillaume!"

"We do what?" one of the men-at-arms asked, puzzled.

"Go back to Sir Guillaume. Now!"

He took his horse from Jake, then walked beside the abbot to the monastery. He did not say anything, but Abbot Planchard seemed to understand from his silence that the young Scot wanted to talk. He told the gatekeeper to look after the destrier, then invited Robbie to leave his sword and shield in the lodge. "Of course you may keep them," the abbot said, "but I thought you might be more comfortable without them. Welcome to St. Sever's."

"St. Sever?" Robbie asked as he unslung the shield from about his neck.

"He is reputed to have mended an angel's wing in this valley. I find that quite hard to believe sometimes, but God likes to test our faith and so I pray to St. Sever every night and thank him for his miracle and ask him to mend me as he mended the white wing."

Robbie smiled. "You need mending?"

"We all do. When we are young it is the spirit that breaks, and when we are old it is the body." Abbot Planchard touched Robbie's elbow to guide him towards a cloister where he picked a spot in the sun and invited his visitor to sit on the low wall between two pillars. "Tell me," he asked, settling on the wall beside Robbie, "are you Thomas? Isn't that the name of the man who leads the English?"

"I'm not Thomas," Robbie said, "but you've heard of us?"

"Oh indeed. Nothing so exciting has happened in these parts since the angel fell," the abbot said with a smile, then turned and asked a monk to bring wine, bread and cheese. "And perhaps some honey! We make very good honey," he added to Robbie. "The lepers tend the hives."

"Lepers!"

"They live behind our house," the abbot said calmly, "a house which you, young man, wanted to plunder. Am I right?"

"Yes," Robbie admitted.

"Instead you are here to break bread with me." Planchard paused, his shrewd eyes searching Robbie's face. "Is there something you wanted to tell me?"

Robbie frowned at that, then looked puzzled. "How did you know?"

Planchard laughed. "When a soldier comes to me, armed and armored, but with a crucifix hanging over his mail, then I know he is a man who is not unmindful of his God. You wear a sign, my son," he pointed at the crucifix, "and even after eighty-five years I can read a sign."

"Eighty-five!" Robbie said in wonderment, but the abbot said nothing. He just waited and Robbie fidgeted for a while and then he blurted out what was on his mind. He described how they had gone to Castillon d'Arbizon, and how they had found the beghard in the dungeons and how Thomas had saved her life. "It's been worrying me," Robbie said, staring at the grass, "and I'm thinking that no good will come to us so long as she lives. The Church condemned her!"

"So it did," Planchard said, then fell silent.

"She's a heretic! A witch!"

"I know of her," Planchard said mildly, "and I heard that she lives."

"She's here!" Robbie protested, pointing south towards the village. "Here in your valley!"

Planchard looked at Robbie, seeing an honest, blunt soul, but one in turmoil, and he sighed to himself, then poured some wine and pushed the board of bread, cheese and honey towards the young man. "Eat," he said gently.

"It isn't right!" Robbie said vehemently.

The abbot did not touch the food. He did sip the wine, then he spoke softly as he stared at the plume of smoke that drifted from the village's warning pyre. "The beghard's sin is not yours, my son," he said, "and when Thomas released her it was not your doing. You worry about other people's sins?"

"I should kill her!" Robbie said.

"No, you should not," the abbot said firmly.

"No?" Robbie sounded surprised.

"If God had wanted that," the abbot said, "then he would not have sent you here to talk to me. God's purposes are not always easy to understand, but I have found that his methods are not as indirect as ours. We complicate God because we do not see that goodness is so very simple." He paused. "You told me that no good could come to you while she lives, but why would God want good to come to you? This region has been at peace, except for bandits, and you disturb it. Would God make you more vicious if the beghard died?"

Robbie said nothing.

"You speak to me," Planchard said more firmly, "of other people's sin, but you do not talk of your own. Do you wear the crucifix for others? Or for yourself?"

"For myself," Robbie said quietly.

"Then tell me of yourself," the abbot said.

So Robbie did.

JOSCELYN, LORD OF BÉZIERS and heir to the great county of Berat, slammed the breastplate onto the table so hard that it started dust from the cracks in the timber.

His uncle, the Count, frowned. "There is no need to beat the wood, Joscelyn," he said placidly. "There is no woodworm in the table. At least I hope not. They treat it with turpentine as a preventative."

"My father swore by a mix of lye and urine," Father Roubert said, "and an occasional scorching." He was sitting opposite the Count,

sifting through the moldering old parchments that had lain undis-
turbed since they had been removed from Astarac a century before.
Some were charred at the edges, evidence of the fire that had been set
in the fallen castle.

"Lye and urine? I should try that." The Count scratched beneath
his woolen hat, then peered up at his angry nephew. "You do know
Father Roubert, Joscelyn? Of course you do." He peered at another
document, saw it was a request that two more watchmen be
appointed to the Astarac town guard, and sighed. "If you could read,
Joscelyn, you could help us."

"I'll help you, uncle," Joscelyn said savagely. "Just let me off the
leash!"

"That can go to Brother Jerome." The Count put the request for
extra watchmen in the big basket which would be carried down to the
room where the young monk from Paris read the parchments. "And
mix in some other documents," he told Father Roubert, "just to con-
fuse him. Those old tax rolls from Lemierre should keep him busy for
a month!"

"Thirty men, uncle," Joscelyn insisted, "that's all I ask! You have
eighty-seven men-at-arms! Just give me thirty!"

Joscelyn, Lord of Béziers, was an impressive figure. He was hugely
tall, broad in the chest and long-limbed, but his appearance was
spoiled by a round face of such vacancy that his uncle sometimes
wondered whether there was any brain at all behind his nephew's pro-
tuberant eyes. He had straw-colored hair that was almost always
marked by the pressure caused by a helmet's leather liner and he had
been blessed with strong arms and sturdy legs, and yet, though Joscelyn was all bone and muscle, and possessed scarcely a single idea to
disturb either, he was not without his virtues. He was diligent, even
if his diligence was directed solely towards the tournament yard
where he was one of the most celebrated fighters in Europe. He had
won the Paris tourney twice, humiliated the best English knights at

the big Tewkesbury gathering, and even in the German states, where men believed no one was better than they, Joscelyn had brought off a dozen top prizes. He had famously put Walther of Siegenthaler on his broad rump twice in one bout, and the only knight who had consistently defeated Joscelyn was the black-armored man called the Harlequin who had ridden grim and relentlessly about the tournament circuit to raise money. But the Harlequin had not been seen for three or four years now and Joscelyn suspected that his absence meant Joscelyn could make himself the champion of Europe.

He had been raised near Paris by the Count's younger brother who had died of the flux seventeen years before. There had been little money in Joscelyn's house and the Count, notoriously mean, had sent the widow hardly an écu to save her distress, yet Joscelyn had made money with his lance and sword, and that, the Count reckoned, was to his credit. And he had brought two men-at-arms with him, both of them hardened warriors, whom Joscelyn paid from his own money and that, the Count thought, showed that he was able to lead men. "But you really should learn to read," he finished his thought aloud. "The mastery of letters civilizes a man, Joscelyn."

"Shit on civilization," Joscelyn said, "there are English bandits in Castillon d'Arbizon and we're doing nothing! Nothing!"

"We're hardly doing nothing," the Count demurred, scratching again under his woolen cap. He had an itch there, and he wondered if it presaged some worse ailment. He made a mental note to consult his copies of Galen, Pliny and Hippocrates. "We've sent word to Toulouse and to Paris," he explained to Joscelyn, "and I shall protest to the seneschal in Bordeaux. I shall protest very firmly!" The seneschal was the English King's regent in Gascony and the Count was not sure he *would* send the man a message, for such a protest might well provoke more English adventurers to seek land in Berat.

"Damn protests," Joscelyn said, "just kill the bastards. They're breaking the truce!"

"They're English," the Count said, "they always break truces. Trust the devil before an Englishman."

"So kill them," Joscelyn persisted.

"I've no doubt we shall," the Count replied. He was deciphering the terrible handwriting of a long-dead clerk who had written a contract with a man called Sestier to line Astarac's castle's drains with elmwood. "In time," he added absently.

"Give me thirty men, uncle, and I'll scour them out in a week!"

The Count discarded the document and picked up another. The ink had turned brown and was badly faded, but he could just make out that it was a contract with a stonemason. "Joscelyn," he asked, still peering at the contract, "how will you scour them out in a week?"

Joscelyn stared at his uncle as though the old man was mad. "Go to Castillon d'Arbizon, of course," he said, "and kill them."

"I see, I see," the Count said, as though grateful for the explanation. "But the last time I was in Castillon d'Arbizon, and that was many years ago, just after the English left, but when I was there, Joscelyn, the castle was made of stone. How will you defeat that with sword and lance?" He smiled up at his nephew.

"For God's sake! They'll fight."

"Oh, I am sure they will. The English like their pleasures, as do you. But these Englishman have archers, Joscelyn, archers. Have you ever encountered an English archer on the tournament field?"

Joscelyn ignored the question. "Only twenty archers," he complained instead.

"The garrison tell us twenty-four," the Count said pedantically. The survivors of Castillon d'Arbizon's garrison had been released by the English and had fled to Berat where the Count had hanged two as an example and then questioned the others. Those others were now all imprisoned, waiting to be taken south and sold as galley slaves. The Count anticipated that source of income with a smile, then was about to put the stonemason's contract in the basket when a word caught his eye and some instinct made him hold on to the document as he turned back to his nephew. "Let me tell you about the English war bow, Joscelyn," he said patiently. "It is a simple thing, made of yew, a peasant's tool, really. My huntsman can use one, but he is the only man in Berat who has ever mastered the weapon. Why do you think that is?" He waited, but his nephew made no answer. "I'll tell you anyway," the Count went on. "It takes years, Joscelyn, many years to master the yew bow. Ten years? Probably that long, and after ten years a man can send an arrow clean through armor at two hundred paces." He smiled. "Splat! A thousand écus of man, armor and weaponry fallen to a peasant's bow. And it isn't luck, Joscelyn. My huntsman can put an arrow through a bracelet at a hundred paces. He can pierce mail coat at two hundred. I've seen him put an arrow through an oak door at a hundred and fifty, and the door was three inches thick!"

"I have plate armor," Joscelyn said sullenly.

"So you do. And at fifty paces the English will pick out the eye slits in your visor and send arrows into your brain. You, of course, might survive that."

Joscelyn did not recognize the insult. "Crossbows," he said.

"We have thirty crossbowmen," the Count said, "and none are as young as they were, and some are ill, and I wouldn't really think they can survive against this young man, what is his name?"

"Thomas of Hookton," Father Roubert interjected.

"Strange name," the Count said, "but he seems to know his business. A man to be treated with care, I'd say."

"Guns!" Joscelyn suggested.

"Ah! Guns," the Count exclaimed as though he had not thought of that himself. "We could certainly take cannon to Castillon d'Arbizon, and I daresay the machines will tear down the castle gate and generally make a regrettable mess, but where are we to find the things? There is one in Toulouse, I'm told, but it needs eighteen horses to move it. We could send to Italy, of course, but they are very expensive things to hire and their expert mechanics are even more expensive, and I very much doubt that they will fetch the things here before the spring. God preserve us till then."

"We can't do nothing!" Joscelyn protested again.

"True, Joscelyn, true," the Count agreed genially. Rain hammered at the horn panels that covered the windows. It was falling in grey swathes all across the town. It cascaded down the gutters, flooded the latrine pits, dripped through thatch and swept like a shallow stream through the town's lower gates. No weather for fighting, the Count thought, but if he did not allow his nephew some freedom then he suspected the young fool would ride off and get himself killed in an ill-considered skirmish. "We could bribe them, of course," he suggested.

"Bribe them?" Joscelyn was outraged by the suggestion.

"It's quite normal, Joscelyn. They're nothing but bandits and they only want money, so I offer them coins to yield the castle. It works often enough."

Joscelyn spat. "They'll take the money then stay where they are and demand more."

"That's very good!" The Count of Berat smiled approvingly at his nephew. "That's precisely what I had concluded. Well done, Joscelyn! So I won't try to bribe them. I have written to Toulouse, though, and requested the service of their gun. No doubt it will be disgustingly expensive, but if it's necessary, we shall unleash it on the English. I hope it doesn't come to that. Have you spoken with Sir Henri?" he asked.

Sir Henri Courtois was the Count's garrison commander and a soldier of experience. Joscelyn had indeed talked with him and been given the same answer that his uncle had just delivered: beware of English archers. "Sir Henri's an old woman," Joscelyn complained.

"With that beard? I doubt it," the Count said, "though I did once see a bearded woman. It was in Tarbes, at the Easter fair. I was very young then, but I distinctly remember her. A great long beard, she had. We paid a couple of coins to see her, of course, and if you paid more you were allowed to tug the beard, which I did, and it was the true thing, and if you paid more still they revealed her breasts which destroyed any suspicion that she was really a man. They were very nice breasts, as I recall." He looked at the stonemason's contract again and at the Latin word that had caught his eye. *Calix*. A memory from his childhood stirred, but would not come.

"Thirty men!" Joscelyn pleaded.

The Count let the document rest. "What we will do, Joscelyn, is what Sir Henri suggests. We shall hope to catch the Englishmen when they are away from their lair. We shall negotiate for the gun at Toulouse. We are already offering a bounty for every English archer captured alive. A generous bounty, so I have no doubt every routier and *coredor* in Gascony will join the hunt and the English will find themselves surrounded by enemies. It won't be a pleasant life for them."

"Why alive?" Joscelyn wanted to know. "Why not dead English archers?"

The Count sighed. "Because then, my dear Joscelyn, the *coredors* will bring in a dozen corpses a day and claim they are Englishmen. We need to talk to the archer before we kill him to make sure he is the real thing. We must, so to speak, inspect the breasts to ensure the beard is real." He stared at the word, *calix*, willing the memory to surface. "I doubt we'll capture many archers," he went on, "they hunt in packs and are dangerous, so we shall also do what we always do when the *coredors* become too impudent. Wait patiently and ambush them when they make a mistake. And they will, but they think we shall make the mistake first. They want you to attack them, Joscelyn, so they can riddle you with arrows, but we have to fight them when they are not expecting a fight. So ride with Sir Henri's men and make sure the beacons are laid and, when the time comes, I will release you. That is a promise."

The beacons were being laid in every village and town of the county. They were great heaps of wood which, when fired, would send a signal of smoke to say that the English raiders were in the vicinity. The beacons warned other nearby communities and also told the watchmen on the tower of Berat's castle where the English were riding. One day, the Count believed, they would come too close to Berat, or be in a place where his men could ambush them, and so he was content to wait until they made that mistake. And they would make it, *coredors* always did, and these English, though they flew the badge of Northampton's Earl, were no better than common bandits. "So go and practice your weapons, Joscelyn," he told his nephew, "because you will use them soon enough. And take that breastplate with you."

Joscelyn left. The Count watched as Father Roubert fed the fire with new logs, then he looked again at the document. The Count of Astarac had hired a stonemason to carve "*Calix Meus Inebrians*" above the gate of Astarac's castle and specified that the date on the contract was to be added to the legend. Why? Why would any man want the words "My Cup Makes Me Drunk" decorating his castle? "Father?" he said.

"Your nephew will get himself killed," the Dominican grumbled.

"I have other nephews," the Count said.

"But Joscelyn is right," Father Roubert said. "They have to be fought, and fought soon. There is a beghard to be burned." Father Roubert's anger kept him awake at night. How dare they spare a heretic? He lay in his narrow bed, imagining the girl's screams as the flames consumed her dress. She would be naked when the cloth had burned and Father Roubert remembered her pale body tied to his table. He had understood temptation then, understood it and hated it and there had been such pleasure in drawing the hot iron up the tender skin of her thighs.

"Father! You're half-asleep," the Count remonstrated. "Look at this." He pushed the stonemason's contract across the table.

The Dominican frowned as he tried to make out the faded handwriting, then nodded as he recognized the phrase. "From the psalms of David," he said.

"Of course! How stupid of me. But why would a man carve '*Calix Meus Inebrians*' over his gateway?"

"The Church Fathers," the priest said, "doubt that the psalmist means drunk, not as we mean it. Suffused with joy, perhaps? 'My cup delights me'?"

"But what cup?" the Count asked pointedly. There was silence except for the sound of rain and the crackle of logs, then the friar looked again at the contract, pushed back his chair and went to the Count's shelves. He took down a great chained book that he placed carefully on the lectern, unclasped the cover and opened the huge, stiff pages. "What book is that?" the Count enquired.

"The annals of St. Joseph's monastery," Father Roubert said. He turned the pages, seeking an entry. "We know," he went on, "that the last Count of Astarac was infected with the Cathar heresy. It's said that his father sent him to be a squire to a knight in Carcassonne and thus he became a sinner. He eventually inherited Astarac and lent his support to the heretics, and we know he was among the last of the Cathar lords." He paused to turn another page. "Ah! Here it is. Montségur fell on St. Joevin's day in the twenty-second year of the reign of Raymond VII." Raymond had been the last great Count of Toulouse, dead now almost a hundred years. Father Roubert thought for a second. "That would mean Montségur fell in 1244."

The Count leaned over the table and picked up the contract. He peered at it and found what he wanted. "And this is dated the eve of St. Nazarius of the same year. Saint Nazarius's feast is at the end of July, yes?"

"It is," Father Roubert confirmed.

"And St. Joevin's day is in March," the Count said, "which proves that the Count of Astarac didn't die in Montségur."

"Someone ordered the Latin carved," the Dominican allowed.

"Maybe it was his son?" He turned the big pages of the annals, flinching at the crudely illuminated capitals, until he found the entry he wanted. "'And in the year of our Count's death, when there was a great plague of toads and vipers,'" he read aloud, "'the Count of Berat took Astarac and slew all that were inside.'"

"But the annals do not say that Astarac himself died?"

"No."

"So what if he lived?" The Count was excited now and had left his chair to start pacing up and down. "And why would he desert his comrades in Montségur?"

"If he did," Father Roubert sounded dubious.

"Someone did. Someone with authority to hire a mason. Someone who wanted to leave a message in stone. Someone who . . ." The Count suddenly stopped. "Why would they describe the date as the eve of St. Nazarius's feast?" he asked.

"Why not?"

"Because that is St. Pantaleon's day. Why not call it that?"

"Because," Father Roubert was about to explain that St. Nazarius was a good deal better known than St. Pantaleon, but the Count interrupted him.

"Because it is the Seven Sleepers' Day! There were seven of them, Roubert! Seven survivors! And they wanted the date inscribed to make that obvious!"

The friar thought the Count was stretching the evidence exceedingly thin, but he said nothing. "And think of the story!" The Count urged him. "Seven young men under threat of persecution, yes? They flee the city, which was it? Ephesus, of course, and hide in a cave! The Emperor, Decius wasn't it? I'm sure it was, and he ordered every cave sealed and years later, over a hundred years later if I remember rightly, the seven young men are found there, and not one of them has aged a day. So seven men, Roubert, fled Montségur!"

Father Roubert replaced the annals. "But a year later," he pointed out, "your ancestor defeated them."

"They could have survived," the Count insisted, "and everyone knows that members of the Vexille family fled. Of course they survived! But think, Roubert," he was unconsciously calling the Dominican by his childhood name, "why would a Cathar lord leave the last stronghold if it not to take the heretics" treasures to safety? Everyone knows the Cathars possessed great treasures!"

Father Roubert tried not to get caught up in the Count's excitement. "The family," he said, "would have taken the treasures with them."

"Would they?" the Count demanded. "There are seven of them. They go their different ways. Some to Spain, others to northern France, one at least to England. Suppose you are hunted, wanted by the Church and by every great lord. Would you take a great treasure with you? Would you risk that it falls into your enemies' hands? Why not hide it and hope that one day whoever of the seven survives can return to recover it?"

The evidence was now stretched impossibly thin and Father Roubert shook his head. "If there was treasure in Astarac," he said, "it would have been found long ago."

"But the Cardinal Archbishop is looking for it," the Count said. "Why else does he want to read our archives?" He picked up the stonemason's contract and held it over a candle so that the three Latin words and the demand to cut the date in the stone were scorched out of existence. He stamped his fist on the charred, glowing edge to extinguish the fire, then put the damaged parchment into the basket of documents that would be given to the monk. "What I should do," he said, "is go to Astarac."

Father Roubert looked alarmed at such hot-headedness. "It is wild country, my lord," he warned, "infested with *coredors*. And not that many miles from the English in Castillon d'Arbizon."

"Then I shall take some men-at-arms." The Count was excited now. If the Grail was in his domain then it made sense that God had placed the curse of barrenness on his wives as a punishment for fail-

ing to search for the treasure. So he would put it right. "You can come
with me," he told Father Roubert, "and I'll leave Sir Henri, the crossbowmen and most of the men-at-arms to defend the town."

"And your nephew?"

"Oh, I'll take him with me! He can command my escort. It will
give him the illusion that he's useful." The Count frowned. "Isn't St.
Sever's near Astarac?"

"Very close."

"I'm sure Abbot Planchard will give us accommodation," the
Count said, "and he's a man who might very well help us!"

Father Roubert thought Abbot Planchard was more likely to tell
the Count he was an old fool, but he could see that the Count was
caught up in the enthusiasm. Doubtless he believed that if he found
the Grail then God would reward him with a son, and perhaps he was
right. And perhaps the Grail needed to be found to put the whole
world right, and so the friar fell to his knees in the great hall and
prayed that God would bless the Count, kill the heretic and reveal the
Grail.

At Astarac.

T HOMAS AND HIS MEN left Astarac in the early afternoon, riding horses that were weighed down with cuts of meat, cooking pots, anything at all that was of value and that could be sold in Castillon d'Arbizon's marketplace. Thomas kept looking back, wondering why he felt nothing for this place, but also knowing he would be back. There were secrets in Astarac and he must unlock them.

Robbie alone rode a horse that was not encumbered with plunder. He had been the last to join the raiders, coming from the monastery with a strangely contented expression. He offered no explanation for his lateness, nor why he had spared the Cistercians. He just nodded at Thomas and fell into the column as it started westwards.

They would be late home. It would probably be dark, but Thomas was not concerned. The *coredors* would not attack, and if the Count of Berat had sent forces to intercept their homeward journey then they should see those pursuers from the ridge tops and so he rode without worries, leaving behind misery and smoke in a shattered village.

"So did you find what you were looking for?" Sir Guillaume asked.

"No."

Sir Guillaume laughed. "A fine Sir Galahad you are!" He glanced at the things hanging from Thomas's saddle. "You go for the Holy Grail and come back with a heap of goatskins and a haunch of mutton."

"That'll roast well with vinegar sauce," Thomas said.

Sir Guillaume looked behind to see a dozen *coredors* had followed them up onto the ridge. "We're going to have to teach those bastards a lesson."

"We will," Thomas said, "we will."

There were no men-at-arms waiting to ambush them. Their only delay occurred when a horse went lame, but it was nothing more than a stone caught in its hoof. The *coredors* vanished as the dusk approached. Robbie was again riding in the vanguard, but when they were halfway home and the sun was a sinking red ball before them, he turned back and fell in beside Thomas. Genevieve was off to one side and she pointedly moved her mare farther away, but if Robbie noticed he made no comment. He glanced at the goatskins draped behind Thomas's saddle. "My father once had a cloak of horseskin," he said by way of breaking the silence that had lasted too long between them, and then, without adding any more details of his father's curious taste in clothing, he looked embarrassed. "I've been thinking," he said.

"A dangerous occupation," Thomas answered lightly.

"Lord Outhwaite let me come with you," Robbie said, "but would he mind if I left you?"

"Left me?" Thomas was surprised.

"I'll go back to him, of course," Robbie said, "eventually."

"Eventually?" Thomas asked, suspicious. Robbie was a prisoner and his duty, if he was not with Thomas, was to go back to Lord Outhwaite in northern England and wait there until his ransom was paid.

"There are things I have to do," Robbie explained, "to put my soul straight."

"Ah," Thomas said, embarrassed himself now. He glanced at the silver crucifix on his friend's chest.

Robbie was staring at a buzzard that quartered the lower hill, looking for small game in the dying light. "I was never one for religion," he said softly. "None of the men in our family are. The women care, of course, but not the Douglas men. We're good soldiers and bad Christians." He paused, plainly uncomfortable, then shot a swift glance at Thomas. "You remember that priest we killed in Brittany?"

"Of course I do," Thomas said. Bernard de Taillebourg had been a Dominican friar and the Inquisitor who had tortured Thomas. The priest had also helped Guy Vexille kill Robbie's brother, and together Thomas and Robbie had chopped him down in front of an altar.

"I wanted to kill him," Robbie said.

"You said," Thomas reminded him, "that there was no sin that some priest could not undamn, and that, I assume, includes killing priests."

"I was wrong," Robbie said. "He was a priest and we shouldn't have killed him."

"He was the bastard turd of the devil," Thomas said vengefully.

"He was a man who wants what you want," Robbie said firmly, "and he killed to get it, but we do the same, Thomas."

Thomas made the sign of the cross. "Are you worried about my soul," he asked caustically, "or yours?"

"I was talking to the abbot in Astarac," Robbie said, ignoring Thomas's question, "and I told him about the Dominican. He said I'd done a dreadful thing and that my name was on the devil's list." That had been the sin Robbie had confessed, though Abbot Planchard was a wise enough man to know that something else worried the young Scot and that the something else was probably the beghard. But Planchard had taken Robbie at his word and become stern with him. "He ordered me to do a pilgrimage," Robbie went on. "He said I had to go to Bologna and pray at the blessed Dominic's tomb, and that I would be given a sign if St. Dominic forgives me for the killing."

Thomas, after his earlier conversation with Sir Guillaume, had already decided that it would be best if Robbie went, and now Robbie was making it easy for him. Yet he pretended to be reluctant. "You can stay through the winter," he suggested.

"No," Robbie said firmly. "I'm damned, Thomas, unless I do something about it."

Thomas remembered the Dominican's death, the fire flickering on the tent walls, the two swords chopping and stabbing at the writhing friar who twitched in his dying blood. "Then I'm damned too, eh?"

"Your soul is your concern," Robbie said, "and I can't tell you what to do. But the abbot told me what I should do."

"Then go to Bologna," Thomas said and hid his relief that Robbie had decided to leave.

It took two days to discover how best Robbie could make the journey, but after talking to a pilgrim who had come to worship at St. Sardos's tomb in the town's upper church they decided he would do best to go back to Astarac and from there strike south to St. Gaudens. Once at St. Gaudens he would be on a well-travelled road where he would find companies of merchants travelling together and they would welcome a young, strong man-at-arms to help protect their convoys. "From St. Gaudens you should go north to Toulouse," the pilgrim said, "and make sure you stop at the shrine of St. Sernin and ask for his protection. The church has one of the whips used to scourge our Lord and if you pay they will let you touch it and you will never suffer blindness. Then you must continue to Avignon. Those roads are well patroled, so you should be safe. And at Avignon you must seek the Holy Father's blessing and ask someone else how to journey farther east."

The most dangerous part of the journey was the first and Thomas promised he would escort Robbie to within sight of Astarac to make sure he was not troubled by any *coredors.* He also gave him a bag of money from the big chest in the hall. "It's more than your share," Thomas told him.

Robbie weighed the bag of gold. "It's too much."

"Christ, man, you have to pay in taverns. Take it. And for God's sake don't gamble it away."

"I'll not do that," Robbie said. "I promised Abbot Planchard I'd give up gambling and he made me take an oath in the abbey."

"And lit a candle, I hope?" Thomas asked.

"Three," Robbie said, then made the sign of the cross. "I'm to give up all sins, Thomas, until I've prayed to Dominic. That's what Planchard said." He paused, then smiled sadly. "I'm sorry, Thomas."

"Sorry? For what?"

Robbie shrugged. "I've not been the best companion." He sounded embarrassed again and he said no more, but that night, when they all ate together in the hall to say farewell to Robbie, the Scotsman made a great effort to be courteous to Genevieve. He even gave her a portion of his mutton, a succulent piece, spiking it on his knife and insisting she let him put it on her plate. Sir Guillaume rolled his surviving eye in astonishment, Genevieve was gracious in her thanks and, next morning, under the lash of a cold north wind, they left to escort Robbie away.

THE COUNT OF BERAT had only visited Astarac once and that had been many years before, and, when he saw the village again, he hardly recognized it. It had always been small, malodorous and poor, but now it had been ravaged. Half the village's thatch had been burned, leaving walls of scorched stone, and a great smear of blood scattered with bones, feathers and offal showed where the villagers' livestock had been butchered. Three Cistercian monks were distributing food from a handcart when the Count arrived, but that charity did not prevent a rush of ragged folk surrounding the Count, dragging off their hats, kneeling and holding out their hands for alms.

"Who did this?" the Count demanded.

"The English, sire," one of the monks answered. "They came yesterday."

"By Christ, but they'll die a hundred deaths for this," the Count declared.

"And I'll inflict them," Joscelyn said savagely.

"I'm almost minded to let you go to them," the Count said, "but what can we do against their castle?"

"Guns," Joscelyn said.

"I have sent for the gun in Toulouse," the Count said angrily, then he scattered a few small coins among the villagers before spurring his horse past them. He paused to stare at the ruins of the castle on its crag, but he did not ride to the old fortress because it was late, the night was near and the air was cold. The Count was also tired and saddle-sore, and the unfamiliar armor he wore was chafing his shoulders and so, instead of climbing the long path to the shattered fortress he went on towards the dubious comforts at the Cistercian abbey of St. Sever.

White-robed monks were trudging home from their work. One carried a great bundle of kindling, while others had hoes and spades. The last grapes were being harvested and two monks led an ox pulling a wagon loaded with baskets of deep purple fruit. They pulled the wagon aside as the Count and his thirty men-at-arms clattered past towards the plain, undecorated buildings. No one in the monastery had been expecting visitors, but the monks greeted the Count without fuss and efficiently found stabling for the horses and provided bedding among the wine presses for the men-at-arms. A fire was lit in the visitors' quarters where the Count, his nephew and Father Roubert would be entertained. "The abbot will greet you after compline," the Count was told, then he was served a meal of bread, beans, wine and smoked fish. The wine was the abbey's own and tasted sour.

The Count dismissed Joscelyn and Father Roubert to their own rooms, sent his squire to wherever the lad could find a bed, then sat alone by the fire. He wondered why God had sent the English to plague him. Was that another punishment for ignoring the Grail? It seemed likely, for he had convinced himself that God had indeed chosen him and that he must perform one great last task and then he would be rewarded. The Grail, he thought, almost in ecstasy. The Grail, the holiest of all holy things, and he had been sent to discover it; he fell to his knees by the open window and listened to the voices of the monks chanting in the abbey church and prayed that his quest would be successful. He went on praying long after the chanting had stopped and thus Abbot Planchard discovered the Count on his knees. "Do I interrupt?" the abbot asked gently.

"No, no." The Count winced with pain from his cramped knees

as he climbed to his feet. He had discarded his armor and wore a fur-lined gown and his customary woolen cap. "I am sorry, Planchard, most sorry to impose on you. No warning, I know. Most inconvenient, I'm sure."

"The devil alone inconveniences me," Planchard said, "and I know you are not sent by him."

"I do pray not," the Count said, then sat and immediately stood again. By rank he was entitled to the room's one chair, but the abbot was so very old that the Count felt constrained to offer it to him.

The abbot shook his head and sat on the window ledge instead. "Father Roubert came to compline," he said, "and talked with me afterwards."

The Count felt a pulse of alarm. Had Roubert told Planchard why they were here? He wanted to tell the abbot himself.

"He is very upset," Planchard said. He spoke French, an aristocrat's French, elegant and precise.

"Roubert's always upset when he's uncomfortable," the Count said, "and it was a long journey and he's not used to riding. Not born to it, you see? He sits his horse like a cripple." He paused, staring open-eyed at the abbot, then let out an explosive sneeze. "Dear me," he said, his eyes watering. He wiped his nose with his sleeve. "Roubert slouches in his saddle. I keep telling him to sit up, but he won't take advice." He sneezed again.

"I do hope you're not catching an ague," the abbot said. "Father Roubert was not upset because of weariness, but because of the beghard."

"Ah, yes, of course. The girl." The Count shrugged. "I rather think he was looking forward to seeing her burn. That would have been a fitting reward for all his hard work. You know he questioned her?"

"With fire, I believe," Planchard said, then frowned. "How odd that a beghard should be this far south. Their haunt is the north. But I suppose he is sure?"

"Entirely! The wretched girl confessed."

"As would I if I were put to the fire," the abbot said acidly. "You know she rides with the English?"

"I heard as much," the Count said. "A bad business, Planchard, a bad business."

"At least they spared this house," Planchard said. "Is that why you came, my lord? To protect us from a heretic and from the English?"

"Of course, of course," the Count said, but then moved a little closer to the truth of his journey. "There was another reason too, Planchard, another reason altogether." He expected Planchard to ask what that reason was, but the abbot stayed silent and, for some reason, the Count felt uncomfortable. He wondered if Planchard would scoff at him. "Father Roubert did not tell you?" he asked.

"He talked of nothing but the beghard."

"Ah," the Count said. He did not quite know how to phrase his quest and so, instead, he plunged into the center of it to see whether Planchard would understand what he was talking about. "'*Calix meus inebrians*,'" he announced, then sneezed again.

Planchard waited until the Count had recovered. "The psalms of David. I love that particular one, especially that wonderful beginning. "'The Lord rules me and denies me nothing.'"

"'*Calix meus inebrians*,'" the Count said, ignoring the abbot's words, "was carved above the gate of the castle here."

"Was it?"

"You had not heard it?"

"One hears so many things in this small valley, my lord, that it is necessary to distinguish between fears, dreams, hopes and reality."

"'*Calix meus inebrians*,'" the Count repeated stubbornly, suspecting that the abbot knew exactly what he was talking about, but wanted to cloud the issue.

Planchard looked at the Count in silence for a while, then nodded. "The tale is not new to me. Nor to you, I suspect?"

"I believe," the Count said awkwardly, "that God sent me here for a purpose."

"Ah, then you are fortunate, my lord!" Planchard sounded impressed. "So many folk come to me seeking God's purposes and all I can tell them is to watch, work and pray, and by doing so I trust they will discover the purpose in their own time, but it is rarely given openly. I envy you."

"It was given to you," the Count retorted.

"No, my lord," the abbot said gravely. "God merely opened a gate onto a field full of stones, thistles and weeds and left me to till it. It has been hard work, my lord, hard work, and I approach my end with most of it still to be done."

"Tell me of the story," the Count said.

"The story of my life?" Planchard countered.

"The story," the Count said firmly, "of the cup that makes us drunk."

Planchard sighed and, for a moment, looked very old. Then he stood. "I can do better than that, my lord," he said, "I can show you."

"Show me?" The Count was astonished and elated.

Planchard went to a cupboard and took out a horn lantern. He lit its wick with a brand from the fire, then invited the excited Count to follow him through a dark cloister and into the abbey church where a small candle burned beneath a plaster statue of St. Benedict, the only decoration in the austere building.

Planchard took a key from under his robe and led the Count to a small door which opened from an alcove that was half hidden by a side altar on the church's north side. The lock was stiff, but at last it gave way and the door creaked open. "Be careful of the steps," the abbot warned, "they are worn and very treacherous."

The lantern bobbed as the abbot went down a steep flight of stone stairs which turned sharp right into a crypt lined with great pillars between which bones were stacked almost to the arched ceiling. There were leg bones, arm bones and ribs stacked like firewood, and between them, like lines of boulders, lay empty-eyed skulls. "The brothers?" the Count asked.

"Awaiting the blessed day of resurrection," Planchard said and went on to the farthest end of the crypt, stooping under a low arch and so into a small chamber where there was an ancient bench and a wooden chest reinforced with iron. He found some half-burned candles in a niche and lit them so that the small room flickered with light. "It was your great-grandfather, God be praised, who endowed this house," he said, taking another key from a pouch under his black robe. "It was small before that and very poor, but your ancestor gave us land to thank God for the fall of the House of Vexille, and those lands are sufficient to support us, but not to make us wealthy. That is good and proper, but we do possess a few small things of value and this, such as it is, is our treasury." He bent to the chest, turned the massive key and lifted the lid.

At first the Count was disappointed for he thought there was nothing inside, but when the abbot brought one of the candles closer the Count saw the chest contained a tarnished silver paten, a leather bag and a single candlestick. The abbot pointed to the bag. "That was given to us by a grateful knight whom we healed in the infirmary. He swore to us it contains St. Agnes's girdle, but I confess I have never even opened the bag. I remember seeing her girdle in Basle, but I suppose she could have had two? My mother had several, but she was no saint, alas." He ignored the two pieces of silver and lifted out an object that the Count had not noticed in the chest's deep shadows. It was a box that Planchard placed on the bench. "You must look at it closely, my lord. It is old and the paint has long faded. I am quite surprised that we did not burn it long ago, but for some reason we keep it."

The Count sat on the bench and lifted the box. It was square, but not deep, big enough to hold a man's glove, but nothing much larger. It was hinged with rusting iron and, when he lifted the lid, he saw it was empty. "This is all?" he asked, his disappointment palpable.

"Look at it, my lord," Planchard said patiently.

The Count looked again. The interior of the wooden box was painted yellow and that paint had lasted better than the exterior sur-

faces, which were very faded, but the Count could see that the box
had once been black and that a coat of arms had been painted on the
lid. The arms were unfamiliar to him and so aged that it was hard to
see them, but he thought there was a lion or some other beast rear-
ing upright with an object held in its outstretched claws. "A yale,"
the abbot said, "holding a chalice."

"A chalice? The Grail, surely?"

"The arms of the Vexille family," Planchard ignored the Count's
question, "and local legend says the chalice was not added until just
before Astarac's destruction."

"Why would they add a chalice?" the Count asked, feeling a small
pulse of excitement.

Again the abbot ignored the question. "You should look, my lord,
at the front of the box."

The Count tipped the box until the candlelight glossed the faded
paint and he saw that words had been painted there. They were indis-
tinct and some letters had been rubbed clear away, but the words were
still obvious. Obvious and miraculous. *Calix Meus Inebrians*. The
Count stared at them, heady with the implications, so heady he could
not speak. His nose was running, so he cuffed it impatiently.

"The box was empty when it was found," Planchard said, "or so
I was told by Abbot Loix, God rest his soul. The story goes that the
box was in a reliquary of gold and silver that was found on the altar
of the castle's chapel. The reliquary, I am sure, was taken back to
Berat, but this box was given to the monastery. As a thing of no value,
I suppose."

The Count opened the box again and tried to smell the interior,
but his nose was foully blocked. Rats scuttled among the bones in the
neighboring crypt, but he ignored the sound, ignored everything, just
dreamed of what this box meant. The Grail, an heir, everything.
Except, he thought, the box was too small to hold the grail. Or maybe
not? Who knew what the Grail looked like?

The abbot reached for the box, intending to return it to the chest, but the Count clutched it tight. "My lord," the abbot said sternly, "the box was empty. Nothing was found in Astarac. That is why I brought you here, to see for yourself. Nothing was found."

"This was found!" the Count insisted. "And it proves the Grail was here."

"Does it?" the abbot asked sadly.

The Count pointed to the faded words on the box's side. "What else does this mean?"

"There is a Grail in Genoa," Planchard said, "and the Benedictines at Lyons once claimed to own it. It is said, God let it not be true, that the real one is in the treasury of the Emperor at Constantinople. It was once reported to be in Rome, and again at Palermo, though that one, I think, was a Saracen cup captured from a Venetian vessel. Others say that the archangels came to earth and took it to heaven, though some insist it still lies in Jerusalem, protected by the flaming sword that once stood sentinel over Eden. It has been seen in Cordoba, my lord, in Nîmes, in Verona and a score of other places. The Venetians claim it is preserved on an island that appears only to the pure of heart, while others say it was taken to Scotland. My lord, I could fill a book with stories of the Grail."

"It was here." The Count ignored everything Planchard had said. "It was here," he said again, "and may still be here."

"I would like nothing more," Planchard admitted, "but where Parsifal and Gawain failed, can we hope to succeed?"

"It is a message from God," the Count averred, still clutching the empty box.

"I think, my lord," Planchard said judiciously, "that it is a message from the Vexille family. I think they made the box and painted it and they left it to mock us. They fled and let us think they had taken the Grail with them. I think that box is their revenge. I should burn it."

The Count would not relinquish the box. "The Grail was here," he maintained.

The abbot, knowing he had lost the box, closed the chest and locked it. "We are a small house, my lord," he said, "but we are not entirely severed from the greater Church. I receive letters from my brethren and I hear things."

"Such as?"

"Cardinal Bessières is searching for a great relic," the abbot said.

"And he is looking here!" the Count said triumphantly. "He sent a monk to search my archives."

"And if Bessières is looking," Planchard warned, "then you may be sure he will be ruthless in God's service."

The Count would not be warned. "I have been given a duty," he asserted.

Planchard picked up the lantern. "I can tell you nothing more, my lord, for I have heard nothing that tells me the Grail is at Astarac, but I do know one thing and I know it as surely as I know that my bones will soon rest with the brethren in this ossuary. The search for the Grail, my lord, drives men mad. It dazzles them, confuses them, and leaves them whimpering. It is a dangerous thing, my lord, and best left to the troubadours. Let them sing about it and make their poems about it, but for the love of God do not risk your soul by seeking it."

But if Planchard's warning had been sung by a choir of angels the Count would not have heard it.

He had the box and it proved what he wanted to believe.

The Grail existed and he had been sent to find it. So he would.

THOMAS NEVER INTENDED to escort Robbie all the way to Astarac. The valley where that poor village lay had already been plundered, and so he meant to stop in the next valley where a slew of plump settlements were strung along the road south from Masseube, and then, when his men were busy about their devil's business, he and a few men would ride with Robbie to the hills overlooking Astarac and, if there were no *coredors* or other enemies in sight, let the Scotsman ride on alone.

Thomas had again taken his whole force except for a dozen men who guarded Castillon d'Arbizon's castle. He left most of his raiders in a small village beside the River Gers and took a dozen archers and as many men-at-arms to escort Robbie the last few miles. Genevieve stayed with Sir Guillaume, who had discovered a great mound in the village that he swore was the kind of place where the old people, the ones who had lived before Christianity lit the world, hid their gold and he had commandeered a dozen shovels and begun to dig. Thomas and Robbie left them to their search and climbed the eastern hills on a winding trail that led through groves of chestnuts where peasants cut staves to support the newly planted vines. They saw no *coredors*; indeed they had seen no enemies all morning, though Thomas wondered how long it would be before the bandits saw the great plume of smoke boiling up from the warning pyre in the village where Sir Guillaume dug into his dreams.

Robbie was in a nervous mood that he tried to cover with careless conversation. "You remember that stilt-walker in London?" he asked. "The one who juggled when he was up on his sticks? He was good. That was a rare place, that was. How much did it cost to stay in that tavern in London?"

Thomas could not remember. "A few pennies, perhaps."

"I mean, they'll cheat you, won't they?" Robbie asked anxiously.

"Who will?"

"Tavern-keepers."

"They'll drive a bargain," Thomas said, "but they'd rather take a penny off you than get nothing. Besides, you can lodge in monasteries most nights."

"Aye, that's true. But you have to give them something, don't you?"

"Just a coin," Thomas said. They had emerged onto the bare summit of the ridge and Thomas looked about for enemies and saw none. He was puzzled by Robbie's odd questions, then realized that the Scotsman, who went into battle with apparent fearlessness, was nevertheless nervous at the prospect of traveling alone. It was one thing to journey at home, where folk spoke your language, but quite another to set off for hundreds of miles through lands where a dozen strange tongues were used. "The thing to do," Thomas said, "is find some other folk going your way. There'll be plenty and they all want company."

"Is that what you did? When you walked from Brittany to Normandy?"

Thomas grinned. "I put on a Dominican's robe. No one wants a Dominican for company, but no one wants to rob one either. You'll be fine, Robbie. Any merchant will want you as company. A young man with a sharp sword? They'll be offering you the pick of their daughters to travel with them."

"I've given my oath," Robbie said gloomily, then thought for a second. "Is Bologna near Rome?"

"I don't know."

"I've a mind to see Rome. Do you think the Pope will ever move back there?"

"God knows."

"I'd like to see it, though," Robbie said wistfully, then grinned at Thomas. "I'll say a prayer for you there."

"Say two," Thomas said, "one for me and one for Genevieve."

Robbie fell silent. The moment for parting had almost come and he did not know what to say. They had curbed their horses, though Jake and Sam rode on until they could see down into the valley where the fires of Astarac's burned thatch still sifted a small smoke into the chill air.

"We'll meet again, Robbie," Thomas said, taking off his glove and putting out his right hand.

"Aye, I know."

"And we'll always be friends," Thomas said, "even if we're on different sides of a battle."

Robbie grinned. "Next time, Thomas, the Scots will win. Jesus, but we should have beaten you at Durham! We were that close!"

"You know what archers say," Thomas said. "Close don't tally. Look after yourself, Robbie."

"I will." They shook hands and just then Jake and Sam turned their horses and kicked back fast.

"Men-at-arms!" Jake shouted.

Thomas urged his horse forward until he could see down the road that led to Astarac and there, not half a mile away, were horsemen. Mailed horsemen with swords and shields. Horsemen under a banner that hung limp so he could not see its device, and squires leading sumpter horses loaded with long clumsy lances. A whole band of horsemen coming straight towards him, or perhaps towards the great plume of smoke that rose from where his men savaged the village in the neighboring valley. Thomas stared at them, just stared. The day had seemed so peaceful, so utterly empty of any threat, and now an enemy had come. For weeks they had been unmolested. Until now.

And Robbie's pilgrimage was forgotten, at least for the moment.

For there was going to be a fight.

And they all rode back west.

Joscelyn, Lord of Béziers, believed his uncle was an old fool and, what was worse, a rich old fool. If the Count of Berat had shared his wealth it would have been different, but he was notoriously mean except when it came to patronizing the Church or buying relics like the handful of dirty straw he had purchased for a chest of gold from the Pope at Avignon. Joscelyn had taken one look at the Christ-child's bedding and decided it was dunged straw from the papal stables, but the Count was convinced it was the first bed of Jesus and now he had come to the miserable valley of Astarac where he was hunting for even more relics. Exactly what, Joscelyn did not know, for neither the Count nor Father Roubert would tell him, but Joscelyn was convinced it was a fool's errand.

Yet, in recompense, he had command of thirty men-at-arms,

though even that was a mixed blessing for the Count had given strict instructions that they were not to ride more than a mile from Astarac. "You are here to protect me," he told Joscelyn, and Joscelyn wondered from what? A few *coredors* who would never dare attack real soldiers? So Joscelyn tried to organize a tournament in the village meadows, but his uncle's men-at-arms were mostly older men, few had fought in recent years and they had become accustomed to a life of comfort. Nor would the Count hire other men, preferring to let his gold gather cobwebs. So even though Joscelyn tried to instill some fighting spirit into the men he had, none would fight him properly, and when they fought each other they did so half-heartedly. Only the two companions he had brought south to Berat had any enthusiasm for their trade, but he had fought them so often that he knew every move they would make and they knew his. He was wasting his time, and he knew it, and he prayed ever more fervently that his uncle would die. That was the only reason Joscelyn stayed in Berat, so he would be ready to inherit the fabulous wealth reputed to be stored in the castle's undercroft and when he did, by God, he would spend it! And what a fire he would make with his uncle's old books and papers. The flames would be seen in Toulouse! And as for the Countess, his uncle's fifth wife, who was kept more or less locked up in the castle's southern tower so that the Count could be sure that any baby she bore would be his and his alone, Joscelyn would give her a proper baby-making ploughing then kick the plump bitch back into the gutter she came from.

He sometimes dreamed of murdering his uncle, but knew that there would inevitably be trouble, and so he waited, content that the old man must die soon enough. And while Joscelyn dreamed of the inheritance, the Count dreamed of the Grail. He had decided he would search what was left of the castle and, because the chapel was where the box had been found, he ordered a dozen serfs to prize up the ancient flagstones to explore the vaults beneath where, as he expected, he found tombs. The heavy triple coffins were dragged from the niches and hacked open. Inside the outer casket, as often as not, was a lead coffin and that had to be split apart with an axe and the metal peeled away. The lead was stored on a cart to be taken to Berat, but the Count expected a far greater profit every time the inner coffin, usually of elm, was splintered open. He found skeletons, yellow and dry, their fingerbones touching in prayer, and in a few of the coffins he found treasures. Some of the women had been buried with necklaces or bangles, and the Count tore away the desiccated shrouds to get what plunder he could, yet there was no Grail. There were only skulls and patches of skin as dark as ancient parchment. One woman still had long golden hair and the Count marvelled at it. "I wonder if she was pretty?" he remarked to Father Roubert. His voice sounded nasal and he was sneezing every few minutes.

"She's awaiting judgement day," the friar, who disapproved of this grave-robbing, said sourly.

"She must have been young," the Count said, looking at the dead woman's hair, but as soon as he tried to lift it from the coffin the fine tresses disintegrated into dust. In one child's coffin there was an old chessboard, hinged so that it could fold into a shallow box. The squares, which on the Count's chessboards in Berat were painted black, were distinguished by small dimples, and the Count was intrigued by that, but much more interested in the handful of ancient coins that had replaced the chess pieces inside the box. They showed the head of Ferdinand, first King of Castile, and the Count marveled at the fineness of the gold. "Three hundred years old!" he told Father Roubert, then pocketed the money and urged the serfs to hammer open another vault. The bodies, once they had been searched, were put back in their wooden coffins and then into their vaults to await the day of judgement. Father Roubert said a prayer over each reburial and something in his tone irritated the Count who knew he was being criticized.

On the third day, when all the coffins had been pilfered and none had proved to hold the elusive Grail, the Count ordered his serfs to dig into the space beneath the apse where the altar had once stood. For a time it seemed there was nothing there except soil packed above the bare rock of the knoll on which the castle had been built, but then, just as the Count was losing heart, one of the serfs pulled a silver casket from the earth. The Count, who was well wrapped up against the cold, was feeling weak. He was sneezing, his nose was running and sore, his eyes were red, but the sight of the tarnished box made him forget his troubles. He snatched it from the serf and scuttled back into the daylight where he used a knife to break the clasp. Inside was a feather. Just a feather. It was yellow now, but had probably once been white, and the Count decided it had to be from the wing of a goose. "Why would someone bury a feather?" he asked Father Roubert.

"St. Sever is supposed to have mended an angel's wing here," the Dominican explained, peering at the feather.

"Of course!" the Count exclaimed, and thought that would explain the yellowish colour for the wing would probably have been colored gold. "An angel's feather!" he said in awe.

"A swan's feather, more like," Father Roubert said dismissively.

The Count examined the silver casket, which was blackened from the earth. "That could be an angel," he said, pointing to a curlicue of tarnished metal.

"It could equally well not be."

"You're not being helpful, Roubert."

"I pray for your success nightly," the friar answered stiffly, "but I also worry about your health."

"It is just a blocked nose," the Count said, though he suspected something worse. His head felt airy, his joints ached, but if he found the Grail all those troubles would surely vanish. "An angel's feather!" the Count repeated wonderingly. "It's a miracle! A sign, surely?" And then there was another miracle, for the man who had discovered the silver box now revealed that there was a wall at the back of the hardpacked earth. The Count thrust the silver box and its heavenly feather into Father Roubert's hands, ran back and clambered up the pile of soil to examine the wall for himself. Only a scrap of it was visible, but that part was made from trimmed stone blocks and, when the Count seized the serf's spade and rapped the stones, he convinced himself that the wall sounded hollow. "Uncover it," he ordered excitedly, "uncover it!" He smiled triumphantly at Father Roubert. "This is it! I know it!"

But Father Roubert, instead of sharing the excitement of the buried wall, was looking up at Joscelyn who, armed in his fine tournament plate, had ridden his horse to the edge of the uncovered vaults. "There is a smoke pyre," Joscelyn said, "in the next valley."

The Count could hardly bear to leave the wall, but he scrambled up a ladder and stared westwards to where, in the pale sky, a dirty plume of smoke drifted southwards. It seemed to come from just across the nearest ridge. "The English?" the Count asked in wonderment.

"Who else?" Joscelyn answered. His men-at-arms were at the bottom of the path that climbed to the castle. They were armored and ready. "We could be there in an hour," Joscelyn said, "and they won't be expecting us."

"Archers," the Count said warningly, then sneezed and afterwards gasped for breath.

Father Roubert watched the Count warily. He reckoned the old man was getting a fever, and it would be his own fault for insisting on making this excavation in the cold wind.

"Archers," the Count said again, his eyes watering. "You must be cautious. Archers are not to be trifled with."

Joscelyn looked exasperated, but it was Father Roubert who answered the Count's warning. "We know they ride in small parties, my lord, and leave some archers behind to protect their fortress. There may only be a dozen of the wretches over there."

"And we may never have another chance like this," Joscelyn put in.

"We don't have many men," the Count said dubiously.

And whose fault was that? Joscelyn wondered. He had told his uncle to bring more than thirty men-at-arms, but the old fool had insisted that would be sufficient. Now the Count was staring at a patch of grubby wall uncovered at the end of the vault and letting his fears overwhelm him. "Thirty men will be enough," Joscelyn insisted, "if the enemy is few."

Father Roubert was staring at the smoke. "Is this not the purpose of the fires, my lord?" he enquired. "To let us know when the enemy is near enough to strike?" That was indeed one purpose of the fires, but the Count wished Sir Henri Courtois, his military leader, was with him to offer advice. "And if the enemy party is small," Father Roubert went on, "then thirty men-at-arms will suffice."

The Count reckoned he would have no peace to explore the mysterious wall unless he gave his permission and so he nodded. "But take care!" he ordered his nephew. "Make a reconnaissance first! Remember the advice of Vegetius!" Joscelyn had never heard of Vegetius so would be hard put to remember the man's advice and the Count might have sensed that for he had a sudden idea. "You'll take Father Roubert and he'll tell you whether it is safe to attack or not. Do you understand me, Joscelyn? Father Roubert will advise you and you will take his advice." That offered two advantages. The first was that the friar was a sensible and intelligent man and so would not let the hot-headed Joscelyn do anything foolish, while second, and better, it would rid the Count of the Dominican's gloomy presence. "Be back by nightfall," the Count commanded, "and keep Vegetius in mind. Above all, keep Vegetius in mind!" These last words were called hurriedly as he clambered back down the ladder.

Joscelyn looked sourly at the friar. He did not like churchmen and he liked Father Roubert even less, but if the friar's company was the price he must pay for a chance to kill Englishmen, then so be it. "You have a horse, father?" he asked.

"I do, my lord."

"Then fetch it." Joscelyn turned his destrier and spurred it back to the valley. "I want the archers alive!" he told his men when he reached them. "Alive, so we can share the reward." And afterwards they would cut off the Englishmen's damned fingers, take out their eyes and then burn them. That was Joscelyn's daydream as he led his men westwards. He would have liked to travel fast, to reach the next valley before the English withdrew, but men-at-arms on their way to battle could not move swiftly. Some of the horses, like Joscelyn's own, were armored with leather and mail, and the weight of the armor, let alone the weight of the riders' armor, inevitably meant that the destriers had to be walked if they were to be fresh for the charge. A few of the men had squires and those lesser beings led packhorses, which carried cumbersome bundles of lances. Men-at-arms did not gallop to war, but lumbered slow as oxen.

"You will bear in mind your uncle's advice, my lord?" Father Roubert remarked to Joscelyn. He spoke to cover his nervousness. The friar was normally a grave and self-contained man, very conscious of his hard-won dignity, but now he found himself in unfamiliar, dangerous, but exciting territory.

"My uncle's advice," Joscelyn responded sourly, "was to heed yours. So tell me, priest, what you know of battle?"

"I have read Vegetius," Father Roubert answered stiffly.

"And who the hell was he?"

"A Roman, my lord, and still considered the supreme authority on military matters. His treatise is called the *Epitoma Rei Militaris*, the essence of military things."

"And what does this essence recommend?" Joscelyn asked sarcastically.

"Chiefly, if I remember aright, that you should look to the enemy's flanks for an opportunity, and that on no account should you attack without a thorough reconnaissance."

Joscelyn, his big tournament helmet hanging from his pommel, looked down on the friar's small mare. "You're mounted on the lightest horse, father," he said with amusement, "so you can make the reconnaissance."

"Me!" Father Roubert was shocked.

"Ride ahead, see what the bastards are doing, then come back and tell us. You're supposed to be giving me advice, aren't you? How the hell can you do that if you haven't made a reconnaissance? Isn't that what your *vegetal* advises? Not now, you fool!" He called these last words because Father Roubert had obediently kicked his mare ahead. "They're not up here," Joscelyn said, "but in the next valley." He nodded towards the smoke that seemed to be thickening. "So wait till we're in the trees on the hill's far side."

In fact they did see a handful of horsemen on the bare summit of the ridge, but the riders were far off and they turned and fled as soon as Joscelyn's men came into view. *Coredors*, as like as not, Joscelyn reckoned. Everyone had heard how the *coredors* were haunting the English in hope of earning one of the Count's rewards for an archer taken alive, though Joscelyn's view was that the only reward any *coredor* should ever fetch was a slow hanging.

The *coredors* had vanished by the time Joscelyn reached the crest. He could see most of the valley ahead now, could see Masseube to the north and the road reaching south towards the high Pyrenees. The smoke plume was directly in front, but the village the English plundered was hidden by trees and so Joscelyn ordered the friar to ride ahead and, to give him some protection, ordered his two personal men-at-arms to accompany him.

Joscelyn and the rest of his men had almost reached the valley floor by the time the Dominican returned. Father Roubert was excited. "They did not see us," he reported, "and can't know we're here."

"You can be sure of that?" Joscelyn demanded.

The friar nodded. His dignity had been replaced by a suddenly discovered enthusiasm for warfare. "The road to the village goes through trees, my lord, and is well shielded from view. The trees thin out a hundred paces from the river and the road crosses it by a ford. It's shallow. We watched some men carry chestnut stakes to the village."

"The English didn't interfere with them?"

"The English, my lord, are delving into a grave mound in the village. There seemed to be no more than a dozen of them. The village itself is another hundred paces beyond the ford." Father Roubert was proud of this report which he considered to be careful and accurate, a reconnaissance of which Vegetius himself might have been proud. "You may approach to within two hundred paces of the village," he concluded, "and arm yourselves in safety before attacking."

It was indeed an impressive report and Joscelyn looked quizzically at his two men-at-arms who nodded to show they agreed. One of them, a Parisian named Villesisle, grinned. "They're ready for butchering," he said.

"Archers?" Joscelyn asked.

"We saw two," Villesisle said.

Father Roubert was saving the best news till last. "But one of the two, my lord," he said excitedly, "was the beghard!"

"The heretic girl?"

"So God will be with you!" Father Roubert said vehemently.

Joscelyn smiled. "So your advice, Father Roubert, is what?"

"Attack!" the Dominican said. "Attack! And God will give us triumph!" He might be a cautious man by nature, but the sight of Genevieve had stirred his soul to battle.

And when Joscelyn reached the edge of the trees on the valley floor he saw that everything seemed to be exactly as the Dominican had promised. Beyond the river the English, apparently ignorant of the presence of enemies, had set no picquets to guard the road that came down from the ridge and instead were digging into the big mound of earth at the center of the village. Joscelyn could see no more than ten men and the one woman. He dismounted briefly and let his squire tighten the buckles of his armor, then he heaved himself into the saddle again where he pulled on his great tournament helm with its yellow and red plume, leather padding, and cross-shaped eye slits. He pushed his left arm through the loops of his shield, made sure his sword was loose in its scabbard, then reached down for his lance. Made of ash, it was sixteen feet long and painted in a spiral of yellow and red, the colors of his lordship at Béziers. Similar lances had broken the best tourney fighters in Europe, now this one would do God's work. His men armed themselves with their own lances, some painted with Berat's colors of orange and white. Their lances were mostly thirteen or fourteen feet long, for none of Berat's men had the strength to carry a great lance like those Joscelyn used in tournaments. The squires drew their swords. Helmet visors were closed, reducing the world to bright slits of sunlight. Joscelyn's horse, knowing it was riding to battle, pawed the ground. All was ready, the unsuspecting English were oblivious of the threat and Joscelyn, at long last, was off his uncle's leash.

And so, with his men-at-arms tight bunched to either side, and with Father Roubert's prayer echoing in his head, he charged.

GASPARD THOUGHT THE HAND of the Lord was on him, for the very first time he attempted to pour the gold into the delicate mold that had once held the wax model of his Mass cup, it worked. He had told his woman, Yvette, that it might take ten or eleven attempts, that he was not even sure he could make the cup for the detail of the filigree was so delicate that he doubted the molten gold would fill every cranny of the mold, but when, with a beating heart, he broke away the fired clay he found that his wax creation had been reproduced almost perfectly. One or two details were lumpish and in some places the gold had failed to make the twist of a leaf or the spine of a thorn, but those defects were soon put right. He filed away the rough edges, then polished the whole cup. That took a week, and when it was done he did not tell Charles Bessières that he had finished, instead he claimed there was still more work to do when in truth he simply could not relinquish the beautiful thing he had made. He reckoned it was the finest piece of goldsmithing ever achieved.

So he made a lid for the cup. It was conical, like the cover of a font, and at its crown he placed a cross, and about its rim he hung pearls, and on its sloping sides he made the symbols of the four evangelists. A lion for St. Mark, an ox for Luke, and angel for Matthew and an eagle for John. That piece, not quite as delicate as the cup itself, also came sweetly from the mould and he filed and polished it, then assembled the whole thing. The golden cup-holder, the ancient green glass cup itself and the new lid hung with pearls. "Tell the Cardinal," he told Charles Bessières as the exquisite thing was packed in cloth, straw and boxes, "that the pearls stand for the tears of Christ's mother."

Charles Bessières could not care what they stood for, but he grudgingly acknowledged that the chalice was a beautiful thing. "If my brother approves of it," he said, "then you'll be paid and freed."

"We can go back to Paris?" Gaspard asked eagerly.

"You can go where you like," Charles lied, "but not till I tell you." He gave his men instructions that Gaspard and Yvette were to be well guarded while he was away, then took the chalice to his brother in Paris.

The Cardinal, when the cup was unwrapped and the three pieces assembled, clasped his hands in front of his breast and just stared. For a long time he said nothing, then he leaned forward and peered at the ancient glass. "Does it seem to you, Charles," he asked, "that the cup itself has a tinge of gold?"

"Haven't looked," was the churlish reply.

The Cardinal carefully removed the lid then lifted the old glass cup from the golden cradle and held it to the light and he saw that Gaspard, in a moment of unwitting genius, had put an almost invisible layer of gold leaf around the cup so that the common glass was given a heavenly sheen of gold. "The real Grail," he told his brother, "is supposed to turn to gold when the wine of Christ's blood is added. This would pass for that."

"So you like it?"

The Cardinal reassembled the chalice. "It is gorgeous," he said reverentially. "It is a miracle." He stared at it. He had not expected anything half as good as this. It was a wonder, so much so that for a brief instant he even forgot his ambitions for the papal throne. "Perhaps, Charles"—there was awe in his voice now—"perhaps it is the real Grail! Maybe the cup I bought was the true object. Perhaps God guided me to it!"

"Does that mean," Charles said, unmoved by the cup's beauty, "that I can kill Gaspard?"

"And his woman," the Cardinal said without removing his gaze from the glorious thing. "Do it, yes, do it. Then you will go south. To Berat, south of Toulouse."

"Berat?" Charles had never heard of the place.

The Cardinal smiled. "The English archer has appeared. I knew he would! The wretched man has taken a small force to Castillon d'Arbizon, which I am told is close to Berat. He is a fruit ripe for the plucking, Charles, so I am sending Guy Vexille to deal with him and I want you, Charles, to be close to Guy Vexille."

"You don't trust him?"

"Of course I don't trust him. He pretends to be loyal, but he is not a man who is comfortable serving any master." The Cardinal lifted the cup again, gazed at it reverentially, then lay it back in the sawdust-filled box in which it had been brought to him. "And you will take this with you."

"That!" Charles looked appalled. "What in Christ's name do I want with that?"

"It is a heavy responsibility," the Cardinal said, handing his brother the box, "but legend insists the Cathars possessed the Grail, so where else must it be discovered but close to the last stronghold of the heretics?"

Charles was confused. "You want me to discover it?"

The Cardinal went to a prie-dieu and knelt there. "The Holy Father is not a young man," he said piously. In fact Clement was only fifty-six, just eight years older than the Cardinal, but even so Louis Bessières was racked by the thought that Pope Clement might die and a new successor be appointed before he had a chance to make his claim with the Grail. "We do not have the luxury of time and so I need the Grail." He paused. "I need a Grail now! But if Vexille knows that Gaspard's cup exists then he will try to take it from you, so you must kill him when he has done his duty. His duty is to find his cousin, the English archer. So kill Vexille, then make that archer talk, Charles. Peel the skin from his flesh inch by inch, then salt him. He'll talk, and when he has told you everything he knows about the Grail, kill him."

"But we have a Grail," Charles said, hefting the box.

"There is a true one, Charles," the Cardinal said patiently, "and if it exists, and if the Englishman reveals where it is, then we shall not need the one you're holding, shall we? But if the Englishman is a dry well, then you will announce that he gave you that Grail. You will bring it to Paris, we shall sing a *Te Deum*, and in a year or two you and I shall have a new home in Avignon. And then, in due time, we shall move the papacy to Paris and the whole world shall marvel at us."

Charles thought about his orders and considered them unnecessarily elaborate. "Why not produce the Grail here?"

"No one will believe me if I find it in Paris," the Cardinal said, his eyes fixed on an ivory crucifix hanging on the wall. "They will assume it is a product of my ambition. No, it must come from a far place and rumors of its discovery must run ahead of its coming so that folk kneel in the street to welcome it."

Charles understood that. "So why not just kill Vexille now?"

"Because he has the zeal to find the true Grail and if it exists, I want it. Men know his name is Vexille, and they know his family once possessed the Grail, so if he is involved in its discovery then it will be all the more convincing. And another reason? He's well born. He can lead men and it will take all his force to prize that Englishman from his lair. Do you think forty-seven knights and men-at-arms will follow you?" The Cardinal had raised Vexille's force from his tenants, the lords who ruled the lands bequeathed to the Church in hope that prayers would wipe away the sins of the men who granted the land. Those men would cost the Cardinal dear, for the lords would not pay rents for a year now. "You and I are from the gutter, Charles," the Cardinal said, "and men-at-arms would despise you."

"There must be a hundred lords who would seek your Grail," Charles suggested.

"A thousand and a thousand men would," the Cardinal agreed mildly, "but once they possessed the Grail they would take it to their King and that fool would lose it to the English. Vexille, so far as he is any man's, is mine, but I know what he will do when he has the Grail. He will steal it. So you will kill him before he has a chance."

"He'll be a hard man to kill," Charles worried.

"Which is why I am sending you, Charles. You and your cut-throat soldiers. Don't fail me."

That night Charles made a new receptacle for the fake Grail. It was a leather tube, of the sort crossbowmen used to carry their quarrels, and he packed the precious cup inside, padded the glass and gold with linen and sawdust, then sealed the tube's lid with wax.

And the next day Gaspard received his freedom. A knife slit his belly, then ripped upwards, so that he died slowly in a pool of blood. Yvette screamed so loudly that she was left voiceless, just gasping for breath, and showed no resistance as Charles cut the dress from her body. Ten minutes later, as a mark of gratitude for what he had just experienced, Charles Bessières killed her quickly.

Then the tower was locked.

And Charles Bessières, the crossbowman's quiver safe at his side, led his hard men south.

I N THE NAME OF THE FATHER, and of the Son, and of the Holy Ghost, amen." Thomas said the words half aloud and crossed himself. Somehow the prayer did not seem sufficient and so he drew his sword, propped it up so the handle looked like a cross and dropped to one knee. He repeated the words in Latin. "*In nomine patris, et filii, et spiritus sancti, amen.*" God spare me, he thought, and he tried to remember when he had last made confession.

Sir Guillaume was amused by his piety. "I thought you said there were few of them?"

"There are," Thomas said, standing and sheathing his sword. "But it doesn't hurt to pray before a fight."

Sir Guillaume made a very sketchy sign of the cross, then spat. "If there's only a few," he said, "we'll murder the bastards."

If, indeed, the bastards were still coming. Thomas wondered if the horsemen had turned back towards Astarac. Who they were he did not know, and whether they were enemies he could not tell. They had certainly not been approaching from Berat for that lay northwards and the riders were coming from the east, but he was certain of one reassuring fact. He outnumbered them. He and Sir Guillaume commanded twenty archers and forty-two men-at-arms and Thomas had estimated the approaching horsemen at less than half those numbers. Many of Thomas's new men-at-arms were routiers who had joined Castillon d'Arbizon's garrison for the opportunity of plunder and they were pleased at the thought of a skirmish that could provide captured horses, weapons and armor, and even, perhaps, the prospect of prisoners to ransom.

"You're sure they weren't *coredors*?" Sir Guillaume asked him.

"They weren't *coredors*," Thomas said confidently. The men on the ridge top had been too well armed, too well armored and too well mounted to be bandits. "They were flying a banner," he added, "but I couldn't see it. It was hanging straight down."

"Routiers, perhaps?" Sir Guillaume suggested.

Thomas shook his head. He could not think why any band of routiers would be in this desolate place or why they would fly a banner. The men he had seen had looked like soldiers on a patrol and, before he had turned tail and galloped back to the village, he had clearly marked the lances bundled on packhorses. Routiers would not just have lances on their sumpter horses, but bundles of clothing and belongings. "I think," he suggested, "that Berat sent men to Astarac after we were there. Maybe they thought we'd go back for a second bite?"

"So they're enemies?"

"Do we have any friends in these parts?" Thomas asked.

Sir Guillaume grinned. "You think twenty?"

"Maybe a few more," Thomas said, "but no more than thirty."

"Perhaps you didn't see them all?"

"We'll find out, won't we?" Thomas asked. "If they come."

"Crossbows?"

"Didn't see any."

"Then let's hope they are coming here," Sir Guillaume said wolfishly. He was as eager as any man to make money. He needed cash, and a lot of it, to bribe and fight and so regain his fief in Normandy. "Maybe it's your cousin?" he suggested.

"Sweet Jesus," Thomas said, "I hadn't thought of that," and he instinctively reached back and touched his yew bow because any mention of his cousin suggested evil. Then he felt a pulse of excitement at the thought that it might truly be Guy Vexille who rode unsuspecting towards the fight.

"If it is Vexille," Sir Guillaume said, fingering the awful scar on his face, "then he's mine to kill."

"I want him alive," Thomas said. "Alive."

"Best tell Robbie that," Sir Guillaume said, "because he's sworn to kill him too." Robbie wanted that revenge for his brother.

"Maybe it isn't him," Thomas said, but he wanted it to be his cousin, and he especially wanted it now for the coming fight promised to be a straightforward trouncing. The horsemen could only approach the village by the ford unless they elected to ride up or downstream to discover another crossing place, and a villager, threatened with a sword held to his baby daughter's eyes, said there was no other bridge or ford within five miles. So the horsemen had to come straight from the ford to the village street and, in the pastures between the two, they must die.

Fifteen men-at-arms would protect the village street. For the moment those men were hidden in the yard of a substantial cottage, but when the enemy came from the ford they would emerge to bar the road, and Sir Guillaume had commandeered a farm cart that would be pushed across the street to make a barrier against the horsemen. In truth Thomas did not expect that the fifteen men would need to fight, for behind the orchard hedges on either side of the road he had deployed his archers. It was the bowmen who would do the initial killing and they had the luxury of readying their arrows, which they thrust point down in the roots of the hedges. Nearest them were the broad-heads, arrows that had a wedge-shaped blade at their tip, and each blade had deep tangs so that once it was imbedded in flesh it could not be pulled out. The archers honed the broad-heads on the whetstones they carried in their pouches to make sure they were razor sharp. "You wait," Thomas told them, "wait till they reach the field marker." There was a white painted stone by the road that showed where one man's pasture ended and another's began, and when the first horsemen reached the stone their destriers would be struck by the broad-heads, which were designed to rip deep, to wound terribly, to drive the horses mad with pain. Some of the destriers would go down then, but others would survive and swerve about the dying beasts to continue the charge,

so when the enemy was close the archers would switch to their bodkin arrows.

The bodkins were made to pierce armor and the best of them had
shafts made of two kinds of wood. The leading six inches of ash or
poplar was replaced with heavy oak that was scarfed into place with
hoof glue, and the oak was tipped with a steel head that was as long
as a man's middle finger, as slender as a woman's little finger and
sharpened to a point. That needle-like head, backed by the heavier oak
shaft, had no barbs: it was just a smooth length of steel that punched
its way through mail and would even penetrate plate armor if it hit
plumb. The broad-heads were to kill horses, the bodkins to kill men,
and if it took a minute for the horsemen to come from the field marker
to the edge of the village, Thomas's twenty archers could loose at least
three hundred arrows and still have twice as many in reserve.

Thomas had done this so many times before. In Brittany, where he
had learned his trade, he had stood behind hedges and helped destroy
scores of enemies. The French had learned the hard way and had taken
to sending crossbowmen ahead, but the arrows just killed them as they
reloaded their clumsy weapons and the horsemen then had no choice
but to charge or retreat. Either way the English archer was king of the
battlefield, for no other nation had learned to use the yew bow.

The archers, like Sir Guillaume's men, were hidden, but Robbie
commanded the rest of the men-at-arms who were the lure. Most of
them were apparently scattered on the mound which was just to the
north of the village street. One or two dug, the rest simply sat as if
they rested. Two others fed the village bonfire, making sure that the
smoke beckoned the enemy onwards. Thomas and Genevieve walked
to the mound and, while Genevieve waited at its foot, Thomas
climbed up to look into the great hole Sir Guillaume had made.
"Empty?"

"Lots of pebbles," Robbie said, "but none of them gold."

"You know what to do?"

Robbie nodded cheerfully. "Wait till they're in chaos," he said, "then charge."

"Don't go early, Robbie."

"We'll not go early," an Englishman called John Faircloth answered. He was a man-at-arms, much older and more experienced than Robbie, and although Robbie's birth entitled him to the command of the small force, Robbie knew well enough to take the older man's advice.

"We'll not let you down," the Scot said happily. His men's horses were picketed just behind the mound. As soon as the enemy appeared they would run down from the small height and mount up, and when the enemy was scattered and broken by the arrows, Robbie would lead a charge that would curl round their rear and so trap them.

"It might be my cousin coming," Thomas said. "I don't know that," he added, "but it might be."

"He and I have a quarrel," Robbie said, remembering his brother.

"I want him alive, Robbie. He has answers."

"But when you have your answers," Robbie said, "I want his throat."

"Answers first, though," Thomas said, then turned as Genevieve called him from the foot of the mound.

"I saw something," she said, "in the chestnut woods."

"Don't look!" Thomas called to those of Robbie's men who had overheard her, then, making a great play of stretching his arms and looking bored, he slowly turned and stared across the stream. For a few heartbeats he could see nothing except two peasants carrying bundles of stakes across the ford and he thought, for a second, Genevieve must have meant those men, then he looked beyond the river and saw three horsemen half hidden by a thicket of trees. The three men probably thought they were well concealed, but in Brittany Thomas had learned to spot danger in thick woods. "They're taking a look at us," he said to Robbie. "Not long now, eh?" He strung his bow.

Robbie stared at the horsemen. "One's a priest," he said dubiously.

Thomas stared. "Just a black cloak," he guessed. The three men had turned and were riding away. They were soon lost to sight in the thicker woods.

"Suppose it's the Count of Berat?" Robbie asked.

"Suppose it is?" Thomas sounded disappointed. He wanted the enemy to be his cousin.

"If we capture him," Robbie said, "there'll be a rare ransom."

"True."

"So would you mind if I stayed until it's paid?"

Thomas was disconcerted by the question. He was used to the idea that Robbie was leaving and so ridding his men of the rancor caused by his jealousy. "You'd stay with us?"

"To get my share of the ransom," Robbie said, bridling. "Is there anything wrong with that?"

"No, no." Thomas hurried to soothe his friend. "You'll get your share, Robbie." He thought maybe he could pay Robbie's share from his existing stock of cash and so spur the Scotsman on his penitential way, but this was not the time to make the suggestion. "Don't charge too early," he warned Robbie again, "and God be with you."

"It's time we had a good fight," Robbie said, his spirits restored. "Don't let your archers kill the rich ones. Leave some for us."

Thomas grinned and went back down the mound. He strung Genevieve's bow, then walked with her to where Sir Guillaume and his men were concealed. "Not long now, lads," he called, climbing onto the farm wagon to see across the yard's wall. His archers were concealed in the pear orchard's hedge beneath him, their bows strung and the first broad-heads resting on their strings.

He joined them and then waited. And waited. Time stretched, slowed, crawled to a halt. Thomas waited so long that he began to doubt any enemy would come, or worse, he feared the horsemen had smelt out his ambush and were circling far up or down stream to ambush him. His other worry was that the town of Masseube, which was not so very far away, might send men to find out why the villagers had lit their warning pyre.

Sir Guillaume shared the anxiety. "Where the hell are they?" he asked when Thomas came back to the yard to climb onto the wagon so he could see across the river.

"God knows." Thomas gazed into the far chestnuts and saw nothing to alarm him. The leaves had just started to change colour. Two pigs were rooting among the trunks.

Sir Guillaume was wearing a full-length hauberk, the mail covering him from shoulder to ankle. He had a scarred breastplate that was tied in place with rope, one plate vambrace that he buckled on his right forearm, and a plain sallet for a helmet. The sallet had a wide sloping brim to deflect downward sword blows, but it was a cheap piece of armor with none of the strength of the best helmets. Most of Thomas's men-at-arms were similarly protected with bits and pieces of armor they had scavenged from old battlefields. None had full plate armor, and all of their mail coats were patched, some with boiled leather. Some carried shields. Sir Guillaume's was made of willow boards covered with leather on which his coat of arms, the three yellow hawks on a blue field, had faded almost to invisibility. Only one other man-at-arms had a device on his shield, in his case a black axe on a white field, but he had no idea whose badge it was. He had taken the shield off a dead enemy in a skirmish near Aiguillon, which was one of the principal English garrisons in Gascony. "Has to be an English shield," the man reckoned. He was a Burgundian mercenary who had fought against the English, been discharged at the truce after the fall of Calais and was now hugely relieved that the yew bows were on his side. "Do you know the badge?" the man asked.

"Never seen it," Thomas said. "How did you get the shield?"

"Sword into his spine. Under the back plate. His buckles had got cut and the back plate was flapping around like a broken wing. Christ, but he screamed."

Sir Guillaume chuckled. He took half a loaf of dark bread from beneath his breastplate and tore off a chunk, then swore as he bit into it. He spat out a scrap of granite that must have broken off the stone when the grain was milled, felt his broken tooth and swore again. Thomas glanced up to see that the sun lay low in the sky. "We'll be late home," he grumbled. "It'll be dark."

"Find the river and follow it," Sir Guillaume said, then flinched with the pain from his tooth. "Jesus," he said, "I hate teeth."

"Cloves," the Burgundian said. "Put cloves in your mouth. Stops the pain."

Then the two pigs among the distant chestnuts raised their heads, stood for a heartbeat and lumbered south in ungainly haste. Something had alarmed them and Thomas held up a warning hand as if the voices of his companions might disturb any approaching horsemen, and just at that moment he saw a gleam of reflected sunlight from the trees across the river and he knew it must come from a piece of armor. He jumped down. "We've got company," he said, and ran to join the other archers behind the hedge. "Wake up," he told them, "the little lambs are coming for their slaughter."

He took his place behind the hedge and Genevieve stood beside him, an arrow on her string. Thomas doubted she would hit anyone, but he grinned at her. "Stay hidden till they reach the field marker," he told her, then peered over the hedge.

And there they were. The enemy, and almost as soon as they appeared Thomas saw that his cousin was not there for the flag, spread now as its carrier trotted from the trees, showed the orange and white leopard badge of Berat instead of the yale of Vexille. "Keep your heads down!" Thomas warned his men as he tried to count the enemy. Twenty? Twenty-five? Not many, and only the first dozen carried lances. The men's shields, each showing the orange leopard on its white field, confirmed what the banner said, that these were the Count of Berat's horsemen, but one man, mounted on a huge black horse that was hung with armor, had a yellow shield with a red mailed fist, a device unknown to Thomas, and that man was also in a full harness of plate and had a red and yellow plume flying high on his helm. Thomas counted thirty-one horsemen. This would not be a fight, it would be a massacre.

And suddenly, oddly, it all seemed unreal to him. He had expected to feel excitement and some fear, but instead he watched the horsemen as though they had nothing to do with him. Their charge was ragged, he noted. When they had first come from the trees they had been riding boot to boot, as men should, but they quickly spread out. Their lances were held upright and would not drop to the killing position until the horsemen were close to their enemy. One lance was tipped with a ragged black pennant. The horses' trappers flapped. The sound was of hooves and the clash of armor as pieces of plate rapped each other. Great clods of earth were slung up behind the hooves; one man's visor went up and down, up and down as his horse rose and fell. Then the onrush of horsemen narrowed as they all tried to cross the ford at its narrowest point and the first white splashes of water rose as high as the saddles.

They came out of the ford. Robbie's men had vanished and the horsemen, thinking that it was now a pursuit of a panicked enemy, touched spurs to destriers and the big horses thumped up the road, stringing out, and then the first of them were at the field marker and Thomas heard a trundling noise as the farm cart was pushed out to block the road.

He stood and instinctively took a bodkin arrow instead of a broadhead. The man with the yellow and red shield rode a horse that had a great protective skirt of mail sewn onto leather and Thomas knew the broad-heads would never pierce it, and then he drew his arm back, the cord was past his ear and the first arrow flew. It wavered as it left the bow, then the air caught the goose-feather fledging and it sped low and fast to bury itself in the black horse's chest and Thomas had a second bodkin on the string, drew, loosed, and a third, drew and loosed and he saw the other arrows flying and was astonished, as ever, that the first arrows seemed to do so little damage. No horses were down, none even slowed, but there were feathered shafts jutting from trappers and armor and he pulled again, released, felt the string whip along the bracer on his left forearm, snatched up a new arrow, then saw the first horses go down. He heard the sound of metal and flesh crashing on the ground and he sent another bodkin at the big black horse and this one drove through the mail and leather to bury itself deep and the horse began frothing blood from its mouth and tossing its head, and Thomas sent his next arrow at the rider and saw it thump into the shield to throw the man back against his high cantle.

Two horses were dying, their bodies forcing the other riders to swerve, and still the arrows came at them. A lance tumbled, skidding along the ground. A dead man, three arrows in his chest, rode a frightened horse that veered across the line of the charge, throwing it into further confusion. Thomas shot again, using a broad-head now to cut down a horse at the rear of the group. One of Genevieve's arrows flew high. She was grinning, her eyes wide. Sam cursed as his cord broke, then stepped back to find another and string it to his bow. The big black horse had slowed to a walk and Thomas put another bodkin into its flank, burying the arrow just ahead of the rider's left knee.

"Horses!" Sir Guillaume called to his men and Thomas knew the Norman reckoned the enemy would never reach his barrier and so had decided to charge them. Where was Robbie? Some of the enemy were turning away, going back to the river and Thomas sped four fast broad-heads at those faint hearts, then loosed a bodkin at the black horse's rider. The arrow glanced off the man's breastplate, then his horse stumbled and went down to its knees. A squire, the man holding the flag of Berat, came to help the rider and Thomas slammed a bodkin into the squire's neck, then two more arrows hit the man who bent backwards over his saddle's cantle and stayed there, dead with three arrows jutting skywards and his flag fallen.

Sir Guillaume's men were hauling themselves into their saddles, drawing swords, taking their places knee to knee, and just then Robbie's force came from the north. The charge was timed well, hitting the enemy at their most chaotic, and Robbie had the sense to charge close to the river, thus cutting off their retreat. "Bows down!" Thomas called. "Bows down!" He did not want his arrows cutting into Robbie's men. He laid his bow by the hedge and drew his sword. It was time to overwhelm the enemy with pure savagery.

Robbie's men hammered into Berat's horsemen with terrible force. They rode properly, knee to knee, and the shock of the men-at-arms threw three enemy horses down. Swords chopped hard down, then each of Robbie's men picked an opponent. Robbie, shouting his war cry, kicked his horse towards Joscelyn.

"Douglas! Douglas!" Robbie was shouting, and Joscelyn was trying to stay in the saddle of a horse that was dying, that was down on its fore knees, and he heard the cry behind him and swept his sword wildly back, but Robbie met the blow on his shield and kept thrusting so that the shield, with its device of the Douglas red heart, struck a huge blow on Joscelyn's helm. Joscelyn had not strapped the helm down, knowing that in a tournament it often helped to take the big steel pot off at the end of a fight to see a half-beaten opponent better, so now it turned on his shoulders, the cross-shaped eye slits vanished and he was in darkness. He flailed his sword into empty air, felt his balance going and then his whole world was a huge ringing blow of steel on steel and he could not see, could not hear, as Robbie thumped his helmet again with his sword.

Berat's men-at-arms were yielding, throwing down swords and offering gauntlets to their opponents. The archers were among them now, hauling men out of their saddles, and then Sir Guillaume's horsemen thundered past to pursue the handful of enemy trying to gallop out of trouble through the ford. Sir Guillaume backswung his sword as he overtook a laggard and the blow ripped the man's helmet clean off his head. The man following Sir Guillaume swept his sword forward and there was a burst of misting blood and the dead man's head went bouncing into the river as the headless body kept riding.

"I yield, I yield!" Joscelyn screamed in pure terror. "I can be ran-

somed!" Those were the words that saved rich men's lives on battlefields and he shouted them again more urgently. "I can be ransomed!" His right leg was trapped under his horse, he was still blinded
by his skewed helmet and all he could hear were thumping hooves,
shouts and the screams of wounded men being killed by archers.
Then, suddenly, he was dazzled by light as his dented helmet was
pulled off and a man stood over him with a sword. "I yield," Joscelyn said hurriedly, then remembered his rank. "Are you noble?"

"I'm a Douglas of the house of Douglas," the man said in bad
French, "and as well born as any in Scotland."

"Then I yield to you," Joscelyn said despairingly, and he could
have wept for all his dreams had been broken in one brief passage of
arrows, terror and butchery.

"Who are you?" Robbie asked.

"I am the Lord of Béziers," Joscelyn said, "and heir to Berat."

And Robbie whooped for joy.

Because he was rich.

THE COUNT OF BERAT wondered if he should have ordered three
or four of the men-at-arms to stay behind. It was not because he
thought he needed protection, but rather it was his due to have an
entourage and the departure of Joscelyn, Father Roubert and all the
horsemen left him only his squire, one other servant and the serfs
who were scrabbling at the earth to clear the mysterious wall which
seemed, the Count thought, to be hiding a cave beneath the place
where the chapel's altar had once stood.

He sneezed again, then felt light-headed so sat on a fallen block
of stone.

"Come by the fire, my lord," his squire suggested. The squire was
the son of a tenant from the northern part of the county and was a
stolid, unimaginative seventeen-year-old who had shown no incli-
nation to ride with Joscelyn to glory.

"Fire?" The Count blinked up at the boy who was called Michel.

"We made a fire, lord," Michel said, pointing to the far end of the vault where a small fire had been conjured from the splintered lids of the coffins.

"Fire," the Count said, for some reason finding it hard to think straight. He sneezed and gasped for breath afterwards.

"It's a cold day, lord," the boy explained, "and the fire will make you feel better."

"A fire," the Count said, confused, then he discovered an unexpected reserve of energy. "Of course! A fire! Well done, Michel. Make a torch and bring it."

Michel went to the fire and found a long piece of elmwood that was burning at one end and gingerly extracted it from the flames. He took it to the wall where the Count was feverishly pushing the serfs aside. At the very top of the wall, which was made from dressed stones, there was a small gap, no bigger than a sparrow would need, and the hole, through which the Count had peered excitedly but uselessly, seemed to lead into a cavern behind. The Count turned as Michel brought the torch. "Give it here, give it here," he said impatiently, then snatched the burning wood and fanned it to and fro to make it flare up. When the elm was burning fiercely, he thrust it into the hole and, to his delight, the wood slipped right through, confirming that there was a space behind; he pushed it inside until it dropped and then he stooped and put his right eye to the gap and stared.

The flames were already becoming feeble in the cavern's stale air, but they threw just enough light to reveal what lay beyond the wall. The Count stared and drew in a breath. "Michel!" he said. "Michel! I can see . . ." Just then the flame guttered out.

And the Count collapsed.

He slid down the ramp of earth, his face white and mouth open, and for a moment Michel thought his master had died, but then the Count gave a sigh. But he stayed unconscious. The serfs gaped at the squire who stared at the Count, then Michel gathered his few wits and ordered the men to carry the Count out of the vault. That was hard, for they had to maneuver his weight up the ladder, but once it was done a handcart was fetched from the village and they pushed the Count north to Saint Sever's monastery. The journey took almost an hour and the Count groaned once or twice and seemed to shiver, but he was still alive when the monks carried him into the infirmary where they placed him in a small whitewashed room equipped with a hearth in which a big fire was lit.

Brother Ramón, a Spaniard who was the monastery's physician, brought a report to the abbot. "The Count has a fever," he said, "and a surplus of bile."

"Will he die?" Planchard asked.

"Only if God wills it," Brother Ramón said, which is what he always said when asked that question. "We shall leech him and then attempt to sweat the fever away."

"And you will pray for him," Planchard reminded Ramón, then he went back to Michel and learned that the Count's men-at-arms had ridden to attack the English in the valley of the River Gers. "You will meet them on their return," the abbot ordered Michel, "and tell them their lord is struck down. Remind the Lord Joscelyn that a message must be sent to Berat."

"Yes, lord." Michel looked worried by this responsibility.

"What was the Count doing when he fainted?" Planchard asked, and so heard about the strange wall beneath the castle chapel.

"Perhaps I should go back," Michel suggested nervously, "and find out what's behind the wall?"

"You will leave that to me, Michel," Planchard said sternly. "Your only duty is to your master and his nephew. Now go and find Lord Joscelyn."

Michel rode to intercept Joscelyn's return and Planchard went in search of the serfs who had brought the Count to the monastery. They were waiting by the gate, expecting some reward, and they fell to their knees as Planchard approached. The abbot spoke first to the oldest man. "Veric, how is your wife?"

"She suffers, sir, she suffers."

"Tell her she is in my prayers," Planchard said truthfully. "Listen, all of you, and listen well." He waited until they were all looking at him. "What you will do now," he told them sternly, "is return to the castle and cover up the wall. Put the earth back. Seal it! Do not dig further. Veric, you know what an *encantada* is?"

"Of course, lord," Veric said, crossing himself.

The abbot bent close to the serf. "If you do not cover the wall, Veric, then a plague of *encantadas* will come from the castle bowels and they will take your children, all of your children," he looked along the line of kneeling men, "they will rise up from the earth, snatch your children and dance them down to hell. So cover the wall. And when it is done, come back to me and I shall reward you." The monastery's poor box contained a few coins and Planchard would give them to the serfs. "I trust you, Veric!" he finished. "Dig no further, just cover up the wall."

The serfs hurried to obey. Planchard watched them go and said a small prayer asking God to forgive him for telling an untruth. Planchard did not believe that enchanted demons lived under Astarac's old chapel, but he did know that whatever the Count had discovered should be hidden and the threat of the *encantadas* should suffice to make certain the work was properly done.

Then, that small crisis resolved, Planchard went back to his room. When the Count had come to the monastery and caused a sudden excitement, the abbot had been reading a letter brought by a messenger just an hour before. The letter had come from a Cistercian house in Lombardy and now Planchard read it again and wondered whether he should tell the brethren about its dreadful contents. He decided not, then he dropped to his knees in prayer.

He lived, he thought, in an evil world.

And God's scourge had come to bring punishment. That was the message of the letter and Planchard could do little except pray. "'*Fiat voluntas tua*,'" he said over and over again. "Thy will be done." And the terrible thing, Planchard thought, was that God's will was being done.

THE FIRST THING was to recover as many arrows as possible. Arrows were scarce as hens' teeth in Gascony. In England, or in England's territory in France, there were always spare arrows. They were made in the shires, bundled into sheaves of twenty-four, and sent wherever archers fought, but here, far from any other English garrison, Thomas's men needed to hoard their missiles and so they went from corpse to corpse collecting the precious arrows. Most of the broad-heads were sunk deep in horseflesh and those heads were mostly lost, but the arrow shafts pulled out cleanly enough and all archers carried spare heads in their pouches. Some men cut into the corpses to retrieve the broad-heads. Other arrows had missed and just lay on the turf and the archers laughed about those. "One of your points here, Sam!" Jake called. "Missed by a bloody mile!"

"That's not mine. Must be Genny's."

"Tom!" Jake had seen the two pigs across the river. "Can I get supper?"

"Arrows first, Jake," Thomas said, "supper afterwards." He bent to a dead horse and cut into the flesh in an attempt to retrieve a broadhead. Sir Guillaume was scavenging pieces of armor, unbuckling greaves and espaliers and chausses from dead men. Another man-at-arms hauled a mail coat from a corpse. Archers were carrying armfuls of swords. Ten enemy horses were either unwounded or so lightly injured as to be worth keeping. The others were dead or else in such pain that Sam dispatched them with a battle-axe blow to the forehead.

It was as complete a victory as Thomas could have wished and, better still, Robbie had captured the man Thomas took to be the enemy leader. He was a tall man with a round, angry face that was shining with sweat. "He's the heir to Berat," Robbie called as Thomas approached, "and his uncle wasn't here."

Joscelyn glanced at Thomas and, seeing his bloody hands and the bow and arrow bag, reckoned him a man of no worth and so looked at Sir Guillaume instead. "Do you lead here?" he demanded.

Sir Guillaume gestured at Thomas. "He does."

Joscelyn seemed bereft of words. He watched, appalled, as his wounded men-at-arms were plundered. At least his own two men, Villesisle and his companion, were both alive, but neither had been able to fight with their accustomed ferocity for the arrows had killed their horses. One of Joscelyn's uncle's men had lost his right hand, another was dying from an arrow in his belly. Joscelyn tried to count the living and dead and reckoned that only six or seven of his men had managed to escape across the ford.

The beghard was plundering with the rest. Joscelyn spat when he realized who she was, then made the sign of the cross, but he went on staring at Genevieve in her silver mail. She was, he thought, as beautiful a creature as he had ever seen.

"She's spoken for," Sir Guillaume said drily, seeing where Joscelyn was looking.

"So what are you worth?" Thomas asked Joscelyn.

"My uncle will pay a great deal," Joscelyn answered stiffly, still not sure that Thomas really was the enemy commander. He was even less sure that his uncle would pay a ransom, but he did not want to suggest that to his captors, nor tell them that his lordship of Béziers would be fortunate to scrape up more than a handful of écus. Béziers was a dirt-poor collection of shacks in Picardy and would be lucky to ransom a captured goat. He looked back at Genevieve, marvelling at her long legs and bright hair. "You had the devil's help in beating us," he said bitterly.

"In battle," Thomas said, "it's good to have powerful friends." He turned to where the ground was horrid with bodies. "Hurry up!" he called to his men. "We want to be home before midnight!"

The men were in a fine mood. They would all have a share of Joscelyn's ransom, even though Robbie would take the greater part, and some of the lesser prisoners would yield a few coins. In addition they had taken helmets, weapons, shields, swords and horses, and only two men-at-arms had received so much as a scratch. It was a good afternoon's work, and they laughed as they retrieved their horses, loaded the captured beasts with plunder, and readied to leave.

And just then a single horseman came across the ford.

Sir Guillaume saw him first and called to Thomas who turned and saw it was a priest who approached. The man had black and white robes, suggesting he was a Dominican. "Don't shoot!" Thomas called to his men. "Bows down! Down!" He walked towards the priest who was mounted on a small mare. Genevieve was already in her saddle, but now she jumped down and hurried to catch up with Thomas.

"His name," Genevieve said softly, "is Father Roubert." Her face was white and her tone bitter.

"The man who tortured you?" Thomas asked.

"The bastard," she said, and Thomas suspected she was fighting back tears; he knew how she was feeling for he had known the same humiliation at the hands of a torturer. He remembered pleading with his torturer and the shame of being so utterly abased to another person. He remembered the gratitude when the pain stopped.

Father Roubert curbed his horse some twenty paces from Thomas and looked at the scattered dead. "Have they been shriven?" he asked.

"No," Thomas said, "but if you want to shrive them, priest, then do it. And afterwards go back to Berat and tell the Count we have his nephew and will negotiate a ransom." He had nothing else to say to the Dominican so he took Genevieve's elbow and turned away.

"Are you Thomas of Hookton?" Father Roubert asked.

Thomas turned back. "What is it to you?"

"You have cheated hell of a soul," the priest said, "and if you do not yield it then I shall demand yours as well."

Genevieve took the bow from her shoulder. "You'll be in hell before me," she called to Roubert.

The friar ignored her, speaking to Thomas instead. "She is the devil's creature, Englishman, and she has bewitched you." His mare twitched and he slapped her neck irritably. "The Church has made its decision and you must submit."

"I've made my decision," Thomas said.

Father Roubert raised his voice so that the men behind Thomas could hear him. "She is a beghard!" he called. "She is a heretic! She has been excommunicated, cast out of God's holy precincts, and as such she is a doomed soul! There can be no salvation for her and none for any man who helps her! You hear me? It is God's Church on earth that talks to you, and your immortal souls, all your immortal souls, are in dire peril because of her." He looked back to Genevieve and could not resist a bitter smile. "You will die, bitch," he said, "in earthly flames that will usher you to the eternal fires of hell."

Genevieve raised her small bow which had a broad-head on the string. "Don't," Thomas said to her.

"He is my torturer," Genevieve said, tears on her cheeks.

Father Roubert sneered at her bow. "You are the devil's whore," he told her, "and worms will inhabit your womb and your breasts will give forth pus and the demons will play with you."

Genevieve loosed the arrow.

She snatched at the shot. She did not aim. Anger made her pluck the cord far back and then she loosed and her eyes were so filled with tears that she could hardly see Father Roubert. In practice her arrows had usually flown madly wide, but at the very last moment, just as she loosed, Thomas tried to knock her arm away; he barely touched her, just tapped her bow hand, and the arrow twitched as it leaped from the string. Father Roubert had been about to insult her toy bow, but instead the arrow flew true and struck him. The broad, tanged head slashed into the priest's throat and the arrow stayed there, its white feathers turning red as blood poured down the shaft. For a heartbeat the priest sat in the saddle, a look of utter astonishment on his face, then a second great gout of blood spurted out over his horse's ears, he made a choking sound and fell hard to the ground.

By the time Thomas reached him the priest was dead.

"I told you he'd go to hell first," Genevieve said, then spat on the corpse.

Thomas made the sign of the cross.

THERE SHOULD HAVE BEEN JUBILATION after the easy victory, but the old mood, the sullen mood, returned to haunt the garrison at Castillon d'Arbizon. They had done well in the fight, but the death of the priest had horrified Thomas's men. Most of them were unrepentant sinners, some had even killed priests themselves, but they were all superstitious and the friar's death was regarded as an evil omen. Father Roubert had ridden forward unarmed, he came to parley, and he had been shot down like a dog. A few men applauded Genevieve. She was a proper woman, they said, a soldier's woman, and the Church could be damned for all they cared, but those men were a small minority. Most of the garrison recalled the priest's last words that had damned their own souls for the sin of harboring a heretic, and those harsh threats brought back the fears that had haunted them when Genevieve's life was first spared. Robbie propounded that view relentlessly and, when Thomas challenged him by asking when the Scot planned to ride to Bologna, Robbie brushed the question off. "I'm staying here," he said, "till I know what ransom I'm getting. I'm not riding away from his money." He jerked a thumb at Joscelyn who had learned of the antagonism inside the garrison and did his best to encourage it by forecasting dire things if the beghard was not burned. He refused to eat at the same table as Genevieve. As a nobleman he was entitled to the best treatment the castle could offer and he slept in a room of his own at the top of the tower, but rather than eat in the hall he preferred to take his meals with Robbie and the men-at-arms and he beguiled them with tales of his tournaments and scared them with dire warnings of what happened to men who protected the enemies of the Church.

Thomas offered Robbie almost all the money in his keeping as his share of Joscelyn's ransom, the final amount to be adjusted when that ransom was negotiated, but Robbie refused it. "You might end up owing me far more," he claimed, "and how do I know you'll pay it? And how will you know where I am?"

"I'll send it to your family," Thomas promised. "You trust me, don't you?"

"The Church doesn't," was Robbie's bitter answer, "so why should I?"

Sir Guillaume tried to ease the tension, but he knew the garrison was falling apart. A fight broke out in the lower hall one night between Robbie's supporters and the men who defended Genevieve, and at the end of it one Englishman was dead and a Gascon had lost an eye to a dagger. Sir Guillaume thumped heads hard, but he knew there would be other fights.

"What do you propose to do about it?" he asked Thomas a week after the skirmish by the River Gers. The air was cold from a north wind, the wind that men believed made them dull and irritable. Sir Guillaume and Thomas were on the keep's battlements, beneath the Earl of Northampton's fading banner. And beneath that red and green flag hung the orange leopard of Berat, but upside down to show the world that the standard had been captured in battle. Genevieve was there too, but sensing that she did not want to hear what Sir Guillaume had come to say she had gone to the farthest corner of the ramparts.

"I'll wait here," Thomas said.

"Because your cousin will come?"

"That's why I'm here," Thomas said.

"And suppose you have no men left?" Sir Guillaume asked.

Thomas said nothing for a while. Eventually he broke the silence. "You too?"

"I'm with you," Sir Guillaume said, "fool that you are. But if your cousin comes, Thomas, he won't come alone."

"I know."

"And he won't be as foolish as Joscelyn was. He won't give you a victory."

"I know." Thomas's voice was bleak.

"You need more men," Sir Guillaume said. "We have a garrison; we need a small army."

"It would help," Thomas agreed.

"But no one will come while she's here," Sir Guillaume warned, glancing at Genevieve. "And three of the Gascons left yesterday." The three men-at-arms had not even waited for their share of Joscelyn's ransom, but had simply ridden away westwards in search of other employment.

"I don't want cowards here," Thomas retorted.

"Oh, don't be such a damned fool!" Sir Guillaume snapped. "Your men will fight other men, Thomas, but they won't fight the Church. They won't fight God." He paused, evidently reluctant to say whatever was on his mind, but then took the plunge. "You have to send her away, Thomas. She has to go."

Thomas stared at the southern hills. He said nothing.

"She has to go," Sir Guillaume repeated. "Send her to Pau. Bordeaux. Anywhere."

"If I do that," Thomas said, "then she dies. The Church will find her and burn her."

Sir Guillaume stared at him. "You're in love, aren't you?"

"Yes," Thomas said.

"Jesus goddamned Christ," Sir Guillaume said in exasperation. "Love! It always leads to trouble."

"Man is born to it," Thomas said, "as the sparks fly upwards."

"Maybe," Sir Guillaume said grimly, "but it's women who provide the bloody kindling."

And just then Genevieve called to them. "Horsemen!" she warned, and Thomas ran across the ramparts and stared down the eastern road and saw that sixty or seventy horsemen were emerging from the woods. They were men-at-arms wearing the orange and white jupons of Berat and at first Thomas assumed they were coming to offer a ransom for Joscelyn, then he saw that they flew a strange banner, not the leopard of Berat, but a Church banner like those carried in processions on holy days. It hung from a cross-staff and showed the blue gown of the Virgin Mary and behind it, on smaller horses, were a score of churchmen.

Sir Guillaume made the sign of the cross. "Trouble," he said curtly, then turned on Genevieve. "No arrows! You hear me, girl? No damn arrows!"

Sir Guillaume ran down the steps and Genevieve looked at Thomas. "I'm sorry," she said.

"For killing the priest? Damn the bastard."

"I rather think they've come to damn us," Genevieve said, and she went with Thomas to the side of the battlements that overlooked Castillon d'Arbizon's main street, the west gate and the bridge across the river beyond. The armed horsemen waited outside the town while the clergy dismounted and, preceded by their banner, trooped up the main street towards the castle. Most of the churchmen were in black, but one was in a white cope, had a mitre and carried a white staff topped with a golden crook. A bishop, no less. He was a plump man with long white hair that escaped from beneath the golden hem of his mitre. He ignored the townsfolk who knelt to him as he called up to the castle. "Thomas!" he shouted. "Thomas!"

"What will you do?" Genevieve asked.

"Listen to him," Thomas said.

He led her down to the smaller bastion above the gate that was already crowded with archers and men-at-arms. Robbie was there and, as Thomas appeared, the Scotsman pointed at him and called down to the bishop, "This is Thomas!"

The bishop struck his staff on the ground. "In the name of God," he called out, "the all-powerful Father, and in the name of the Son, and in the name of the Holy Ghost, and in the name of all the saints, and in the name of our Holy Father, Clement, and by virtue of the power which has been granted us to loose and to bind in heaven as it is loosed and bound upon earth, I summon you, Thomas! I summon you!"

The bishop had a fine voice. It carried clearly, and the only other sound, except for the wind, was the murmur as a handful of Thomas's men translated the French into English for the benefit of the archers. Thomas had assumed that the bishop would speak in Latin and that he alone would know what was being said, but the bishop wanted everyone to understand his words.

"It is known that you, Thomas," the bishop resumed, "sometime baptized in the name of the Father, and of the Son, and of the Holy Ghost, have fallen from the society of Christ's body by committing the sin of giving comfort and shelter to a condemned heretic and murderer. So now, with grief in our heart, we deprive you, Thomas, as we will deprive all your accomplices and supporters, of the communion of the body and the blood of our Lord Jesus Christ." He banged his staff on the ground again and one of the priests rang a small handbell. "We separate you," the bishop went on, his voice echoing from the castle's high keep, "from the society of all Christians and we exclude you from all holy precincts." Again the staff struck the cobbles and the bell rang. "We banish you from the bosom of our holy mother the Church in heaven and upon earth." The bell's clear tone echoed back from the keep's stones. "We declare you, Thomas, to be excommunicated and we judge you to be condemned to eternal fire with Satan and all his angels and all the reprobates. We pronounce you accursed in this wicked fact and we charge all those who favor and love our Lord Jesus Christ to hold you for punishment." He thumped his staff a last time, glared defiantly at Thomas and then turned away, followed by the priests and their banner.

And Thomas felt numb. Cold and numb. Empty. It was as though the foundations of the earth had vanished to leave an aching void above the blazing gates of hell. All the certainties of life, of God, of salvation, of eternity, were gone, had been blown away like the fallen leaves rustling in the town's gutters. He had been changed into a true hellequin, excommunicated, cut off from the mercy, the love and the company of God.

"You heard the bishop!" Robbie broke the silence on the rampart. "We're charged to arrest Thomas or else share his damnation." And he put his hand on his sword and would have drawn it if Sir Guillaume had not intervened.

"Enough!" the Norman shouted. "Enough! I am second-in-command here. Does anyone dispute that?" The archers and men-at-arms had drawn away from Thomas and Genevieve, but no one intervened on Robbie's behalf. Sir Guillaume's scarred face was grim as death. "The sentries will stay on duty," he ordered, "the rest of you to your quarters. Now!"

"We have a duty . . ." Robbie began and then involuntarily stepped back as Sir Guillaume turned on him in fury. Robbie was no coward, but no one could have withstood Sir Guillaume's anger at that moment.

The men went reluctantly, but they went, and Sir Guillaume slammed home his half-drawn sword. "He's right, of course," he said gloomily as Robbie went down the steps.

"He was my friend!" Thomas protested, trying to hold on to one piece of certainty in a world turned inside out.

"And he wants Genevieve," Sir Guillaume said, "and because he can't have her he's persuaded himself his soul is doomed. Why do you think the bishop didn't excommunicate all of us? Because then we'd all be in the same hell with nothing to lose. He divided us, the blessed and the damned, and Robbie wants his soul to be safe. Can you blame him?"

"What about you?" Genevieve asked the Norman.

"My soul withered years ago," Sir Guillaume said grimly, then he turned and gazed down the main street. "They'll be leaving men-at-arms outside the town to take you when you leave. But you can go out by the small gate behind Father Medous's house. They won't be guarding that, and you can cross the river at the mill. You'll be safe enough in the woods."

For a moment Thomas did not comprehend what Sir Guillaume

was saying, then it struck him with awful force that he was being told to go. To run. To hide. To leave his first command, to abandon his new wealth, his men, everything. He stared at Sir Guillaume, who shrugged. "You can't stay, Thomas," the older man said gently. "Robbie or one of his friends will kill you. My guess is that a score of us would support you, but if you stay it will be a fight between us and them and they'll win."

"You'll stay here?"

Sir Guillaume looked uncomfortable, then nodded. "I know why you came here," he said. "I don't believe the damn thing exists nor, if it does, do I think we have a cat's chance of finding it. But we can make money here, and I need money so, yes, I'm staying. But you're going, Thomas. Go west. Find an English garrison. Go home." He saw the reluctance on Thomas's face. "What in Christ's name else can you do?" he demanded. Thomas said nothing and Sir Guillaume glanced at the soldiers waiting beyond the town gate. "You can take the heretic to them, Thomas, and give her over to the burning. They'll lift your excommunication then."

"I won't do that," Thomas said fiercely.

"Take her down to the soldiers," Sir Guillaume said, "and kneel to the bishop."

"No!"

"Why not?"

"You know why not."

"Because you love her?"

"Yes," Thomas said, and Genevieve took his arm. She knew he was suffering, just as she had suffered when the Church withdrew the love of God from her, but she had come to terms with the horror. Thomas had not and she knew it would take him time.

"We shall survive," she said to Sir Guillaume.

"But you must leave," the Norman insisted.

"I know," Thomas could not keep the heartbreak from his voice.

"I'll bring you supplies tomorrow," Sir Guillaume promised. "Horses, food, cloaks. What else do you need?"

"Arrows," Genevieve said promptly, then she looked at Thomas as if expecting him to add something, but he was still too shocked to think properly. "You'll want your father's writings, won't you?" she suggested gently.

Thomas nodded. "Wrap them up for me?" he asked Sir Guillaume. "Wrap them in leather."

"Tomorrow morning, then," Sir Guillaume said. "Wait by the hollow chestnut on the hill."

Sir Guillaume escorted them out of the castle, through the back alleys behind the priest's house to where a small door had been let through the town wall to give access to a path which led to the watermill on the river. Sir Guillaume shot the bolts and opened the gate warily, but no soldiers waited outside and so he led them down to the mill and there he watched as Thomas and Genevieve crossed the stone sill of the mill pond. From there they climbed into the woods.

Thomas had failed. And he was damned.

Part Two

FUGITIVE

I T RAINED ALL NIGHT. It was a pelting rain driven by a cold
wind that snatched the leaves from the oaks and chestnuts and
swirled spitefully into the ancient tree that had been broken by lightning and hollowed by time. Thomas and Genevieve tried to shelter
in the trunk, flinching once when a burst of thunder sounded in the
sky. No lightning showed, but the rain slashed down even more forcefully. "It's my fault," Genevieve said.

"No," Thomas said.

"I hated that priest," she said. "I knew I shouldn't shoot, but I
remembered all he did to me." She buried her face on his shoulder so
her voice became muffled and Thomas could hardly hear her. "He
would stroke me when he wasn't burning me. Stroke me like a child."

"Like a child?"

"No," she said bitterly, "like a lover. And when he'd hurt me he'd
say prayers for me and tell me I was precious to him. I hated him."

"I hated him too," Thomas said, "for what he did to you." He had
his arms about her. "And I'm glad he's dead," he added, and then
reflected that he himself was as good as dead. He had been sent to
hell, cut off from salvation.

"So what will you do?" Genevieve asked in the shivering dark.

"I won't go home."

"So where will you go?"

"Stay with you. If you want." Thomas thought of saying that she
was free to go wherever she wished, but he knew she had entwined
her fate in his so he did not try to persuade her to leave him, nor did
he want her to leave him. "We'll go back to Astarac," he suggested
instead. He did not know what good that would do, but he knew he
could not just crawl home defeated. Besides, he was damned now. He

had nothing to lose and all eternity to gain. And perhaps the Grail would redeem him. Perhaps now that he was doomed, he would find the treasure and it would restore his soul to grace.

Sir Guillaume arrived soon after dawn, escorted by a dozen men who Sir Guillaume knew would not betray Thomas. Jake and Sam were among them and both wanted to accompany Thomas, but he refused. "Stay with the garrison," he told them, "or go back west and find another English fort." It was not that he did not want company, but he knew it would be difficult enough to feed himself and Genevieve without having two other mouths to worry about. Nor did he have any prospect to offer them except danger, hunger and the certainty of being hunted across southern Gascony.

Sir Guillaume had brought two horses, food, cloaks, Genevieve's bow, four sheaves of arrows and a fat purse of coins. "But I couldn't get your father's manuscript," he confessed, "Robbie took it."

"He stole it?" Thomas asked indignantly.

Sir Guillaume shrugged as if the fate of the manuscript was unimportant. "Berat's men-at-arms have gone," he said, "so the road west is safe, and I sent Robbie east this morning to look for livestock. So ride west, Thomas. Ride west and go home."

"You think Robbie wants to kill me?" Thomas asked, alarmed.

"Arrest you, probably," Sir Guillaume said, "and give you to the Church. What he really wants, of course, is to have God on his side and he believes if he finds the Grail then all his problems will be over." Sir Guillaume's men looked surprised at the mention of the Grail and one, John Faircloth, began a question, but Sir Guillaume cut him off. "And Robbie's persuaded himself that you're a sinner," he said to Thomas. "Sweet Christ," he added, "but there's nothing worse than a young man whose just found God. Except a young woman who finds God. They're insufferable."

"The Grail?" John Faircloth insisted. There had been plenty of wild rumors about why the Earl of Northampton had sent Thomas and his men to Castillon d'Arbizon, but Sir Guillaume's careless admission had been the first confirmation.

"It's a madness Robbie's got in his skull," Sir Guillaume explained firmly, "so take no damned notice."

"We should stay with Thomas," Jake put in. "All of us. Begin again."

Sir Guillaume knew enough English to understand what Jake had said and he shook his head. "If we stay with Thomas," he said, "then we have to fight Robbie. That's what our enemy wants. He wants us divided."

Thomas translated for Jake. "And he's right," he added forcibly.

"So what do we do?" Jake wanted to know.

"Thomas goes home," Sir Guillaume pronounced doggedly, "and we stay long enough to get rich and then we go home too." He tossed Thomas the reins of the two horses. "I'd like to stay with you," he said.

"Then we all die."

"Or we'll all be damned. But go home, Thomas," he urged, throwing down a fat leather bag. "There's enough money in that purse to pay your passage, and probably enough to persuade a bishop to lift the curse. The Church will do anything for money. You'll do fine, and in a year or two come and find me in Normandy."

"And Robbie?" Thomas asked. "What will he do?"

Sir Guillaume shrugged. "He'll go home in the end. He'll not find what he's looking for, Thomas, and you know that."

"I don't know that."

"Then you're as mad as he is." Sir Guillaume pulled off his gauntlet and held out his hand. "You don't blame me for staying?"

"You should stay," Thomas said. "Get rich, my friend. You're in command now?"

"Of course."

"Then Robbie will have to pay you a third share of Joscelyn's ransom."

"I'll keep some for you," Sir Guillaume promised, then he clasped Thomas's hand, turned his horse and led his men away. Jake and Sam, as farewell gifts, threw down two more sheaves of arrows, and then the horsemen were gone.

Thomas felt his anger simmer as he and Genevieve rode eastwards in a soft drizzle that soon soaked through their new cloaks. He was angry at himself for having failed, though the only way he could have succeeded was by putting Genevieve on a pile of firewood and torching her, and he could never do that. He was bitter at Robbie for having turned against him, though he understood the Scotsman's reasons and even considered that they were good ones. It was not Robbie's fault that he was attracted to Genevieve, and it was no bad thing for a man to have a care for his soul. So most of all Thomas was furious at life, and that rage helped to take his mind off their discomfort as the rain grew heavy again. They tended southwards as they went east, sticking to the woods where they were forced to duck beneath low branches. Where there were no trees they used the higher ground and kept a lookout for mailed horsemen. They saw none. If Robbie's men were in the east then they were keeping to the low ground and so Thomas and Genevieve were alone.

They avoided farms and villages. That was not difficult for the country was sparsely populated and the higher ground was given to pasture rather than cultivation. They saw a shepherd in the afternoon who sprang up, surprised, from behind a rock and fished a leather sling and a stone from his pocket before he saw the sword at Thomas's side and swiftly hid the sling and knuckled his forehead as he bowed. Thomas paused to ask the man if he had seen any soldiers and Genevieve translated for him, reporting the man had seen nothing. A mile beyond the frightened shepherd Thomas put an arrow into a goat. He retrieved the arrow from the carcass, which he skinned, gutted and jointed. That night, in the roofless shelter of an old cottage built at the head of a wooded valley, they lit a fire with flint and steel, then roasted goat ribs in the flames.

Thomas used his sword to cut branches from a larch, which he fashioned into a crude lean-to against one wall. It would keep the rain off for a night, and he made a bed of bracken beneath the makeshift shelter.

Thomas remembered his journey from Brittany to Normandy with Jeanette. Where was the Blackbird now, he wondered? They had travelled in the summer, living off his bow, avoiding every other living person, and it had been a happy time. Now he did the same with Genevieve, but the winter was coming. He did not know how hard that winter would be, but Genevieve said she had never known snow in these foothills. "It falls to the south," she said, "in the mountains, but here it is just cold. Cold and wet."

The rain was intermittent now. Their horses were picketed on a patch of thin grass beside the stream that trickled past the ruins. A crescent moon sometimes showed through the clouds to silver the high wooded ridges on either side of the valley. Thomas walked a half-mile downstream to listen and watch, but he saw no other lights and heard nothing untoward. They were safe, he reckoned, from men if not from God, and so he went back to where Genevieve was trying to dry their heavy cloaks in the small heat of the fire. Thomas helped her, draping the woolen cloth over a frame of larch sticks. Then he crouched by the flames, watching the red embers glow, and he thought of his doom. He remembered all the pictures he had seen daubed on church walls: pictures showing souls tumbling towards hell with its grinning demons and roaring fires.

"You are thinking of hell," Genevieve said flatly.

He grimaced. "I was," he said and he wondered how she had known.

"You really think the Church has the power to send you there?" she asked and, when he did not reply, she shook her head. "Excommunication means nothing."

"It means everything," Thomas said sullenly. "It means no heaven and no God, no salvation and no hope, everything."

"God is here," Genevieve said fiercely. "He is in the fire, in the sky, in the air. A bishop cannot take God away from you. A bishop cannot suck the air from the sky!"

Thomas said nothing. He was remembering the bishop's staff striking the cobbles and the sound of the small handbell echoing from the castle walls.

"He just said words," Genevieve said, "and words are cheap. They said the same words to me, and that night, in the cell, God came to me." She put a piece of wood onto the fire. "I never thought I would die. Even as it came close I never thought it would happen. There was something inside me, a sliver, that said it would not. That was God, Thomas. God is everywhere. He is not a dog on the Church's leash."

"We only know God through His Church," Thomas said. The clouds had thickened, obscuring the moon and the last few stars, and in the dark the rain became harder and there was a grumble of thunder from the valley's high head. "And God's Church," he went on, "has condemned me."

Genevieve took the two cloaks from their sticks and bundled them up to keep the worst of the rain from their weave. "Most people don't know God through the Church," she said. "They go and they listen to a language they don't understand, and they say their confession and they bow to the sacraments and they want the priest to come to them when they are dying, but when they are really in trouble they go to the shrines the Church doesn't know about. They worship at springs, at holy wells, in deep places among the trees. They go to wise women or to fortune-tellers. They wear amulets. They pray to their own God and the Church never knows about it. But God knows because God is everywhere. Why would the people need a priest when God is everywhere?"

"To keep us from error," Thomas said.

"And who defines the error?" Genevieve persisted. "The priests! Do you think you are a bad man, Thomas?"

Thomas thought about the question. The quick answer was yes because the Church had just expelled him and given his soul to the demons, but in truth he did not think he was bad and so he shook his head. "No."

"Yet the Church condemns you! A bishop says words. And who knows what sins that bishop does?"

Thomas half smiled. "You are a heretic," he said softly.

"I am," she said flatly. "I'm not a beghard, though I could be one, but I am a heretic, and what choice do I have? The Church expelled me, so if I am to love God I must do it without the Church. You must do the same now, and you will find that God still loves you however much the Church might hate you." She grimaced as the rain beat the last small flames out of their fire, then they retreated to the larch shelter where they did their best to sleep under layers of cloaks and mail coats.

Thomas's sleep was fitful. He dreamed of a battle in which he was being attacked by a giant who roared at him, then he woke with a start to find that Genevieve was gone and that the roaring was the bellow of thunder overhead. Rain seethed on the larch and dripped through to the bracken. A slither of lightning pierced the sky, showing the gaps in the branches that half sheltered Thomas, and he wriggled out from beneath the larch and stumbled in the dark to find the broken hovel's doorway. He was about to shout Genevieve's name when another crack of thunder tore the sky and echoed from the hills, so near and so loud that Thomas reeled sideways as if he had been struck by a warhammer. He was bare-footed and wearing nothing but a long linen shirt that was sopping wet. Three lightning whips stuttered to the east and in their light Thomas saw the horses were white-eyed and trembling and so he crossed to them, patted their noses and made sure their tethers were still firm. "Genevieve!" he shouted. "Genevieve!"

Then he saw her.

Or rather, in the instant glare of a splintering streak of lightning,

he saw a vision. He saw a woman, tall and silver and naked, standing with her arms raised to the sky's white fire. The lightning went,
yet the image of the woman stayed in Thomas's head, glowing, and
then the lightning struck again, slamming into the eastern hills, and
Genevieve had her head back, her hair was unbound, and the water
streamed from it like drops of liquid silver.

She was dancing naked beneath the lightning.

She did not like to be naked with him. She hated the scars that
Father Roubert had seared into her arms and legs and down her back,
yet now she danced naked, a slow dance, her face tilted back to the
downpour, and Thomas watched in each successive lightning flash
and he thought she was indeed a *draga*. She was the wild silver creature of the dark, the shining woman who was dangerous and beautiful
and strange. Thomas crouched, gazing, thinking that his soul was in
greater peril still for Father Medous had said the *dragas* were the
devil's creatures, yet he loved her too; and then the thunder filled the
air to shake the hills and he squatted lower, his eyes fast closed. He
was doomed, he thought, doomed, and that knowledge filled him with
utter hopelessness.

"Thomas." Genevieve was stooping in front of him now, her
hands cradling his face. "Thomas."

"You're a *draga*," he said, his eyes still closed.

"I wish I was," she said. "I wish flowers would grow where I
walked. But I'm not. I just danced under the lightning and the thunder spoke to me."

He shuddered. "What did it say?"

She put her arms round him, comforting him. "That all will be
well."

He said nothing.

"All will be well," Genevieve said again, "because the thunder
does not lie if you dance to it. It is a promise, my love, it is a promise. That all will be well."

*　　*　　*

SIR GUILLAUME HAD SENT one of the captured men-at-arms to Berat to inform the Count that Joscelyn and thirteen other men were prisoners and that ransoms needed to be negotiated. Joscelyn had reported that his uncle had been at Astarac, but Sir Guillaume assumed the old man must have returned to his castle.

Yet it seemed he had not, for four days after Thomas and Genevieve had left, a peddler came to Castillon d'Arbizon and said that the Count of Berat was sick with the fever, perhaps dying, and that he was in the infirmary of Saint Sever's monastery. The man-at-arms sent to Berat returned the next day with the same news and added that no one in Berat possessed the authority to negotiate Joscelyn's freedom. All that Sir Henri Courtois, the garrison commander, could do for Joscelyn was send a message to Astarac and hope that the Count was well enough to cope with the news.

"Now what do we do?" Robbie asked. He sounded aggrieved for he was eager to see the ransom's gold. He and Joscelyn sat in the great hall. They were alone. It was night. A fire burned in the hearth.

Joscelyn said nothing.

Robbie frowned. "I could sell you on," he suggested. That was done often enough. A man took a prisoner whose ransom would be considerable, but rather than wait for the money he would sell the prisoner to a richer man who would pay a lesser sum and then endure the long negotiations before realizing his profit.

Joscelyn nodded. "You could," he agreed, "but you won't make much money."

"The heir to Berat and Lord of Béziers?" Robbie asked scornfully. "You're worth a big ransom."

"Béziers is a pig field," Joscelyn said scornfully, "and the heir to Berat is worth nothing, but Berat itself is worth a fortune. A fortune." He stared at Robbie in silence for a few heartbeats. "My uncle is a fool," he went on, "but a very rich one. He keeps coins in his cellars.

Barrel after barrel of coins, filled to the top, and two of those barrels are crammed with nothing but genoins."

Robbie savored the thought. He imagined the money sitting in the dark, the two barrels filled with the marvellous coins of Genoa, coins made of pure gold, each tiny genoin sufficient to keep a man fed and clothed and armed for a year. Two barrels!

"But my uncle," Joscelyn went on, "is also a mean man. He won't spend money except on the Church. If he had a choice then he would rather that I was dead, that one of my brothers was his heir and that his coins were undiminished. At night, sometimes, he takes a lantern down to the castle cellars and stares at his money. Just stares at it."

"You're telling me," Robbie said bitterly, "that you won't be ransomed?"

"I'm telling you," Joscelyn said, "that so long as my uncle is the Count, then so long will I be your prisoner. But if I was the Count?"

"You?" Robbie was not sure where the conversation was going and sounded puzzled.

"My uncle is sick," Joscelyn said, "and perhaps dying."

Robbie thought about that and saw what Joscelyn was suggesting. "And if you were the Count," he said slowly, "then you could negotiate your own ransom?"

"If I was Count," Joscelyn said, "I would ransom myself and my men. All of them. And I'd do it quickly."

Again Robbie thought. "How big are the barrels?" he asked after a while.

Joscelyn held a hand a couple of feet above the floor. "It is the biggest hoard of gold in Gascony," he said. "There are ducats and écus, florins and agnos, deniers and genoins, pounds and moutons."

"Moutons?"

"Gold ones," Joscelyn said, "thick and heavy. More than enough for a ransom."

"But your uncle may live," Robbie said.

"One prays so," Joscelyn said piously, "but if you would let me send two men to Astarac they could discover his state of health for us? And they could, perhaps, persuade him to offer a ransom?"

"But you said he would never pay." Robbie was pretending not to understand, or perhaps he did not want to acknowledge what Joscelyn was suggesting.

"He might be persuaded," Joscelyn said, "out of his lingering affection for me. But only if I send men to him."

"Two men?"

"And if they fail," Joscelyn said innocently, "then of course they will return to their captivity here, so what can you lose? But you cannot let them travel unarmed. Not in a country beset by *coredors*."

Robbie stared at Joscelyn, trying to read his face in the firelight, then a question occurred to him. "What was your uncle doing at Astarac?"

Joscelyn laughed. "The stupid old fool was looking for the Holy Grail. He thought I didn't know, but one of the monks told me. The Holy goddamned Grail! He's mad. But he thinks God will give him a son if he finds it."

"The Grail?"

"God knows where he got the idea. He's mad! Mad with piety."

The Grail, Robbie thought, the Grail. At times he had doubted Thomas's search, thinking it a lunacy, but now it seemed that other men shared the madness, which confirmed that the Grail might truly exist. And the Grail, Robbie thought, should not go to England. Anywhere but England.

Joscelyn seemed unaware of how his words had affected Robbie. "You and I," he said, "shouldn't be on different sides. We're both enemies of England. They're the ones who caused the trouble. It was the English who came here," he tapped the table to emphasize his point, "and they started the killing, and for what?"

For the Grail, Robbie thought, and he imagined taking the holy relic back to Scotland. He imagined the armed might of Scotland, given power by the Grail, sweeping in bloody triumph through England.

"You and I should be friends," Joscelyn said, "and you can show me a gesture of friendship now." He looked up at his shield, which hung on the wall, but it had been hung upside down so that the red fist pointed downwards. Thomas had put it there as the symbol that the shield's owner had been taken prisoner. "Take that down," Joscelyn said bitterly.

Robbie glanced at Joscelyn, then walked to the wall and used his sword to dislodge the shield which fell with a clatter. He propped it, right way up, against the stones.

"Thank you," Joscelyn said, "and remember, Robbie, that when I'm Count of Berat I'm going to need good men. You're not sworn to anyone, are you?"

"No."

"The Earl of Northampton?"

"No!" Robbie protested, remembering the Earl's unfriendliness.

"So think of serving me," Joscelyn said. "I can be generous, Robbie. Hell, I'll start by sending a priest to England."

Robbie blinked, confused by Joscelyn's words. "You'd send a priest to England? Why?"

"To carry your ransom, of course," Joscelyn said with a smile. "You'll be a free man, Robbie Douglas." He paused, watching Robbie closely. "If I'm Count of Berat," he added, "I can do that."

"If you're Count of Berat," Robbie said cautiously.

"I can ransom every prisoner here," Joscelyn said expansively, "ransom you and hire as many of your men as want employment. Just let me send my two men to Astarac."

Robbie talked with Sir Guillaume in the morning and the Norman saw no reason why two men-at-arms should not talk with the Count at Astarac so long as they swore to return to their captivity when their errand was done. "I just hope he's well enough to listen to them," Sir Guillaume said.

So Joscelyn sent Villesisle and his companion, his own sworn men. They rode in armor, with swords and with careful instructions.

And Robbie waited to become rich.

THE WEATHER CLEARED. The grey clouds dissipated into long streaks that were a beautiful pink in the evenings and next night they faded to a clear sky in which the wind went to the south and became warm.

Thomas and Genevieve stayed in the broken cottage for two days. They dried their clothes and let the horses eat the last of the year's grass. They rested. Thomas felt no urge to reach Astarac quickly, for he did not expect to find anything there, but Genevieve was certain that the local folk would have tales to tell and, at the very least, they should listen. But for Thomas it was enough that he and Genevieve were alone for the first time. They had never really been alone even in the castle, for when they went behind the tapestry there was always the knowledge that others were sleeping in the hall just beyond. And Thomas had not realized until now how burdened he had been by decisions. Whom to send out on raids, whom to leave behind, whom to watch, whom to trust, whom to keep apart, who needed the reward of a few coins if they were to stay loyal, and always, ever present, the worry that he had forgotten something, that his enemy might be planning some surprise that he had not foreseen. And all the time the real enemy had been close by: Robbie, seething with righteous indignation and tortured desire.

Now Thomas could forget it all, but not for long, for the nights were cold and the winter was coming, and on the second day in their refuge he saw horsemen on the southern heights. There were half a dozen of them, ragged-looking men, two with crossbows slung on their shoulders. They did not look down into the valley where Thomas and Genevieve sheltered, but he knew that eventually someone would come here. It was the time of year when wolves and *core-dors* came down from the high mountains to seek easier plunder in the foothills. It was time to go.

Genevieve had questioned Thomas about the Grail, hearing how his father, the clever, half-mad priest, had perhaps stolen it from his own father who was the exiled Count of Astarac, but how Father Ralph had never once admitted the theft or the ownership, instead he had merely left a tangle of strange writings that only added to the mystery. "But your father," Genevieve said on the morning they were readying to leave, "wouldn't have taken it back to Astarac, would he?"

"No."

"So it isn't there?"

"I don't know if it even exists," Thomas said. They were sitting beside the stream. The horses were saddled and the arrow sheaves tied to the cantles. "I think the Holy Grail is a dream that men have, a dream that the world can be made perfect. And if it existed," he went on, "then we'd all know the dream can't come true." He shrugged, then began scraping at a patch of rust on his mail.

"You don't think it exists, yet you look for it?" Genevieve asked.

Thomas shook his head. "I look for my cousin. I want to learn what he knows."

"Because you do believe in it, don't you?"

He paused in his work. "I want to believe. But if my father had it then it ought to be in England, and I've searched everywhere he might have hidden it. But I'd like to believe." He thought for a moment. "And if I found it," he went on, "then the Church must take us back."

Genevieve laughed. "You are like a wolf, Thomas, who dreams of nothing but joining the flock of sheep."

Thomas ignored that. He gazed up at the eastern skyline. "It's all that's left. The Grail. I've failed as a soldier."

Genevieve was scornful. "You will get your men back. You will win, Thomas, because you are a wolf. But I think you will find the Grail too."

He smiled at her. "Did you see that under the lightning?"

"I saw darkness," she said vehemently, "a real darkness. Like a shadow that is going to cover the world. But you lived in it, Thomas, and you shone." She was gazing into the stream, an expression of solemnity on her long face. "Why should there not be a Grail? Perhaps that is what the world waits for, and it will sweep all the rottenness away. All the priests." She spat. "I don't think your Grail will be at Astarac, but perhaps there will be answers to questions."

"Or more questions."

"Then let's find out!"

They rode eastwards again, climbing through trees to the high, bare uplands and always going cautiously, avoiding settlements, but late in the morning, to cross the valley of the Gers, they rode through the village where they had fought Joscelyn and his men. The villagers must have recognized Genevieve, but they made no trouble for no one ever interfered with armed riders, not unless they were soldiers themselves. Thomas saw a newly dug patch of earth next to one of the pear orchards and reckoned that was where the skirmish's dead had been buried. Neither of them said anything as they passed the place where Father Roubert had died, though Thomas made the sign of the cross. If Genevieve saw the gesture she ignored it.

They forded the river and climbed through the trees to the wide flat crest that overlooked Astarac. There were woods to their right and a jumbled summit of rocks on higher ground to the left and Thomas instinctively went towards the woods, seeking their cover, but Genevieve checked him. "Someone's lit a fire," she said, and pointed to a tiny wisp of smoke coming from deep among the trees.

"Charcoal-burners?" Thomas suggested.

"Or *coredors*," she countered, turning her horse away. Thomas followed, giving one reluctant glance at the wood. Just as he did, he saw a movement there, something furtive, the kind of motion he had learned to look for in Brittany, and he instinctively pulled his bow from the sheath that held it to his saddle.

Then the arrow came.

It was a crossbow bolt. Short, squat and black, and its ragged leather vane made a whirring noise as it flew and Thomas kicked his heels back and shouted a warning to Genevieve just as the bolt seared in front of his horse to thump her mare in the haunch. The mare bolted, blood red on its white hide and with the quarrel's stub sticking from the wound.

Genevieve somehow stayed in the saddle as her horse bolted northwards, spraying blood as it went. Two more quarrels flew past Thomas, then he twisted in his saddle to see four horsemen and at least a dozen men on foot coming from the wood. "Go for the rocks!" he shouted at Genevieve. "The rocks!" He doubted their horses could outrun the *coredors*, not with Genevieve's mare pumping out blood with every stride.

He could hear the pursuing horses. He could hear their hooves drumming on the thin turf, but then Genevieve was among the rocks and she swung herself out of the saddle and scrambled up the boulders. Thomas dismounted beside her horse, but instead of following her he strung his bow and snatched an arrow from his bag. He shot once, shot again, the arrows whipping low, and one rider was falling back from his horse and the second man was dead with an arrow in his eye and the other two swerved away so violently that one horse lost its footing and spilled its rider. Thomas flicked an arrow at the surviving horseman, missed, and sent his fourth at the unsaddled man, sticking the bodkin high on the man's back.

The men on foot were following as fast as they could, but they were still some way off and that gave Thomas time to pull all his spare arrows and his purse of money from his horse's saddle. He rescued Genevieve's bag from her mare, tied the two horses' reins together and looped the knot over a boulder in the hope it would hold them, then climbed up the steep jumble of rocks. Two crossbow bolts banged on stone near him, but he was scrambling fast and knew only too well how hard it was to hit a moving man. He found Genevieve in a gully near the top. "You killed three!" she said in wonderment.

"Two," he said. "The others are just wounded." He could see the man he had hit in the back crawling towards the distant woods. He looked around and reckoned Genevieve had found the best refuge possible. Two vast boulders formed the sides of the gully, their massive flanks touching at the back, while in front was a third boulder that served as a parapet. It was time, Thomas thought, to teach these bastards the power of the yew bow and he stood up behind the makeshift parapet and hauled back the cord.

He drove his arrows with a cold fury and a terrible skill. The men had been coming in a bunch and Thomas's first half-dozen arrows could not miss, but slashed into the ragged *coredors* one after the other, and then they had the sense to scatter, most turning and running away to get out of range. They left three men on the ground and another two limping. Thomas sent a final arrow at a fugitive, missing the man by an inch.

Then the crossbows were released and Thomas ducked down beside Genevieve as the iron quarrels clanged and cracked on the gully's boulders. He reckoned there were four or five crossbows and they were shooting at a range just outside the reach of his bow; he could do nothing except peer round the boulder and watch through a crack that was little more than a hand's breadth wide. After a few moments he saw three men running towards the rocks and he loosed an arrow through the crack, then stood and shot two more shafts before ducking fast as the quarrels hammered on the high boulders and tumbled to fall beside Genevieve. His arrows had driven the three men away, though none had been hit. "They'll all go away soon,"

Thomas said. He had seen no more than twenty men pursuing and he had killed or wounded nearly half of them, and while that would doubtless make them angry, it would also make them cautious. "They're just bandits," Thomas said, "and they want the reward for capturing an archer." Joscelyn had confirmed to him that the Count had indeed offered such a reward, and Thomas was sure that bounty was on the minds of the *coredors*, but they were discovering just how difficult it would be to earn it.

"They'll send for help," Genevieve said bitterly.

"Maybe there aren't any more of them," Thomas suggested optimistically, then he heard one of the horses whinny and he guessed that a *coredor*, one he had not seen, had reached the two animals and was untying their reins. "God damn them," he said, and jumped over the boulder and began leaping from stone to stone down the front of the hill. A crossbow bolt slammed just behind him while another drove a spark from a boulder in front, then he saw a man leading both horses away from the rocks and he paused and drew. The man was half hidden by Genevieve's mare, but Thomas loosed anyway and the arrow flashed beneath the mare's neck to strike the man's thigh. The *coredor* fell, still holding the reins, and Thomas turned and saw one of the four crossbowmen was aiming up at Genevieve. The man shot and Thomas loosed in return. He was at the limit of his big bow's range, but his arrow went perilously close to the enemy and that near escape persuaded all the crossbowmen to back away. Thomas, his arrow bag banging awkwardly against his right thigh, knew they were terrified of his bow's power and so, instead of returning to his eyrie in the high rocks, he ran towards them. He shot two more arrows, feeling the strain in his back muscles as he hauled the string far back, and the white-feathered shafts arched through the sky to plummet down around the crossbowmen. Neither shaft hit, but the men backed off still farther and Thomas, when he was sure they were at a safe range, turned back to rescue the horses.

It had not been a man he wounded, but a boy. A snub-nosed child, maybe ten or eleven, who was lying on the turf with tears in his eyes and a scowl on his face. He gripped Thomas's reins as though his life depended on it, and in his left hand there was a knife that he waved in feeble threat. The arrow was through the boy's right thigh, high up, and the pain on his victim's face made Thomas think that the bodkin point had probably broken the bone.

Thomas kicked the knife out of the boy's hand. "Do you speak French?" he asked the lad, and received a gob of spittle in reply. Thomas grinned, took the reins back then hauled the boy to his feet. The child cried out with pain as the arrow tore at his wound, and Thomas looked at the surviving *coredors* and saw that all the fight had gone from them. They were staring at the boy.

Thomas guessed the boy had come with the three men who had run to the rocks while he was crouched behind the boulder. They had doubtless been hoping to steal the two horses for that, at least, would give them some small profit on what had turned out to be a disastrous foray. Thomas's arrows had turned the men back, but the boy, smaller, nimbler and faster, had reached the rocks and tried to be a hero. Now, it seemed, he was a hostage, for one of the *coredors*, a tall man in a leather coat and with a cracked sallet crammed onto his wildly tangled hair, held out both hands to show he carried no weapons and walked slowly forwards.

Thomas kicked the boy down to the ground when the man was thirty paces away, then he half drew the bow. "Far enough," he told the man.

"My name is Philin," the man said. He was broad in the chest, long-legged, with a sad, thin face that had a knife or sword scar running across his forehead. He had a knife sheathed at his belt, but no other weapons. He looked like a bandit, Thomas thought, yet there was something about Philin's eyes which spoke of better times, even of respectability. "He is my son," Philin added, nodding at the boy.

Thomas shrugged as if he did not care.

Philin took off his cracked helmet and stared briefly at the dead men on the pale grass. There were four of them, all killed by the long arrows, while two more were wounded and groaning. He looked back to Thomas. "You are English?"

"What do you think this is?" Thomas asked, hefting the bow. Only the English carried the long war bow.

"I have heard of the bows." Philin admitted. He spoke a badly accented French and sometimes hesitated as he searched for a word. "I have heard of them," he went on, "but I had not seen one until today."

"You've seen one now," Thomas said vengefully.

"I think your woman is wounded," Philin said, nodding up to Genevieve's hiding place.

"And you think I'm a fool," Thomas said. Philin wanted him to turn his back so that the crossbows could creep near again.

"No," Philin said. "What I think is that I want my boy to live."

"What do you offer for him?" Thomas asked.

"Your life," Philin said. "If you keep my son then we shall bring other men here, many men, and we shall surround you and wait for you. You will both die. If my son dies then you will die in such agony, Englishman, that all the torments of hell will seem a relief afterwards. But let Galdric live and you both live. You and the heretic."

"You know who she is?" Thomas was surprised.

"We know everything that happens between Berat and the mountains," Philin said.

Thomas glanced back up the mound of rocks, but Genevieve was hidden. He had planned to beckon her down, but instead he stepped away from the boy. "You want me to take out the arrow?" he asked Philin.

"The monks at Saint Sever's will do that," Philin said.

"You can go there?"

"Abbot Planchard will always take a wounded man."

"Even a *coredor*?"

Philin looked scornful. "We are just landless men. Evicted. Accused of crimes we did not do. Well," he smiled suddenly and Thomas almost smiled back, "some we did not do. What do you think we should have done? Gone to the galleys? Been hanged?"

Thomas knelt beside the boy, put his bow down and drew his knife. The boy glared at him, Philin called out in alarm, but then went silent as he saw that Thomas meant the child no harm. Instead Thomas cut the arrow head from the shaft and put the precious scrap of metal into his haversack. Then he stood. "Swear on your boy's life," he ordered Philin, "that you will keep your word."

"I swear it," Philin said.

Thomas gestured towards the high rocks where Genevieve sheltered. "She is a *draga*," he said. "Break your oath, Philin, and she will make your soul shriek."

"I will not harm you." Philin said gravely, "and they," he looked at the other *coredors*, "will not harm you either."

Thomas reckoned he had little choice. It was either trust Philin or resign himself to a siege in a high place where there was no water and so he stepped away from the boy. "He's yours."

"Thank you," Philin said gravely. "But tell me . . ." These last three words checked Thomas who had turned to lead the horses back to the rocks. "Tell me, Englishman, why you are here? Alone?"

"I thought you knew everything that happened between Berat and the mountains?"

"I know by asking questions," Philin said, stooping to his son.

"I'm a landless man, Philin, a fugitive. Accused of a crime I did commit."

"What crime?"

"Giving refuge to a heretic."

Philin shrugged as if to suggest that crime ranked very low in the hierarchy of evils that had driven the *coredors* to outlawry. "If you are truly a fugitive," he said, "you should think of joining us. But look after your woman. I did not lie. She is wounded."

He was right. Thomas took the horses back to the rocks and he called Genevieve's name and when she did not answer he climbed up to the gully and found her with a crossbow bolt in her left shoulder. It had pierced the silver mail and shattered a rib just above her left breast, close to the armpit, and she was lying there, surrounded by the ugly black quarrels, breathing shallowly, her face paler than ever and she cried out when Thomas lifted her. "I'm dying," she said, but there was no blood in her mouth and Thomas had seen many others live after such wounds. He had seen them die too.

He gave her a lot of pain as he carried her down the rocks, but once at the foot she found some small strength to help herself as Thomas lifted her into the saddle. Blood ran down her mail, trickling between the rings. She slouched there, eyes dull, and the *coredors* came close to stare at her in wonderment. They stared at Thomas too, and made the sign of the cross as they looked at the big bow. They were all thin men, victims of the region's poor harvests and of the difficulty of finding food when they were fugitives, but now that Philin had ordered them to put up their weapons, they were not threatening. They were, instead, pathetic. Philin spoke to them in the local language and then, with his son mounted on one of the scrawny horses with which the *coredors* had pursued Thomas and Genevieve, he started down the hill towards Astarac.

Thomas went with him, leading Genevieve's horse. The blood had clotted on the mare's haunch and, though she walked stiffly, she did not seem badly injured and Thomas had left the bolt in her flesh. He would deal with it later. "Are you their leader?" he asked Philin.

"Only of the men you saw," the big man said, "and maybe no longer."

"No longer?"

"The *coredors* like success," Philin said, "and they don't like burying their dead. No doubt there are others who think they can do better than me."

"What about those other injured men?" Thomas asked, jerking his head back up the hill. "Why aren't they going to the abbey?"

"One didn't want to, he'd rather go back to his woman, and the others? They'll probably die." Philin looked at Thomas's bow. "And some of them refuse to go down to the abbey; they think they'll be betrayed and captured. But Planchard will not betray me."

Genevieve was swaying in her saddle so that Thomas had to ride close alongside to give her support. She said nothing. Her eyes were still dull, her skin pale and her breathing almost undetectable, but she gripped the pommel firmly enough and Thomas knew there was still some life in her. "The monks may not treat her," he said to Philin.

"Planchard takes everyone," Philin said, "even heretics."

"Planchard is the abbot here, yes?"

"He is," Philin confirmed, "and also a good man. I was one of his monks once."

"You?" Thomas could not hide his surprise.

"I was a novice, but I met a girl. We were staking out a new vineyard and she brought the willow slips to tie the vines and . . ." Philin shrugged as if the rest of the tale was too familiar to bear repetition. "I was young," he finished instead, "and so was she."

"Galdric's mother?" Thomas guessed.

Philin nodded. "She's dead now. The abbot was kind enough. He told me I had no vocation and let me go. We became the abbey's tenants, just a small farm, but the other villagers didn't like me. Her family had wanted her to marry someone else, they said I was no good for anything and after she died they came to burn me out. I killed one of them with a hoe and they said I had started the fight and branded me a murderer, so here I am. It was either this or be hanged in Berat." He led his son's horse across a small stream that tumbled from the hill.

"It's the wheel of fortune, isn't it? Round and round, up and down, but I seem to be down more than up. And Destral will blame me."

"Destral?"

"Our leader. His name means 'axe,' and that's what he kills with."

"He's not here?"

"He sent me to see what was happening in Astarac," Philin said. "There were men in the old castle, digging. Destral thinks there's treasure there."

The Grail, Thomas thought, the Grail, and he wondered if it had already been found, then dismissed the thought for surely that news would have gone through the countryside like lightning.

"But we never reached Astarac," Philin went on. "We camped in the woods and were just about to leave when we saw you instead."

"And thought you'd become rich?"

"We would have got forty coins for you," Philin said, "all of them gold."

"Ten more than Judas got," Thomas said lightly, "and his were only silver." Philin had the grace to smile.

They reached the monastery just after midday. The wind was cold, gusting from the north and blowing the kitchen smoke above the gateway where two monks accosted them. They nodded to Philin, allowing him to take his son to the infirmary, but then barred Thomas's path. "She needs help," Thomas insisted angrily.

"She is a woman," one of the monks said, "she cannot enter here."

"There is a place in the back," the other monk said and, pulling his white hood over his head, he led Thomas around the side of the buildings and through some olive trees to where a cluster of wooden huts was surrounded by a high fence of palings. "Brother Clement will receive you," the monk said, then hurried away.

Thomas tied the two horses to an olive tree, then carried Genevieve to the gate in the fence. He kicked it with his boot, waited and kicked again, and after the second kick the gate creaked open and a small, white-robed monk with a wrinkled face and a straggling beard smiled up at him.

"Brother Clement?"

The monk nodded.

"She needs help," Thomas said.

Clement just gestured inside and Thomas carried Genevieve into what he at first took to be a farmyard. It smelt like one, though he could see no dungheap, but the thatched buildings looked like small barns and stables, then he noticed the gray-robed people sitting in doorways. They stared at him hungrily, and others came to the small windows when the news of his arrival spread. His immediate impression was that they were monks, then he saw there were women among the robed figures and he looked back to the gate where a small table was piled with wooden clappers. They were pieces of wood attached to a handle by a strip of leather and, if the handle was shaken, the wooden flaps would make a loud noise. He had noticed them when Brother Clement beckoned him inside, but now the strange objects made sense. The clappers were carried by lepers to warn folk of their approach and the table was set so that anyone from this compound going into the wider world could take one. Thomas checked, frightened. "Is this a lazar house?" he asked Brother Clement.

The monk nodded cheerfully, then plucked at Thomas's elbow. Thomas resisted, fearing the dreadful contagion of the gray-robed lepers, but Brother Clement insisted and pulled him to a small hut to one side of the yard. The hut was empty except for a straw mattress in one corner and a table on which jars, pestles and an iron balance stood. Brother Clement gestured at the mattress.

Thomas laid Genevieve down. A dozen of the lepers crowded at the doorway and gaped at the newcomers until Brother Clement shooed them away. Genevieve, oblivious of the stir her arrival had caused, sighed, then blinked at Thomas. "It hurts," she whispered.

"I know," he said, "but you must be brave."

Brother Clement had rolled up his sleeves and now he gestured that Genevieve's mail coat must be taken off. That would be hard for the crossbow quarrel was still in her flesh and was jutting through the polished mail. But the monk seemed to know what to do for he pushed Thomas aside and first moved Genevieve's arms so they were reaching above her head, then he took hold of the quarrel's leather vanes. Genevieve moaned, then Brother Clement, with extraordinary delicacy, eased the bloody and broken mail and the leather jerkin that supported it clear up over the bolt. Then he reached down with his left hand and put it under the jerkin's skirt, right up until he was holding the bolt and his left arm was supporting the armor to keep it from touching the quarrel and he nodded at Thomas, looked expectant, then jerked his head as if to suggest that Thomas should simply pull Genevieve out of the mail coat. The monk nodded approvingly as Thomas took hold of her ankles, then nodded encouragement.

Thomas shut his eyes and pulled. Genevieve screamed. He stopped pulling and Brother Clement made some guttural noises that suggested Thomas was being squeamish and so he pulled again, sliding her out of the mail, and when he opened his eyes he saw that her body was clear of the iron rings, though her outstretched arms and head were still encased by their folds. But the bolt was clear of the armor and Brother Clement, making clucking noises, eased the mail coat from her arms and tossed it aside.

The monk went back to the table while Genevieve cried aloud and turned her head from side to side in an effort to quell the pain of the wound that had started to bleed again. Her linen shirt was red from armpit to waist.

Brother Clement knelt by her. He put a water-soaked pad on her forehead, patted her cheek, made some more clucking noises that seemed to soothe Genevieve and then, still smiling, he put his left knee on her breast, both hands on the quarrel and pulled. She screamed, but the bolt came out, bloody and dripping, and Brother Clement had a knife with which he slashed the linen to reveal the wound onto which he dropped the wet pad. He motioned that Thomas should hold it in place.

Thomas did while the monk busied himself at the table. He came back with a lump of moldy bread that he had softened in water. He put it on the wound, then pressed it down hard. He gave Thomas a strip of sacking and mimed that it should be wrapped about Genevieve's chest like a bandage. It hurt her, for Thomas had to sit her up to do it, and once she was upright Brother Clement cut away the rest of her bloodied linen shift, then Thomas wrapped the sacking about her breasts and shoulder, and only when the moldy, blood-soaked poultice was strapped tight was she allowed to rest. Brother Clement smiled as if to say that it was all well done, then he closed his hands prayerfully and put them beside his face to suggest that Genevieve should sleep.

"Thank you," Thomas said.

Brother Clement opened his mouth in a big smile and Thomas saw the monk had no tongue. A rat rustled in the thatch and the small monk seized a triple-pronged eel spear and began jabbing violently at the straw which only succeeded in tearing great holes in the roof.

Genevieve slept.

Brother Clement went to see to his lepers' needs, then came back with a brazier and a clay pot in which he had some embers. He lit a bundle of tinder in the brazier, fed the fire with wood and, when it was smoking and red hot, he shoved the quarrel that had wounded Genevieve into the glowing heart of the fire. The leather vanes scorched and stank. Brother Clement nodded happily and Thomas understood that the little monk was curing her wound by punishing the thing that had caused it. Then, when the offending quarrel had been punished by fire, Brother Clement tiptoed to Genevieve's side, peered at her and smiled happily. He pulled two dirty blankets from under the table and Thomas spread them over her.

He left her sleeping. He had to water the horses, let them graze and then stable them in the monastery's wine press. He hoped to see Abbot Planchard, but the monks were at prayer and they were still in the abbey church after Thomas, imitating Brother Clement, had made the mare scream by jerking the quarrel from her haunch. He had to step smartly back to avoid her lashing rear hooves. When she had settled he soaked the wound in water, patted her neck, then carried the saddles, bridles, arrows, bows and bags to the shed where Genevieve was now awake. She lay propped against a sack and Brother Clement, making his little clucking noises, was feeding her a soup of mushrooms and sorrel. He gave Thomas a happy smile, then tipped his head towards the yard from where came the sound of singing. It was the lepers, and Brother Clement hummed along with their tune.

There was more soup and bread for Thomas. After he had eaten, and when Brother Clement had gone to wherever he spent his nights, Thomas lay beside Genevieve. "It still hurts," she said, "but not like it did."

"That's good."

"It didn't hurt when the arrow hit. It was just like getting a punch."

"You'll get better," he said fervently.

"Do you know what they were singing?" she asked.

"No."

"The song of Herric and Alloise. They were lovers. A very long time ago." She reached up and traced a finger down the long unshaven line of his jaw. "Thank you," she said.

After a while she slept again. Small shafts of moonlight came through the ragged thatch and Thomas could see sweat on her forehead. But at least she was breathing more deeply and, after a time, Thomas fell asleep.

He slept badly. Sometimes in the night he dreamed of horses' hooves and of men shouting and he woke to find it was no dream, but real, and he sat up as the monastery's bell began to toll the alarm. He pushed off the blankets, thinking he should go to see what had caused the disturbance, but then the bell stopped its clamor and the night became quiet again.

And Thomas slept once more.

T HOMAS WOKE WITH A START, realizing there was a man standing above him. It was a tall man, his looming height outlined against the pale light of dawn showing in the hut doorway. Thomas instinctively twisted away and reached for his sword, but the man stepped back and made a hushing sound. "I did not mean to wake you," he said softly in a voice that was deep and held no threat.

Thomas sat up to see it was a monk who had spoken. He could not see the monk's face for it was dark in the hut, but then the tall, white-robed man stepped forward again to peer at Genevieve. "How is your friend?" he asked.

Genevieve was sleeping. A strand of golden hair shivered at her mouth with every breath. "She was feeling better last night," Thomas said softly.

"That's good," the monk said fervently, then stepped back again to the doorway. He had picked up Thomas's bow as he stooped to look at Genevieve and now he examined the bow in the thin grey light. Thomas, as ever, felt uncomfortable when a stranger handled the weapon, but he said nothing and, after a while, the monk propped the bow against Brother Clement's medicine table. "I would like to talk with you," the monk said. "Shall we meet in the cloisters in a few moments?"

It was a cold morning. A dew lay on the grass between the olive trees and on the lawn in the cloister's center. There was a circular communal trough at one corner of the cloisters where the monks, with one prayer service already behind them, splashed their faces and hands, and Thomas first looked for the tall monk among the washing men, but then saw him sitting on a low wall between two pillars of the southern arcade. The monk gestured to him and Thomas saw that he was very old, with a face deeply lined and somehow full of kindness. "Your friend," the old monk said when Thomas joined him, "is in excellent hands. Brother Clement is a most skilled healer, but he and Brother Ramón don't agree about things, so I have to keep them apart. Ramón looks after the infirmary and Clement tends the lepers. Ramón is a proper physician, trained at Montpellier, so of course we have to defer to him, but he seems to have no remedies other than prayer and copious bleeding. He uses them for every ailment, while Brother Clement, I suspect, uses his own kind of magic. I should probably disapprove of that, but I am forced to say that if I was sick I would prefer Brother Clement to treat me." He smiled at Thomas. "My name is Planchard."

"The abbot?"

"Indeed. And you are most welcome to our house. I am sorry I could not greet you yesterday. And Brother Clement tells me you were alarmed at being in the lazar house? There's no need. My experience is that the condition is not promoted by contact with others. I have been visiting the lepers for forty years and have yet to lose a finger, and Brother Clement lives and worships with them and he has never been touched by the disease." The abbot paused and made the sign of the cross and Thomas at first thought the old man was warding off the evil thought of catching leprosy, then he saw that Planchard was looking at something across the cloister. He followed the Abbot's gaze and saw a body being carried on a stretcher. It was obviously a corpse for the face was covered with a white cloth and there was a crucifix balanced on the chest which fell off after a few steps so that the monks had to stop and retrieve it. "We had excitement here last night," Planchard said mildly.

"Excitement?"

"You probably heard the bell? It was rung too late, I fear. Two men came to the monastery after dark. Our gate is never shut, so they had no trouble entering. They tied the gatekeeper hand and foot, then went to the infirmary. The Count of Berat was there. He was attended by his squire and three of his men-at-arms who had survived a horrid little fight in the next valley," the Abbot waved a hand towards the west, but if he knew or suspected that Thomas had been involved in that fight, he made no comment, "and one of the men-at-arms was sleeping in the Count's chamber. He woke up when the killers came, and so he died and then the Count's throat was cut and the two killers ran for their lives." The old abbot recounted these events in a flat voice, as though foul murders were commonplace in Saint Severt's.

"The Count of Berat?" Thomas asked.

"A sad man," Planchard said. "I quite liked him, but I fear he was one of God's fools. He was astonishingly learned, but possessed no sense. He was a hard master to his tenants, but good to the Church. I used to think he was trying to buy his way into heaven, but actually he was seeking a son and God never rewarded that desire. Poor man, poor man." Planchard stared as the dead Count was carried to the gatehouse, then smiled gently at Thomas. "Some of my monks insisted you must be the murderer."

"Me!" Thomas exclaimed.

"I know it was not you," Planchard said. "The real murderers were seen leaving. Galloping into the night." He shook his head. "But the brothers can get very excited and, alas, our house has been much disturbed of late. Forgive me, I did not ask your name."

"Thomas."

"A good name. Just Thomas?"

"Thomas of Hookton."

"That sounds very English," Planchard said. "And you are what? A soldier?"

"An archer."

"Not a friar?" Planchard asked in grave amusement.

Thomas half smiled. "You know about that?"

"I know that an English archer called Thomas went to Castillon d'Arbizon dressed as a friar. I know he spoke good Latin. I know he took the castle, and I know that he then spread misery in the countryside. I know he caused many tears, Thomas, many tears. Folk who struggled all their lives to build something for their children saw it burned in minutes."

Thomas did not know what to say. He stared at the grass. "You must know more than that," he said after a while.

"I know that you and your companion are excommunicated," Planchard said.

"Then I should not be here," Thomas said, gesturing at the cloister. "I was excluded from holy precincts," he added bitterly.

"You are here at my invitation," Planchard said mildly, "and if God disapproves of that invitation then it will not be long before he has a chance to demand an explanation from me."

Thomas looked at the abbot who endured his scrutiny patiently. There was something about Planchard, Thomas thought, that reminded him of his own father, though without the madness. But there was a saintliness and a wisdom and an authority in the old lined face and Thomas knew he liked this man. Liked him very much. He looked away. "I was protecting Genevieve," he muttered, explaining away his excommunication.

"The beghard?"

"She's no beghard," Thomas said.

"I would be surprised if she was," Planchard said, "for I very much doubt if there are any beghards in these parts. Those heretics congregate in the north. What are they called? The Brethren of the Free Spirit. And what is it they believe? That everything comes from God, so everything is good! It's a beguiling idea, is it not? Except when they say everything they mean exactly that, everything. Every sin, every deed, every theft."

"Genevieve is no beghard," Thomas repeated the denial, though the firmness of his tone did not reflect any conviction.

"I'm sure she's a heretic," Planchard said mildly, "but which of us is not? And yet," his mild tone vanished as his voice became stern, "she is also a murderer."

"Which of us is not?" Thomas echoed.

Planchard grimaced. "She killed Father Roubert."

"Who had tortured her," Thomas said. He drew up his sleeve and showed the abbot the burn scars on his arm. "I too killed my torturer and he too was a Dominican."

The abbot gazed up at the sky that was clouding over. Thomas's confession of murder did not seem to disturb him, indeed his next words even suggested he was ignoring it completely. "I was reminded the other day," he said, "of one of the psalms of David. *'Dominus reget me et nihil mihi deerit.'*"

"*'In loco pascuae ibi conlocavit,'*" Thomas finished the quotation.

"I can see why they thought you were a friar," Planchard said, amused. "But the implication of the psalm, is it not, is that we are sheep and that God is our shepherd? Why else would He put us in a pasture and protect us with a staff? But what I have never fully understood is why the shepherd blames the sheep when they become ill."

"God blames us?"

"I cannot speak for God," Planchard said, "only for the Church. What did Christ say? *'Ego sum pastor bonus, bonus pastor animam suam dat pro ovibus.'*" He paid Thomas the compliment of not translating the words which meant: "I am the good shepherd and the good shepherd gives his life for the sheep." "And the Church," Planchard went on, "continues Christ's ministry, or it is supposed to, yet some churchmen are sadly enthusiastic about culling their flock."

"And you are not?"

"I am not," Planchard said firmly, "but don't let that weakness in me persuade you that I approve of you. I do not approve of you, Thomas, and I do not approve of your woman, but nor can I approve of a Church that uses pain to bring the love of God to a sinful world. Evil begets evil, it spreads like a weed, but good works are tender shoots that need husbandry." He thought for a while, then smiled at Thomas. "But my duty is clear enough, is it not? I should give both of you to the Bishop of Berat and let his fire do God's work."

"And you," Thomas said bitterly, "are a man who does his duty."

"I am a man who tries, God help me, to be good. To be what Christ wanted us to be. Duty is sometimes imposed by others and we must always examine it to see if it helps us to be good. I do not approve of you, either of you, but nor do I see what good will come from burning you. So I will do my duty to my conscience which does not instruct me to send you to the bishop's fire. Besides," he smiled again, "burning you would be an awful waste of Brother Clement's endeavors. He tells me he is calling a bone-setter from the village and she will try to repair your Genevieve's rib, though Brother Clement warns me that ribs are very hard to mend."

"Brother Clement talked to you?" Thomas asked, surprised.

"Dear me, no! Poor Brother Clement can't talk at all! He was a galley slave once. The Mohammedans captured him in a raid on Leghorn, I think, or was it Sicily? They tore his tongue out, I assume because he insulted them, and then they cut off something else which is why, I suspect, he became a monk after he was rescued by a Venetian galley. Now he tends to the beehives and looks after our lepers. And how do we talk to each other? Well, he points and he gestures and he makes drawings in the dust and somehow we manage to understand one another."

"So what will you do with us?" Thomas asked.

"Do? Me? I shall do nothing! Except pray for you and to say farewell when you leave. But I would like to know why you are here."

"Because I was excommunicated," Thomas said bitterly, "and my companions wanted nothing more to do with me."

"I mean why you came to Gascony in the first place," Planchard asked patiently.

"The Earl of Northampton sent me," Thomas said.

"I see," Planchard said, his tone implying he knew Thomas was evading the question. "And the Earl had his reasons, did he?"

Thomas said nothing. He saw Philin across the cloister and raised a hand in greeting and the *coredor* smiled back; the smile suggesting that his son, like Genevieve, was recovering from the arrow wound.

Planchard persisted. "The Earl had reasons, Thomas?"

"Castillon d'Arbizon was once his property. He wanted it back."

"It was his property," Planchard said tartly, "for a very short time, and I cannot think that the Earl is so bereft of land that he needs send men to defend an insignificant town in Gascony, especially after a truce was signed at Calais. He must have sent you to break that truce for a very special reason, don't you think?" He paused, then smiled at Thomas's obduracy. "Do you know any more of that psalm which begins *'Dominus reget me'*?"

"Some," Thomas said vaguely.

"Then perhaps you know the words *'calix meus inebrians'*?"

" 'My cup makes me drunk,' " Thomas said.

"Because I looked at your bow this morning, Thomas," Planchard said, "out of nothing but idle curiosity. I have heard so much about the English war bow, but I have not seen one for many years. But yours, I noticed, had something which I suspect most bows do not. A silver plate. And on the plate, young man, was the badge of the Vexilles."

"My father was a Vexille," Thomas said.

"So you're nobly born?"

"Bastard born," Thomas said. "He was a priest."

"Your father was a priest?" Planchard sounded surprised.

"A priest," Thomas confirmed, "in England."

"I heard some of the Vexilles had fled there," Planchard said, "but that was many years ago. Before my memories begin. So why does a Vexille return to Astarac?"

Thomas said nothing. Monks were going to work, carrying hoes and stakes out of the gate. "Where were they taking the dead Count?" he asked, trying to evade the abbot's question.

"He must go to Berat, of course, to be buried with his ancestors," Planchard said, "and his body will be stinking by the time it gets to the cathedral. I remember when his father was buried: the smell was so bad that most of the mourners fled into the open air. Now, what was my question? Ah yes, why does a Vexille return to Astarac?"

"Why not?" Thomas answered.

Planchard stood and beckoned him. "Let me show you something, Thomas." He led Thomas to the abbey church where, as he entered, the abbot dipped his finger into the stoup of holy water and made the sign of the cross as he genuflected towards the high altar. Thomas, almost for the first time in his life, did not make the same obeisance. He was excommunicated. The old things had no power for him now because he had been cut off from them. He followed the abbot across the wide empty nave to an alcove behind a side altar and there Planchard unlocked a small door with a big key. "It will be dark downstairs," the old man warned, "and I have no lantern, so step carefully."

A dim light found its way down the stairs and when Thomas reached the bottom Planchard held up a hand. "Wait here," he said, "and I will bring you something. It is too dark to see in the treasury."

Thomas waited. His eyes became accustomed to the gloom and he saw there were eight arched openings in the undercroft and then he saw that it was not just a vault, but an ossuary and the realization made him take a step back in sudden horror. The arches were stacked with bones. Skulls gazed at him. At the eastern end there was an arch only half filled, the rest of its space waiting for the brethren who prayed each day in the church above. This was the cellar of the dead, heaven's antechamber.

He heard the click of a lock turning, then the abbot's footsteps returned and Planchard held out a wooden box. "Take it to the light," he said, "and look at it. The Count tried to steal it from me, but when he returned here with the fever I took it back from him. Can you see it properly?"

Thomas held the box up to the small light that came down the stairwell. He could see that the box was old, that its wood had dried out, and that it had once been painted inside and out, but then, on the front, he saw the remnants of the words he knew so well, the words that had haunted him ever since his father had died: *Calix Meus Ine-brians*.

"It is said," the Abbot took the box back from Thomas, "that it was found in a precious reliquary on the altar of the chapel in the Vexille castle. But it was empty when it was found, Thomas. Do you understand that?"

"It was empty," Thomas repeated.

"I think I know," Planchard said, "what brings a Vexille to Astarac, but there is nothing here for you, Thomas, nothing at all. The box was empty." He put the box back, locked the heavy chest and led Thomas back up to the church. He secured the treasury door, then beckoned Thomas to sit with him on a stone ledge that ran all around the otherwise bare nave. "The box was empty," the abbot insisted, "though no doubt you are thinking it was filled once. And I think you came here to find the thing that filled it."

Thomas nodded. He was watching two novices sweep the church, their birch bristles making small scratching noises on the wide flagstones. "I also came," he said, "to find the man who killed, who murdered my father."

"You know who did that?"

"My cousin. Guy Vexille. I'm told he calls himself the Count of Astarac."

"And you think he is here?" Planchard sounded surprised. "I have never heard of such a man."

"I think that if he knows I am here," Thomas said, "then he'll come."

"And you will kill him?"

"Question him," Thomas said. "I want to know why he thought my father possessed the Grail."

"And did your father possess it?"

"I don't know," Thomas said truthfully. "I think he may have believed he did. But he was also mad at times."

"Mad?" The question was asked very gently.

"He didn't worship God," Thomas said, "but fought him. He pleaded, shouted, screamed and wept at God. He saw most things very clearly, but God confused him."

"And you?" Planchard asked.

"I'm an archer," Thomas said, "I have to see things very clearly."

"Your father," Planchard said, "opened the door to God and was dazzled, while you keep the door shut?"

"Maybe," Thomas said defensively.

"So what is it, Thomas, that you hope to achieve if you find the Grail?"

"Peace," Thomas said. "And justice." It was not an answer he had thought about, but almost a dismissal of Planchard's question.

"A soldier who seeks peace," Planchard said, amused. "You are full of contradictions. You have burned and killed and stolen to make peace." He held up a hand to still Thomas's protest. "I have to tell you, Thomas, that I think it would be best if the Grail were not found. If I were to discover it I would hurl it into the deepest sea, down among the monsters, and tell no one. But if another person finds it, then it will merely be another trophy in the wars of ambitious men. Kings will fight for it, men like you will die because of it, churches will grow rich on it, and there will be no peace. But I don't know that. Maybe you're right? Maybe the Grail will usher in an age of plenty and peacefulness, and I pray it does. Yet the discovery of the crown of thorns brought no such splendors, and why should the Grail be more powerful than our dear Lord's thorns? We have vials of his blood in Flanders and England, yet they do not bring peace. Is the Grail more precious than his blood?"

"Some men think so," Thomas said uncomfortably.

"And those men will kill like beasts to possess it," Planchard said. "They will kill with all the pity of a wolf savaging a lamb, and you tell me it will bring peace?" He sighed. "Yet perhaps you're right. Perhaps this is the time for the Grail to be found. We need a miracle."

"To bring peace?"

Planchard shook his head. He said nothing for a while, just stared at the two sweepers and looked very solemn and immensely sad. "I have not told this to anyone, Thomas," he broke his long silence, "and you would be wise to tell no one either. In time we shall all know and by then it will be too late. But not long ago I received a letter from a brother house in Lombardy and our world is about to change utterly."

"Because of the Grail?"

"I wish it were so. No, because there is a contagion in the east. A dreadful contagion, a pestilence that spreads like smoke, that kills whoever it touches and spares no one. It is a plague, Thomas, that has been sent to harrow us." Planchard gazed ahead, watching the dust dance in a shaft of slanting sunlight that came down from one of the high, clear windows. "Such a contagion must be the devil's work," the abbot went on, making the sign of the cross, "and it is horrid work. My brother abbot reports that in some towns of Umbria as many as half the folk have died and he advises me to bar my gates and allow no travelers inside, but how can I do that? We are here to help people, not to shut them away from God." He looked higher, as if seeking divine aid among the great beams of the roof. "A darkness is coming, Thomas," he said, "and it is a darkness as great as any mankind has ever seen. Perhaps, if you find the Grail, it will give light to that darkness."

Thomas thought of Genevieve's vision beneath the lightning, of a great darkness in which there was a point of brilliance.

"I have always thought," Planchard went on, "that the search for the Grail was a madness, a hunt for a chimera that would bring no good, only evil, but now I learn that everything is going to change. Everything. Perhaps we shall require a wondrous symbol of God's love." He sighed. "I have even been tempted to wonder whether this coming pestilence is sent by God. Perhaps he burns us out, purges us, so that those who are spared will do His will. I don't know." He shook his head sadly. "What will you do when your Genevieve is well?"

"I came here," Thomas said, "to find out all I could about Astarac."

"Of the beginning and end of man's labors," Planchard said with a smile, "there is no end. Would you resent advice?"

"Of course not."

"Then go far away, Thomas," the abbot said firmly, "go far away. I do not know who killed the Count of Berat, but it is not hard to guess. He had a nephew, a stupid but strong man, whom you took prisoner. I doubt the Count would have ransomed him, but now the nephew is himself the Count and can arrange his own ransom. And if he seeks what his uncle sought then he will kill any rival, and that means you, Thomas. So take care. And you must go soon."

"I am unwelcome here?"

"You are most welcome," Planchard insisted, "both of you. But this morning the Count's squire went to report his master's death and the boy will know you are here. You and the girl. He may not know your names, but the two of you are . . . what shall I say? Noticeable? So if anyone wants to kill you, Thomas, they will know where to look for you. Which is why I tell you to go far away. This house has seen enough murder and I want no more." He stood and placed a gentle hand on Thomas's head. "Bless you, my son," he said, then walked out of the church.

And Thomas felt the darkness closing.

JOSCELYN WAS THE COUNT OF BERAT.

He kept remembering that, and each remembrance gave him a surge of pure joy. Count of Berat! Lord of money.

Villesisle and his companion had returned from Astarac with news that the old man had died in his sleep. "Before we even reached the monastery," Villesisle told Joscelyn in front of Robbie and Sir Guillaume, though later, in private, he confessed that things had not gone quite so well and that blood had been shed.

"You're a fool," Joscelyn snarled. "What did I tell you?"

"To stifle him."

"So you drench the damn room with his blood instead?"

"We didn't have a choice," Villesisle claimed sullenly. "One of his men-at-arms was there and tried to fight. But what does it matter? The old man's dead, isn't he?"

He was dead. Dead and rotting, and that was what really mattered. The fourteenth Count of Berat was on his way to heaven or to hell and so the county of Berat with its castles, fiefs, towns, serfs, farm-lands and hoarded coin all belonged to Joscelyn.

Joscelyn possessed a new authority when he met with Robbie and Sir Guillaume. Before, when he had been wondering whether or not his uncle would ransom him, he had done his best to be courteous for his future depended on the goodwill of his captors, but now, though he was not rude to them, he was aloof and that was fitting for they were mere adventurers and he was one of the richest nobles of south-ern France. "My ransom," he declared flatly, "is twenty thousand florins."

"Forty," Sir Guillaume insisted immediately.

"He's my prisoner!" Robbie turned on Sir Guillaume.

"So?" Sir Guillaume bridled. "You'll settle for twenty when he's worth forty?"

"I'll settle for twenty," Robbie said and it was, in truth, a fortune, a ransom worthy of a royal duke. In English money it would be close to three thousand pounds, sufficient to set a man up in luxury for life.

"And three thousand florins more," Joscelyn offered, "for the cap-tured horses and my men-at-arms."

"Agreed," Robbie said before Sir Guillaume could object.

Sir Guillaume was disgusted at Robbie's ready acceptance. The Norman knew the twenty thousand florins was a fine ransom, more than he had ever dared hope for as he had watched the few horsemen approach the ford and the waiting ambush, but even so he believed that Robbie had acquiesced far too quickly. It usually took months to negotiate a ransom, months of haggling, of messengers carrying offer and counter-offer and rejection and threat, yet Joscelyn and Robbie had settled the whole thing in moments. "So now," Sir Guillaume said, watching Joscelyn, "you stay here until the money arrives."

"Then I shall stay here for ever," Joscelyn said calmly. "I have to enter into my inheritance," he explained, "before the money will be released."

"So I just let you go?" Sir Guillaume asked scornfully.

"I'll go with him," Robbie said.

Sir Guillaume looked at the Scotsman, then back to Joscelyn, and he saw allies. It must have been Robbie, Sir Guillaume thought, who had taken down Joscelyn's reversed shield, a gesture the Norman had noticed, but decided to ignore. "You'll go with him," he said flatly, "and he's your prisoner, eh?"

"He's my prisoner," Robbie said.

"But I command here," Sir Guillaume insisted, "and a share of the ransom is mine. Ours." He waved a hand to indicate the rest of the garrison.

"It will be paid," Robbie said.

Sir Guillaume looked into Robbie's eyes and saw a young man who would not meet his gaze, a young man whose allegiances were uncertain, who proposed riding to Berat with Joscelyn. Sir Guillaume suspected Robbie would not come back and so the Norman went to the niche where the crucifix hung, the same crucifix that Thomas had held in front of Genevieve's eyes. He took it from the wall and laid it on the table in front of Robbie. "Swear on that," he demanded, "that our share will be paid."

"I do so swear it," Robbie said solemnly and laid his hand on the cross. "By God and my mother's own life, I swear it." Joscelyn, watching, seemed amused.

Sir Guillaume gave in. He knew he could have kept Joscelyn and the other prisoners, and that in the end a means of conveying all the ransom money would be found if he did keep them, but he also knew that he would face weeks of unrest. Robbie's supporters, and there were many of them, especially among the routiers who had joined the garrison, would claim that by waiting he risked losing all the money, or else they would suggest that he was planning to take the cash and cheat them, and Robbie would encourage that unrest and in the end the garrison would fall apart. It was probably going to fall apart anyway for, without Thomas, there was no compelling reason to stay. The men had never known that the Grail was their quest, but they had sensed Thomas's urgency, sensed that he had a cause, and that what they did had a meaning; now, Sir Guillaume knew, they were just another band of routiers who were lucky enough to hold a castle. None of them would stay long, Sir Guillaume thought. Even if Robbie did not pay his share Sir Guillaume could still ride away much richer than he had arrived, but if Robbie kept faith then Sir Guillaume would have enough money to raise the men he needed to gain his revenge on those who had stolen his lands in Normandy.

"I expect the money to be here within a week," Sir Guillaume said.

"Two," Joscelyn said.

"One week!"

"I shall try," Joscelyn said off-handedly.

Sir Guillaume pushed the crucifix across the table. "One week!"

Joscelyn looked at Sir Guillaume for a long time, then placed a finger on the broken body of Christ. "If you insist," he said. "One week."

Joscelyn left next morning. He rode in full armor, his banner, horses and men-at-arms restored to him, and with him rode Robbie Douglas and sixteen other men-at-arms, all of them Gascons who had served Thomas, but who now preferred to take gold from the Count of Berat. Sir Guillaume was left with the men who had come to Castillon d'Arbizon, but at least that meant he had the archers. He stood on the castle's topmost rampart and watched Joscelyn ride away. John Faircloth, the English man-at-arms, joined him there. "Is he leaving us?" he asked, meaning Robbie.

Sir Guillaume nodded. "He's leaving us. We'll not see him again."

"So what do we do?" Faircloth asked, in French this time.

"Wait for the money, then go."

"Just go?"

"What else in God's name can we do? The Earl of Northampton doesn't want this town, John. He'll never send anyone to help us. If we stay here, we die."

"And we go or die without the Grail," Faircloth said. "Is that why the Earl sent us here? He knew about the Grail?"

Sir Guillaume nodded. "The knights of the round table," he said, amused, "that's us."

"And we abandon the search?"

"It's a madness," Sir Guillaume said forcefully, "a goddamned madness. It doesn't exist, but Thomas thought it might and the Earl thought it worth an effort. But it's pure moonstruck idiocy. And Robbie's caught up in it now, but he won't find it because it isn't there to be found. There's just us and too many enemies, so we'll take our money and go home."

"What if they don't send the money?" Faircloth asked.

"There's honor, isn't there?" Sir Guillaume said. "I mean we plunder, thieve, rape and kill, but we never cheat each other over ransoms. Sweet Jesus! No one could ever trust anyone else if that happened." He paused, staring at Joscelyn and his entourage who had stopped at the valley's end. "Look at the bastards," he said, "just watching us. Wondering how to get us out of here."

The horsemen were indeed taking a last look at Castillon d'Arbizon's tower. Joscelyn saw the impudent standard of the Earl of Northampton lift and fall in the small breeze, then he spat onto the road. "Are you really going to send them money?" he asked Robbie.

Robbie looked startled at the question. "Of course," he said. Once he had been paid the agreed ransom then honor insisted that he would have to pass on Sir Guillaume's share. It had never occurred to him to do otherwise.

"But they fly the flag of my enemy," Joscelyn pointed out. "So if you send them the money, what's to stop me taking it back?" He looked at Robbie, waiting for a response.

Robbie tried to work out the ramifications of the suggestion, testing them against his honor, but so long as the money was sent, he thought, then honor was satisfied. "They didn't ask for a truce," he said hesitantly, and it was the answer Joscelyn wanted because it suggested Joscelyn could start a fight the moment the money was paid. He smiled and rode on.

They reached Berat that evening. A man-at-arms had ridden ahead, warning the town of their new lord's approach, and a delegation of consuls and priests met Joscelyn a half-mile from the eastern gate. They knelt to welcome him and the priests presented the Count with some of the cathedral's precious relics. There was a rung from Jacob's ladder, the bones of one of the fishes used to feed the five thousand, St. Gudule's sandal, and a nail used to crucify one of the two thieves who had died with Christ. All had been gifts to the town from the old Count, and now the new Count was expected to dismount and pay the precious relics, all encased in silver or gold or crystal, due reverence. Joscelyn knew what he was expected to do, but instead he leaned on his pommel and glowered at the priests. "Where is the bishop?" he demanded.

"He is ill, lord."

"Too ill to welcome me?"

"He is sick, lord, very sick," one of the priests said, and Joscelyn stared at the man for an instant, then abruptly accepted the explanation. He dismounted, knelt briefly, made the sign of the cross towards the proffered relics, then nodded curtly at the consuls who held out the town's ceremonial keys on a cushion of green velvet. Joscelyn was supposed to take the keys and then return them with a kind word, but he was hungry and thirsty so he clambered up into his saddle and spurred past the kneeling consuls.

The cavalcade entered the town by its western gate where the guards went on their knees to their new lord, and then the horsemen climbed to the saddle between the two hills on which Berat was built. To their left now, on the lower hill, was the cathedral, a long, low church that lacked tower or spire, while to their right a cobbled street stretched to the castle on the taller hill. The street was hung with painted signs that forced the horsemen to ride in single file, while on either side of them the citizens knelt and called out blessings. One woman strewed vine leaves on the cobbles while a tavern-keeper offered a tray of wine pots that got spilled when Joscelyn's horse sidled into the man.

The street opened into the marketplace, which was dirty with trampled vegetables and stinking from the dung of cows, sheep and goats. The castle was ahead now and its gates swung open as the guards recognized the banner of Berat carried by Joscelyn's squire.

Then it all became confusing for Robbie. His horse was taken by a servant and he was eventually given a room in the east tower where there was a bed and a fire, and later that evening there was a raucous feast to which the dowager Countess was invited. She proved to be a small, plump and pretty girl, and at the feast's end Joscelyn took her by the wrist and led her to his new bedchamber, the old Count's room, and Robbie stayed in the hall where the men-at-arms stripped three serving girls naked and took their turns with them. Others, encouraged by Joscelyn before he disappeared, were dragging bundles of old parchments from the shelves and feeding them to the big fire that blazed mightily and bright. Sir Henri Courtois watched, said nothing, but became as drunk as Robbie.

Next morning the rest of the shelves were emptied. The books were thrown out of a window into the castle yard where a new fire burned. The shelves were hacked down and followed the books and parchments out of the window. Joscelyn, in high spirits, supervised the room's cleansing, and in between he received visitors. Some had been servants of his uncle: the huntsmen, armorers, cellarers and clerks who wanted to make sure their jobs were safe. Some were lesser lords from his new domain who came to swear fealty by placing their hands between the Count's, swearing the oath of allegiance and then receiving the kiss that made them Joscelyn's own men. There were petitioners wanting justice and even more desperate men who had been owed money by the late Count and who now dared hope that his nephew would honor the debts. There were a dozen priests from the town who wanted the new Count to give them money to say Masses for his uncle's soul and Berat's consuls climbed the stairs in their red and blue robes with arguments why the town's tax yield should be lower; and amidst it all Joscelyn was roaring at his men to burn more books, to feed more parchments to the fire, and when a young and nervous monk appeared to protest that he had not yet finished searching the muniments, Joscelyn chased him from the hall and so found the monk's lair, which was full of still more documents. All were burned, leaving the monk in tears.

It was then, as the newly discovered hoard of parchments was flaring high to scatter burning scraps throughout the courtyard and threaten the thatched roof of the castle's mews, that the bishop, apparently not sick at all, arrived. He came with a dozen other clergymen, and with them was Michel, the old Count's squire.

The bishop hammered his staff on the cobblestones to get Joscelyn's attention and when the new Count deigned to notice him the bishop pointed the staff at Joscelyn. A hush fell over the courtyard as men realized a drama was unfolding. Joscelyn, the fire gleaming from his round face, looked belligerent. "What do you want?" he demanded of the bishop who had not, he thought, shown sufficient deference.

"I want to know," the bishop demanded, "how your uncle died."

Joscelyn took a few paces towards the deputation, the sound of his boots echoing from the castle walls. There were at least a hundred men in the courtyard and some of them, having suspected that the old Count had been murdered, made the sign of the cross, but Joscelyn looked quite unconcerned. "He died," he said loudly, "in his sleep, of a sickness."

"It is a strange sickness," the Bishop said, "that leaves a man with a slit throat."

A murmur sounded in the yard and swelled to a roar of indignation. Sir Henri Courtois and some of the old Count's men-at-arms put hands to their sword hilts, but Joscelyn was equal to the challenge. "What do you accuse me of?" he snarled at the bishop.

"I accuse you of nothing," the bishop said. He was not willing to pick a fight with the new Count, not yet, but instead attacked through Joscelyn's hirelings. "But I do accuse your men. This man," he drew Michel forward, "saw them cut your uncle's throat."

A murmur of disgust sounded in the yard and some of the men-at-arms moved towards Sir Henri Courtois as if assuring him of their support. Joscelyn ignored the protest and instead looked for Villesisle. "I sent you," he said loudly, "to seek an audience with my dear uncle. And now I hear that you killed him?"

Villesisle was so taken aback by the accusation that he said nothing. He just shook his head in denial, but so uncertainly that every man there was sure of his guilt. "You want justice, bishop?" Joscelyn called over his shoulder.

"Your uncle's blood cries for it," the bishop said, "and the legitimacy of your inheritance depends on it."

Joscelyn drew his sword. He was not in armor, just breeches, boots and a belted woolen jerkin, while Villesisle wore a leather coat that would be proof against most sword strokes, but Joscelyn jerked his blade to indicate that Villesisle should draw his own weapon. "A trial by combat, bishop," he said.

Villesisle backed away. "I only did what you . . ." he began, then had to retreat fast because Joscelyn had attacked him with two quick strokes. Villesisle became frightened that this was no dumb show put on to placate a troublesome bishop, but a real fight. He drew his sword. "My lord," he pleaded with Joscelyn.

"Make it look good," Joscelyn said softly, "and we can sort everything out afterwards."

Villesisle felt a surge of relief, then grinned and made an attack of his own that Joscelyn parried. The watching men were fanning out to make a half-circle around the fire in front of which the two men could fight. Villesisle was no novice, he had fought in tournaments and skirmishes, but he was wary of Joscelyn who was taller and stronger, and Joscelyn attacked now, making use of those advantages, scything his sword in massive strokes that Villesisle parried desperately. Each clash of blades echoed twice, once from the castle's curtain wall and once from the big keep, one triple ring fading as the next began, and Villesisle was backing away, backing away, and then he leaped aside to let one of Joscelyn's murderous cuts waste itself on the smoky air and immediately pressed forward, lunging with the point, but Joscelyn had been waiting for it and he turned the lunge and bulled forward, throwing Villesisle off his feet so that he sprawled on the cobbles and Joscelyn loomed over him. "I might have to imprison you after this," he said almost in a whisper, "but not for long." Then he raised his voice. "I ordered you to go and talk with my uncle. Do you deny it?"

Villesisle was happy to play along with the deception. "I do not deny it, lord," he said.

"Say it again!" Joscelyn ordered. "Louder!"

"I do not deny it, lord!"

"Yet you cut his throat," Joscelyn said, and he motioned for Villesisle to stand and, once his opponent was up, he moved fast forward, scything the sword, and again the triple rings sounded in the yard. The swords were heavy, the strokes clumsy, yet the men watching reckoned Joscelyn had the greater skill, though Sir Henri Courtois wondered whether Villesisle was using all his skill. He slashed now, but did not try to close on his opponent and it was no trouble for Joscelyn to step back. The burning books and parchments roared beside him, starting sweat from his forehead and he cuffed it away. "If I draw blood from this man, bishop," Joscelyn called out, "will you take that as a sign of his guilt?"

"I will," the Bishop said, "but it will not be sufficient punishment."

"The punishment can wait for God to give," Joscelyn said and he grinned at Villesisle who grinned back. Then Joscelyn stepped carelessly towards his opponent, opening his right side to a blow; Villesisle understood he was being invited to make a swing and so give the appearance that the fight was real and he obliged, swinging his great, awkward blade in the expectation that Joscelyn would parry it, but instead Joscelyn stepped back and used his sword to propel the blow onwards so that Villesisle was spun around, carried by the heavy blade's momentum and Joscelyn, cold-eyed and quick as lightning, brought his own blade back and gave it the merest flick of a wrist and the tip of the sword sliced into Villesisle's throat. It stuck there, caught on Villesisle's gullet, and Joscelyn pushed it forward, twisted the steel, pushed again and he was smiling as he did it and the blood was streaming down the blade, cascading from its edges and Joscelyn still smiled as Villesisle, a look of utter astonishment on his face, fell to his knees. His sword fell with a clang. Breath was bubbling red at the rent in his throat and now Joscelyn gave the sword a great shove so that it tore down into Villesisle's chest. The dying man was caught there, suspended by the sword that had been rammed down his windpipe, and then Joscelyn gave the blade another twist, put both hands on the hilt and ripped the steel free with a monstrous heave that made Villesisle's body shudder and blood fountain up across Joscelyn's arms.

The spectators let out a breath as Villesisle fell sideways and died. His blood trickled between the yard's cobbles to hiss where it met the fire.

Joscelyn turned and looked for the second man, Villesisle's murderous companion, and that man tried to run, but he was caught by the other men-at-arms and thrust into the open space where he fell to his knees and begged Joscelyn for mercy. "He wants mercy," Joscelyn called to the bishop. "Would you give it to him?"

"He deserves justice," the bishop said.

Joscelyn wiped his bloody sword on the skirts of his jerkin, then sheathed it and looked at Sir Henri Courtois. "Hang him," he ordered curtly.

"Lord . . ." the man began an appeal, but Joscelyn turned and kicked him in the mouth so hard that he dislocated the man's jaw and, when the man recovered his balance, Joscelyn raked his foot back, half tearing off an ear with his spur. Then, in an apparent paroxysm of rage, Jocelyn leaned down to haul the bleeding man upright. He held him at arm's length for a heartbeat and then, with all the strength of a man trained to the tournament, he threw him backwards. The man screamed as he tripped and fell into the fire. His clothes flared. The spectators gasped, some even looked away as the burning man tried to stagger free of the flames, but Joscelyn, risking being burned himself, thrust him back in. The man screamed again. His hair caught fire and blazed bright, he jerked in terrible spasms and then collapsed into the hottest part of the fire.

Joscelyn turned on the bishop. "Satisfied?" he asked, then walked away, brushing embers from his sleeves.

The bishop was not done. He caught up with Joscelyn in the great hall, which had now been stripped of its books and shelves, and where the new Count, thirsty after his exertions, was pouring himself red wine from a jug. Joscelyn turned a sour look on the bishop.

"The heretics," the Bishop said. "They are in Astarac."

"There are probably heretics everywhere," Joscelyn said carelessly.

"The girl who killed Father Roubert is there," the bishop insisted, "and the man who refused our orders to burn her."

Joscelyn remembered the golden-haired girl in the silver armor. "That girl," he said, interest in his voice, then he drained the cup and poured another. "How do you know they're there?" he asked.

"Michel was there. He was told by the monks."

"Ah yes," Joscelyn said, "Michel." He stalked towards his uncle's squire with murder in his eyes. "Michel," Joscelyn said, "who tells stories. Michel who runs to the bishop instead of coming to his new lord."

Michel hurriedly stepped back, but the bishop saved him by stepping in front of Joscelyn. "Michel serves me now," he said, "and to lay a hand on him is to attack the Church."

"So if I kill him, as he deserves," Joscelyn sneered, "you'll burn me, eh?" He spat towards Michel, then turned away. "So what do you want?" he asked the bishop.

"I want the heretics captured," the bishop said. He was nervous of this new and violent Count, but he forced himself to be brave. "I demand in the name of God and in the service of His Holy Church that you send men to find the beghard who was known as Genevieve and the Englishman who calls himself Thomas. I want them brought here. I want them burned."

"But not before I have talked with them." A new voice spoke, a voice as cutting as it was cold, and the Bishop and Joscelyn, indeed every man in the hall, turned to the door where a stranger had appeared.

Joscelyn had been aware, ever since he had stalked away from the courtyard, of the sound of hooves, but he had thought nothing of it. The castle had been loud with comings and goings all morning, but now he realized that strangers must have arrived in Berat and a half-dozen of them were now in the doorway of the hall. Their leader was the man who had spoken and he was taller even than Joscelyn, and spare, with a hard, long, sallow face that was framed with black hair. He was dressed all in black. Black boots, black breeches, black jerkin, black cloak, black broad-brimmed hat and a sword scabbard sheathed in black cloth. Even his spurs were made from black metal and Joscelyn, who had as much religion in his soul as an inquisitor possessed mercy, felt a sudden urge to make the sign of the cross. Then, when the man removed his hat, he recognized him. It was the Harlequin, the mysterious knight who had made so much money on the tournament fields of Europe, the one man Joscelyn had never beaten. "You're the Harlequin," Joscelyn said, accusation in his tone.

"I am sometimes known by that name," the man said, and the bishop and all his clergy made the sign of the cross for the name meant that this man was beloved by the devil. Then the tall man took another step forward and added, "But my real name, my lord, is Guy Vexille."

The name meant nothing to Joscelyn, but the bishop and his clergy all crossed themselves a second time and the bishop held out his staff as if to defend himself.

"And what the hell are you doing here?" Joscelyn demanded.

"I have come," Vexille said, "to bring light to the world."

And Joscelyn, fifteenth Count of Berat, shivered. He did not know why. He just knew he was frightened of the man called the Harlequin who had come to bring light to the darkness.

THE BONE-SETTER CLAIMED she could not do much, and whatever she did do caused Genevieve excruciating pain, but after it was done, and when her shoulder and left breast were soaked with new blood, Brother Clement gently cleaned her and then poured honey onto the wound, which he bound up with sacking again. The good thing was that Genevieve was suddenly ravenously hungry and she ate whatever Thomas brought her, though God knew that was little enough for his own raid on Astarac had left the village bereft of food and the monastery's supplies had been depleted to feed the villagers. Still, there was some cheese, pears, bread and honey, and Brother Clement made more mushroom soup. The lepers, clappers sounding, went into the woods to find the mushrooms that were served to all the monks. Twice a day some of them rattled their way around the back of the monastery and up a flight of steps into a bare stone room where a small window overlooked the altar of the abbey church. This was where they were permitted to worship and Thomas, on his second and third day after his talk with Abbot Planchard, went with them. He did not go willingly, for his excommunication meant he was no longer welcome in any church, but Brother Clement would pluck his arm insistently, then smile with genuine pleasure when Thomas indulged him.

Genevieve came with him on the day after the bone-setter had made her scream. She could walk well enough, though she was still weak and could scarcely move her left arm. Yet the arrow had missed her lungs and that, Thomas decided, was why she had lived. That and Brother Clement's care. "I thought I was going to die," she confessed to Thomas.

He remembered the coming plague. He had heard no more about it and, for the moment, he did not tell Genevieve. "You won't die," he told her, "but you must move the arm."

"I can't. It hurts."

"You must," he said. When his own arms and hands had been scarred by the torturer he had thought he would never use them again, but his friends, Robbie chief among them, had forced him to practice with the bow. It had seemed hopeless at first, yet little by little the ability had come back. He wondered where Robbie was now, whether he had stayed at Castillon d'Arbizon, and that thought frightened him. Would Robbie seek him here at Astarac? Had friendship really turned to hate? And if not Robbie, who else might come? The news of his presence in the monastery would spread in the unseen way such news always did, tales told in taverns, peddlers carrying the gossip from one village to the next, and soon enough someone in Berat would take notice. "We have to go soon," he told Genevieve.

"Where?"

"A long way away. England, perhaps?" He knew he had failed. He would not find the Grail here and, even if his cousin did come, how could Thomas defeat him? He was one man with only a wounded woman to help him and Guy Vexille travelled with a whole *conroi* of men-at-arms. The dream was over and it was time to go.

"I'm told it's cold in England," Genevieve said.

"The sun always shines," Thomas said gravely, "the harvest never fails and fish jump straight from the rivers into the frying pan."

Genevieve smiled. "Then you must teach me English."

"You know some already."

"I know goddamn," she said, "and I know goddamn bloody, bloody goddamn and Christ goddamn bloody help us."

Thomas laughed. "You've learned archers' English," he said, "but I'll teach you the rest."

He decided they would leave next day. He made a bundle of his arrows, then he cleaned the caked blood from Genevieve's coat of mail. He borrowed a pair of pincers from the monastery's carpenter and did his best to mend the mail where the crossbow bolt had pierced it, bending and closing the shattered links until at least they were crudely joined, though the rent was still obvious. He tethered the horses in the olive grove to let them graze and then, because it was still early in the afternoon, he walked south to the castle. He was determined to have one last glimpse of the stronghold where his ancestors had been lords.

He met Philin as he left the monastery. The *coredor* had brought his son from the infirmary and, with the boy's leg firmly splinted with a half-dozen of the chestnut stakes used to hold the monastery's vines, he had put him on a horse and was leading him southwards. "I don't want to stay here too long," he told Thomas. "I'm still wanted for murder."

"Planchard would give you sanctuary," Thomas insisted.

"He would," Philin agreed, "but that wouldn't stop my wife's family sending men to kill me. We're safer in the hills. His leg will mend there as well as anywhere. And if you're looking for refuge . . . ?"

"Me?" Thomas was surprised by the offer.

"We can always use a good archer."

"I think I'll go home. Home to England."

"God look after you anyway, my friend," Philin said, then he struck off to the west and Thomas walked south through the village where some of the folk made the sign of the cross which was evidence enough that they knew who he was, but none tried to take revenge on him for the harm his men had caused. They might have wanted such a revenge, but he was tall, strong and wearing a long sword at his belt. He climbed the path to the ruins and noticed that three men had followed him. He paused to face them, but they made no hostile move, just watched him from a safe distance.

It was a good place for a castle, Thomas thought. Certainly better than Castillon d'Arbizon. Astarac's stronghold was built on a crag and could only be approached by the narrow path he had climbed to the broken gate. Once past the gate the crag had originally been topped by a curtain wall encircling the courtyard, though that was now nothing more than heaps of mossy stone that were never higher than a man's waist. An oblong of broken walls with a semi-circular extension at their eastern end showed where the chapel had been and Thomas, walking the wide flagstones beneath which his ancestors were buried, saw that those stones had been disturbed recently. Raw marks betrayed where they had been prized up. He thought of trying to raise one of the flagstones himself, but knew he had neither the time nor the tools, and so he walked on to the western side of the crag where the old keep had stood, a broken tower now, hollow to the wind and rain. He turned when he reached the old tower and saw how his three followers had lost interest in him when he left the chapel. Were they there to guard something? The Grail? That thought seethed like a bolt of fire in his veins, but then he dismissed it. There was no Grail, he thought. It was his father's madness that had touched him with its hopeless dream.

A shattered stair was built into one flank of the tower and Thomas took it as far as he could climb, which was only to where the missing first floor had spanned the hollow shaft. There was a great gaping hole in the tower wall there, a wall that was over five feet thick, and Thomas could walk into the space. He stared down the valley, following the line of the stream with his eyes and he tried once more to feel some sense of belonging. He tried to snare the echoes of his ancestors, but there was nothing. He had felt emotion when he went back to Hookton, the little of it that remained, but here, nothing. And the thought that Hookton, like this castle, was in ruins made him wonder if there was a curse on the Vexilles. The country folk here claimed that *dragas*, the devil's women, left flowers where they walked, but did the Vexilles leave ruins? Maybe the Church was right after all. Maybe he deserved to be excommunicated. He turned to look west in the direction he must travel if he was to go home.

And saw the horsemen.

They were on the western ridge, way to the north of him, coming, he thought, from the direction of Berat. There was a large band of them, and they were soldiers right enough for what had caught his eye was the glint of light reflecting from a helmet or mail coat.

He stared, not wanting to believe what he saw, and then, coming to his senses, he ran. He went down the stairs, across the weed-thick courtyard, out through the ruined gate where he barged past the three men, and then down the path. He ran through the village and then northwards and he was out of breath by the time he banged on the gate of the lazar house. Brother Clement opened it and Thomas pushed past him. "Soldiers," he said in curt explanation, then he went into the hut and picked up his bow, the bundled arrows, their cloaks and mail and bags. "Come quick," he told Genevieve, who was carefully ladling some of Brother Clement's newly gathered honey into small jars. "Don't ask," he told her, "just come. Bring the saddles."

They went back outside to the olive grove, but Thomas, looking around, saw soldiers on the road in the valley north of St. Sever's. Those men were still some way off, but if they saw two people riding from the monastery they would be bound to follow, which meant there could be no escape now, just concealment. He hesitated, thinking.

"What is it?" Genevieve asked.

"Soldiers. Probably from Berat."

"There, too." She was looking south, towards the castle, and Thomas saw the villagers hurrying towards the monastery for refuge and that surely meant there were armed men approaching their houses.

He swore. "Leave the saddles," he told her and, when she had dropped them, he pulled her round the back of the monastery, following the lepers' path to the church. Someone had begun to toll the monastery bell to warn the brethren that armed strangers had come to their valley.

And Thomas knew why. Knew that if they were found they would both burn in the holy fire and so he ran into the lepers' part of the church and climbed the short flight of stairs to the window that overlooked the altar. He pushed his bow through, sent the arrows after it, then the rest of the baggage, and clambered up himself. It was a tight fit, but he squeezed through and dropped clumsily and painfully onto the flagstones. "Come on!" he urged Genevieve. People were coming into the church, thronging the door at the far end of the nave.

Genevieve hissed with pain as she scrambled through the small window. She looked frightened at the drop, but Thomas was beneath and he caught her. "This way." He picked up his bow and bags and led her down the side of the choir and then behind the side altar where the statue of St. Benedict stared sadly towards the frightened villagers.

The door in the alcove was locked as Thomas expected it to be, but they were hidden here and he did not think anyone had noticed them slip through the shadowed choir. He raised his right leg and kicked his heel against the lock. The noise was huge, a drum bang echoing in the church, and the door shook violently, but did not open. He kicked again, harder, then a third time and was rewarded by a splintering noise as the lock's tongue tore out the old wood of the frame. "Tread carefully," he warned her, and he led her down the stairs into the darkness of the bone house. He groped his way to the eastern end, where the arched niche was only half full of bones, and he threw his belongings to the back of the pile, then hoisted Genevieve up. "Go to the back," he told her, "and start digging."

He knew he could not climb up himself without spilling dozens of ribs and thigh bones and arm bones, and so he went along the cellar and pulled down stacks of bones. Skulls bounced and rolled, arms and legs clattered, and when the cellar was a mess of scattered skeletons he went back to Genevieve, scrambled up and helped her delve down into the old bones closest to the wall. They made a hole there, pulling the rib cages and pelvises and shoulder-blades apart, scrabbling ever deeper until at last they had made a deep, dark hiding place among the dead.

And there, in the blackness, cradled by the bones, they waited.

And heard the broken door squeal on its hinges. Saw the small flickering light of a lantern cast grotesque shadows on the arched ceiling.

And heard the mailed footsteps of the men who had come to find them, to take them and to kill them.

S IR HENRI COURTOIS was ordered to take thirty-three crossbowmen and forty-two men-at-arms to Castillon d'Arbizon
where he was to lay siege to the castle. Sir Henri accepted the orders
glumly. "I can lay siege," he told Joscelyn, "but I can't capture the castle. Not with that small force."

"The English managed it," Joscelyn said acidly.

"Your uncle's garrison was sleeping," Sir Henri said, "but Sir Guillaume d'Evecque will not be so obliging. He's got a reputation, a good
one." Sir Henri knew who commanded at Castillon d'Arbizon
because Robbie had told him, and had also told him how many men
were under Sir Guillaume's command.

Joscelyn jabbed a finger into the older man's chest. "I do not want
one more archer raiding my territory. Stop them. And give the bastards this." He handed Sir Henri a sealed parchment. "It gives them
two days to leave the castle," Joscelyn explained airily, "and if they
agree to its terms, you can let them go."

Sir Henri took the parchment, but paused before putting it in his
pouch. "And the ransom?" he asked.

Joscelyn glared at him, but honor decreed that Sir Guillaume
should receive a third of the money that had ransomed the new Count
and Sir Henri's question was therefore a proper one and so Joscelyn
answered it, but curtly. "The ransom's there," he said, nodding at the
parchment, "all there."

"It's here?" Sir Henri asked, astonished, for the message plainly
contained no coins.

"Just go!" Joscelyn snapped.

Sir Henri left the same day that Guy Vexille took his own men to
Astarac. Joscelyn was glad to see the back of the Harlequin, for Vex-

ille was an uncomfortable presence even though his men-at-arms were a welcome addition to the Count's forces. Vexille had brought forty-eight soldiers, all well mounted, well armored and well armed, and he had surprised Joscelyn by not demanding a single écu as payment. "I have my own funds," he had said coldly.

"Forty-eight men-at-arms?" Joscelyn wondered aloud. "That takes money."

"They were a heretic family, my lord," his uncle's old chaplain had maintained, as if that explained the Harlequin's wealth, but Vexille had come equipped with a letter from Louis Bessières, Cardinal Archbishop of Livorno, and that proved he was no heretic. Not that Joscelyn would have cared if Vexille worshiped wooden idols every night and sacrificed weeping virgins at each dawn. He was far more worried by the fact that the Vexilles had once been the lords of Astarac. He confronted Vexille with that, unable to hide his fear that the black-dressed knight had come to reclaim his ancestral lands.

The Harlequin had merely looked bored. "Astarac has been in your lordship's fief for a hundred years," he said, "so how could I hold that honor?"

"Then why are you here?" Joscelyn demanded.

"I fight for the Church now," Vexille said, "and my task is to hunt a fugitive who must be taken to justice. And when he is found, my lord, we shall leave your domain." He turned because a sword had just been drawn, the sound of the blade scraping on the scabbard's throat unnaturally loud in the great hall.

Robbie Douglas had just entered the room. He now pointed the drawn weapon at Vexille. "You were in Scotland," he said threateningly.

Vexille looked the young man up and down and seemed unworried by the blade. "I have visited many countries," he said coldly, "including Scotland."

"You killed my brother."

"No!" Joscelyn placed himself between the two men. "You swore my oath, Robbie."

"I swore an oath to kill that bastard!" Robbie said.

"No," Joscelyn said again, and he took Robbie's blade in his hand and forced it down. In truth Joscelyn would not have been upset if Robbie had died, but if Guy Vexille was killed his black-cloaked men-at-arms might take vengeance on Joscelyn and his men. "You can kill him when he's finished here. That is a promise."

Vexille smiled at the promise. He and his men left next morning, and Joscelyn was pleased to be rid of them. It was not just Guy Vexille he found chilling, but also his companions, especially the one who did not carry a lance or shield. His name was Charles, a man of startling ugliness, who looked as though he had been plucked from some dark gutter, brushed down, given a knife and released to spread fear. Charles led his own smaller band of a dozen men-at-arms who all rode with Vexille when he went south to Astarac.

So Sir Henri had gone to rid the county of the impudent English garrison at Castillon d'Arbizon and Vexille was hunting his heretic in Astarac, which left Joscelyn free to enjoy his inheritance in Berat. Robbie Douglas was one of his many companions, and for the next few days they simply enjoyed themselves. There was money to be spent on clothes, weapons, horses, wine, women, anything that caught Joscelyn's fancy, but some things could not be purchased in Berat itself and so a craftsman was summoned to the castle. The man's usual job was making plaster saints that were sold to churches, convents, and monasteries, but his task in the castle was to make casts of Joscelyn's body. He wrapped the Count's arms in greased muslin, coated them with plaster, then did the same for Joscelyn's legs and trunk. A tailor had also been summoned and he made measurements of the Count's body that were noted down by a clerk. So many inches from shoulder to hip bone, from hip bone to knee, from shoulder to elbow, and when the measurements were taken they were copied onto a parchment and sealed in a great box in which the plaster casts were packed in sawdust, and the box was dispatched under the guard of four men-at-arms to Milan where Antonio Givani, the finest armorer in Christendom, was commanded to make a complete set of plate armor. "Let it be a masterpiece," Joscelyn dictated the letter to a clerk, "the envy of all other knights," and he sent a generous payment in genoins with a promise of many more if the armor arrived before spring.

He had paid Robbie his ransom in the same coins, but on the night that the men-at-arms left for Turin, Robbie was foolish enough to admire a set of ivory dice that Joscelyn had purchased in the town. "You like them?" Joscelyn asked. "I'll roll you for them. Highest number keeps the dice."

Robbie shook his head. "I've sworn an oath to keep from gambling," he explained.

Joscelyn thought that the funniest thing he had heard in months. "Women make oaths," he said, "and monks have to, but warriors only make oaths of brotherhood for battle."

Robbie blushed. "I promised a priest," he said.

"Oh, sweet Jesus!" Joscelyn leaned back in his chair. "You can't face risk, is that it? Is that why the Scots lose to the English?" Robbie's temper flared, but he had the sense to curb it and said nothing. "Risk," Joscelyn said airily, "is the soldier's fate. If a man can't abide risk he can't be a soldier."

"I'm a soldier," Robbie said flatly.

"Then prove it, my friend," Joscelyn said, rolling the dice across the table.

So Robbie played and lost. And lost the next night. And the next. And on the fourth night he gambled the money that was supposed to be sent to England to purchase his ransom and he lost that too, and next day Joscelyn heard that the Italian gunners, whom his uncle had summoned from Toulouse, had come to the castle with their machine and Joscelyn paid them their fee out of the money he had won from

Robbie. "How soon can you go to Castillon d'Arbizon?" he demanded of the Italians.

"Tomorrow, sire?"

"The thing is ready?" Joscelyn asked, walking round the wagon on which the gun, shaped like a flask with a narrow neck and a bulbous body, was lashed.

"It's ready," the Italian, whose name was Gioberti, confirmed.

"You have powder?"

Gioberti gestured at the second wagon, loaded perilously high with kegs.

"And missiles? Balls?"

"Bolts, my lord," Gioberti corrected him, and pointed at yet another wagon. "We have more than enough."

"Then we shall all go!" Joscelyn said enthusiastically. He was fascinated by the cannon, a thing as ugly as it was impressive. It was nine feet long, four feet across the bulbous breech, and had a squat, evil air. It looked devilish, an unnatural thing, and he was tempted to demand a demonstration right there in the castle's courtyard, but he understood that such a demonstration would take precious time. Better to watch the device in action against the stubborn fools in Castillon d'Arbizon.

Sir Henri Courtois was already beginning that siege. When he reached the town he left his crossbowmen and men-at-arms outside the western gate and rode to the castle with only a young priest for company. He called up to the sentinels on the wall and, when Sir Guillaume saw it was only a single man-at-arms and a priest who wanted entrance he gave permission for the gates to be opened.

Sir Guillaume met the two men in the courtyard where Sir Henri dismounted and named himself. Sir Guillaume returned the courtesy, then the two men sized each other up. Each recognized the other as a soldier like himself. "I come from the Count of Berat," Sir Henri said formally.

"Bring the money, did you?" Sir Guillaume demanded.

"I brought what I was ordered to bring and I doubt it will make you happy," Sir Henri said, then he took a long professional look at the archers and men-at-arms who had come to see the visitors. Tough bastards, he thought, before looking back to Sir Guillaume. "I'm tired," he said. "Been riding all day. Do you have any wine in this place?"

"Berat's short of wine, is he?" Sir Guillaume asked.

"He's short of sense," Sir Henri said, "but not of wine."

Sir Guillaume smiled. "Inside," he said, then led his guest up the keep stairs to the upper hall and, because this conversation would affect the destiny of all the garrison, he allowed those men who were not on guard to follow and listen.

Sir Guillaume and Sir Henri sat either side of the long table. The priest, who was there as a token that Sir Henri meant no harm, sat as well, while the men-at-arms and archers stood against the wall. The fire was revived, wine and food served, and as that was being done Sir Henri unlooped the shield from about his neck, unbuckled his breastplate and backplate and laid them all on the floor. He stretched, then nodded thanks for the wine which he drained. Finally he took the sealed parchment from his pouch and pushed it across the table.

Sir Guillaume lifted the seal with his knife, unfolded the document and read it. He did so slowly, for he was not a good reader, and when he had read it twice he looked angrily at Sir Henri. "What the hell does this mean?"

"I've not seen it," Sir Henri confessed. "May I?" He reached for the parchment and the watching men of the garrison made a low threatening noise, sensing Sir Guillaume's fury.

Sir Henri could not read so he gave the parchment to the priest who tilted it towards one of the high narrow windows. The priest was a very young man and nervous. He read it, glanced at the horribly scarred Sir Guillaume and looked even more nervous.

"Tell us what it says," Sir Henri said. "No one's going to kill you."

"It says two things," the priest said. "That Sir Guillaume and his men have two days to leave Castillon d'Arbizon unmolested."

"The other thing," Sir Guillaume snarled.

The priest frowned. "It is a draft of money from a man called Robert Douglas," he explained to Sir Henri, "and if Sir Guillaume presents it to Jacques Fournier then he will be paid six thousand, six hundred and sixty florins." He put the document onto the table as though it was smeared with poison.

"Who, in Christ's name," Sir Guillaume asked, "is Jacques Fournier?"

"A goldsmith in Berat," Sir Henri explained, "and I doubt Jacques has that much cash in his cellars."

"Robbie arranged this?" Sir Guillaume asked angrily.

"Robbie Douglas is sworn to the Lord of Berat now," Sir Henri said. He had watched the brief ceremony when Robbie had sworn his allegiance, he had seen the kisses exchanged and noticed the look of triumph on Joscelyn's face. "This is my lord's doing."

"He thinks we're fools?"

"He thinks you won't dare show your faces in Berat," Sir Henri said.

"Cheated! Jesus Christ! We've been cheated!" Sir Guillaume glared at his visitors. "Is this what passes for honor in Berat?" he demanded, and when Sir Henri offered no answer, Sir Guillaume thumped the table. "I could hold you two prisoner!" The men around the walls growled their agreement.

"You could," Sir Henri agreed equably, "and I wouldn't blame you. But the Count won't ransom me and he certainly won't ransom *him*." He nodded at the timid priest. "We'll just be two more mouths to feed."

"Or two more corpses to bury," Sir Guillaume retorted.

Sir Henri shrugged. He knew that the offer of money from the goldsmith's cellars was dishonorable, but it was not of his doing.

"So you can tell your master," Sir Guillaume said, "that we'll leave this castle when we have six thousand, six hundred and sixty florins. And every week you make us wait the price goes up by another hundred."

His men murmured approval. Sir Henri did not seem surprised by the decision. "I'm here," he told Sir Guillaume, "to make sure you don't leave. Unless you wish to go today or tomorrow?"

"We stay," Sir Guillaume said. It was not a decision he had thought about, and he might have chosen differently had he been given the time to think, but being cheated of money was a sure way to rouse his pugnacity. "We stay, damn it!"

Sir Henri nodded. "Then I stay also." He pushed the parchment across the table. "I'll send a message to my lord and tell him that it would be sensible for young Douglas to pay the coins, that it will save money and lives if he does."

Sir Guillaume took the parchment and thrust it into his jerkin. "You're staying?" he asked. "Where?"

Sir Henri looked at the men against the wall. These were not men he could surprise by a sudden escalade. Besides, Sir Henri's own men were mostly the forces of the old Count and they had grown lazy, no match for this garrison. "You can hold the castle," he told Sir Guillaume, "but you don't have enough men to garrison the two town gates. You're leaving that to the constables and watchmen. So I'll take over from them. You can always fight your way through, of course, but I'll have crossbowmen on the gate towers and men-at-arms under the arches."

"You've faced English bowmen?" Sir Guillaume asked threateningly.

Sir Henri nodded. "In Flanders," he said, "and I didn't enjoy it. But how many archers can you afford to lose in a street brawl?"

Sir Guillaume acknowledged the sense of that. Send his archers against the town gates and they would be fighting at close quarters, shooting up from gardens, yards and windows, and Sir Henri's crossbowmen would be crouched behind their pavises or behind windows in the houses and some of their quarrels would be bound to hit. In a few minutes Sir Guillaume could lose four or five bowmen and that would seriously weaken him. "You can have the town gates," he allowed.

Sir Henri poured himself more wine. "I've got forty-two men-at-arms," he revealed, "and thirty-three crossbows, and all the usual servants and women and clerks. They all need shelter. Winter's coming."

"So freeze," Sir Guillaume suggested.

"We could do that," Sir Henri agreed, "but I propose you let us use the houses between the west gate and St. Callic's church, and I'll guarantee we won't use any building east of Wheelwright's Alley or south of Steep Street."

"You know the town?" Sir Guillaume asked.

"I was castellan here once. Long time ago."

"Then you know about the mill gate?" Sir Guillaume was referring to the small door in the town wall that led to the water mill, the gate that Thomas and Genevieve had used to escape.

"I know about it," Sir Henri said, "but it's too close to the castle and if I put men to guard it then your archers can skewer them from the tower's top." He paused to drink the wine. "If you want me to besiege you, I can. I'll close my men up to the castle and let the crossbows practice on your sentries, but you know and I know that we'll only kill men and you'll still be inside. I assume you have food?"

"More than enough."

Sir Henri nodded. "So I'll stop your horsemen leaving by the two big gates. You can still slip men out of the mill gate, but so long as they don't interfere with me, I'll not notice them. You've got nets in the mill pond?"

"We do."

"I'll leave them alone," Sir Henri offered. "I'll tell my men the mill's out of bounds to them."

Sir Guillaume thought about it, drumming his fingers on the table's edge. There was a continual small murmur from the men against the wall as the French conversation was translated into English. "You can have the houses between the west gate and St. Callic's church," Sir Guillaume agreed after a moment, "but what about the taverns?"

"Essential things," Sir Henri acknowledged.

"My men like the Three Cranes."

"It's a good house," Sir Henri said.

"So your men stay away from it," Sir Guillaume demanded.

"Agreed, but they can use the Bear and Butcher?"

"Agreed," Sir Guillaume said, "but we'd also better insist now that no man can carry swords or bows to either."

"Knives only," Sir Henri said, "that's sensible." Neither man wanted drunken soldiers conducting wild forays in the night. "And if any problems crop up," Sir Henri added, "I'll come and talk to you." He paused, frowning as he tried to remember something. "You were in Flanders, weren't you? With the Count of Coutances?"

"I was in Flanders," Sir Guillaume confirmed, "with that spavined, gutless bastard." The Count, his liege lord, had treacherously turned against him and taken his land.

"They're all bastards," Sir Henri said. "But the old Count of Berat wasn't bad. He was mean, of course, and spent his life poking into books. Books! What use are they? He knew every book in Christendom, he did, and had read most of them twice, but he didn't have the sense of a chicken! You know what he was doing in Astarac?"

"Looking for the Holy Grail?" Sir Guillaume asked.

"Exactly," Sir Henri said and both men laughed. "Your friend's there now," Sir Henri added.

"Robbie Douglas?" Sir Guillaume asked coldly. He had no love for Robbie now.

"Not him, he's at Berat. No, the archer and his heretic woman."

"Thomas?" Sir Guillaume could not hide his surprise. "At Astarac? I told him to go home."

"Well, he didn't," Sir Henri said. "He's in Astarac. Why didn't he just burn the girl?"

"He's in love."

"With the heretic? So he's a prick-for-brains, is he? He won't have either soon."

"He won't?"

"Some bastard's come from Paris. Got a small army. Gone to catch him, which means there'll be fires in Berat's marketplace before long. You know what a priest told me once? That women burn brighter then men. Strange that." Sir Henri pushed his chair back and stood. "So we're agreed?"

"We're agreed," Sir Guillaume said and leaned over the table to shake the other man's hand. Then Sir Henri picked up his armor and shield and beckoned the priest to follow him to the courtyard where he gazed up at the sky. "Looks like rain."

"Get your armor under cover," Sir Guillaume advised, knowing the advice was not needed.

"And light some fires, eh? Coldest autumn I can remember here."

Sir Henri went. The gates slammed shut and Sir Guillaume climbed laboriously to the top of the castle keep. But he was not looking to watch where his amenable enemy was going, but east towards unseen Astarac, and wondering what he could do to help Thomas.

Nothing, he thought, nothing. And doubtless, he reckoned, the bastard from Paris was Guy Vexille, the man called the Harlequin, who had once given Sir Guillaume three wounds. Three wounds needing vengeance, but Sir Guillaume could do nothing now. For he was besieged and Thomas, he reckoned, was doomed.

CHARLES BESSIÈRES AND A HALF-DOZEN of his men went to the ossuary beneath the abbey church in search of plunder. One carried a burning candle and, by its uncertain light, they began hauling down the serried bones, evidently expecting to discover treasure, though all they revealed were more bones, but then one of them discovered the small chamber at the vault's western end and shouted in triumph because it contained the big iron-bound chest. One of the men forced the chest's lock with his sword and Bessières seized the silver paten and the candlestick. "Is that all?" he asked, disappointed. Another of his men found the grail box, but none of them could read and even if they could they would not have understood the Latin inscription and when they saw the box was empty they hurled it back down the vault to fall among the scattered bones. Charles Bessières then picked up the leather bag that supposedly contained St. Agnes's girdle. He swore when he found it contained nothing but a length of embroidered linen, but the bag was big enough to hold the plundered silver. "They've hidden their wealth," Bessières said.

"Or they're poor," one of his men suggested.

"They're bloody monks! Of course they're rich." Bessières hung the bag of silver at his waist. "Go and find their damned abbot," he told two of his men, "and we'll beat the truth out of the bastard."

"You will do nothing of the sort." A new voice spoke and the men in the treasury chamber turned to see that Guy Vexille had come down to the ossuary. He was holding a lantern and its light glinted dark from his black-lacquered plate armor. He held the lantern high and looked at the tumbled bones. "Have you no respect for the dead?"

"Fetch the abbot." Charles Bessières ignored Vexille's question and spoke to his men instead. "Bring him here."

"I have already sent for the abbot," Vexille said, "and you will not beat any truth from him."

"You don't command me," Bessières bridled.

"But I command my sword," Vexille said calmly, "and if you cross me then I shall slit your belly open and spill your foul guts to feed the worms. You are here merely as your brother's watchman, nothing else, but if you wish to do something useful then go to the lazar house and search it for the Englishman. But don't kill him! Bring him to me. And put that silver back where you found it." He nodded at the neck of the candlestick that protruded from the leather bag at Bessières's waist.

Vexille was alone and facing seven men, but such was his confidence that none thought to oppose him. Even Charles Bessières, who feared few men, meekly put the silver down. "But I'm not leaving this valley empty-handed," he growled as a parting defiance.

"I trust, Bessières," Vexille said, "that we shall leave this valley with the greatest treasure of Christendom in our keeping. Now go."

Vexille grimaced when the men went. He put the lantern on the floor and started putting the bones back in their alcoves, but he stopped when footsteps sounded on the steps. He turned then and watched as Planchard, tall and white-robed, came down to the ossuary.

"I apologize for this," Vexille said, indicating the bones. "They were ordered to leave the abbey untouched."

Planchard said nothing about the desecration; he just made the sign of the cross and then stooped to retrieve the bag of silver. "This passes for our treasury," he said, "but we have never been a wealthy house. Still, you are welcome to steal these poor things."

"I did not come here to steal," Vexille said.

"Then why are you here?" Planchard demanded.

Vexille ignored the question. "My name," he said instead, "is Guy Vexille, Count of Astarac."

"So your men told me," Planchard said, "when they summoned me to your presence." He said the last words calmly as if to suggest he took no offense at such an indignity. "But I think I would have recognized you anyway."

"You would?" Vexille sounded surprised.

"Your cousin was here. A young Englishman." The abbot carried the silver back to the chest, then rescued the strip of linen, which he kissed reverently. "The two of you," he went on, "bear a remarkable resemblance to each other."

"Except he's bastard born," Vexille said angrily, "and a heretic."

"And you are neither?" Planchard asked calmly.

"I serve Cardinal Archbishop Bessières," Vexille said, "and His Eminence sent me here to find my cousin. Do you know where he is?"

"No," Planchard said. He sat down on the bench and took a small string of prayer beads from a pocket of his white gown.

"He was here though?"

"Certainly he was here last night," Planchard said, "but where he is now?" The abbot shrugged. "I advised him to leave. I knew men would come searching for him, if only for the pleasure of watching him burn, so I told him to hide himself. I would suggest that he is gone to the woods and your search will be difficult."

"It was your duty," Vexille said harshly, "to give him to the Church."

"I have always tried to do my duty to the Church," Planchard said, "and sometimes I have failed, but doubtless God will punish me for those failings."

"Why was he here?" Vexille asked.

"I think you know that, my lord," Planchard said, and there was, perhaps, a hint of mockery in the last two words.

"The Grail," Vexille said. Planchard said nothing. He just counted his prayer beads, running them through his thumb and forefinger as he looked at the tall young man in black armor. "The Grail was here," Vexille said.

"Was it?" Planchard asked.

"It was brought here," Vexille insisted.

"I know nothing of it," Planchard said.

"I think you do," Vexille retorted. "It was brought here before the fall of Montségur, brought here to keep it safe. But then the French crusaders came to Astarac and the Grail was taken away again."

Planchard smiled. "This all happened before I was born. How would I know of it?"

"Seven men took the grail away," Vexille said.

"The seven dark lords," Planchard said, smiling. "I have heard that story."

"Two of them were Vexilles," Guy Vexille said, "and four of them were knights who had fought for the Cathars."

"Seven men fleeing the forces of France and the Church's crusaders," Planchard said musingly, "into a Christendom that hated them. I doubt they survived."

"And the seventh man," Vexille ignored the abbot's words, "was the Lord of Mouthoumet."

"Which was always an insignificant fief," Planchard said dismissively, "scarce able to support two knights from its mountain pastures."

"The Lord of Mouthoumet," Vexille went on, "was a heretic." He turned suddenly for a noise had come from deep in the ossuary. It had sounded something like a stifled sneeze and was followed by a rattle of bones. He lifted the lantern and walked back to where the arches had been desecrated.

"There are rats here," Planchard said. "The abbey's drains cross the end of the vault and we believe some of the brickwork has collapsed. You often hear strange noises down here. Some of the more superstitious brethren believe they are made by ghosts."

Vexille was standing among the bones, the lantern held high, listening. He heard nothing more and so turned back to the abbot. "The Lord of Mouthoumet," he said, "was one of the seven. And his name was Planchard." Vexille paused. "My lord," he added mockingly.

Planchard smiled. "He was my grandfather. He did not ride with the others, but went to Toulouse and threw himself on the mercy of the Church. He was lucky, I think, not to be burned, but he was reconciled with the true faith even though it cost him his fief, his title and what passed for his fortune. He died in a monastery. The tale was told in our family, of course it was, but we never saw the Grail and I can assure you that I know nothing of it."

"Yet you are here," Guy Vexille accused the abbot harshly.

"True," Planchard acknowledged. "And I am here by design. I first entered this house as a young man and I came here because the tales of the dark lords intrigued me. One of them was supposed to have taken the Grail, and the others were sworn to protect him, but my grandfather claimed he never saw the cup. Indeed, he thought it did not exist, but was merely invented to tantalize the Church. The crusaders had destroyed the Cathars and the revenge of the dark lords was to make them think they had destroyed the Grail along with the heresy. That, I think, is the devil's work."

"So you came here," Vexille asked scornfully, "because you did not believe the Grail existed?"

"No, I came here because if ever the descendants of the dark lords were to seek the Grail then they would come here, I knew that, and I wanted to see what would happen. But that curiosity died long ago. God gave me many years, He was pleased to make me abbot, and He has enfolded me in His mercy. And the Grail? I confess I searched for memories of it when I first came here, and my abbot chided me for that, but God brought me to my senses. I now think my grandfather was right and that it is a tale invented to spite the Church and a mystery to make men mad."

"It existed," Vexille said.

"Then I pray to God that I find it," Planchard said, "and when I do I shall hide it in the deepest ocean so that no more folk will ever die in its pursuit. But what would you do with the Grail, Guy Vexille?"

"Use it," Vexille said harshly.

"For what?"

"To cleanse the world of sin."

"That would be a great work," Planchard said, "but even Christ could not achieve it."

"Do you abandon weeding between the vines simply because the weeds always grow back?" Vexille asked.

"No, of course not."

"Then Christ's work must go on," Vexille said.

The abbot watched the soldier for a time. "You are Christ's instrument? Or Cardinal Bessières's tool?"

Vexille grimaced. "The Cardinal is like the Church, Planchard. Cruel, corrupt and evil."

Planchard did not contradict him. "So?"

"So a new Church is needed. A clean Church, a sinless Church, a Church filled with honest men who live in God's fear. The Grail will bring that."

Planchard smiled. "The Cardinal, I am sure, would not approve."

"The Cardinal sent his brother here," Vexille said, "and doubtless he has orders to kill me when I have been useful."

"And your usefulness is what?"

"To find the Grail. And to do that I must first find my cousin."

"You think he knows where it is?"

"I think his father possessed it," Guy Vexille said, "and I think the son knows of it."

"He thinks the same of you," Planchard said. "And I think the two of you are like blind men who each thinks the other can see."

Vexille laughed at that. "Thomas," he said, "is a fool. He brought men to Gascony for what? To find the Grail? Or to find me? But he failed and now he's a fugitive. A good few of his men have pledged their allegiance to the Count of Berat and the rest are trapped at Castillon d'Arbizon and how long will they last? Two months? He has failed, Planchard, failed. He might be blind, but I see, and I will have him and I will take what he knows. But what do you know?"

"I have told you. Nothing."

Vexille paced back to the chamber and stared at the abbot. "I could put you to the torture, old man."

"You could," Planchard agreed mildly, "and I would doubtless scream to be spared the torment, but you will find no more truth in those screams than I have told you willingly here." He tucked his beads away and stood to his full height. "And I would beg you in the name of Christ to spare this community. It knows nothing of the Grail, it can tell you nothing, and it can give you nothing."

"And I will spare nothing," Vexille said, "in the service of God. Nothing." He drew his sword. Planchard watched expressionless, and did not even flinch as the sword was pointed at him. "Swear on this," Vexille said, "that you know nothing of the Grail."

"I have told you all I know," Planchard said and, instead of touching the sword, he raised the wooden crucifix that hung about his neck, and kissed it. "I will not swear on your sword, but I do make oath on my dear Lord's cross that I know nothing of the Grail."

"But your family still betrayed us," Vexille said.

"Betrayed you?"

"Your grandfather was one of the seven. He recanted."

"So he betrayed you? By cleaving to the true faith?" Planchard frowned. "Are you telling me you keep the Cathar heresy, Guy Vexille?"

"We come to bring light to the world," Vexille said, "and to purge it of the Church's foulness. I have kept the faith, Planchard."

"Then you are the only man who has," Planchard said, "and it is an heretical faith."

"They crucified Christ for heresy," Vexille said, "so to be named a heretic is to be one with Him." Then he rammed the blade forward, into the base of Planchard's throat, and the old man, amazingly, did not appear to put up any struggle, but just clutched his crucifix as the blood surged from his throat to turn his white robe red. He took a long time to die, but eventually he slumped over and Vexille withdrew his sword and wiped the blade clean on the hem of the abbot's robe. He sheathed the blade and picked up the lantern.

He glanced about the ossuary, but saw nothing to worry him and so he climbed the stairs. The door shut, cutting off all light. And Thomas and Genevieve, hidden in the dark, waited.

*   *   *

THEY WAITED ALL NIGHT. It seemed to Thomas he did not sleep at all, but he must have dozed for he woke once when Genevieve sneezed. Her wound was hurting, but she said nothing of it, just waited and half slept.

They had no idea when morning came for it was pitch dark in the ossuary. They had heard nothing all night. No footsteps, no screams, no chanted prayers, just the silence of the tomb. And still they waited until Thomas could abide the wait no longer and he wriggled out of their hole, across the bones and down to the floor. Genevieve stayed where she was as Thomas felt his way through the scattered bones to the stairs. He crept up, listened at the top for a while, heard nothing and so eased the broken door open.

The abbey church was empty. He knew it was morning for the light came from the east, but it was hard to tell how high the sun had risen for the light was soft-edged, diffuse, and Thomas guessed there was a morning fog.

He went back down to the ossuary. He kicked something wooden as he crossed the floor and he stooped to find the empty grail box. For a moment he was tempted to return it to its chest, then he decided to keep it. It would just fit into his bag, he reckoned. "Genevieve!" he called softly. "Come."

She pushed their bags, his bow and the arrows, the mail and their cloaks across the bones, then followed, wincing at the pain in her shoulder. Thomas had to help her put on the mail and he hurt her when he lifted her arm. He put on his own, draped the cloaks about their shoulders, then strung his bow so he could wear it on his back. He belted his sword in place, put the box in his bag, which he hung from his belt, and then, carrying the arrow sheaves, turned to the stairs and saw, because just enough light spilled from the open door, the white robe in the treasury chamber. He motioned Genevieve to stay where she was and crept up the vault. Rats scampered away as he came to the low arch and there he stopped and stared. Planchard was dead.

"What is it?" Genevieve asked.

"The bastard killed him," Thomas said in astonishment.

"Who?"

"The abbot!" He spoke in a whisper and, though he was excommunicated, he made the sign of the cross. "He killed him!" He had listened to the end of Vexille and Planchard's conversation and had been puzzled that the abbot fell silent, and equally puzzled that he had only heard one set of feet climb the stairs, but he had never imagined this. Never. "He was a good man," he said.

"And if he's dead," Genevieve said, "they'll blame us. So come on! Come!"

Thomas hated to leave the bloody corpse in the cellar, but knew he had no choice. And Genevieve was right, they would be blamed. Planchard had died because his grandfather had recanted a heresy, but no one would believe that, not when two condemned heretics were there to blame.

He led her up the stairs. The church was still empty, but now Thomas thought he could hear voices beyond the open western door. There was a fog outside and some of it was spilling into the nave and spreading gently across the flagstones. He thought of going back to the ossuary and hiding again, then wondered whether his cousin would make a more thorough search of the whole monastery today and that decided him to keep going. "This way." He took Genevieve's hand and led her to the southern side of the church where a door led to the inner cloister. It was the door the monks used when they came for prayers, a devotion that had evidently been denied them this morning.

Thomas pushed the door, flinching when its hinges creaked, and peered through. At first he thought the cloister, like the church, was empty; then he saw a group of black-cloaked men at its far side. They were standing at a doorway, evidently listening to someone inside, and none looked round as Thomas and Genevieve flitted under the shadowed arcade and chose a door at random. It opened onto a corridor and at its end they found themselves in the monastery kitchen where two monks were stirring a vast cauldron above a fire. One of them saw Genevieve and looked as if he was about to protest at a woman's presence, but Thomas hissed at him to be silent. "Where are the other monks?" Thomas asked.

"In their cells," the frightened cook replied, then watched as the two of them ran across the kitchen, past the table with its cleavers and spoons and bowls and beneath the hooks where two goat carcasses hung, and disappeared out of the far door, which led into the olive grove where Thomas had abandoned their horses. Those horses were gone.

The gate to the lazar house was open. Thomas glanced at it, then turned westwards, but Genevieve plucked at his cloak and pointed through the fog and Thomas saw a black-cloaked rider beyond the trees. Was the man part of a cordon? Had Vexille placed men all about the monastery? It seemed likely and it seemed even more likely that the horseman would turn and see them, or that the two kitchen monks might raise the alarm, but then Genevieve plucked his cloak again and led him across the olive grove and into the lazar house.

It was empty. All men feared lepers and it seemed to Thomas that Vexille must have driven them away so his men could search the sheds. "We can't hide here," he whispered to Genevieve. "They'll search again."

"We don't hide," she said, and she went into the biggest shed and came out with two gray robes. Thomas understood then. He helped drape one robe over Genevieve, pulling its hood over her golden hair, donned the other and then took two clappers from the handful left on the table. Genevieve, meanwhile, had put the arrow sheaves and Thomas's bow on a sledge that the lepers used to gather firewood and Thomas heaped some of the firewood over the weapons and put the sledge's looped rope over his shoulders. "Now we go," Genevieve said.

Thomas hauled the sledge, which ran easily on the damp ground. Genevieve went ahead and, once out of the gate, she turned north and west, hoping to avoid the horseman. The fog was their ally, a gray cloak in which their own cloaks melded. A tongue of woodland reached from the western ridge and Genevieve walked towards it, not sounding the clapper, but just watching. She hissed once and Thomas went still. A horse's hooves sounded; he heard them go away, and he hauled on. He turned after a while and saw that the monastery had vanished. The trees ahead were gaunt black shapes in the vapor. They were following a track that the lepers used when they went to gather mushrooms from the woods. The trees came closer, then the thud of hooves sounded once more and Genevieve rattled her clapper in warning.

But the horseman was not deterred. He came from behind them and Thomas shook his own clapper as he turned. He kept his head low so his face would not be seen under the robe's hood. He saw the horse's legs, but not the rider. "Mercy, kind sir," he said, "mercy."

Genevieve reached out her hands as if seeking charity, and the scars on her skin left by Father Roubert looked grotesque. Thomas did the same, revealing his own scars, the skin white and ridged. "Alms," he said, "of your kindness, sir, alms."

The unseen horseman stared at them and they dropped to their knees. The horse's breath came as great clouds of thicker fog. "Have pity on us." Genevieve spoke in the local tongue, using a rasping voice. "For God's sake, have pity."

The horseman just sat there and Thomas dared not look up. He felt the abject fear of a defenseless man at the mercy of a mailed rider, but he also knew that the man was torn by indecision. He had doubtless been ordered to look for two people escaping the monastery, and he had found just such a couple, but they appeared to be lepers and his fear of leprosy was fighting with his duty. Then, suddenly, more clappers sounded and Thomas sneaked a look behind him to see a group of gray-shrouded figures coming from the trees, sounding their warnings and calling out for alms. The sight of more lepers, coming to join the first two, was more than the horseman could take. He spat at them, then wrenched his reins to turn away. Thomas and Genevieve waited, still on their knees, until the man was half cloaked in the fog and then they hurried on to the trees where at last they could throw down the clappers, strip off the stinking gray robes and retrieve the bow and arrow sheaves. The other lepers, driven from their refuge at the monastery, just stared at them. Thomas took a handful of coins from those Sir Guillaume had given him and left them on the grass. "You have not seen us," he said to them, and Genevieve repeated the words in the local language.

They walked on west, climbing out of the fog, keeping to the trees until there were no more woods, only a rocky slope going up to the ridge. They scrambled up, trying to stay behind boulders or in gullies, while behind them the fog burned off the valley. The roof of the abbey church appeared first, then the other roofs, and by mid-morning the whole monastery was visible, but Thomas and Genevieve were already on the crest, going south. If they had kept going westwards they would descend into the valley of the River Gers where the villages lay thick, while to the south was emptier, wilder country and that was where they were headed.

At midday they stopped to rest. "We have no food," Thomas said.

"Then we go hungry," Genevieve said. She smiled at him. "And where are we going?"

"Castillon d'Arbizon," Thomas said, "eventually."

"Going back there!" She was surprised. "But they threw us out: why would they take us back?"

"Because they need us," Thomas said. He did not know that, not for sure, but he had listened to Vexille talking to Planchard and had learned that some of the garrison had gone over to the Count of Berat, and he reckoned Robbie must have led that group. He could not imagine Sir Guillaume breaking his allegiance to the Earl of Northampton, but Robbie had no allegiance outside of Scotland. It was Thomas's guess that the men left at Castillon d'Arbizon were his own men, the men he had recruited outside Calais, the Englishmen. So he would go there, and if he found the castle slighted and the garrison dead then he would go on, ever westwards, until he reached the English possessions.

But first they would go southwards for that was where the great woods stretched in folds across the ridges running out of the mountains. He picked up his baggage and, as he did, the grail box, which had been stuffed into his archer's bag on top of the spare arrow heads, sharpening stone and cords, fell out. He sat again and picked up the box. "What is it?" Genevieve asked.

"Planchard believed it was the box that held the Grail," he told her, "or maybe the box that was supposed to make men think it had held the Grail." He stared at the fading inscription. Now that he could see the box properly, in the sunlight, he saw that the lettering had been in red and that where the paint had been rubbed away there was still a faint impression on the wood. There was another faint impression inside the box, a circle of dust that had been forced into the wood as if something had rested there a long time. The two iron hinges were rusted and fragile, and the wood so dry that it weighed almost nothing.

"Is it real?" Genevieve asked.

"It's real," Thomas said, "but whether it ever held the Grail, I don't know." And he thought how often he had said those last three words whenever he talked about the Grail.

Yet he knew more now. He knew that seven men had fled Astarac in the previous century, back when the forces of France, wearing the crusaders' cross, had come to burn a heresy from the southland. The men had fled, claiming to take a treasure, and they had pledged to defend it, and now, so many years later, only Guy Vexille had kept the twisted faith. And had Thomas's father really possessed the Grail? That was why Guy Vexille had gone to Hookton and murdered his way through the village, just as he had now murdered Planchard. The descendants of the dark lords were being purged for betraying the trust, and Thomas knew exactly what would happen to him if his cousin caught him.

"It's a strange shape for a Grail," Genevieve said. The box was shallow and square, not tall as though a stemmed cup had once been stored in it.

"Who knows what the Grail looks like?" Thomas asked, and then he put the box into his haversack and they walked on southwards. Thomas constantly glanced behind and around mid-afternoon he saw dark-cloaked men riding up to the ridge from the monastery. There were a dozen of them and he guessed they would use the ridge as a lookout. Guy Vexille must have searched the monastery again and found nothing so now he was spreading his net wider.

They hurried. As evening approached they were in sight of the jumbled rocks where Genevieve had been wounded; the woodlands were not far ahead now, but Thomas kept looking behind, expecting the dozen riders to appear at any moment. Instead, more men appeared to the east, another twelve climbing the track which led across the ridge, and Thomas and Genevieve ran across the grass and vanished into the trees just moments before the new horsemen appeared on the crest.

The two lay in the undergrowth, catching their breath. The twelve new riders sat in the open, waiting, and after a while the first horsemen appeared like a line of beaters. They had been searching the open part of the ridge, hoping to flush Thomas and Genevieve out of cover, and Thomas understood that his cousin had foreseen exactly what he would do, had foreseen that he would try to reach Castillon d'Arbizon, or at least journey west towards the other English garrisons, and now his men were combing all the landscape west of Astarac. And even as Thomas watched, his cousin came into sight, leading another score of men who joined the others on the grassy crest. There were now over forty men-at-arms on the high ground, all in mail or plate, all cloaked in black, all with long swords.

"What do we do?" Genevieve breathed the question.

"Hide," Thomas said.

They wriggled backwards, trying to make no sound, and when

they were deep in the trees Thomas led her eastwards. He was going back towards Astarac because he doubted Guy would expect that, and when they reached the edge of the high ground and could see the valley spread out in front of them, Thomas sidled north again to see what his pursuers were doing.

Half of them had gone on westwards to block the tracks crossing the neighboring valley, but the rest, led by Vexille, were riding towards the trees. They would be the beaters again, hoping to drive Thomas and Genevieve out towards the other men-at-arms and, now that the horsemen were closer, Thomas could see that some of them were carrying crossbows.

"We're safe for the moment," Thomas told Genevieve when he rejoined her in the rocky gully where she sheltered. He reckoned he had slipped inside his cousin's cordon that was driving outwards, and the farther it went the wider that cordon would become and the easier it would be to slip between its gaps. But that must wait till morning because the sun was already sinking towards the western clouds, touching them pink. Thomas listened to the sound of the woods, but heard nothing alarming, only the scrabble of claws on bark, the wing beats of a pigeon and the sigh of the wind. The black-cloaked riders had gone westwards, but to the east, down in the valley, their work was visible. There were still soldiers down there and those men had fired the lazar house so that its smoke smeared all the sky above the monastery, and they had also burned what remained of the village, reckoning the flames would drive anyone concealed in the cottages into the open. More men were in the ruins of the castle, and Thomas wondered what they did there, but he was much too far away to see.

"We have to eat," he told Genevieve.

"We have nothing," she said.

"Then we'll look for mushrooms," Thomas said, "and nuts. And we need water."

They found a tiny streamlet to the south and they both slaked their thirst by thrusting their faces against a rock down which the water trickled, then Thomas made a bed of bracken in the streamlet's gully and, when he was satisfied that they would be well hidden there, he left Genevieve and went in search of food. He carried his bow and had a half-dozen arrows in his belt, not just for defense, but in hope of seeing a deer or pig. He found some mushrooms in the leaf mould, but they were small and black-veined and he was not sure whether they were poisonous. He went farther, looking for chestnuts or game, always creeping, always listening, and always keeping the edge of the ridge in sight. He heard a noise and turned fast and thought he saw a deer, but the shadows were lengthening and he could not be certain; he put an arrow on the string anyway and crept to where he had seen the flickering movement. This was the rutting season and the stags should be in the woods, looking for others to fight. He knew he dared not light a fire to cook the meat, but he had eaten raw liver before and it would be a feast this night. Then he saw the antlers and he moved to one side, half crouching, trying to bring the stag's body into view and just then the crossbow shot and the bolt hissed past him to thump into a tree and the stag took off in great bounds as Thomas twisted round, hauling back the bowcord, and saw the men drawing their swords.

He had walked into a trap.

And he was caught.

Part Three

THE
DARKNESS

T HE SEARCH OF THE MONASTERY had yielded nothing except the body of Abbot Planchard and Guy Vexille, on being told of the old man's death, loudly blamed his missing cousin. He had then ordered a search of all the buildings, commanded that the village and lazar house be fired to make certain no fugitives were hiding in either, and then, reluctantly convinced that his prey had fled, he sent horsemen to search all the nearby woods. The discovery of a pair of discarded lepers' robes and two wooden clappers in the western woods suggested what had happened and Vexille confronted the horsemen who had been guarding that side of the monastery. Both men swore they had seen nothing. He did not believe them, but there was little to be gained by challenging their assertions and so, instead, he sent horsemen to rake every path which led towards the English possessions in Gascony. When he ordered Charles Bessières to add his men to the search, however, Bessières refused. He claimed his horses were lame and his men tired. "I don't take your orders," Bessières snarled. "I'm here for my brother."

"And your brother wants the Englishman found," Vexille insisted.

"Then you find him, my lord," Bessières said, making the last two words sound like an insult.

Vexille rode west with all his men, knowing that Bessières probably wanted to stay behind to plunder the village and monastery, and that was precisely what Charles Bessières did, though he found little enough. He sent six of his men to rake through the pathetic belongings that the villagers had saved from the new flames, and they discovered some pots and pans that might sell for a few sous, but what they really wanted were the coins that the villagers would have hidden when they saw armed men coming. Everyone knew that peasants hoarded small amounts of cash, and buried it when mailed raiders appeared, and so Bessières's men tortured the serfs to make them reveal the hiding places and, in so doing, discovered something far more intriguing. One of Charles's men spoke the language of southern France and he had been sawing at a prisoner's fingers when the man blurted out that the old Count had been digging in the castle ruins and had uncovered an ancient wall beneath the chapel but then had died before he was able to delve farther. That interested Bessières, because the man suggested there was something behind the wall, something that had excited the old Count and which the abbot, God save his soul, had wanted hidden and so, once Vexille had vanished westwards, Bessières led his men up to the old fortress.

It took less than an hour to prize up the flagstones and reveal the vault, and in another hour Bessières had pulled out the old coffins and seen that they had already been plundered. The man from the village was fetched and he showed where the Count had been digging and Bessières ordered his men to uncover the wall. He made them work fast, wanting to finish the job before Guy Vexille returned and accused him of desecrating his family's graves, but the wall was stoutly made and well mortared, and it was not until one of his men fetched the blacksmith's heaviest hammer from the plunder taken from the burned village that he made real progress. The hammer crashed on the stones, chipping and dislodging them, until at last they were able to get an iron spike between the lower blocks and the wall came tumbling down.

And inside, on a stone pillar, was a box.

It was a wooden box, perhaps big enough to hold a man's head, and even Charles Bessières felt a surge of excitement as he saw it. The Grail, he thought, the Grail, and he imagined riding north with the prize that would give his brother the papacy. "Out of the way," he snarled at a man reaching for the treasure, then he stooped into the low space and took the wooden box from its pedestal.

The chest was cunningly made, for it seemed to have no lid. On one side—Bessières assumed it was the top—was inset a silver cross that had become tarnished over the years, but there was no writing on the box and no clue as to what might be inside. Bessières shook it and heard something rattle. He paused then. He was thinking that perhaps the real Grail was in his hands, but if the box proved to hold something else then this might be a good time to take the fake Grail from the quiver at his belt and pretend he had discovered it beneath Astarac's ruined altar.

"Open it," one of his men said.

"Shut your mouth," Bessières said, wanting to think some more. The Englishman was still at large, but he would probably be caught, and suppose he had the Grail and the one at his hip was thus revealed as a fake? Bessières faced the same dilemma that had puzzled him in the ossuary when he'd had a simple chance to kill Vexille. Produce the Grail at the wrong time and there would be no easy life in the papal palace at Avignon. So it was best, he thought, to wait for the Englishman's capture and thus make sure there was only one Grail to be carried to Paris. Yet perhaps this box contained the treasure?

He carried it up to the daylight and there he drew his knife and hacked at the box's well-made joints. One of his men offered to use the blacksmith's hammer to splinter the wood apart, but Bessières cursed him for a fool. "You want to break what's inside?" he asked. He cuffed the man aside and went on working with the knife until he finally succeeded in splitting one side away.

The contents were wrapped in white woolen cloth. Bessières eased them out, daring to hope that this was the great prize. His men crowded around expectantly as Bessières unwound the old, threadbare cloth.

To find bones.

A skull, some foot bones, a shoulder-blade and three ribs. Bessières stared at them, then cursed. His men began to laugh and Bessières, in his anger, kicked the skull so that it flew down into the vault, rolled for a few paces, and then was still.

He had blunted his good knife to find the few remaining bones of the famous healer of angels, St. Sever.

And the Grail was still hidden.

THE *COREDORS* HAD BEEN INTRIGUED by the activity around Astarac. Whenever armed men pillaged a town or village there would be fugitives who made easy pickings for desperate and hungry outlaws, and Destral, who led close to a hundred *coredors*, had watched the harrowing of Astarac and noted the folk fleeing the soldiers and watched where they went.

Most of the *coredors* were fugitives themselves, though not all. Some were just men down on their luck, others had been discharged from the wars and a handful had refused to accept their given place as serfs belonging to a master. In summer they preyed on the flocks taken to the high pastures and ambushed careless travelers in the mountain passes, but in winter they were forced to lower ground to find victims and shelter. Men came and went from the band, bringing and taking their women with them. Some of the men died of disease, others took their plunder and left to make a more honest living, while a few were killed in fights over women or wagers, though very few died in fights with outsiders. The old Count of Berat had tolerated Destral's band so long as they did no great damage, reckoning it a waste of money to hire men-at-arms to scour mountains riven with gullies and thick with caves. Instead he put garrisons wherever there was wealth to attract *coredors* and made sure the wagons carrying his tax tribute from the towns were well guarded. Merchants, traveling away from the main roads, took care to move in convoy with their own hired soldiers, and what was left was the *coredors'* pickings, which sometimes they had to fight for because routiers encroached on their territory.

A routier was almost a *coredor*, except that routiers were better organized. They were soldiers without employment, armed and experienced, and routiers would sometimes take a town and ransack it, garrison it, keep it till it was wrung dry and then travel again. Few lords were willing to fight them for the routiers were trained soldiers and formed small vicious armies that fought with the fanaticism of men who had nothing to lose. Their predations stopped whenever a war started and the lords offered money for soldiers. Then the routiers would take a new oath, go to war and fight until a truce was called, and then, knowing no trade except killing, they would go back to the lonelier stretches of countryside and find a town to savage.

Destral hated routiers. He hated all soldiers for they were the natural enemies of *coredors*, and though, as a rule, he avoided them, he would allow his men to attack them if he had a great advantage in numbers. Soldiers were a good source for weapons, armor and horses, and so, on the evening when the smoke from the burning village and lazar house was smearing the sky above Astarac, he allowed one of his deputies to lead an attack on a half-dozen black-cloaked men-at-arms who had strayed a short way into the trees. The attack was a mistake. The riders were not alone, there were others just beyond the woods, and suddenly the gloom beneath the trees was loud with horses' hooves and the scrape of swords leaving scabbards.

Destral did not know what was happening at the wood's edge. He was deeper among the trees in a place where a limestone crag reared up from the oaks and a small stream fell from the heights. Two caves offered shelter, and this was where Destral planned to spend his winter, high enough in the hills to offer protection, but close enough to the valleys so his men could raid the villages and farms, and it was here that the two fugitives from Astarac had been brought. The pair had been captured at the edge of the ridge and escorted back to the clearing in front of the caves where Destral had prepared fires, though he would not light the wood until he was sure the soldiers were dealt with. Now, in the evening's twilight, he saw his men had brought him a greater prize than he had dared dream of because one of the two captives was an English archer and the other was a woman, and women were always scarce among the *coredors*. She would have her uses, but the Englishman would have a greater value. He could be sold. He also possessed a bag of money, a sword and a mail coat, which meant his capture, for Destral, was a triumph made even sweeter because this was the same man who had killed half a dozen of his men with his arrows. The *coredors* searched Thomas's haversack and stole his flint and steel, the spare bowcords and the few coins Thomas had stored there, but they threw away the spare arrow heads and the empty box which they considered a thing of no value. They stripped him of his arrows and gave his bow to Destral who tried to draw it and became enraged when, despite his strength, he could not haul the string back more than a few inches. "Just chop off his fingers," he snarled, throwing down the bow, "and strip her naked."

Philin intervened then. A man and a woman had seized Genevieve and were hauling the mail shirt over her head, ignoring her shrieks of pain, and Thomas was trying to break away from the two men holding his arms, when Philin shouted that they were all to stop.

"Stop?" Destral turned on Philin in disbelief at the challenge. "You've gone soft?" he accused Philin. "You want us to spare him?"

"I asked him to join us," Philin said nervously. "Because he let my son live."

Thomas did not understand any of the conversation, which was being held in the local tongue, but it was plain that Philin was pleading for his life, and it was equally plain that Destral, whose nickname came from the great axe that was slung on his shoulder, was in no mood to grant the request. "You want him to join us?" Destral roared. "Why? Because he spared your son? Jesus Christ, but you're a weak bastard. You're a lily-livered piece of snot-nosed shit." He unslung the axe, looped the cord tied to its handle about his wrist, and advanced on the tall Philin. "I let you lead men and you have half of them killed! That man and his woman did that, and you'd have him join us? If it wasn't for the reward I'd kill him now. I'd slit his belly and hang him by his own rotten guts, but instead he'll lose a finger for every man of mine he killed." He spat towards Thomas then pointed the axe at Genevieve. "Then he can watch her warm my bed."

"I asked him to join us," Philin repeated stubbornly. His son, his leg in a splint and with crude crutches cut from oak boughs beneath his shoulders, swung across to stand beside his father.

"Will you fight for him?" Destral asked. He was not as tall as Philin, but he was broad across the shoulders and had a squat brute strength. His face was flat with a broken nose and he had eyes like a mastiff; eyes that almost glowed with the thought of violence. His beard was matted, strung with dried spittle and scraps of food. He swung the axe so its head glittered in the dying light. "Fight me," he said to Philin, his voice hungry.

"I just want him to live," Philin said, unwilling to draw a sword on his mad-eyed leader, but the other *coredors* had smelt blood, plenty of it, and they were making a rough circle and egging Destral on. They grinned and shouted, wanting the fight, and Philin backed away until he could go no farther.

"Fight!" the men shouted. "Fight!" Their women were screaming as well, shouting at Philin to be a man and face the axe. Those closest to Philin shoved him hard forward so that he had to jump aside to stop himself colliding with Destral who, scornful, slapped him in the face and then tugged his beard in insult.

"Fight me," Destral said, "or else slice off the Englishman's fingers yourself."

Thomas still did not know what was being said, but the unhappy look on Philin's face told him it was nothing good. "Go on!" Destral said. "Cut off his fingers! Either that, Philin, or I'll cut off *your* fingers."

Galdric, Philin's son, drew his own knife and pushed it towards his father. "Do it," the boy said, and when his father would not take the knife he looked at Destral. "I'll do it!" the boy offered.

"Your father will do it," Destral said, amused, "and he'll do it with this." He unlooped the wrist strap and offered the axe to Philin.

And Philin, too terrified to disobey, took the weapon and walked towards Thomas. "I'm sorry," he spoke in French.

"For what?"

"Because I have no choice." Philin looked miserable, a humiliated man, and he knew the other *coredors* were enjoying his shame. "Put your hands on the tree," he said, then repeated the order in his own language and the men holding Thomas forced his arms up until both his crooked hands were flat against the bark. They held Thomas by the forearms as Philin came close. "I'm sorry," Philin said again. "You must lose your fingers."

Thomas watched him. Saw how nervous he was. Understood that the axe blow, when it came, was as likely to chop him at the wrist instead of the fingers. "Do it quickly," he said.

"No!" Genevieve shouted and the couple holding her laughed.

"Quickly," Thomas said, and Philin drew the axe back. He paused, licked his lips, took one last anguished look into Thomas's eyes, then swung.

Thomas had let the men force him against the tree; he didn't try to pull away from them until the axe came. Only then did he use his huge strength to tear himself from their grasp. The two men, astonished by the power of an archer trained to use the long yew bow, flailed as Thomas snatched the axe out of the air and with a bellow of rage turned it on the man holding Genevieve. His first swing split that man's skull, the woman instinctively let go of Genevieve's other arm and Thomas wheeled back to beat down the men who had been holding his arms against the tree. He was screaming his war cry, the battle shout of England: "St. George! St. George!" and he lashed the heavy blade at the nearest man just as the horsemen came from the trees.

For a heartbeat the *coredors* were caught between the need to overwhelm Thomas and the danger of the horsemen, then they realized the riders were by far the more dangerous enemy and they did what all men instinctively did when faced by galloping men-at-arms. They ran for the trees and Guy Vexille's black-robed riders spurred among them, swinging swords and killing with brutal ease. Destral, oblivious of their threat, had run straight at Thomas and Thomas thrust the axehead into the squat man's face, shattering the bridge of his nose and hurling him backwards, then Thomas let go of the clumsy weapon, seized his bow and arrow bag and snatched Genevieve's wrist.

They ran.

There was safety in the trees. The trunks and low branches stopped the horsemen running free in the wood, and the darkness was coming fast to obscure their view, but in the clearing the horsemen were wheeling, cutting, wheeling again, and the *coredors* who had failed to escape into the trees were dying like sheep savaged by wolves.

Philin was beside Thomas now, but his son, on his awkward crutches, was still in the clearing and a horseman saw the boy, turned and lined his sword. "Galdric!" Philin shouted, and he started to run to save the boy, but Thomas tripped him, then put an arrow on the string.

The rider was holding the sword low, intending to jab the point into the small of Galdric's back. He touched his horse with his spurs and it accelerated just as the arrow whipped from the shadows to slice his throat open. The horse wheeled away, its rider spilling from the saddle in a stream of blood. Thomas shot a second arrow that flashed past the boy to spit Destral through one eye, then he looked for his cousin among the horsemen, but it was so dim now that he could not make out any faces.

"Come!" Genevieve urged him. "Come!"

But Thomas, instead of running with her, dashed back into the clearing. He scooped up the empty grail box, looked for his bag of money, plucked up a sheaf of his arrows, then heard Genevieve's cry of warning as hooves came towards him and he swerved to one side, doubled back, then ran into the trees. The pursuing rider, confused by Thomas's quick evasions, spurred forward again, then veered away as Thomas ducked under a low branch. Other *coredors* were fleeing to the caves, but Thomas ignored that refuge and struck south beside the crag. He led Genevieve by the hand while Philin carried Galdric on his shoulders. A handful of the braver horsemen made a brief effort to follow, but some of the surviving *coredors* had their crossbows and the bolts thumping out of the dark persuaded the riders to be content with their small victory. They had killed a score of bandits, captured as many more and, what was better, taken a dozen of their women. And in doing it they had lost only one man. They took the arrow from his throat, draped his body on his horse and, with their captives tied by strips of cloth, went back northwards.

While Thomas ran. He still had his mail coat, his bow, a bag of arrows and an empty box, but everything else was lost. And he was running in the dark.

To nowhere.

FAILURE WAS HARD, and Guy Vexille knew he had failed. He had sent riders into the woods to beat any fugitives out to the open ground and instead they had become tangled in a bloody, one-sided brawl with *coredors* that had left one of his men dead. The body was taken down to Astarac where, early next morning, Guy Vexille buried the man. It was raining. The rain had begun at midnight, a steady downpour that flooded the grave, which had been scraped between the olive trees. The bodies of the captured *coredors*, all of them beheaded the previous night, were lying abandoned at the edge of the olive grove, but Vexille was determined his own man should have a grave. The body had been stripped of everything except his shirt and now the man was rolled into the shallow hole where his head flopped back into the rainwater to expose the wound in his neck. "Why wasn't he wearing his gorget?" Vexille asked one of the men who had attacked the *coredors*. A gorget was a piece of plate covering the throat and

Vexille remembered that the dead man had been proud of the piece of armor that he had scavenged from some forgotten battlefield.

"He was."

"A lucky sword thrust then?" Vexille asked. He was curious. All knowledge was useful, and few scraps of knowledge so useful as those that helped a man live in the chaos of battle.

"It wasn't a sword," the man said, "he got an arrow."

"Crossbow?"

"Long arrow," the man said, "went straight through the gorget. Must have hit plumb." The man made the sign of the cross, praying that he would not suffer a similar fate. "The archer got away," he went on. "Ran into the woods."

And that was when Vexille realized Thomas must have been among the *coredors*. It was possible that one of the bandits had been using a hunting bow, but not likely. He demanded to know where the arrow was, but it had been thrown away, no one knew where, so in the morning mist Vexille led his men up to the ridge and then south to the clearing where the bodies still lay. Rain pelted down, dripping from the horses' trappers and finding its way beneath men's armor so that the metal and leather chafed chilled skins. Vexille's men grumbled, but Vexille himself seemed oblivious of the weather. Once at the clearing he looked at the scatter of corpses, then saw what he was looking for. A squat, bearded man had an arrow in his eye and Vexille dismounted to look at the shaft, which proved to be a long ash arrow fledged with goose feathers. Vexille pulled it free, tugging it from the dead man's brains. It had a long, needle-like head, and that suggested it was English, then he looked at the fledging. "Did you know," he said to his men, "that the English only use feathers from one wing of a goose?" He stroked the damp feathers, which were held in place by twine and by glue that had a greenish tinge. "Either the right wing," he said, "or the left, doesn't matter, but you don't mix feathers from both wings on one arrow." He suddenly snapped the arrow in a surge of frustration. Goddamn it! It was an English arrow and that meant Thomas had been here, so damned close, and now was gone. But where?

One of his men proposed riding westwards to rake the valley of the Gers, but Vexille snarled at the suggestion. "He's no fool. He'll be miles away by now. Miles." Or perhaps he was just yards away, watching from among the trees or from the rocky heights of the crag, and Vexille stared into the woods and tried to put himself into Thomas's place. Would he run back to England? But why would he ever have come here in the first place? Thomas had been excommunicated, thrown out from his companions, sent into the wilderness, but instead of fleeing home to England he had come east to Astarac. But there was nothing in Astarac now. It had been harrowed, so where would Thomas go? Guy Vexille looked into the caves, but they were empty. Thomas was gone.

Vexille returned to the monastery. It was time to leave and he went there to gather the rest of his men. Charles Bessières had also assembled his few soldiers who were mounted on horses heavy with plunder. "And where are you going?" Vexille asked him.

"Wherever you go, my lord," Bessières said with sarcastic courtesy, "to help you find the Englishman. So where do we look?" He asked the question caustically, knowing that Guy Vexille had no ready answer.

Vexille said nothing. The rain still fell steadily, turning the roads into quagmires. On the northern road, that led eventually to Toulouse, a group of travellers had appeared. They were all on foot, thirty or forty of them, and it was apparent that they were coming to seek shelter and help from the monastery. They looked like fugitives for they were pushing four handcarts loaded with chests and bundles. Three old people, too weak to struggle through the cloying mud, were riding on the carts. Some of Bessières's men, hoping for more easy plunder, were spurring towards them and Guy Vexille headed them off. The folk, seeing Vexille's lacquered armor and the prancing yale on his shield, knelt in the mud. "Where are you going?" Vexille demanded.

"To the monastery, lord," one of the men said, hauling off his hat and bowing his head.

"And where are you from?"

The man said they were from the valley of the Garonne, two days' journey to the east, and further questioning elicited that they were four craftsmen and their families: a carpenter, a saddler, a wheelwright and a mason, all from the same town.

"Is there trouble there?" Vexille wanted to know. He doubted it would concern him, for Thomas would surely not have travelled eastwards, but anything strange was of interest to him.

"There is a plague, lord," the man said. "People are dying."

"There's always plague," Vexille said dismissively.

"Not like this, lord," the man said humbly. He claimed that hundreds, maybe thousands, were dying and these families, at the very first onslaught of the contagion, had decided to flee. Others were doing the same, the man said, but most had gone north to Toulouse while these four families, all friends, had decided to look to the southern hills for their safety.

"You should have stayed," Vexille said, "and taken refuge in a church."

"The church is filled with the dead, lord," the man said, and Vexille turned away in impatience. Some disease in the Garonne was not his business, and if common folk panicked, that was nothing unusual. He snarled at Charles Bessières's men to leave the fugitives alone, and Bessières snapped back, saying that they were wasting their time. "Your Englishman's gone," he sneered.

Vexille heard the sneer, but ignored it. Instead, he paused a moment, then gave Charles Bessières the courtesy of taking him seriously. "You're right," he said, "but gone where?"

Bessières was taken aback by the mild tone. He leaned on his saddle pommel and stared at the monastery as he thought about the question. "He was here," he said eventually, "he went, so presumably he found what he wanted?"

Vexille shook his head. "He ran from us, that's why he went."

"So why didn't we see him?" Bessières asked belligerently. The rain dripped from the broad metal brim of his sallet, a piece of armor he had adopted to keep his head dry. "But he's gone, and taken whatever he found with him. And where would you go if you were him?"

"Home."

"Long way," Bessières said. "And his woman's wounded. If I was him I'd find friends and find them fast."

Vexille stared at the grim Charles Bessières and wondered why he was being so unusually helpful. "Friends," Vexille repeated.

"Castillon d'Arbizon," Charles Bessières spelled it out.

"They threw him out!" Vexille protested.

"That was then," Bessières said, "but what choices does he have now?" In truth Charles Bessières had no idea whether Thomas would go to Castillon d'Arbizon, but it was the most obvious solution, and Charles had decided he needed to find the Englishman fast. Only then, when he was certain that no true Grail had been discovered, could he reveal the fake chalice. "But if he hasn't gone to his friends," he added, "he's certainly going west towards the other English garrisons."

"Then we'll cut him off," Vexille said. He was not convinced that Thomas would go to Castillon d'Arbizon, but his cousin would surely go west, and now Vexille had a new worry, one put there by Bessières, that Thomas had found what he sought.

The Grail could be lost and the scent was cold, but the hunt must go on.

They all rode west.

IN THE DARK THE RAIN came like vengeance from heaven. A downpour that thrashed on the trees and dripped to the floor of the wood and soaked the fugitives and lowered their already low spirits. In one brief passage of unexpected violence the *coredors* had been broken apart, their leader killed and their winter encampment ruined.

Now, in the utter blackness of the autumn night, they were lost, unprotected and frightened.

Thomas and Genevieve were among them. Genevieve spent much of the night doubled over, trying to contain the pain of her left shoulder that had been exacerbated when the *coredors* tried and failed to strip her of the mail shirt, but when the first thin, damp light showed a path through the trees she stood and followed Thomas as he went westwards. At least a score of the *coredors* followed, including Philin, who was still carrying his son on his shoulders. "Where are you going?" Philin asked Thomas.

"Castillon d'Arbizon," Thomas said. "And where are you going?"

Philin ignored the question, walking in silence for a few paces, then he frowned. "I'm sorry," he said.

"What for?"

"I was going to cut your fingers off."

"Didn't have much choice, did you?"

"I could have fought Destral."

Thomas shook his head. "You can't fight men like that. They love fighting, feed on it. He'd have slaughtered you and I'd still have lost my fingers."

"I'm sorry, though."

They had worked their way across the highest part of the ridge and now could see the gray rain slashing all across the valley ahead, and across the next ridge and further valley. Thomas wanted to look at the landscape ahead before they descended the slope and so he ordered them all to rest, and Philin put his son down. Thomas turned to the tall man. "What did your boy say to you when he offered you the knife?"

Philin frowned as if he did not want to answer, then shrugged. "He told me to cut off your fingers."

Thomas hit Galdric hard across the head, making the boy's head ring and prompting a cry of pain. Thomas slapped him a second time, hard enough to hurt his own hand. "Tell him," Thomas said, "to pick fights with people his own size."

Galdric began crying, Philin said nothing and Thomas looked back to the valley ahead. He could see no horsemen there, no riders on the roads or mailed soldiers patrolling the wet pastures, and so he led the group on downwards. "I heard"—Philin spoke nervously, his son back on his shoulders—"that the Count of Berat's men are besieging Castillon d'Arbizon?"

"I heard the same," Thomas said curtly.

"You think it's safe to go there?"

"Probably not," Thomas said, "but there's food in the castle, and warmth and friends."

"You could walk farther west?" Philin suggested.

"I came here for something," Thomas said, "and I haven't got it." He had come for his cousin, and Guy Vexille was close; Thomas knew he could not double back on Astarac and face him because Vexille's mounted men-at-arms held all the advantages in open country, but there was a small chance in Castillon d'Arbizon. A chance, at least, if Sir Guillaume was in command and Thomas's friends were the men making up the shrunken garrison. And at least he would be back among archers, and so long as he had them by his side he believed he could offer his cousin a fight to remember.

The rain poured on as they crossed the valley of the Gers, and became even harder as they climbed the next ridge through thick chestnuts. Some of the *coredors* fell behind, but most kept up with Thomas's quick pace. "Why are they following me?" Thomas asked Philin. "Why are you following me?"

"We need food and warmth too," Philin said. Like a dog that had lost its master he had attached himself to Thomas and Genevieve, and the other *coredors* were following him, and so Thomas stopped on the ridge's top and stared at them. They were a band of thin, ragged, hungry and beaten men, with a handful of bedraggled women and miserable children. "You can come with me," he said, and waited for Philin to translate, "but if we get to Castillon d'Arbizon you become soldiers. Proper soldiers! You'll have to fight. Fight proper. Not skulk in the woods and run away when it gets hard. If we get into the castle you'll have to help defend it, and if you can't face that, then go away now." He watched them as Philin interpreted: most looked sheepish, but none turned away. They were either brave, Thomas thought, or so hopeless that they could think of no alternative but to follow him.

He walked on towards the next valley. Genevieve, her hair plastered to her skull, kept pace with him. "How will we get into the castle?" she asked.

"Same way I did before. Across the weir and up to the wall."

"They won't guard that?"

Thomas shook his head. "Too close to the ramparts. If they put men on that slope they'll be picked off by archers. One by bloody one." Which did not mean that the besiegers might not have occupied the mill, but he would face that problem once he reached Castillon d'Arbizon.

"And when we're inside?" she asked. "What then?"

"I don't know," Thomas said honestly.

She touched his hand as if to indicate that she was not criticizing, but merely curious. "It seems to me," she said, "that you are like a hunted wolf, and you're going back to your lair."

"True," Thomas said.

"And the huntsmen will know you are there. They will trap you."

"Also true," Thomas said.

"Then why?" she asked.

He did not answer for a while, then he shrugged and tried to tell her the truth. "Because I've been beaten," he said, "because they killed Planchard, because I've got nothing to bloody lose, because if I'm on those ramparts with a bow then I can kill some of them. And

I bloody will. I'll kill Joscelyn; I'll kill my cousin." He slapped the yew shaft, which was unstrung to preserve the cord from the rain. "I'll kill them both. I'm an archer, and a bloody good one, and I'd rather be that than a fugitive."

"And Robbie? You'll kill him?"

"Maybe," Thomas said, unwilling to consider the question.

"So the wolf," she said, "will kill the hounds? Then die?"

"Probably," Thomas said. "But I'll be with friends." That was important. Men he had brought to Gascony were under siege and, if they would take him back, he would stay with them to the end. "And you don't have to come," he added to Genevieve.

"You goddamn fool," she said, her anger matching his. "When I was going to die, you came. You think I will leave you now? Besides, remember what I saw under the thunder."

Darkness and a point of light. Thomas smiled in grim amusement. "You think we'll win?" he asked. "Maybe. I do know I'm on God's side now, whatever the Church thinks. My enemies killed Planchard and that means they're doing the devil's work."

They were going downhill, coming towards the end of the trees and the first of the vineyards and Thomas paused to search the landscape ahead. The *coredors* straggled in behind him, dropping exhausted on the wet forest floor. Seven carried crossbows, the rest had a variety of weapons, or none at all. One woman, red-haired and snub-nosed, carried a falchion, a broad-bladed, curved sword, and she looked as if she knew how to use it.

"Why are we stopping?" Philin asked, though he was grateful for the respite because his son was a heavy burden.

"To look for the hunters," Thomas said, and he stared a long time at the vineyards, meadows and small woods. A stream glinted between two pastures. There was no one in sight. There were no serfs digging ditches or herding pigs towards the chestnuts and that was worrying. Why would serfs stay home? Only because there were armed men around and Thomas looked for them.

"There," Genevieve said, pointing, and to the north, by a bend in the glistening stream, Thomas saw a horseman in the shadow of a willow.

So the hunters were waiting for him and once he was out of the trees they would surround him, chop down his companions and take him to his cousin.

It was time to hide again.

JOSCELYN LOVED THE GUN. It was a thing of ugly beauty; a solid, bulbous, thunderous lump of clumsy killing machine. He wanted more of them. With a dozen such devices, he thought, he could be the greatest lord of Gascony.

It had taken five days to drag the gun to Castillon d'Arbizon where Joscelyn had discovered that the siege, if it could even be called that, was going nowhere. Sir Henri claimed he had contained the garrison by penning them into the castle, but he had made no effort to attack. He had built no scaling ladders, nor positioned his crossbowmen close enough to pick the English archers off the ramparts. "Been dozing, have you?" Joscelyn snarled.

"No, lord."

"Paid you off, did they?" Joscelyn demanded. "Bribed you perhaps?" Sir Henri bridled at such an affront to his honor, but Joscelyn ignored him. Instead he ordered the crossbowmen to advance halfway up the main street and find windows or walls from where they could shoot at the men on the castle ramparts, and five of the crossbowmen were dead and another six were wounded by the long English arrows before the day ended, but Joscelyn was content. "Got them worried," he claimed, "and tomorrow we'll begin slaughtering them."

Signor Gioberti, the Italian master gunner, decided to place his cannon just inside the town's west gate. There was a convenient stretch of level cobbles there, and on them he put the two vast baulks of timber that supported the wooden frame that cradled the jar-shaped weapon. The spot was a good twenty yards outside the range of the

English archers, so his men were safe and, better still, the gate's archway, ten paces behind the gun, provided shelter from the intermittent showers so his men could mix the gunpowder safely.

It took all morning to emplace the gun and its frame, which had to be lifted from the wagon by a crane that Gioberti's men constructed from stout pieces of oak. The runners beneath the frame had been greased with pig lard, and Gioberti placed a tub of the white fat beside the gun so that the runners could be kept lubricated as the frame recoiled whenever the gun was fired.

The cannon's missiles were carried on a separate wagon and each needed two men to lift it from their bed. The missiles were iron bolts, four feet long; some were shaped like arrows with stubby metal vanes while the rest were simple bars, each as thick across as a man's upper arm. The powder came in barrels, but it needed stirring because the heavy saltpeter, which made up about two-thirds of the mix, had sunk to the bottom of the tubs while the lighter sulphur and charcoal had risen to the top. The stirring was done with a long wooden spoon, and when Signor Gioberti was satisfied, he ordered eight cupfuls to be placed in the dark recess of the gun.

That breech, where the explosion would take place, was contained by the great jar-like bulge of the cannon's rear. That bulbous piece of iron was painted on one side with an image of St. Eloi, the patron saint of metal, and on the other with St. Maurice, the patron of soldiers, while below the saints was the gun's name, Hell Spitter. "She's three years old, lord," Gioberti told Joscelyn, "and as well behaved as a properly beaten woman."

"Well behaved?"

"I've seen them split, lord." Gioberti indicated the bulbous breech and explained that some guns tore themselves apart when they were fired, shattering scraps of hot metal to decimate the crew. "But Hell Spitter? She's as sound as a bell. And that's who made her, lord, bellfounders in Milan. They're hard to cast right, very hard."

"You can do it?" Joscelyn enquired, imagining a cannon foundry in Berat.

"Not me, lord. But you can hire good men. Or find bell-founders. They know how to do it, and there's a way of making sure they do a proper job."

"What's that?" Joscelyn asked eagerly.

"You make the gun's makers stand by the breech when the first shot is fired, my lord. That concentrates them on their work!" Gioberti chuckled. "I had Hell Spitter's founders standing by her and they didn't flinch. Proves she's well made, my lord, well made."

A fuse, made from linen soaked with a mix of oil and gunpowder and protected by a sewn linen sheath, was placed with one end in the powder and the other trailing through the gun's narrow neck where the missile would be placed. Some gunners, Gioberti said, preferred a hole drilled through the big breech, but he was of the opinion that such a hole dissipated part of the gun's force and he preferred to light the fuse from the gun's mouth. The white linen tube was held in place by a handful of wet loam slapped into the narrow neck, and only when that loam had set slightly did Gioberti allow two of his men to bring one of the arrow-shaped bolts, which was lifted up to the flaring mouth and carefully pushed back so that its long black length rested in the cannon's narrow neck. Now more loam was brought, newly mixed from river water and from sand and clay that were carried in the third wagon, and the loam was packed all around the missile to make a tight seal. "It holds in the explosion, lord," Gioberti said, and explained that without the loam to seal the barrel much of the powder's explosive force would waste itself as it vented past the missile. "Without the loam," he said, "it just spits the bolt out. No force at all."

"You will let me fire the fuse?" Joscelyn asked, as eager as a small child with a new toy.

"So you should, my lord," Gioberti said, "but not yet. The loam must set hard."

That took almost three hours, but then, as the sun sank behind the town and lit the eastern face of the castle, Gioberti declared everything was ready. The barrels of powder were safely stored in a nearby house where no trace of fire could reach them, the gunners had taken shelter in case the breech burst, and the thatch in front of the gun on either side of the street had been wetted down by men with buckets. The cannon had been wedged upwards so that it was pointing at the top of the castle's entrance arch, but the bolt, the Italian said, should fall slightly as it flew and thus strike the very centre of the gate. He ordered one of his men to bring a lighted brand from the hearth of the Bear and Butcher tavern and when he had been given the fire and he was sure all had been done that should be done, he bowed to Joscelyn and held out the burning wood. A priest said a prayer of blessing, then scuttled into the alley beside the tavern. "Just touch the fire to the fuse, my lord," Gioberti said, "then you and I can go to the gate rampart and watch."

Joscelyn looked at the thick black arrow head protruding from the barrel to fill the gun's flared mouth, then at the fuse beneath, and he touched the fire to the linen sleeve and the powder inside began to fizz. "Back, lord, if you please," Gioberti said. A little trail of smoke was coming from the linen sleeve, which shriveled and turned black as it shrank towards the throat. Joscelyn wanted to watch the fire vanish into the gun's neck, but Signor Gioberti dared to pull his lordship's sleeve in his urgency and Joscelyn meekly followed the Italian up to the gate rampart from where he stared at the castle. Up on the keep the Earl of Northampton's flag stirred in the small wind, but not for much longer, Joscelyn thought.

Then the world shook. The noise was such that Joscelyn thought he stood in the heart of thunder, a thunder that gave a palpable blow to his eardrums so sudden and strong he involuntarily jumped, and then the whole street ahead of him, all the space between the walls and the dampened thatch, filled with smoke in which bright shards of charcoal and shattered scraps of loam, all trailing fire like comets, arched and fell. The town's gateway shuddered, and the noise of the explosion echoed back from the castle to drown the screech of Hell Spitter's ponderous frame recoiling on its greased runners. Dogs began howling in the shuttered houses and a thousand startled birds took to the sky. "Sweet God!" Joscelyn said, amazed, his ears ringing from the thunder that still rolled about the valley. "Dear Christ!" The gray-white smoke drifted away from the street and with it came a stench so hideous, so rotten, that Joscelyn almost gagged. Then, through the foul-smelling smoke's remnants, he could see that one leaf of the castle's gates was hanging askew. "Do it again," he ordered, his voice sounding muffled to himself because his ears were full of echoes.

"Tomorrow, lord," Gioberti said. "It takes time to set the loam. We'll load tonight and shoot at daybreak."

Next morning the gun fired three shots, all of them solid bars of rusted iron that succeeded in tearing the castle's gates off their hinges. It began to rain and the drops hissed and steamed when they hit Hell Spitter's metal. The townsfolk cowered in their houses, flinching every time the massive noise of the gun shook their window shutters and made their kitchen pots rattle. The castle's defenders had vanished from the battlements and that emboldened the crossbowmen who moved even closer.

The gate was gone, though Joscelyn could still not see into the castle's courtyard for that lay higher than the gun, but he assumed the garrison would know that an assault must come through the gate and doubtless they were preparing defenses. "The trick of it," he declared at midday, "is not to give them time."

"They've had time," Sir Henri Courtois pointed out. "They've had all morning."

Joscelyn ignored Sir Henri who he thought was nothing but a timid old man who had lost his appetite for battle. "We attack this evening," Joscelyn decreed. "Signor Gioberti will fire an iron into the courtyard and we shall follow while the noise still cows them."

He picked forty men-at-arms, the best he had, and he ordered them

to be ready at sunset and, to ensure that the defenders had no warning of his attack, he had men hack holes in the house walls so that
the attackers could approach the castle through the town's buildings.
By going through the walls, sneaking from house to house, the attackers could get within thirty paces of the gate without being seen and,
as soon as the gun fired, they were to erupt from their hiding place
and charge the castle's archway. Sir Henri Courtois offered to lead the
attack, but Joscelyn refused. "It needs young men," he said, "men
without fear." He glanced at Robbie. "Will you come?"

"Of course, my lord."

"We'll send a dozen crossbowmen first," Joscelyn decreed. "They
can shoot a volley into the courtyard and then get out of our way."
They would also, he hoped, draw the arrows of any English archers
who might be waiting.

Sir Henri drew a diagram on a kitchen table with a scrap of charcoal to show Joscelyn what lay inside the courtyard. The stables, he
said, were to the right and should be avoided for they led nowhere.
"Facing you, lord," he said, "are two doorways. The one on the left
leads down to the dungeons and, once down there, there is no other
way out. The one on the right is at the top of a dozen steps and that
leads to the halls and battlements."

"So that's the one we want?"

"Indeed, lord." Sir Henri hesitated. He wanted to warn Joscelyn that
Sir Guillaume was an experienced soldier, that he would be ready. The
siege proper had only just begun, the gun had been working for less
than a day, and that was when a garrison was at its most alert. Sir Guillaume would be waiting, but Sir Henri knew that any caution would
only incur Joscelyn's dismissive scorn and so he said nothing.

Joscelyn ordered his squire to prepare his armor, then gave Sir
Henri a careless glance. "When the castle is taken," he said, "you will
be castellan again."

"Whatever your lordship orders," Sir Henri said, taking the insult
of his demotion calmly.

The attackers gathered in St. Callic's church where a Mass was said and a blessing given to the men in their mail coats, and afterwards they filed through the crude doorways hacked in the house walls, climbing the hill, going secretly to a wheelwright's shop that opened onto the square in front of the castle. They crouched there, weapons ready. Men pulled on helmets, said their silent prayers and waited. Most had shields, but some preferred to go without, claiming they could move faster. Two had huge axes, weapons to strike terror in a small space. They touched their talismans, said more prayers and waited impatiently for the roar of the huge gun. None peered around the doorway for Joscelyn was watching them and he had given strict orders that they were to stay hidden until the gun fired. "There is still a reward for every archer taken alive," he reminded them, "but I'll give it for dead archers too."

"Keep your shields up," Robbie put in, thinking of the long English arrows.

"They'll be dazed," Joscelyn said, "and cowering from the noise. We just go in and kill them."

Pray God that was true, Robbie thought, and he felt a twinge of guilt that he was fighting against Sir Guillaume, whom he liked, but he had sworn his new allegiance and he was convinced he was fighting for God, for Scotland and for the true faith.

"Five gold coins apiece," Joscelyn said, "for the first five men up the steps and into the keep." Why the hell did the gun not fire? He was sweating. It was a cool day, but he was hot because the greased leather coat under his plate armor was thick. That armor was the best that any of the attackers owned, but it was also the heaviest and Joscelyn knew it would be a struggle to keep up with the men in the lighter mail. No matter. He would join the fight where it was thickest and he relished the thought of cutting down screaming, desperate archers. "And no prisoners," he said, wanting his day to be crowned by death.

"Sir Guillaume?" Robbie suggested. "Can we take him captive?"

"Does he have estates?" Joscelyn asked.

"No," Robbie admitted.

"Then what ransom can he promise?"

"None."

"So no prisoners!" Joscelyn called to his attackers. "Kill them all!"

"But not their women," a man suggested.

"Not their women," Joscelyn agreed, and regretted that the golden-haired beghard was not in the castle. Well, there would be other women. There were always other women.

The shadows lengthened. It had rained all morning, but the sky had cleared since and the sun was low, very low, and Joscelyn knew that Signor Gioberti was waiting until the last bright rays shone clean through the gate to dazzle the defenders. Then would come the noise, the evil-smelling smoke, the terrible crash of the iron striking the courtyard wall and, while the defenders were still stunned by the tumult, the armored men would erupt in pitiless fury through the gate. "God is with us," Joscelyn said, not because he believed it, but because he knew such a sentiment was expected of him. "Tonight we feast on their food and women." He was talking too much because he was nervous, but he did not realize it. This was not like a tournament where the loser could walk away, however bruised and cut. This was death's playground and, though he was supremely confident, he was also apprehensive. Let the defenders be sleeping, or eating, he thought, but let them not be ready.

And just then the world was filled with thunder, flame-seared iron screamed through the gate, smoke boiled up the street and the waiting, thank Christ, was over.

They charged.

S IR GUILLAUME, the moment the gun first appeared in Castillon d'Arbizon, had readied the garrison for an attack. He gave orders that ten archers were to be in the courtyard at all times, five on each side of the yard so their arrows would slant in at the open space where the cannon's bolts had demolished the main gate. The castle's curtain wall, which was undamaged, sheltered them from any crossbowmen in the town. Then, during the morning that the gun demolished the gate, Sir Guillaume tore down most of the stable walls, but left the posts supporting the roof in place so that the archers had a place to shelter their bow-strings when it rained. The horses were taken up the steps into the lower hall, which became their new stables.

The timber from the stable wall, the byres and the shattered main gates were used to make a barricade across the courtyard. It was not as high as Sir Guillaume would have liked, and there was not enough timber to make it heavy enough to withstand a determined assault, but any kind of obstacle would slow down a man in armor and give the archers time to place another arrow on their cords. The first iron bolts shot from the gun were added to the barricade, and then a barrel of rancid olive oil was fetched up from the undercroft. With that, Sir Guillaume was ready.

He suspected Joscelyn would attack sooner rather than later. Sir Guillaume had spent enough time in the new Count of Berat's company to understand that Joscelyn was an impatient man, too eager for victory, and Sir Guillaume also reckoned the attack would either come at dusk or dawn and so, as the first full day of the gun's firing tore down the gates and cracked the bastion at one side of the archway, he made sure the whole garrison was armored and ready well before dusk.

In mid-afternoon he had been certain the attack would come very soon for, in the long space between the gun's shots, he had crouched on the undamaged part of the gate rampart and heard the strange sounds of hammers and splintering, and he guessed the enemy was breaking a path through the house walls so they could approach the open space in front of the castle unseen. And when evening came and the gun did not fire, Sir Guillaume knew it must be waiting until the attackers were ready. He crouched by the gate and heard the chink of armor from the houses across the square, and when he peered round the arch he saw that more men than usual had gathered on the ramparts above the west gate to watch the castle. They might as well have sounded a trumpet, he thought scornfully, to announce their intentions. He ducked out of sight just a heartbeat before a crossbow quarrel slammed into the arch where he had been lurking.

He went back to his men-at-arms. "They're coming," he told them and he pushed his left forearm into the leather loops of his shield that showed the faded badge of the three hawks.

There was a relief in that knowledge. Sir Guillaume hated being besieged, and he had hated the calm menace of the first days when Sir Henri had kept to their agreement for, even though that was a safe period, there was still the frustration of being mewed up in a castle. Now he could kill some of the besiegers, and to a soldier like Sir Guillaume that was far more satisfying. When the gun had first come to the town Sir Guillaume had wondered whether Joscelyn would offer him terms, but then, when the gun first fired to wrench the heavy gates askew, he understood that Joscelyn, hot-blooded, incautious and ungenerous, wanted nothing but death.

So now he would give it to him.

"When the gun fires," Sir Guillaume instructed his men, "that's when they'll come," and he squatted beside the gate, on the enemy's side of the barricade, and hoped he was right. He waited, watching the sunlight creep across the flagstones of the courtyard. He had eighteen fit archers and all of them were behind the barricade, while sixteen men-at-arms waited with Sir Guillaume. The rest had deserted, all but half a dozen men who were ill. The town was quiet except for a barking dog that suddenly yelped as it was struck to silence. Beat them off here, Sir Guillaume thought, and then what? He had no doubt he would beat them off, but he was still hugely outnumbered and his garrison was far from any help. Perhaps, if the besiegers were well beaten here, then Joscelyn would talk terms. Sir Henri Courtois would certainly take an honorable surrender, Sir Guillaume thought, but did Sir Henri have influence over the hot-headed Joscelyn?

Then the gun fired, the noise of it seeming to shake the castle, and an iron bar hammered through the gateway to drive a great chunk of stone and white dust from the tower wall next to the steps leading into the keep. Sir Guillaume tensed, his ears ringing with the echo of the terrible sound, and then he heard the cheers and the sound of heavy boots on the cobbles of the square outside and he prized the loosened lid from the barrel of oil and then kicked the tub over so that the greenish liquid spilt across the flagstones by the gateway. Just then he heard a voice bellowing outside. "No prisoners!" the man's voice was distorted by a helmet with a closed visor. "No prisoners!"

"Archers!" Sir Guillaume called, though he doubted they needed to be alerted. In Thomas's absence the bowmen were led by Jake who did not much like the responsibility, but he liked Sir Guillaume and wanted to fight well for him. Jake said nothing to his archers; they did not need any orders. Instead they waited with bows half drawn, bodkin arrows on their strings, and then the gateway was filled with a group of crossbowmen, and behind them were the men-at-arms, already shouting their battle cries, and Jake, as ordered, waited a heartbeat until the first men slipped on the olive oil and only then did he shout, "Loose!"

Eighteen arrows tore into the chaos. The first attackers through the gate were sprawling on the stones, the men behind tripped over them and then the arrows ripped into the confusion. The assault was still ten paces from the barricade, yet already it was checked because the castle's narrow gateway was blocked by the dying and the dead. Sir Guillaume stood to one side, sword drawn, doing nothing as yet, just letting the archers finish their work. He was astonished at how fast they had another arrow on the string, then watched as the second and third flights pierced mail and skewered flesh. A crossbowman crawled out from the tangle and bravely tried to raise his weapon, but Sir Guillaume took two steps and brought his sword hard down on the nape of the man's unprotected neck. The other crossbowmen, evidently sent in the front rank to deliver a volley at his archers, were dead or dying. Joscelyn's men-at-arms were mingled with them, arrows jutting from mail and shields, and in the gateway the crush of men could make no headway. Jake now directed his arrows at them, volley after volley, and then Sir Guillaume waved his men-at-arms forward. "They want no prisoners," he shouted to them, "you hear me? No prisoners!"

Sir Guillaume and his men were attacking from the left side of the courtyard, so Jake took his archers to the right and shot only through the gateway at the few figures left under the arch. And after a few seconds all the arrows stopped, for so many of the attackers were dead, and those that lived were trapped by Sir Guillaume's sudden assault from the corner of the yard.

It was a massacre. The attackers, already half beaten by the arrows, had assumed any defenders would be behind the barricade, and instead the men-at-arms came from their flank, and Sir Guillaume's men, informed that the enemy had wanted all their deaths, were in no mood to offer mercy. "Bastard." John Faircloth stabbed at a fallen man-at-arms, working his sword through a rent in the man's mail. "Bastard," he said again, cutting the throat of a crossbowman. A Burgundian was using an axe, crushing helmets and skulls with one efficient blow after another, spattering the oil-slicked stone with brains and blood. One enemy rose snarling from the pile, a big man, strong and useful, who stepped on bodies to carry the fight to the garrison, but Sir Guillaume took the man's sword blow on his shield and plunged his own sword into the man's throat. The man stared at Sir Guillaume, his eyes wide, his lips trying to frame an obscenity, but there was nothing in his mouth except a lump of blood, thick as lard; then he wavered and fell, and Sir Guillaume was already past him to kill another man-at-arms. And now the archers, discarding their bows, had come to join the slaughter, using axes, swords or knives to despatch the wounded. Shouts for mercy echoed in the courtyard, screams sounded, and the few unwounded attackers at the rear of the assault heard them, heard the triumphant English shouts. "St. George! St. George!" They fled. One man, dazed by a sword blow to his helmet, fled the wrong way and John Faircloth met him with a sword thrust that ripped through the iron rings of his mail to rip his belly open. "Bastard," Faircloth said, dragging his blade free.

"Clear the gate!" Sir Guillaume said. "Pull them clear!" He did not want his men to be shot by the crossbowmen outside the castle while they plundered the corpses of their armor and weapons, and so they dragged the bodies to the side of the yard. There were no wounded enemy that Sir Guillaume could see. It was the enemy that had shouted the call for no prisoners and the garrison had obeyed them. And now the attack was over.

Yet the danger was not past. There were still two bodies in the archway. Sir Guillaume knew the crossbowmen lower in the town could see into the gateway, so, using his shield to protect his body, he stooped and sidled into the arch and dragged the first body back towards the yard. There was no sign of Joscelyn and that was a pity. Sir Guillaume had dreamed of taking the Count prisoner for a second time, and then he would have doubled Joscelyn's ransom, doubled it again and then doubled it a third time. Bastard, Sir Guillaume thought, and a crossbow bolt slammed high into his shield, banging the top edge against Sir Guillaume's helmet. He crouched lower, grabbed the last man's ankle and pulled, and the man stirred and tried to fight back so Sir Guillaume hammered the shield's pointed lower edge into the man's groin and the man gasped, then stopped struggling.

It was Robbie. Once Sir Guillaume had him in the courtyard and was safe from the crossbowmen in the town, he could see that Robbie had not been wounded. Instead he had been stunned, probably by an arrow that had struck the lower edge of his helmet and left a fierce dent in the thick rim, which had thumped onto Robbie's skull and hurled him back. One inch lower and there would have been a dead Scotsman. As it was there was a very confused Scotsman who twitched in search of his sword as he realized where he was.

"Where's my money," Sir Guillaume growled, threatening Robbie with the Scotsman's own sword.

"Oh, Jesus," Robbie groaned.

"He's no damned use to you. If you want mercy, son, ask me. Ask them!" Sir Guillaume pointed at the archers and men-at-arms who were stripping the dead and injured of their weapons, armor and clothes. Cross-eyed Jake was grinning because one of the enemy dead had been wearing a ruby ring. Jake had sawn off the finger and now held the jewel aloft in triumph. Sam, the proud new owner of a fine coat of German-made mail, came to look at Robbie. He spat to show his opinion of the Scotsman.

Robbie, tears in his eyes because of his humiliation, looked at the dead men, their undershirts laced with blood. Forty attackers had crossed the square outside the castle and over half of them were dead. He looked up at Sir Guillaume. "I'm your prisoner," he said, and he wondered how he was supposed to pay one ransom to Lord Outhwaite in England and another to Sir Guillaume.

"You're bloody not my prisoner," Sir Guillaume said in crude English, then he changed back to French. "I heard the shout outside. No prisoners. And you might remember that when we do take prisoners, we don't get ransoms. We just get pieces of parchment. Is that what honor means in Scotland?"

Robbie looked up into the savage, one-eyed face and shrugged. "Just kill me," he said wearily. "Kill me and go to hell."

"Your friend wouldn't like that," Sir Guillaume said and saw the puzzlement on Robbie's face. "Your friend Thomas," he explained. "He likes you. He wouldn't want you dead. Got a soft spot for you, he has, because he's a goddamned fool. So I'll let you live. Get on your feet." Sir Guillaume prodded Robbie up. "Now go to Joscelyn and tell that spavined bastard that he can pay us what you owe us and then we'll leave. Got that? He pays the money, then you watch us ride away."

Robbie wanted to ask for the sword that belonged to his uncle and concealed a precious relic of St. Andrew in its hilt, but he knew he would be refused and so, still dazed, he went back to the arch, followed by the jeers of the archers. Sir Guillaume bellowed at the crossbowmen in the town that the man coming out was one of their own. "Perhaps they'll shoot you anyway," he said to Robbie, then shoved him out into the dusk.

None of the crossbowmen shot at Robbie who, with an aching head and a throbbing groin, stumbled down the street. The survivors of the attack were gathered by the still smoking gun; some of them had arrows in their arms or legs. Joscelyn was there, bare-headed; his hair had been flattened by the helmet's liner and his round face was slick with sweat and red with anger. He had been among the last to crowd into the gateway, had seen the chaos in front and had then been knocked over by an arrow strike on his breastplate. He had been astonished by the force of the blow, like being kicked by a horse, and the plate had a bright gouge in it. He had struggled up only to be hit by a second arrow which, like the first, had failed to pierce the thick plate, but he was knocked back again, and then the panic of the survivors had enveloped him and he had stumbled away with them. "They let you go?" he greeted Robbie who he saw had a dark bruise on his forehead.

"They sent me with a message, lord," Robbie said. "If they receive their money," he went on, "they will leave without more fighting."

"It's your money!" Joscelyn snarled. "So you pay them. Do you have it?"

"No, lord."

"Then we damned well kill them. We damned well kill them all!" Joscelyn turned on Signor Gioberti. "How long will it take you to bring down the whole archway?"

Gioberti thought for a second. He was a small man, nearly fifty, with a deeply lined face. "A week, lord," he estimated. One of his bolts had hit the side of the arch and ripped out a barrowload of stones, suggesting that the castle was in ill repair. "Maybe ten days," he amended his answer, "and in another ten days I can bring down half the curtain wall."

"We'll crush them in ruins," Joscelyn snarled, "then slaughter the damned lot." He turned on his squire. "Is my supper ready?"

"Yes, lord."

Joscelyn ate alone. He had thought he would eat in the castle's hall this night and listen to the screams of the archers having their fingers cut off, but fate had decreed otherwise. So now he would take his time, reduce the castle to rubble, then have his revenge.

And next morning Guy Vexille and Charles Bessières came to Castillon d'Arbizon with over fifty men. It seemed that Vexille had failed to find his heretic but, for reasons Joscelyn neither cared about nor understood, he believed the man and his beghard woman would be coming to the besieged castle.

"You catch them," Joscelyn said, "and the man's yours. But the woman's mine."

"She belongs to the Church," Vexille said.

"Mine first," Joscelyn insisted. "the Church can play with her next and the devil can have her afterwards."

The gun fired and the castle gateway trembled.

*   *   *

THOMAS AND HIS COMPANIONS spent a wet night under the trees. In the morning three of the *coredors* had vanished with their women, but fourteen men were left with eight women, six children and, most usefully, seven crossbows. They were all old bows with goat-leg levers to draw the string, which meant they were less powerful than the steel-shafted bows that used cranked handles to draw the cord, but in a fight the old sort were quick to reload and lethal enough at short distances.

The horsemen had gone from the valley. It took Thomas most of the morning to satisfy himself of that, but eventually he saw a pig-herder bringing his animals towards the woods and, shortly after that, the road leading south beside the stream was suddenly busy with folk who looked like fugitives for they were carrying huge loads and pushing handcarts piled with goods. He guessed the horsemen had got bored waiting for him and had attacked a nearby town or village instead, but the sight of the people reassured him that no soldiers were close and so they went on westwards.

The next day, as they took a high southern route that kept them away from the valleys and roads, he heard the gun in the distance. At first he thought it was a strange kind of thunder, an abrupt clap with no fading rumble, but there were no dark clouds in the west, and then it sounded again, and at midday a third time and he realized it was a cannon. He had seen cannons before, but they were uncommon, and he feared what the strange device might do to his friends in the castle. If they were still his friends.

He hurried, tending north now towards Castillon d'Arbizon, but forced to take care each time he came to an open valley or a place where horsemen might lie in ambush. He shot a roe deer that evening and they each had a morsel of the uncooked liver for they dared not light a fire. At dusk, when he carried the roe back to their encampment, he had seen the smoke to the northwest and known it came from the cannon, and that meant he was very close, so close that he stayed on guard till the heart of the night, then woke Philin and made him serve as a sentry.

It was raining in the morning. The *coredors* were miserable and hungry and Thomas tried to cheer them by promising them that warmth and food were not far off. But the enemy were also nearby and he went cautiously. He dared not leave his bow strung, for the rain would weaken the string. He felt naked without an arrow on the cord. The sound of the gun, firing every three or four hours, grew louder, and by the early afternoon Thomas could hear the distinct crash of the missiles striking stone. But then, as he breasted a rise and the rain at last ended, he saw that the Earl of Northampton's flag still hung drab and damp on the keep's high staff and that gave him encouragement. It did not denote safety, but it promised an English garrison to fight at his side.

They were close now, perilously close. The rain might have stopped, but the ground was slippery and Thomas fell twice as he scrambled down the steep wooded slope which led to the river that curled about the castle's crag. He planned to approach the castle as he had escaped it, by crossing the weir beside the mill, but as he reached the foot of the slope, where the trees grew close to the mill pond, he saw his fears had been justified and that the enemy had anticipated him for a crossbowman was standing in the mill's doorway. The man, wearing a chain mail coat, was beneath a small thatched porch that hid him from any archers on the castle battlements though, when Thomas looked up the hill, he saw no archers there. The besiegers doubtless had crossbows in the town and would shoot at any man who exposed himself.

"Kill him." Genevieve was crouching beside Thomas and had seen the lone crossbowman across the river.

"And warn the others?"

"What others?"

"He's not alone there," Thomas said. He reckoned the miller and his family must have gone because the spillway chute had been low-ered and the great waterwheel was motionless, but the besiegers would not have posted a single man to guard the difficult route across the weir's top. There were probably a dozen men there. He could shoot the first, that was no problem, but then the others would shoot at him from the door and from the two windows facing the river and he would have no chance of crossing the weir. He stared for a long time, thinking, then went back to Philin and the *coredors* who were hiding farther up the slope. "I need flint and steel," he told Philin.

The *coredors* travelled frequently and needed to make fires every night so several of the women had flint and steel, but one also had a leather pouch filled with the powder made from puffball fungi. Thomas thanked her, promised her a reward for the precious powder, then went downstream until he was hidden from the sentry stand-ing under the mill's porch. He and Genevieve searched the under-growth for small scraps of kindling and for newly fallen chestnut leaves. He needed twine so he pulled a strand from the shirt Genevieve wore beneath her mail coat, then piled some kindling on a flat stone, liberally sprinkled it with powder, and gave the steel and flint to Genevieve. "Don't light it yet," he told her. He did not want smoke drifting out of the almost bare trees to alert the men across the river.

He took the thicker scraps of kindling and bound them to the head of a broad-head arrow. It took time, but after a while he had a thick bunch of kindling that he would protect with the big chestnut leaves. A fire arrow had to be burning well, but the rush of its flight could extinguish the flames and the leaves would help prevent that. He wet the leaves in a puddle, placed them over the dry twigs, tied the twine off, then shook the arrow to make certain the bunched kindling was secure. "Light it now," he told Genevieve.

She rapped the flint and the puffball powder flared instantly, then the kindling took and a brief, bright flame shot up. Thomas let the fire grow, held the arrow to it, let it catch and then held it an instant so that all the kindling was burning. The ash shaft blackened as he edged downhill until he could see the mill's thatched roof.

He drew. The fire scorched his left hand so he could not draw to the bow's full extent, but the distance was short. He prayed no one was staring out of the mill's windows, said another prayer to St. Sebastian that the arrow would fly properly, and loosed.

The broad-head flew. It arched from the trees, trailing smoke, and thumped into the thatch halfway up the roof. The sound must have alerted the men inside the mill, but at that moment the gun fired in the town and that much greater noise would probably have distracted them.

He stamped out Genevieve's small fire, then led her back upstream and beckoned Philin and the men with the crossbows to creep down to the wood's edge. Now he waited.

The mill's thatch was damp. It had been raining heavily and the mossy straw was dark with moisture. Thomas could see a wisp of smoke coming from where the arrow had buried itself in the dirty, ragged roof, but there were no flames. The crossbowman was still in the doorway, yawning. The river had been swollen by the rain and was pouring over the weir in a thick, green-white rill that would tug at the ankles as they tried to cross. Thomas looked back to the mill roof and thought the smoke was dying. He would have to do it all again, and keep doing it until he was discovered or the fire caught, and just as he was making up his mind to take Genevieve back downstream to find new kindling, the roof suddenly emitted a surge of smoke. It thickened fast, billowing up like a small rain cloud, then a flame appeared in the thatch and Thomas had to hush the *coredors* who had begun to cheer. The fire spread with extraordinary rapidity. The arrow must have carried the kindling into the drier layer beneath the dark, wet straw and the flames now burst through the black, moss-covered outer sheath. In only seconds half the roof was ablaze and Thomas knew this was a fire that would never be extinguished.

It would set light to the beams, the roof would collapse, and then the mill's great wooden workings would burn until there was nothing left but a smoke-blackened stone shell.

Then the men burst out of the door. "Now," Thomas said, and his first broad-head seared across the stream and threw a man back through the door, and the *coredors* were loosing their crossbows that gave clicks as the cords were freed. The bolts clattered on stone, struck a man in the leg, and Thomas's second and third arrows were on the way before the crossbows shot again. One of the men from the mill succeeded in scrambling away behind the burning building, doubtless going to alert the other besiegers, and Thomas knew time was short, but more men came from the mill and he shot again, saw he had put an arrow through a woman's neck, had no time for regrets, pulled the cord and loosed again. Then the doorway was empty and he pulled one of the crossbowmen away from bank and told the others to keep shooting at anyone who showed in the doorway. "Cross now!" he called to Philin.

Thomas and the crossbowman negotiated the weir first. The stone sill was about as broad as a man's foot, and it was slippery, but they edged across, the water fierce against their feet. Philin, his son on his shoulders, led the other *coredors* across as Thomas, at last gaining the town bank, sent an arrow into the flamelit interior of the mill. There were bodies by the doorway. Some still moved. The woman he had shot looked at him with wide, dead eyes. A crossbow bolt hammered down from the wood which lay between the mill and the town wall above and the quarrel narrowly missed Thomas to splash into the mill pond, but then a white-feathered arrow hissed down from the keep's rampart and slashed into the trees where the crossbowman was hidden. No more bolts came.

A woman slipped on the weir and screamed as she fell down its face into the churning white water. "Leave her!" Philin shouted.

"Up the path!" Thomas yelled. "Go, go!" He sent one of the *coredors* up first because the man was armed with an axe; Thomas had told him to hack through the small gate in the wall at the hill's top. He turned to the crossbowmen over the river whose aim was now obscured by the folk scrambling up the town bank. "Come on!" he called to them, and though none spoke English they understood him well enough, and then a great crash sounded from the mill as a section of the roof collapsed and a gout of sparks and flames erupted from the fallen joists and rafters.

And at that instant the mill's last defender came running from the doorway. He was a tall man, dressed in leather rather than mail, and his hair was smoking from the fire and his face, as ugly as any Thomas had ever seen, was fixed in a rictus of hate. The man leaped the barrier of dead and dying and for a second Thomas thought the man was charging him, but then he twisted away in an attempt to escape and Thomas pulled the cord, loosed, and the arrow plunged between the man's shoulder-blades and hurled him forward. The wounded man had been carrying a belt which had a sword, a knife and a crossbowman's quiver attached to it, and the belt skidded away in the wet leaves. Thomas thought that any spare missiles would always be welcome and so he ran to pick up the belt, and the man, who had to be dying, snatched at Thomas's ankle. "Bastard," the man said in French, "bastard!"

Thomas kicked the man in the face, breaking his teeth, then stamped down with his heel to break some more. The dying man released his grip and Thomas kicked him again, just to keep him still. "Up the hill!" he shouted. He saw that Genevieve had crossed the weir safely and he tossed her the belt with its weapons and quarrel-case, then followed her up the path towards the small gate behind St. Sardos's church. Would the enemy be guarding it? But if they were, that enemy was in trouble, for more archers were on the castle's tower now and they were shooting down into the town. They were standing, shooting, ducking down and Thomas could hear the sound of crossbow bolts banging into the castle's stone.

The path was steep and wet. Thomas kept glancing to his left, looking for enemy, but none showed on the slope. He hurried, lost his footing, saw the wall so close ahead and climbed on. Genevieve was in the gate now, looking back for him, and Thomas scrambled the last few feet and ran through the splintered gate, following Genevieve down the dark alley and out into the square. A crossbow bolt spat into the cobbles, bounced up, and someone was shouting and he saw men-at-arms in the main street, was aware of an arrow sizzling past him just as he saw that half the gate arch had been destroyed, that a pile of rubble half obscured the castle's entrance, that a pile of naked corpses was lying in the square under the castle's curtain wall and that crossbow quarrels were skidding across the stones. Then he jumped the rubble, bounced off the remaining part of the arch and was safe inside the yard where his feet flew from beneath him because the stones were slippery. He slid a few feet, then banged against a timber barricade stretching across the yard.

And Sir Guillaume, one eyed, evil-looking, was grinning at him. "Took your time coming, didn't you?" the Frenchman said.

"Bloody hell," Thomas said. The *coredors* were all there except for the woman who had fallen from the weir. Genevieve was safe. "I thought you'd need help," he said.

"You think you can help us?" Sir Guillaume said. He lifted Thomas to his feet and enfolded his friend in an embrace. "I thought you were dead," he said, and then, embarrassed at this display of feeling, he jerked his head at the *coredors* and their children. "Who are they?"

"Bandits," Thomas said, "hungry bandits."

"There's food in the upper hall," Sir Guillaume said, and then Jake and Sam were there, grinning, and they escorted Thomas and Genevieve up the stairs where the *coredors* stared at the cheese and salt meat. "Eat," Sir Guillaume said.

Thomas remembered the naked corpses in the town square. Were they his men? Sir Guillaume shook his head. "Bastards attacked us," he said, "and the bastards died. So we stripped them and threw them over the wall. Rats are eating them now. Big bastards, they are."

"The rats?"

"Big as cats. So what happened to you?"

Thomas told him as he ate. Told of going to the monastery, of Planchard's death, of the fight in the wood, and of the slow journey back to Castillon d'Arbizon. "I knew Robbie wasn't here," he explained, "so I reckoned only my friends would be left."

"Nice to die among friends," Sir Guillaume said. He glanced up at the hall's high narrow windows, judging the progress of the day by the angle of the light. "Gun won't fire for another couple of hours."

"They're knocking down the gate arch?"

"That's what they seem to be doing," Sir Guillaume said, "and maybe they want to bring down the whole curtain wall? That would make it easier for them to get into the courtyard. It'll take them a month, though." He looked at the *coredors*. "And you bring me extra mouths to feed."

Thomas shook his head. "They'll all fight, even the women. And the children can pick up the crossbow bolts." There were plenty of those strewn about the castle and, once the vanes had been straightened, they would serve the *coredors'* crossbows well enough. "First thing, though," Thomas went on, "is to get rid of that bloody gun."

Sir Guillaume grinned. "You think I haven't thought about doing that? You reckon we've just been sitting on our backsides playing dice? But how do you do it? A sally? If I take a dozen men down the street half of them will be spitted by quarrels by the time we reach the tavern. Can't be done, Thomas."

"Kindling," Thomas said.

"Kindling," Sir Guillaume repeated flatly.

"Kindling and twine," Thomas said. "Make fire arrows. They're not storing their damned gunpowder in the open air, are they? It's in a house. And houses burn. So we burn the bloody town down. All of it. I doubt our arrows can reach the houses by the gun, but if we get an east wind the fire will spread fast enough. It'll slow them anyway."

Sir Guillaume stared at him. "You're not as daft as you look, are you?"

Then a gasp made both men turn round. Genevieve, sitting close by, had been toying with the quarrel-case that Thomas had snatched up at the mill. The lid, which fitted neatly over the circular leather case, had been sealed with wax and that had intrigued her so she had scraped the wax away, lifted the lid, and found something inside, something which had been carefully wrapped in linen and padded with sawdust. She had shaken the sawdust off, then unwrapped the linen.

And everyone in the room now gazed at her in awe.

For she had found the Grail.

JOSCELYN DECIDED he hated Guy Vexille. Hated the man's air of competence, the slight sneer that always seemed to be on his face and which, without words being said, seemed to condemn whatever Joscelyn did. He also hated the man's piety and self-control. Joscelyn would have liked nothing better than to order Vexille away, but his men were a valuable addition to the besieging force. When the assault came, when there was a charge across the rubble of the castle gateway, Vexille's black-cloaked men-at-arms could well mean the difference between defeat and victory. So Joscelyn endured Vexille's presence.

Robbie also endured it. Vexille had killed his brother and Robbie had sworn to take vengeance for that, but by now Robbie was so confused that he did not know what his oaths meant any more. He had sworn to go on pilgrimage, yet here he was, still in Castillon d'Arbizon; he had sworn to kill Guy Vexille, yet the man lived; he had sworn allegiance to Joscelyn, and now he recognized that Joscelyn was a brainless fool, brave as a pig, but with no trace of religion or honor. The one man he had never sworn an oath to was Thomas, yet that was the man he wished well in the unfolding tragedy.

And at least Thomas lived. He had managed to cross the weir, despite the guard Guy Vexille had placed on the mill. Vexille had come to Castillon d'Arbizon, discovered the river crossing was unguarded, and put the sour, dour Charles Bessières in command at the mill. Bessières had accepted the order because it kept him away from both Vexille and Joscelyn, but then he had failed, and Robbie had been astonished at the delight he had felt when he realized that Thomas had again outwitted them, and that Thomas lived and was back in the castle. He had seen Thomas run across the square, the air humming with crossbow bolts, and he had almost cheered when he saw his friend make the safety of the castle

Robbie had seen Genevieve too and he did not know what to think about that. In Genevieve he saw something he wanted so badly that it was like an ache. Yet he dared not admit it, for Joscelyn would just laugh at him. If Robbie had a choice, and his oaths meant he had none, he would have gone to the castle and begged Thomas's forgiveness, and doubtless he would have died there.

For Thomas, though he lived, was trapped. Guy Vexille, cursing that Charles Bessières had failed at such a simple task, had put men in the woods across the river so that there was now no escape across the weir. The only way out of the castle was down the main street and out the town's west gate or north to the smaller gate by St. Callic's church, which opened onto the water meadows where the townsfolk grazed their cattle, and Joscelyn and Vexille, between them, had well over a hundred men-at-arms waiting for just such an attempt. Crossbowmen were placed in every vantage point in the town, and meanwhile the gun would gnaw and hammer and undermine the castle-gate bastions until, in time, there would be a rough path across the ruins and into the castle's heart. Then the slaughter could begin and Robbie must watch his friends die.

Half the castle's gateway was already down and Signor Gioberti had now realigned his bulbous gun so that its missiles would strike the right-hand side of the arch. The Italian reckoned it would take a week to bring the whole gate down, and he had advised Joscelyn that it would be best to spend still more time on widening the breach by bringing down those sections of the curtain wall either side of the ruined arch so that the attackers were not channeled into a narrow space which the archers could fill with feathered death.

"Pavises," Joscelyn said, and he had ordered the town's two carpenters to make more of the big willow shields that would protect the crossbowmen as they ran to the breach. Those crossbowmen could then shoot up at the archers while the men-at-arms streamed past them. "One week," Joscelyn told the Italian, "you've got one week to bring down the gate, then we attack." He wanted it over fast for the siege was proving more expensive and more complicated than he had ever imagined. It was not just the fighting that was difficult, but he had to pay carters to bring hay and oats for all the men-at-arms' horses, and he had to send men to scavenge for scarce food in a district that had already been plundered by the enemy, and each day brought new unforeseen problems that gnawed at Joscelyn's confidence. He just wanted to attack and get the wretched business over.

But the defenders attacked first. At dawn, on the day after Thomas reached Castillon d'Arbizon, when there was a chill northeasterly wind blowing under a leaden sky, fire arrows seared from the tower ramparts to plunge into the town's thatch. Arrow after arrow trailed smoke, and the besiegers woke to the danger as the townfolk screamed for hooks and water. Men used the long-handled hooks to pull the thatch from the roofs, but more arrows came and within minutes three houses were ablaze and the wind was pushing the flames towards the gate where the gun was already loaded and the loam was setting.

"The powder! The powder!" Signor Gioberti shouted, and his men began carrying the precious barrels out of the house near the gun, and smoke billowed across them and frightened folk got in their way so that one man slipped and spilt a whole barrel of unmixed powder across the roadway. Joscelyn came from his commandeered house and shouted at his men to fetch water, while Guy Vexille was ordering that buildings should be pulled down to make a firebreak, but the townspeople held the soldiers up and now the fires were roaring, a dozen more houses were ablaze and their thatch had become furnaces that spread from roof to roof. Panicked birds fluttered inside the smoke and rats, in their scores, fled out of thatch and cellar doors. Many of the besieging crossbowmen had made themselves eyries inside the roofs from where they could shoot through holes piercing the thatch, and they now stumbled down from the attics. Pigs squealed as they were roasted alive and then, just when it seemed the whole town would burn and when the first flying sparks were settling on the roofs near the cannon, the heavens opened.

A crash of thunder tore across the sky and then the rain slashed down. It fell so hard that it blotted out the view of the castle from the town gate. It turned the street into a watercourse, it soaked the powder barrels and it extinguished the fires. Smoke still poured upwards, but the rain hissed on glowing embers. The gutters ran with black water and the fires died.

Galat Lorret, the senior consul, came to Joscelyn and wanted to know where the townsfolk should shelter. Over a third of the houses had lost their roofs and the others were crowded with billeted soldiers. "Your lordship must find us food," he told Joscelyn, "and we need tents." Lorret was shivering, perhaps with fear or else from the onset of a fever, but Joscelyn had no pity for the man. Indeed he was so enraged at being given advice by a commoner that he struck Lorret, then struck him again, driving him back into the street with a flurry of blows and kicks.

"You can starve!" Joscelyn screamed at the consul. "Starve and shiver. Bastard!" He punched the old man so hard that Lorret's jaw was broken. The consul lay in the wet gutter, his official robes soaking with the ash-blackened water. A young woman came from the undamaged house behind him; she had glazed eyes and a flushed face. She vomited suddenly, pouring the contents of her stomach into the gutter beside Lorret. "Get out!" Joscelyn screamed at her. "Put your filth somewhere else!"

Then Joscelyn saw that Guy Vexille, Robbie Douglas and a dozen men-at-arms were staring open-mouthed at the castle. Just staring. The rain was lessening and the smoke was clearing and the castle's shattered frontage could be seen again, and Joscelyn turned to see what they gazed at. He could see the armor hanging from the keep's battlements, the mail coats stripped from his dead men and hung there as an insult, and he could see the captured shields, including Robbie's red heart of Douglas, hanging upside down among the hauberks, but Guy Vexille was not staring at those trophies. Instead he was looking at the lower rampart, at the half-broken parapet above the castle gate, and there, in the rain, was gold.

Robbie Douglas risked the archers in the castle by walking up the street to see the golden object more clearly. No arrows came at him. The castle appeared deserted, silent. He walked almost to the square until he could see the thing clearly and he peered in disbelief and then, with tears in his eyes, he fell to his knees. "The Grail," he said, and suddenly other men had joined him and were kneeling on the cobbles.

"The what?" Joscelyn asked.

Guy Vexille pulled off his hat and knelt. He stared upwards and it seemed to him that the precious cup glowed.

For in the smoke and destruction, shining like the truth, was the Grail.

THE CANNON DID NOT FIRE again that day. Joscelyn was not happy about that. The new Count of Berat did not care that the defenders had a cup, they could have had the whole true cross, the tail of Jonah's whale, the baby Jesus' swaddling clothes, the crown of thorns and the pearly gates themselves and he would happily have buried the whole lot under the castle's shattered masonry, but the priests with the besiegers went on their knees to him, and Guy Vexille did the same, and that obeisance from a man he feared gave Joscelyn pause.

"We have to talk with them," Vexille said.

"They are heretics," the priests said, "and the Grail must be saved from them."

"What am I supposed to do?" Joscelyn demanded. "Just ask for it?"

"You must bargain for it," Guy Vexille said.

"Bargain!" Joscelyn bridled at the thought, then an idea came. The Grail? If the thing existed, and everyone about him believed it did, and if it really was here, in his domain, then there was money to be made from it. The cup would need to go to Berat, of course, where fools like his dead uncle would pay mightily to see it. Big jars at the castle gate, he thought, and lines of pilgrims throwing in money to be allowed to see the Grail. There was, he thought, profit in that gold, and plainly the garrison wanted to talk for, after displaying the cup, they had shot no more arrows.

"I will go and talk with them," Vexille said.

"Why you?" Joscelyn demanded.

"Then you go, my lord," Vexille said deferentially.

But Joscelyn did not want to face the men who had held him prisoner. The next time he saw them he wanted them to be dead, and so he waved Vexille on his way. "But you'll offer them nothing!" he warned. "Not unless I agree to it."

"I will make no agreement," Vexille said, "without your permission."

Orders were given that the crossbowmen were not to shoot and then Guy Vexille, bare-headed and without any weapons, walked up the main street past the smoking wreckage of the houses. A man was sitting in an alley and Vexille noticed that his face was sweating and blotched with dark lumps and his clothes were stained with vomit. Guy hated such sights. He was a fastidious man, scrupulously clean, and the stench and diseases of mankind repelled him: they were evidences of a sinful world, one that had forgotten God. Then he saw his cousin come onto the broken rampart and take the Grail away.

A moment later Thomas crossed the rubble that filled the gateway. Like Guy he wore no sword, nor had he brought the Grail. He wore his mail, which was rusting now, frayed at the hem and crusted with dirt. He had a short beard for he had long lost his razor and it gave him, Guy thought, a grim and desperate look. "Thomas," Guy greeted him, then gave a small bow, "cousin."

Thomas looked past Vexille to see three priests watching from halfway down the street. "The last priests who came here excommunicated me," he said.

"What the Church does," Guy said, "it can undo. Where did you find it?"

For a moment it looked as if Thomas would not answer, then he shrugged. "Under the thunder," he said, "at the lightning's heart."

Guy Vexille smiled at the evasion. "I do not even know," he said, "whether you have the Grail. Perhaps it is a trick? You put a golden cup on the wall and we just make an assumption. Suppose we are wrong? Prove it to me, Thomas."

"I can't."

"Then show it to me," Guy begged. He spoke humbly.

"Why should I?"

"Because the Kingdom of Heaven depends on it."

Thomas seemed to sneer at that answer, then he looked curiously at his cousin. "Tell me something first," he said.

"If I can."

"Who was the tall, scarred man I killed at the mill?"

Guy Vexille frowned for it seemed a very strange question, but he could see no trap in it and he wanted to humour Thomas so he answered. "His name was Charles Bessières," he said cautiously, "and he was the brother of Cardinal Bessières. Why do you ask?"

"Because he fought well," Thomas lied.

"Is that all?"

"He fought well, and he very nearly took the Grail from me," Thomas embroidered the untruth. "I just wondered who he was." He shrugged and tried to work out why a brother of Cardinal Bessières should have been carrying the Grail.

"He was not a man worthy of having the Grail," Guy Vexille said.

"Am I?" Thomas demanded.

Guy ignored the hostile question. "Show it to me," he pleaded. "For the love of God, Thomas, show it to me."

Thomas hesitated, then he turned and raised a hand and Sir Guillaume, armored in captured plate from head to foot and with a drawn sword, came from the castle with Genevieve. She carried the Grail and had a wine skin tied to her belt. "Not too close to him," Thomas warned her, then looked back to Guy. "You remember Sir Guillaume d'Evecque? Another man sworn to kill you?"

"We are meeting under a truce," Guy reminded him, then he nodded at Sir Guillaume whose only response was to spit on the cobbles. Guy ignored the gesture, gazing instead at the cup in the girl's hands.

It was a thing of ethereal, magical beauty. A thing of lace-like delicacy. A thing so far removed from this smoke-stinking town with its rat-chewed corpses that Guy had no doubts that this was the Grail. It was the most sought-after object in Christendom, the key to heaven itself, and Guy almost dropped to his knees in reverence.

Genevieve took off the pearl-hung lid and tipped the stemmed gold goblet over Thomas's hands. A thick green glass cup fell out of the golden filigree and Thomas held it reverently. "This is the Grail, Guy," he said. "That golden confection was just made to hold it, but this is it."

Guy watched it hungrily, but dared make no move towards it. Sir Guillaume wanted only the smallest excuse to lift his sword and ram it forward and Guy had no doubt that archers were watching him from behind the slits in the high tower. He said nothing as Thomas took the skin from Genevieve's belt and poured some wine into the cup. "See?" Thomas said, and Guy saw that the green had darkened with the wine, but that it also now possessed a golden sheen that had not been there before. Thomas let the wine skin drop to the ground and then, with his eyes on his cousin's eyes, he lifted the cup and drained it. "'*Hic est enim sanguis meus*,'" Thomas said angrily. They were the words of Christ. "This is my blood." Then he gave the cup to Genevieve and she walked away with it, followed by Sir Guillaume. "A heretic drinks from the Grail," Thomas said, "and there's worse to come."

"Worse?" Guy asked gently.

"We shall put it under the gate arch," Thomas said. "And when your cannon brings down the rest of the bastions then the Grail will be crushed. What you'll get is a twisted piece of gold and some broken glass."

Guy Vexille smiled. "The Grail cannot be broken, Thomas."

"Then you risk that belief," Thomas said angrily and turned away.

"Thomas! Thomas, I beg you," Guy called. "Listen to me."

Thomas wanted to keep walking, but he reluctantly turned back for his cousin's tone had been pleading. It had been the voice of a broken man, and what did it hurt Thomas if he heard more? He had made the threat. If the attack continued then the Grail would be broken. Now, he supposed, he must let his cousin make whatever offer he wanted, though he did not intend to make that easy. "Why should I listen," he asked, "to the man who killed my father? Who killed my woman?"

"Listen to a child of God," Guy said.

Thomas almost laughed, but he stayed.

Guy took a breath, framing what he wanted to say. He stared up at the sky where low clouds threatened more rain. "The world is beset by evil," he said, "and the Church is corrupt, and the devil does his work unhindered. If we have the Grail we can change that. The Church can be cleansed, a new crusade can scour the world of sin. It will bring the Kingdom of Heaven to earth." He had been staring skywards as he spoke, but now looked at Thomas. "That is all I want, Thomas."

"So my father had to die for that?"

Guy nodded. "I wish it had not been necessary, but he was hiding the Grail. He was an enemy of God."

Thomas hated Guy then, hated him more than ever, hated him even though his cousin was speaking low and reasonably, his voice filled with emotion. "Tell me," Thomas said, "what you want now."

"Your friendship," Guy said.

"Friendship!"

"The Count of Berat is evil," Guy said. "He's a bully, a fool, a man who ignores God. If you lead your men out of the castle I will turn on him. By nightfall, Thomas, you and I will be lords of this place, and tomorrow we shall go to Berat and reveal the Grail and invite all men of God to come to us." Guy paused, watching Thomas's hard face for any reaction to the words. "March north with me," he went on, "Paris will be next. We shall rid ourselves of that foolish Valois King. We shall take the world, Thomas, and open it to the love of God. Think of it, Thomas! All the grace and beauty of God poured onto the world. No more sadness, no more sin, just the harmony of God in a world of peace."

Thomas pretended to think about it, then frowned. "I'll attack Joscelyn with you," he said, "but I would want to talk with Abbot Planchard before I marched north."

"With Abbot Planchard?" Guy could not hide his surprise. "Why?"

"Because he's a good man," Thomas said, "and I trust his advice."

Guy nodded. "Then I shall send for him. I can have him here by tomorrow."

Thomas felt such anger then that he could have attacked Guy with his bare fists, but he held the rage in check. "You can have him here by tomorrow?" he asked instead.

"If he'll come."

"Doesn't have much choice, does he?" Thomas said, the fury in his voice now. "He's dead, cousin, and you killed him. I was there, in the ossuary, hiding. I heard you!"

Guy looked astonished, then incensed, but he had nothing to say.

"You lie like a child," Thomas said scornfully. "You lie about one good man's death? Then you lie about everything." He turned and walked away.

"Thomas!" Guy called after him.

Thomas turned back. "You want the Grail, cousin? Then you fight for it. Maybe just you and me? You and your sword against me and my weapon."

"Your weapon?" Guy asked.

"The Grail," Thomas said curtly and, ignoring his cousin's pleas, walked back to the castle.

"So what did he offer?" Sir Guillaume asked.

"All the kingdoms of the earth," Thomas said.

Sir Guillaume sniffed suspiciously. "I smell something holy in that answer."

Thomas smiled. "The devil took Christ into the wilderness and offered him all the kingdoms of the earth if he would give up his mission."

"He should have accepted," Sir Guillaume said, "and saved us a pile of trouble. So we can't leave?"

"Not unless we fight our way out."

"The ransom money?" Sir Guillaume asked hopefully.

"I forgot to ask about it."

"Much bloody use you are," Sir Guillaume retorted in English, then he switched back to French and sounded more cheerful. "But at least we have the Grail, eh? That's something!"

"Do we?" Genevieve asked.

The two men turned to her. They were in the upper hall, bare of furniture now because the table and stools had been taken down to reinforce the barricade in the courtyard. All that was left was the big iron-bound chest that had the garrison's money inside and there was plenty of that after a season of raiding. Genevieve sat on the chest; she had the beautiful golden Grail with its green cup, but she also had the box that Thomas had brought from St. Sever's monastery, and now she took the cup from its golden nest and placed it in the box. The lid would not close because the glass cup was too big. The box, whatever it might have been made for, had not been made for this Grail. "Do we have the Grail?" she asked, and Thomas and Sir Guillaume stared at her as she showed how the cup would not fit in the box.

"Of course it's the Grail," Sir Guillaume said dismissively.

Thomas went to Genevieve and took the cup. He turned it in his hands. "If my father did have the Grail," he asked, "how did it end up with Cardinal Bessières's brother?"

"Who?" Sir Guillaume demanded.

Thomas stared at the green glass. He had heard that the Grail in Genoa Cathedral was made of green glass, and no one believed that was real. Was this the same grail? Or another green-glass fake? "The man I took it from," he said, "was the brother of Cardinal Bessières, and if he already had the Grail, then what was he doing in Castillon d'Arbizon? He would have taken it to Paris, or to Avignon."

"Sweet Jesus Christ," Sir Guillaume said. "You mean that isn't real?"

"One way to find out," Thomas said, and he held the cup high. He

saw the tiny specks of gold on the glass and he thought it was a beautiful thing, an exquisite thing, an old thing, but was it the real thing?
And so he raised his hand higher, held the cup for another heartbeat
and then let it drop to the floorboards.

Where the green glass shattered into a thousand fragments.

"Sweet Jesus Christ," Sir Guillaume said, "sweet Jesus goddamned
bloody Christ."

I T WAS ON THE MORNING after the fire had burned out so much of Castillon d'Arbizon that the first people died. Some died in the night, some at dawn, and the priests were busy carrying the consecrated wafers to houses where they would offer the last rites. The shrieks of bereaved families were loud enough to wake Joscelyn who snarled at his squire to go and silence the wretched noise, but the squire, who slept on straw in a corner of Joscelyn's room, was shivering and sweating and his face had grown evil-looking dark lumps that made Joscelyn wince. "Get out!" he shouted at the squire and then, when the young man did not move, he kicked him towards the door. "Out! Out! Oh, Jesus! You shat yourself! Get out!"

Joscelyn dressed himself, pulling breeches and a leather coat over his linen shirt. "You're not ill, are you?" he said to the girl who had shared his bed.

"No, lord."

"Then get me bacon and bread, and mulled wine."

"Mulled wine?"

"You're a serving girl, aren't you? So damn well serve me, then clean up that damned mess." He pointed at the squire's bed, then pulled on his boots and wondered why he had not been woken by the cannon which usually fired at cock-crow. The loam in the gun's barrel set overnight and Signor Gioberti was of the opinion that the dawn shot did the most damage, yet this morning it had still not been fired. Joscelyn strode into the parlor of the house, shouting for the gunner.

"He's sick." It was Guy Vexille who answered. He was sitting in a corner of the room, sharpening a knife and evidently waiting for Joscelyn. "There is a contagion."

Joscelyn strapped on his sword belt. "Gioberti's sick?"

Guy Vexille sheathed the knife. "He's vomiting, my lord, and sweating. He has swellings in his armpits and groin."

"His men can fire the damned gun, can't they?"

"Most of them are sick as well."

Joscelyn stared at Vexille, trying to understand what he was hearing. "The gunners are sick?"

"Half the town seems to be sick," Vexille said, standing. He had washed, put on clean black clothes and oiled his long black hair so that it lay sleek along his narrow skull. "I heard there was a pestilence," he said, "but I didn't believe it. I was wrong, God forgive me."

"A pestilence?" Joscelyn was scared now.

"God punishes us," Vexille said calmly, "by letting the devil loose, and we could not hope for a clearer sign from heaven. We have to assault the castle today, lord, seize the Grail and thus end the plague."

"Plague?" Joscelyn asked, then heard a timid knock on the door and hoped it was the serving girl bringing him food. "Come in, damn you," he shouted, but instead of the girl it was Father Medous who looked frightened and nervous.

The priest went on his knees to Joscelyn. "People are dying, lord," he said.

"What in God's name do you expect me to do?" Joscelyn asked.

"Capture the castle," Vexille said.

Joscelyn ignored him, staring at the priest. "Dying?" he asked helplessly.

Father Medous nodded. There were tears on his face. "It is a pestilence, lord," he said. "They sweat, vomit, void their bowels, show black boils and they're dying."

"Dying?" Joscelyn asked again.

"Galat Lorret is dead; his wife is ill. My own housekeeper has the sickness." More tears rolled down Medous's face. "It is in the air, lord, a pestilence." He stared up at Joscelyn's blank, round face, hoping that his lord could help. "It is in the air," he said again, "and we need doctors, my lord, and only you can command them to come from Berat."

Joscelyn pushed past the kneeling priest, ducked out into the street and saw two of his men-at-arms sitting in the tavern door with swollen faces running with sweat. They looked at him dully and he turned away, hearing the wailing and screeching of mothers watching their children sweat and die. Smoke from the previous day's fire drifted thin through the damp morning and everything seemed covered in soot. Joscelyn shivered, then saw Sir Henri Courtois, still healthy, coming from St. Callic's church and he almost ran and embraced the old man in his relief. "You know what's happening?" Joscelyn asked.

"There is a pestilence, my lord."

"It's in the air, yes?" Joscelyn asked, snatching at what Father Medous had told him.

"I wouldn't know," Sir Henri said tiredly, "but I do know that more than a score of our men are sick with it, and three are already dead. Robbie Douglas is sick. He was asking for you, my lord. He begs you to find him a physician."

Joscelyn ignored that request and sniffed the air instead. He could smell the remnants of the fires, the stench of vomit and dung and urine. They were the smells of any town, the everyday smells, yet somehow they seemed more sinister now. "What do we do?" he asked helplessly.

"The sick need help," Sir Henri said. "They need physicians." And gravediggers, he thought, but did not say it aloud.

"It's in the air," Joscelyn said yet again. The stink was rank now, besieging him, threatening him, and he felt a tremor of panic. He could fight a man, fight an army even, but not this silent insidious reek. "We go," he decided. "Any man untouched by the disease will leave now. Now!"

"Go?" Sir Henri was confused by the decision.

"We go!" Joscelyn said firmly. "Leave the sick behind. Order the men to get ready and saddle their horses."

"But Robbie Douglas wants to see you," Sir Henri said. Joscelyn was Robbie's lord and so owed him the duty of care, but Joscelyn was in no mood to visit the sick. The sick could damn well look after themselves and he would save as many men from the horror as he could.

They left within the hour. A stream of horsemen galloped out of the town, fleeing the contagion and riding for the safety of Berat's great castle. Almost all of Joscelyn's crossbowmen, abandoned by their knights and men-at-arms, followed and many of the townsfolk were also leaving to find a refuge from the pestilence. A good number of Vexille's men vanished too, as did those few gunners who were not touched by the plague. They abandoned Hell Spitter, stole sick men's horses and rode away. Of Joscelyn's healthy men only Sir Henri Courtois stayed. He was middle-aged, he had lost his fear of death, and men who had served him for many years were lying in agony. He did not know what he could do for them, but what he could, he would.

Guy Vexille went to St. Callic's church and ordered the women who were praying to the image of the saint and to the statue of the Virgin Mary to get out. He wanted to be alone with God and, though he believed the church was a place where a corrupted faith was practiced, it was still a house of prayer and so he knelt by the altar and stared at the broken body of Christ that hung above the altar. The painted blood flowed thick from the awful wounds and Guy gazed at that blood, ignoring a spider that span a web between the lance cut in the Saviour's side and the outstretched left hand. "You are punishing us," he said aloud, "scourging us, but if we do your will then you will spare us." But what was God's will? That was the dilemma, and he rocked back and forth on his knees, yearning for the answer. "Tell me," he told the man hanging on the cross, "tell me what I must do."

Yet he knew already what he must do: he must seize the Grail and release its power; but he hoped that in the church's dim interior, beneath the painting of God enthroned in the clouds, a message would come. And it did, though not as he had wanted. He had hoped for a voice in the darkness, a divine command that would give him surety of success, but instead he heard feet in the nave and when he looked round he saw that his men, those that remained and were not sick, had come to pray with him. They came one by one as they heard he was at the altar, and they knelt behind him and Guy knew that such good men could not be beaten. The time had come to take the Grail.

He sent a half-dozen men through the town with orders to find every soldier, every crossbowman, every knight and man-at-arms who could still walk. They must arm themselves," he said, "and we meet by the gun in one hour."

He went to his own quarters, deaf to the cries of the sick and their families. His servant had been struck by the sickness, but one of the sons of the house where Guy had his room was still fit and Guy ordered him to help with his preparations.

First he put on leather breeches and a leather jerkin. Both garments had been made tight-fitting so that Vexille had to stand still while the clumsy boy tied the laces at the back of the jerkin. Then the lad took handfuls of lard and smeared the leather so it was well greased and would let the armor move easily. Vexille wore a short mail haubergeon over the jerkin that provided extra protection for his chest, belly and groin, and that too needed greasing. Then, piece by piece, the black plate armor was buckled into place. First came the four cuisses, the rounded plates that protected the thighs, and beneath them the boy buckled the greaves that ran from knee to ankle. Vexille's knees were protected by roundels and his feet by plates of steel attached to boots that were buckled to the greaves. A short leather skirt on which were riveted heavy square plates of steel was fastened about his waist, and when that was adjusted Vexille lifted the plate gorget into place about his neck and waited as the youth did up the two buckles behind. Then the lad grunted as he lifted the breast-and backplates over Vexille's head. The two heavy pieces were joined by short leather straps that rested on his shoulders and the plates were secured by more straps at his sides. Then came the rerebraces that protected his upper arms, and the vambraces that sheathed his forearms, the espaliers to cover his shoulders and two more roundels that armored his elbow joints. He flexed his arms as the boy worked, making sure that the straps were not so tight that he could not wield a sword. The gauntlets were of leather that had been studded with overlapping steel plates that looked like scales; then came the sword belt with its heavy black scabbard holding the precious blade made in Cologne.

The sword was a whole ell in length, longer than a man's arm, and the blade was deceptively narrow, suggesting the sword might be fragile, but it had a strong central rib that stiffened the long steel and made it into a lethal lunging weapon. Most men carried cutting swords that blunted themselves on armor, but Vexille was a master with the thrusting blade. The art was to look for a joint in the armor and ram the steel through. The handle was sheathed with maple wood and the pommel and handguard were of steel. It bore no decoration, no gold leaf, no inscriptions on the blade, no silver inlay. It was simply a workman's tool, a killing weapon, a fit thing for this day's sacred duty.

"Sir?" the boy said nervously, offering Vexille the big tournament helm with its narrow eye slits.

"Not that one," Vexille said. "I'll take the bascinet and the coif." He pointed to what he wanted. The big tournament helm gave very restricted vision and Vexille had learned to distrust it in battle for it prevented him seeing enemies at his flanks. It was a risk to face archers without any visor, but at least he could see them, and now he pulled the mail coif over his head so that it protected the nape of his neck and his ears, then took the bascinet from the boy. It was a simple helmet, with no rim and with no faceplate to constrict his vision. "Go and look after your family," he told the boy, and then he picked up his shield, its willow boards covered with boiled, hardened leather on which was painted the yale of the Vexilles carrying its

Grail. He had no talisman, no charm. Few men went to battle without such a precaution, whether it was a lady's scarf or a piece of jewelry blessed by a priest, but Guy Vexille had only one talisman, and that was the Grail.

And now he went to fetch it.

ONE OF THE *COREDORS* was the first to fall ill in the castle and by the night's end there were more than a score of men and women vomiting, sweating and shivering. Jake was one of them. The cross-eyed archer dragged himself to a corner of the courtyard and propped his bow beside him and put a handful of arrows on his lap, and there he suffered. Thomas tried to persuade him to go upstairs, but Jake refused. "I'll stay here," he insisted. "I'll die in the open air."

"You won't die," Thomas said. "Heaven won't take you and the devil doesn't need any competition." The small joke failed to raise a smile on Jake's face, which was discolored by small red lumps that were rapidly darkening to the colour of a bruise. He had taken down his breeches because he could not contain his bowels and the most he would let Thomas do for him was to bring him a bed of straw from the ruins of the stables.

Philin's son also had the sickness. His face was showing pink spots and he was shivering. The disease seemed to have come from nowhere, but Thomas assumed it had been brought on the east wind that had fanned the flames in the town before the rain killed the fires. Abbot Planchard had warned him of this, of a pestilence coming from Lombardy, and here it was and Thomas was helpless. "We must find a priest," Philin said.

"A physician," Thomas said, though he knew of none and did not know how one could be got into the castle even if he could be found.

"A priest," Philin insisted. "If a child is touched by a consecrated wafer it cures him. It cures everything. Let me fetch a priest."

It was then Thomas realized the gun had not fired and that no bored crossbowman had clattered a quarrel against the castle's stones,

and so he let Philin go out of the ruined gateway in search of Father
Medous or one of the other priests in the town. He did not expect to
see the tall man again, yet Philin returned within half an hour to say
that the town was as badly stricken as the castle and that Father
Medous was anointing the sick and had no time to come to the
enemy garrison. "There was a dead woman in the street," Philin told
Thomas, "just lying there with her teeth clenched."

"Did Father Medous give you a wafer?"

Philin showed him a thick piece of bread, then carried it up to his
son who was in the upper hall with most of the sick. A woman wept
that her husband could not receive the last rites and so, to console her
and to give hope to the ill, Genevieve carried the golden cup around
the pallets and touched it to the hands of the sick and told them it
would work a miracle.

"We need a goddamned miracle," Sir Guillaume said to Thomas.
"What the hell is it?" The two had gone to the castle's tower from
where, unthreatened by any crossbows, they gazed down at the abandoned gun.

"There was a plague in Italy," Thomas said, "and it must have
come here."

"Jesus Christ," Sir Guillaume said. "What kind of plague?"

"God knows," Thomas said. "A bad one." For a moment he was
assailed with the fear that the pestilence was a punishment for breaking the green-glass Grail, then he remembered that Planchard had
warned him of the disease long before he had found the cup. He
watched a man wrapped in a bloody sheet stagger into the main street
and fall down. He lay still, looking as though he were already in his
winding sheet.

"What in God's name is happening?" Sir Guillaume asked, making the sign of the cross. "Have you ever seen anything like it?"

"It's God's wrath," Thomas said, "punishing us."

"For what?"

"For being alive," Thomas said bitterly. He could hear wailing from the town, and he saw the people fleeing the pestilence. They had their goods in wheelbarrows or handcarts and they pushed past the gun, out of the gate, across the bridge and off to the west.

"Pray for snow," Sir Guillaume said. "I've often noticed that snow stops sickness. Don't know why."

"It doesn't snow here," Thomas said.

Genevieve joined them, still holding the golden cup. "I fed the fire," she said. "It seems to help."

"Help?"

"The sick," she said. "They like the warmth. It's a huge fire." She pointed to the smoke coming from the vent in the keep's side. Thomas put an arm around her and searched her face for any signs of the reddish spots, but her pale skin was clear. They stood watching the people cross the bridge and take the westwards road and, while they watched, they saw Joscelyn lead a stream of mounted men-at-arms away to the north. The new Count of Berat did not look back, he just rode as if the devil himself was on his heels.

And perhaps he was, Thomas thought, and he looked for any sign of his cousin among the disappearing horsemen, but did not see him. Perhaps Guy was dying?

"Is the siege over?" Sir Guillaume wondered aloud.

"Not if my cousin lives," Thomas said.

"How many archers do you have?"

"Twelve who can pull a cord," Thomas said. "Men-at-arms?"

"Fifteen." Sir Guillaume grimaced. The only consolation was that none of the garrison was tempted to flee for they were all stranded far from any friendly troops. Some of the *coredors* had gone when they learned from Philin that no besiegers were watching the castle, but Thomas did not regret their loss. "So what do we do?" Sir Guillaume asked.

"Stay here till our sick recover," Thomas said. "Or till they die," he added. "Then we go." He could not leave men like Jake to suffer alone. The least he could do was stay and keep them company on their passage to heaven or hell.

Then he saw that passage to the next world might come quicker than he expected, for men-at-arms were gathering at the foot of the street. They carried swords, axes and shields, and their appearance meant only one thing. "They want the Grail," he said.

"Jesus Christ, give it to them." Sir Guillaume said fervently. "Give them all the pieces."

"You think that will satisfy them?"

"No," Sir Guillaume admitted.

Thomas leaned over the battlements. "Archers!" he shouted, then ran to pull on his mail coat and strap on his sword and gather his bow and arrow bag.

For the siege was not done.

THIRTY-THREE KNIGHTS and men-at-arms advanced up the street. The leading twelve, among whom was Guy Vexille, carried the pavises that should have sheltered the crossbowmen, but only six of those archers were left and Guy had ordered them to follow him, keeping a good ten paces behind, and so the vast crossbow shields, each taller than a man, served to protect his men-at-arms.

They moved slowly, shuffling to keep close and to stay behind the thick, heavy pavises that were being pushed along the cobbles so that no arrow could fly beneath and pin a man's ankle. Guy Vexille waited for the thudding of the arrows striking the wood, then realized that Thomas had either lost all his archers or, far more likely, was waiting for the moment when the pavises were dropped.

They climbed through a town of the dying and the dead, a town stinking of fire and ordure. There was a man lying dead in a soiled sheet; they kicked his corpse aside and walked on. The men in the second rank held their shields aloft, protecting the three ranks from arrows shot from the castle's high keep, but still no missiles came.

Guy wondered if everyone in the castle was dead and he imagined walking its empty halls like a knight of old, a Grail-searcher come to his destiny, and he shuddered with pure ecstasy at the thought of claiming the relic; then the group of men were crossing the open space in front of the castle and Guy reminded them to stay close and to keep the pavises overlapping as they struggled over the mound of rubble thrown down by Hell Spitter. "Christ is our companion," he told his men. "God is with us. We cannot lose."

The only sounds were the cries of women and children in the town, the scrape of pavises and the clanking of armored feet. Guy Vexille moved one of the heavy shields aside and glimpsed a makeshift barricade stretching across the courtyard, but he also saw archers bunched at the top of the steps which led into the keep and one of those men drew back his string and Guy hastily closed up the chink between the shields. The arrow struck the pavise and knocked it back and Guy was astonished by the arrow's force, and even more astonished when he looked up and saw a hand's breadth of needle-pointed arrow protruding through the pavise that was twice as thick as an ordinary shield. More arrows struck, their sound an irregular drumbeat, and the heavy pavises shook from the impact. A man cursed, wounded in the cheek by an arrow that had pierced the timber layers, but Guy steadied his men. "Stay together," he said, "go slow. When we're through the gate we go to the barricade. We can pull it down. Then the front rank charges the steps. Keep hold of the pavises till we reach the archers." His own pavise jarred on a stone and he lifted the big wooden handle to hoist the shield over the small obstacle and an arrow immediately slammed into the rubble, missing his foot by an inch. "Stay firm," he told his men, "stay firm. God is with us." The pavise rocked back, struck high by two arrows, but Guy forced it upright, took another step, climbing now for he was crossing the rubble in the shattered gateway. They moved the big shields in small jerks, forcing them against the power of the arrow hits. It

seemed there were no archers on the keep's ramparts for no arrows
came down from the sky, just from the front where they were stopped
by the big shields. "Stay close," Guy told his men, "stay close and
trust in God," and then, from where they had been hidden behind the
remaining curtain wall to the right of the gate, Sir Guillaume's men-
at-arms howled and charged.

Sir Guillaume had seen how the attackers were hiding behind the
pavises and had reckoned those great shields would blind them, and
so he had thrown down one end of the barricade and taken ten men
to the corner of the yard behind the curtain wall, a place where the
stable dungheap lay, and now, as Guy's men appeared through the
arch, Sir Guillaume attacked. It was the same tactic he had used to
such effect against Joscelyn's attack, only this time the plan was to
charge, kill and wound, and immediately retreat. He had told his men
that idea over and over again. Break the pavise wall, he had said, then
let the archers do the rest of the slaughter while they got back to the
gap in the barricade, and for an instant it all seemed to work. The
onslaught did surprise the attackers, who reeled back in disarray. An
English man-at-arms, a wild man who loved nothing better than a
fight, split a skull with an axe while Sir Guillaume thrust his sword
into another man's groin, and the men holding the pavises instinctively turned towards the threat and that meant the shields turned
with them and opened their left sides to the archers on the top of the
steps.

"Now!" Thomas called, and the arrows flew.

Guy had not foreseen this, but he was ready. In his rear rank was
a man called Fulk, a Norman, who was loyal as a dog and fierce as an
eagle. "Hold them, Fulk!" Vexille shouted. "Front rank with me!" An
arrow had glanced off one of his rerebraces, wounding a man behind,
and two of the front rank were staggering with arrows through their
mail, but the rest followed Guy Vexille as he closed up the pavise wall
and headed towards the gap at the end of the barricade. Sir Guil-

laume's men should have retreated, but they were locked in battle now, lost in the excitement and terror of close combat; they were fending blows with their shields, trying to find chinks in enemy armor. Guy ignored them and went past the barricade, and then, with the heavy pavise still protecting him, he advanced on the steps. Five men went with him; the rest were attacking Sir Guillaume's few men, who were now seriously outnumbered. The archers had turned on the six men coming to the steps and were wasting their arrows on the huge shields, and then the six crossbowmen, unnoticed in the confusion, appeared in the gateway and shot a volley that tore into the English bowmen. Three went down instantly; another found himself holding a broken bow that had been shattered by a quarrel.

And Guy, shouting that God was with him, discarded the pavise and charged up the steps.

"Back!" Thomas shouted. "Back!" There were three men-at-arms waiting to defend the stairway, but first his archers had to get through the door and Guy had trapped one man, tangling his legs with the sword so he fell, then making him scream when the long blade rammed up his groin. Blood cascaded down the steps. Thomas thrust his bowstave at Guy's chest, pushing him back, then Sam seized Thomas and dragged him back into the doorway. After that it was a scramble up the stairs, always twisting to the right, past the three men-at-arms who waited at the top. "Hold them," Thomas said to the three. "Sam! Up top! Quick!"

Thomas stayed on the stairs. Sam and the other seven archers who were left would know what to do once they reached the keep's battlements, while for Thomas the most important thing was to stop Guy's men climbing the steps up to the first hall. The attackers had to come with the stairway's central spine on their right and that would restrict their sword arms, while Thomas's men, fighting downwards, would have more space to wield their weapons, except Guy's first man up was left-handed and he carried a short-handled, broadbladed axe that he chopped into a man-at-arm's foot and brought him down in a clatter of shield, sword and mail. The axe fell again, there was a brief scream, then Thomas loosed an arrow at three paces' range and the axeman was falling back, the shaft in his throat. A crossbow bolt followed, screeching along the curve of the wall, and Thomas saw Genevieve had collected four of the *coredors'* bows and was waiting for another target.

Sir Guillaume was now in desperate trouble. He was outnumbered and cornered. He shouted at his men to lock shields and to brace themselves against the yard's corner where the dungheap obstructed him. Then Guy's men came in a rush and the shields went up to meet swords and axes. Sir Guillaume's men thrust the shields forward to rock the enemy back and lunged their swords at bellies or chests, but one of the enemy, a big man showing the symbol of a bull on his jupon, had a mace, a great ball of iron on a stout handle that he used to beat down an Englishman's shield until it was nothing but splintered pieces of willow held together by the leather cover and the shield's holder had a crushed forearm. Yet still the Englishman tried to ram the broken shield into his attacker's face, until another Frenchman rammed a sword into his guts and he fell to his knees. Sir Guillaume seized the mace, hauled it towards him and the enemy came fast, tripping on his victim. Sir Guillaume hit him in the face with the hilt of his sword, the crosspiece sinking into an eye, but the man fought on, blood and jelly on his cheek, and two more enemy were coming behind him, prizing the short line of defenders apart. An Englishman was on his knees, being hammered on the helmet by two swords, then he bent forward and vomited and one of the Frenchmen shoved the sword blade behind his back-plate, in the gap between plate and helmet, and the Englishman screamed as his spine was flayed open. The man with the mace, one-eyed now, was trying to stand and Sir Guillaume kicked him in the face, kicked him again, and still he would not stay down so Sir Guillaume rammed his sword into the man's breast, ripping through mail, but then a Frenchman thrust a sword at Sir Guillaume's breast and the blow hurled him back onto the dungheap. "They're dead men!" Fulk shouted. "They're dead men!" And just then the first volley of arrows came from the keep's battlements.

The arrows slashed into the backs of Fulk's men-at-arms. Some wore plate and the arrows, coming at a steep angle, glanced off that armor, but the bodkin points drove through mail and leather and suddenly four of the attackers were dead and three were wounded, and then the archers turned their bows on the crossbowmen in the gate. Sir Guillaume, unwounded, managed to stand. His shield was split and he threw it away, then the man with the bull on his jupon raised himself onto his knees and grappled with him, arms about his waist, trying to pull him down. Sir Guillaume used both hands to hammer the heavy pommel of his sword onto the man's helmet, yet he was still hauled down, falling with a crash, and he let go of his sword as the big man tried to throttle him. Sir Guillaume felt with his left hand to find the bottom of the man's breastplate, drew his dagger with his right and stabbed up into the big man's belly. He felt the knife go through leather, then puncture skin and muscle and he worked the blade, ripping at the man's guts as the coarse, sweat-reddened, bloodied, one-eyed face snarled at him.

More arrows flew, thumping with a sickening thud into Fulk's remaining men. "Here!" Guy Vexille was in the doorway at the top of the steps. "Fulk! Here! Leave them! Here!"

Fulk repeated the order in his roaring voice. So far as he could see only three of the defenders were alive in the corner of the courtyard, but if he stayed to finish them off then the archers on the tower would kill all his men. Fulk had an arrow in the thigh, but he felt no pain as he stumbled up the steps and into the big doorway where, at last, he was safe from the arrows. Guy now had fifteen men left. The others were dead or else still in the yard, wounded. One man, already struck by two arrows, tried to crawl to the steps and two more arrows thudded into his back, throwing him down. He twitched, and his mouth opened and closed in spasms until a last arrow broke his spine.

An archer whom Guy had not noticed before, a man who had been lying on a bed of straw, struggled a few paces across the yard and used a knife to cut the throat of a wounded man-at-arms, but then a crossbow bolt flashed from the gate to strike the archer and throw him onto his victim's body. The archer vomited, jerked for a few heartbeats and then was still.

Sir Guillaume was helpless. He had two men left, not nearly enough to attack the doorway, and Sir Guillaume himself was bruised, bleeding and feeling strangely and suddenly weak. His stomach gave a heave and he retched emptily, then staggered back onto the wall. John Faircloth was lying on the dungheap, bleeding from the belly, unable to talk as he died. Sir Guillaume wanted to say something comforting to the dying Englishman, but a wave of nausea swept over him. He retched again, and his armor felt curiously heavy. All he wanted to do was lie down and rest. "My face," he said to one of the two survivors, a Burgundian, "look at my face," and the man obeyed and flinched when he saw the red blotches. "Oh, sweet Jesus," Sir Guillaume said, "sweet goddamn Jesus," and he slumped down by the wall and reached for his sword as if the familiar weapon would give him solace.

"Shields," Guy said to his men. "Two of you with shields, hold them high, go up the stairs, and we'll come behind and cut their legs out." That was the best way to take a stairway, to chop the vulnerable ankles of the defenders, but when they tried it they discovered the two remaining men-at-arms were using shortened lances that Sir Guillaume had placed on the landing to defend the steps, and they hammered the lances on the shields, driving the men back, and an arrow and a crossbow bolt took one man in the helmet so that blood spilled down from beneath its rim to sheet his face. He fell back and Guy pulled him down the steps and put him beside the corpse of the axeman he had dragged off the stairway.

"We need crossbows," Fulk said. His blunt face was bruised and there was blood in his beard. He went to the doorway and bellowed for the crossbowmen to run to the steps. "Come fast!" he shouted, then spat out a bloody tooth. "It's safe! The archers are dead," he lied, "so come now!"

The crossbowmen tried, but Sam and his archers on the battlements had been waiting for them and four of the six were hit by arrows. A loaded crossbow clattered across the stones, hit the barricade and tripped the pawl so that its bolt buried itself in a corpse. One crossbowman tried to run back through the arch and was hurled onto the rubble by an arrow, yet two of the bowmen managed to reach the steps unharmed.

"There are few of them," Guy told his men, "and God is with us. We need one effort, just one, and the Grail is ours. Your reward will be glory or heaven. Glory or heaven." He had the best armor so he decided he would lead the next attack with Fulk beside him. The two crossbowmen would be immediately behind, ready to shoot the bowmen waiting behind the curve of the stairway. Once the stairway was clear Guy would hold the base of the keep. With luck, he thought, the Grail would be in whatever room they reached, but if it was another floor up then they must do it all again, but he was certain they would reach the prize and, once it was gained, he would fire the castle. The wooden floors would burn readily enough and the flames and smoke would kill the archers on the battlements and Guy would be victorious. He could leave, the Grail would be his and the world would be changed.

Just one last effort.

Guy took a small shield from one of his men-at-arms. It was scarcely bigger than a serving platter, intended only to fend off sword blows in a mêlée, and he began the attack by pushing it round the corner, hoping to draw the arrows and then rush the steps while the bowmen upstairs had empty strings, but the archers were not drawn by the ruse and so Guy nodded to Fulk who had snapped off the head and feathered end of the arrow in his thigh, leaving the shortened shaft sticking clean through the muscle. "I'm ready," Fulk said.

"Then we go," Guy said, and the two men crouched behind their shields and climbed the winding stair, treading on the blood of their comrades, and they turned the bend and Guy braced himself for an arrow's strike. None came, and he peered over the shield and saw nothing but empty steps ahead and knew God had given him victory. "For the Grail," he told Fulk, and the two men hurried, just a dozen steps to go and the crossbowmen were behind them, and then Guy smelt the burning. He thought nothing of it. The stair turned and he could see the hallway opening up ahead and he shouted his war cry and then the fire came.

It had been Genevieve's idea. She had given her crossbow to Philin and gone up to the hall where the sick lay and she had seized one of the breastplates captured from Joscelyn's assault and raked into its shallow bowl a bucket full of glowing embers from the fire. One of the *coredor* women helped her, scooping smoldering cinders and ash into a great cooking pot, and they carried the fire downstairs, the breastplate burning Genevieve's hands, and when the first two men came into view they hurled the red hot scraps down the stairs. The ash did the greatest damage. It drifted, hot dust, and some got into the eyes of the crossbowman behind Fulk and he flinched away, his weapon dropped as he pawed the burning scraps from his face, and the crossbow struck the step, fired itself and the bolt went through Fulk's ankle. Fulk fell into a scatter of red-hot embers and scrambled backwards to free himself of the pain and Guy was alone on the stairs, ash half blinding him, and he lifted the shield as though that would protect his eyes and it was struck by an arrow with such force that it threw him back. The arrow was half through the shield. A crossbow bolt cracked against the wall. Guy staggered, trying to gain his balance, trying to see through the ash-induced tears and the thick smoke, and then Thomas led his few men in a charge. Thomas carried one of the shortened lances that he rammed at Guy, throwing him all the way down the stairs, while the man-at-arms with Thomas stabbed a sword two-handed into Fulk's neck.

Vexille's men at the foot of the stairs should have stopped the charge, but they were taken aback by the sight of Guy staggering down, by Fulk's screaming and by the stench of fire and burning flesh and they backed out of the door as the enemy came howling out of the smoke. Thomas only led five men, but they were enough to panic Guy's small band who seized their master and fled back into the courtyard's fresh air. Thomas followed, thrusting the lance forward, and he caught Guy plumb on the breastplate so that he was thrown back down the outer steps to sprawl on the courtyard's stones. Then the arrows came from the battlements, plunging through mail and plate. The attackers could not go back up the steps, because Thomas was there and the doorway was filled with armed men and smoke, and so they fled. They ran for the town and the arrows followed them through the archway and hurled two of them onto the rubble. Then Thomas shouted for the archers to stop shooting. "Rest strings!" he yelled. "You hear me, Sam? Rest strings! Rest strings!"

He let the shortened lance fall and held out his hand. Genevieve gave him his bow and Thomas took a broad-head from his arrow bag and looked down the steps to where his cousin, abandoned by his men, struggled to stand in his heavy black armor. "You and me," Thomas said, "your weapon against mine."

Guy looked left and right and saw no help. The courtyard was stinking of vomit, dung and blood. It was thick with bodies. He backed away, going to the gap at the edge of the barricade and Thomas followed, coming down the steps and staying within a dozen paces of his enemy. "Lost your appetite for battle?" Thomas asked him.

Guy rushed him then, hoping to get within the range of his long sword's blade, but the broad-head hit him smack on the breastplate and he was brutally checked by it, stopped dead by the sheer force of the big bow, and Thomas already had another arrow on the string. "Try again," Thomas said.

Guy backed away. Back through the barricade, past Sir Guillaume and his two men who did nothing to interfere with him. Thomas's archers had come down from the battlements and were on the steps, watching. "Is your armor good?" Thomas asked Guy. "It needs to be. Mind you, I'm shooting broad-heads. They won't pierce your armor." He loosed again and the arrow hammered into the plates at Guy's groin and bent him over and threw him back onto the rubble. Thomas had another arrow ready.

"So what will you do now?" Thomas asked. "I'm not defenseless like Planchard. Like Eleanor. Like my father. So come and kill me."

Guy got to his feet and backed over the rubble. He knew he had men in the town and if he could just reach them then he would be safe, but he dared not turn his back. He knew he would fetch an arrow if he did and a man's pride did not allow a wound in the back. You died facing the enemy. He was outside the castle now, backing slowly across the open space and he prayed one of his men would have the wit to fetch a crossbow and finish Thomas off, but Thomas was still coming towards him, smiling, and the smile was of a man come to his sweet revenge.

"This one's a bodkin," Thomas said, "and it's going to hit you in the chest. You want to raise the shield?"

"Thomas," Guy said, then raised the small shield before he could say anything more because he had seen Thomas draw the big bow, and the string was released and the arrow, headed with heavy oak behind the needle-sharp blade, slammed through the shield, through the breastplate, mail and leather to lodge against one of Guy's ribs. The impact jarred him back three paces, but he managed to keep his feet, though the shield was now pinned to his chest and Thomas had another arrow nocked.

"In the belly this time," Thomas said.

"I'm your cousin," Guy said, and he wrenched the shield free, tearing the arrow head from his chest, but he was too late and the arrow punched his stomach, driving through plate steel and iron mail and greased leather, and this arrow sank deep. "The first was for my father," Thomas said, "that one was for my woman, and this one's for

Planchard." He shot again and the arrow pierced Guy's gorget and hurled him back onto the cobbles. He still had the sword and he tried to lift it as Thomas came close. He also tried to speak, but his throat was filled with blood. He shook his head, wondering why his sight was going misty, and he felt Thomas kneel on his sword arm and he felt the punctured gorget being prized up and he tried to protest, but only spewed blood, then Thomas put the dagger under the gorget and rammed it deep into Guy's gullet. "And that one's for me," Thomas said.

Sam and a half-dozen archers joined him by the body. "Jake's dead," Sam said.

"I know."

"Half the bloody world's dead," Sam said.

Maybe the world was ending, Thomas thought. Perhaps the terrible prophecies of the Book of Revelation were coming true. The four dread horsemen were riding. The rider on the white horse was God's revenge on an evil world, the red horse carried war, the black horse was saddled by famine while the pale horse, the worst, brought plague and death. And perhaps the only thing that could turn the riders away was the Grail, but he did not have the Grail. So the horsemen would run free. Thomas stood, picked up his bow and started down the street.

Guy's surviving men were not staying to fight the archers. They fled like Joscelyn's men, going to find a place where no plague filled the streets, and Thomas stalked a town of the dying and the dead, a town of smoke and filth, a place of weeping. He carried an arrow on the string, but no one challenged him. A woman called for help, a child cried in a doorway, and then Thomas saw a man-at-arms, still in mail, and he half drew the bow, then saw the man had no weapons, only a pail of water. He was an older man, gray-haired. "You must be Thomas?" the man said.

"Yes."

"I'm Sir Henri Courtois." He pointed at a nearby house. "Your friend is in there. He's sick."

Robbie lay on a fouled bed. He was shaking with a fever and his face was dark and swollen. He did not recognize Thomas. "You poor bastard," Thomas said. He gave his bow to Sam. "And take that too, Sam," he said, pointing to the parchment that lay on a low stool beside the bed, and then he lifted Robbie in his arms and carried him back up the hill. "You should die among friends," he told the unconscious man.

The siege, at last, was over.

SIR GUILLAUME DIED. Many died. Too many to bury, so Thomas had the corpses carried to a ditch in the fields across the river and he covered them with brushwood and set the heap on fire, though there was not enough fuel to burn the bodies, which were left half roasted. Wolves came and ravens darkened the sky above the ditch that was death's rich feast.

Folk came back to the town. They had sought refuge in places that were struck as badly as Castillon d'Arbizon. The plague was everywhere, they said. Berat was a town of the dead, though whether Joscelyn lived no one knew and Thomas did not care. Winter brought frost and at Christmas a friar brought news that the pestilence was now in the north. "It is everywhere," the friar said, "everyone is dying." Yet not everyone died. Philin's son, Galdric, recovered, but just after Christmas his father caught the disease and was dead in three agonizing days.

Robbie lived. It had seemed he must die for there had been nights when he appeared not to breathe, yet he lived and slowly he recovered. Genevieve looked after him, feeding him when he was weak and washing him when he was filthy, and when he tried to apologize to her she hushed him. "Speak to Thomas," she said.

Robbie, still weak, went to Thomas and he thought the archer looked older and fiercer. Robbie did not know what to say, but Thomas did. "Tell me," he said. "When you did what you did, you thought you were doing the right thing?"

"Yes," Robbie said.

"Then you did no wrong," Thomas said flatly, "and that's an end of it."

"I should not have taken that," Robbie said, pointing to the parchment on Thomas's lap, the Grail writings left by Thomas's father.

"I got it back," Thomas said, "and now I'm using it to teach Genevieve to read. It isn't any use for anything else."

Robbie stared into the fire. "I'm sorry," he said.

Thomas ignored the apology. "And what we do now is wait until everyone is well, then we go home."

They were ready to leave by St. Benedict's Day. Eleven men would go home to England, and Galdric, who had no parents now, would travel as Thomas's servant. They would go home rich, for most of the money from their plunders was still intact, but what they would find in England, Thomas did not know.

He spent the last night in Castillon d'Arbizon listening as Genevieve stumbled over the words of his father's parchment. He had decided to burn it after this night, for it had led him nowhere. He was making Genevieve read the Latin, for there was little English or French in the document, and though she did not understand the words it did give her practice in deciphering the letters. "'*Virga tua et baculus tuus ipsa consolobuntur me,*'" she read slowly, and Thomas nodded and knew the words *calix meus inebrians* were not far ahead, and he thought that the cup *had* got him drunk, drunk and wild and all to no purpose. Planchard had been right. The search made men mad.

"'*Pono coram me mensam,*'" Genevieve read, "'*ex adverso hostium meorum.*'"

"It's not *pono,*" Thomas said, "but *pones.* '*Pones coram me mensam ex adverso hostium meorum.*'" He knew it by heart and now translated for her. "'Thou preparest a table for me in the presence of my enemies.'"

She frowned, a long pale finger on the writing. "No," she insisted, "it does say '*pono.*'" She held out the manuscript to prove it.

The firelight flickered on the words that did indeed say "*pono coram me mensam ex adverso hostium meorum.*" His father had written it and Thomas must have looked at the line a score of times, yet he had never noticed the mistake. His familiarity with the Latin had led him to skip across the words, seeing them in his head rather than on the parchment. *Pono.* "I prepare a table." Not thou preparest, but I prepare, and Thomas stared at the word and knew it was not a mistake.

And knew he had found the Grail.

Epilogue

The Grail

T HE BREAKING WAVES drove up the shingle, hissed white and scraped back. On and on, ever and ever, the gray-green sea beating at England's coast.

A small rain fell, soaking the new grass where lambs played and buck hares danced beside the hedgerows where anemones and stitchwort grew.

The pestilence had come to England. Thomas and his three companions had ridden through empty villages and heard cows bellowing in agony for there was no one to take the milk from their swollen udders. At some villages archers waited at barricaded streets to turn all strangers away and Thomas had dutifully ridden around such places. They had seen pits dug for the dead; pits half filled with corpses that had received no last rites. The pits were edged with flowers for it was springtime.

In Dorchester there was a dead man in the street and no one to bury him. Some houses had been nailed shut and painted with a red cross to show that the folk inside were sick and must be left there to die or recover. Outside the town the fields went unplowed, seed stayed in the barns of dead farmers, and yet there were larks above the grass and the kingfishers darting along the streams and plovers tumbling beneath the clouds.

Sir Giles Marriott, the old lord of the manor, had died before the plague struck, and his grave was in the village church, but if any of the surviving villagers saw Thomas ride by, they did not greet him. They sheltered from God's wrath and Thomas, Genevieve, Robbie and Galdric rode on down the lane until they were beneath Lipp Hill and ahead was the sea, and the shingle, and the valley where Hookton had once stood. It had been burned by Sir Guillaume and Guy Vexille back when they were allies, and now there was nothing but thorns looping over the lumpy remains of the cottages, and hazels and thistles and nettles growing in the scorched black, roofless walls of the church.

Thomas had been in England for a fortnight. He had ridden to the Earl of Northampton, and he had knelt to his lord, who had first had servants examine Thomas to make sure he did not carry the dark marks of the pestilence, and Thomas had paid his lord one-third of the money they had brought from Castillon d'Arbizon, and then he had given him the golden cup. "It was made for the Grail, my lord," he said, "but the Grail is gone."

The Earl admired the cup, turning it and holding it up so that it caught the light, and he was amazed at its beauty. "Gone?" he asked.

"The monks at Saint Sever's," Thomas lied, "believe it was taken to heaven by an angel whose wing had been mended there. It is gone, lord."

And the Earl had been satisfied, for he was the possessor of a great treasure even if it was not the Grail, and Thomas, promising to return, had gone away with his companions. Now he had come to the village of his childhood, the place he had learned to master the bow, and to the church where his father, the mad Father Ralph, had preached to the gulls and hidden his great secret.

It was still there. Hidden in the grass and nettles that grew between the flagstones of the old church, a thing discarded as being of no value. It was a clay bowl which Father Ralph had used to hold the mass wafers. He would put the bowl on the altar, cover it with a linen cloth and carry it home when mass was done. "I prepare a table," he had written, and the altar was the table and the bowl was the thing he set it with and Thomas had handled it a hundred times and thought nothing of it, and when he had last been in Hookton he had picked it up from the ruins and then, disdaining it, he had thrown it back among the weeds.

Now he found it again among the nettles and he took it to Genevieve who placed it in the wooden box and closed the lid, and the fit of the thing was so perfect that the box did not even rattle when it was shaken. The base of the bowl matched the slight dis-colored circle in the old paint of the box's interior. The one had been made for the other. "What do we do?" Genevieve asked. Robbie and Galdric were outside the church, exploring the ridges and lumps that betrayed where the old cottages had been. Neither knew why Thomas had come back to Hookton. Galdric did not care, and Robbie, quieter now, was content to stay with Thomas until they all rode north to pay Lord Outhwaite the ransom that would release Robbie back to Scotland. If Outhwaite lived.

"What do we do?" Genevieve asked again, her voice a whisper.

"What Planchard advised me," Thomas said, but first he took a skin wine from his bag, poured a little wine into the bowl and made Genevieve drink from it, then he took the bowl and drank himself. He smiled at her. "That rids us of excommunication," he said, for they had drunk from the bowl that caught Christ's blood from the cross.

"Is it really the Grail?" Genevieve asked.

Thomas took it outside. He held Genevieve's hand as they walked towards the sea and, when they reached the shingle inside the hook where the Lipp Stream curved across the beach by the place where the fishing boats had been hauled up when Hookton still had villagers, he smiled at her, then hurled the bowl as hard as he could. He threw it across the stream to the hook of shingle on the far side and the bowl crunched down into the stones, bounced, ran a few feet and was still.

They waded the stream, climbed the bank and found the bowl undamaged.

"What do we do?" Genevieve asked again.

It would cause nothing but madness, Thomas thought. Men would fight for it, lie for it, cheat for it, betray for it and die for it. The Church would make money from it. It would cause nothing but evil, he thought, for it stirred horror from men's hearts, so he would do what Planchard had said he would do. "'Hurl it into the deepest sea,'" he quoted the old abbot, "'down among the monsters, and tell no one.'"

Genevieve touched the bowl a last time, then kissed it and gave it back to Thomas who cradled it for a moment. It was just a bowl of peasant's clay, red-brown in color, thickly made and rough to the touch, not perfectly round, with a small indentation on one side where the potter had damaged the unfired clay. It was worth pennies, perhaps nothing, yet it was the greatest treasure of Christendom and he kissed it once and then he drew back his strong archer's right arm, ran down to the sucking sea's edge and threw it as far and as hard as he could. He hurled it away and it span for an instant above the gray waves, seemed to fly a heartbeat longer as though it were reluctant to let go of mankind, and then the bowl was gone.

Just a white splash, instantly healed, and Thomas took Genevieve's hand and turned away.

He was an archer, and the madness was over. He was free.

HISTORICAL NOTE

I HAVE ALLOWED A SURFEIT of rats to appear here and there in *Heretic*, though I am persuaded they were probably innocent of spreading the plague. There is argument among the medical historians as to whether the Black Death (named for the color of the buboes, or swellings, which disfigured the sick) was bubonic plague, which would have been spread by fleas from rats, or some form of anthrax, which would have come from cattle. Fortunately for me, Thomas and his companions did not need to make that diagnosis. The medieval explanation for the pestilence was mankind's sin added to an unfortunate astrological conjunction of the planet Saturn, always a baleful influence. It caused panic and puzzlement for it was an unknown disease that had no cure. It spread north from Italy, killing its victims within three or four days and mysteriously sparing others. This was the first appearance of the plague in Europe. There had been other pandemics, of course, but nothing on this scale, and it would continue its ravages, at intervals, for another four hundred years. The victims did not call it the Black Death; that name was not to be used till the 1800s. They just knew it as the "pesti-lence."

It killed at least one-third of the European population. Some com-munities suffered a mortality bill of more than 50 percent, but the overall figure of one-third seems to be accurate. It struck as hard in rural areas as in towns, and whole villages vanished. Some of them can still be detected as ridges and ditches in farmland, while in other places there are lone churches, standing in fields with no apparent purpose. They are the plague churches, all that remain of the old vil-lages.

Only the opening and closing passages of *Heretic* are based on real history. The plague happened, as did the siege and capture of Calais, but everything in between is fictional. There is no town of Berat, nor a bastide called Castillon d'Arbizon. There is an Astarac, but what-ever was built there now lies under the waters of a great reservoir. The fight which begins the book, the capture of Nieulay and its tower, did happen, but the victory gained the French no advantage for they were unable to cross the River Ham and engage the main English army. So the French withdrew, Calais fell and the port remained in English hands for another three centuries. The story of the six burghers of Calais being condemned to death, then reprieved, is well known and Rodin's statue of the six, in front of the town's hall, commemorates the event.

Thomas's language difficulties in Gascony were real enough. The aristocracy there, as in England, used French, but the common folk had a variety of local languages, chiefly Occitan, from which the mod-ern Languedoc comes. Languedoc simply means "the language of oc," because *oc* was the word for yes, and it is closely related to Catalan, the language spoken just across the Pyrenees in northern Spain. The French, conquering the territory to their south, tried to suppress the language, but it is still spoken and is now enjoying something of a revival.

As for the Grail? Long gone, I suspect. Some say it was the cup

Christ used at the Last Supper, and others that it was the bowl used to catch his blood from the "dolorous blow," the lance wound given to his side during the crucifixion. Whatever it was, it has never been found, though rumors persist and some say it is hidden in Scotland. It was, nevertheless, the most prized relic of medieval Christendom, perhaps because it was so mysterious, or else because, when the Arthurian tales received their final form, all the old Celtic tales of magic cauldrons became confused with the Grail. It has also been a golden thread through centuries of stories, and will go on being that, which is why it is probably best if it remains undiscovered.